OH S#!T IT'S KIM & KIM

writer
Magdalene Visaggio

pencils & inks
Eva Cabrera

colorist
Claudia Aguirre

letterer
Zakk Saam

issue #1 edited by
Katy Rex & Joe Corallo

issues #2-5 edited by
Joe Corallo

Linguist
Kirsten Thompson

cover art
Phillip Sevy

for this edition, additional design
Phil Smith

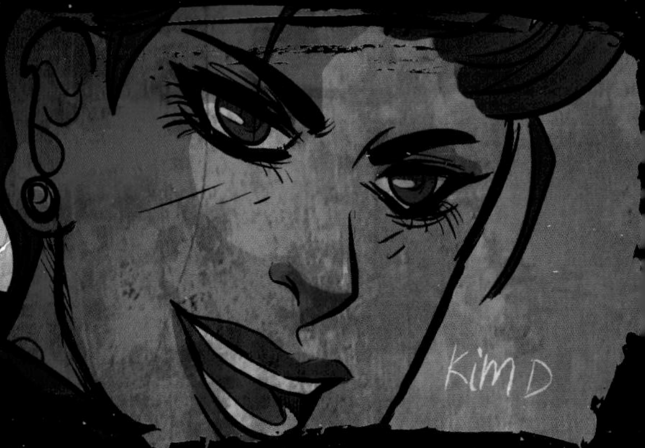
Kim D

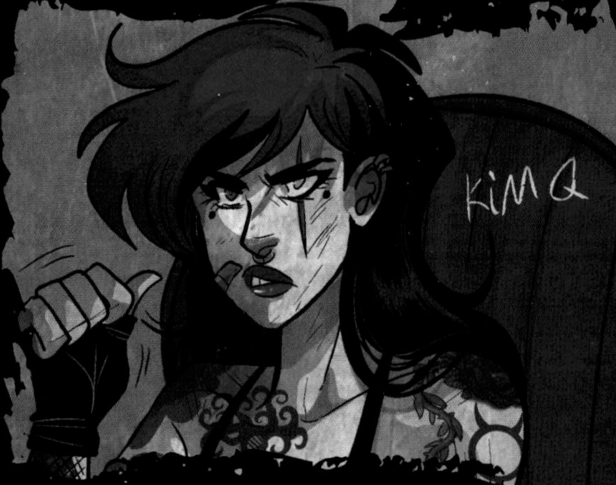
Kim Q

ORIGINAL CONCEPT BY
MAGDALENE VISAGGIO

SPECIAL THANKS TO:
Ryan Cady & Tini Howard

BLACK MASK
PUBLISHED BY BLACK MASK STUDIOS LLC
MATT PIZZOLO | BRETT GUREWITZ | STEVE NILES

PREVIOUSLY IN: KIM AND KIM VOLUME 1
"THIS GLAMOROUS HIGH-FLYING ROCK STAR LIFE"

ISSUE 1: Kim & Kim are twenty-something besties out to make a name for themselves in the wild world o interdimensional cowboy law enforcement. In a massive "screw you" to their parents and the authorities, decide to hijack some high stakes bounty -- and end up in way over their heads.

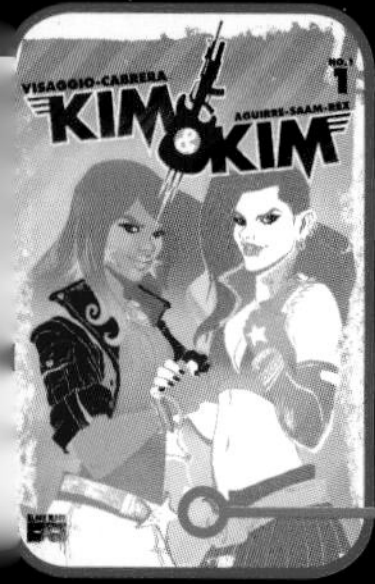
VISAGGIO-CABRERA
KIM & KIM
1

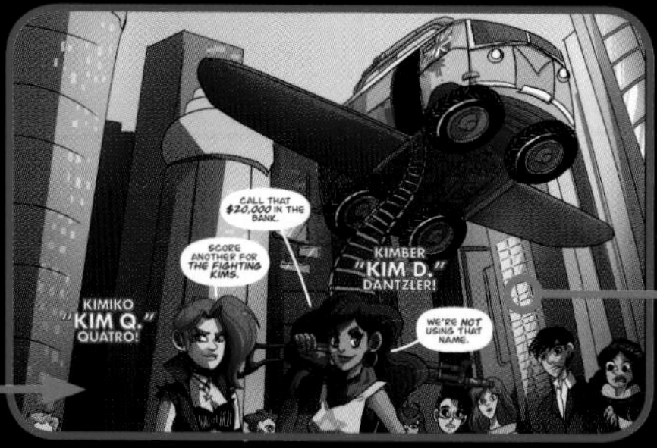
KIMIKO
"KIM Q."
QUATRO!
SCORE ANOTHER FOR THE FIGHTING KIMS.
CALL THAT $20,000 IN THE BANK.
KIMBER
"KIM D."
DANTZLER!
WE'RE NOT USING THAT NAME.

Meet Kim Q. (left) and Kim D. (right).

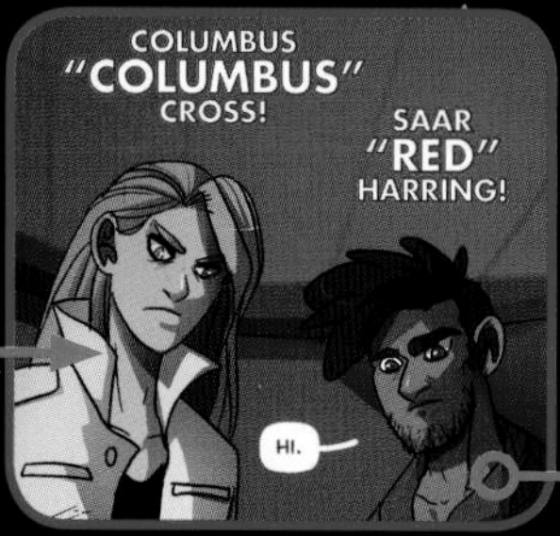
COLUMBUS
"COLUMBUS"
CROSS!
SAAR
"RED"
HARRING!
HI.

Meet the Frenemies.

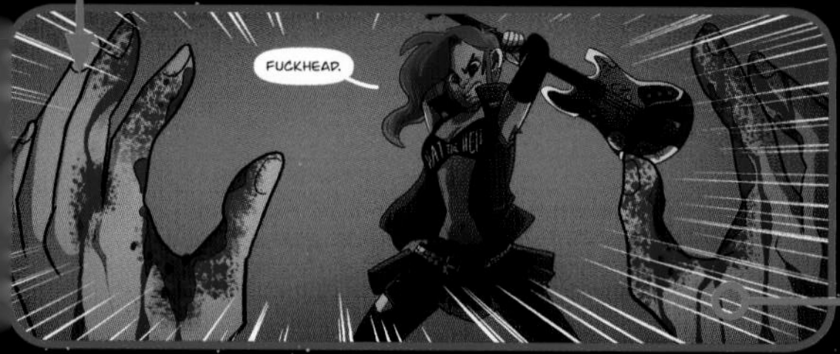
FUCKHEAD.

Kim Q. is violent and likes to bash people with her guitar.

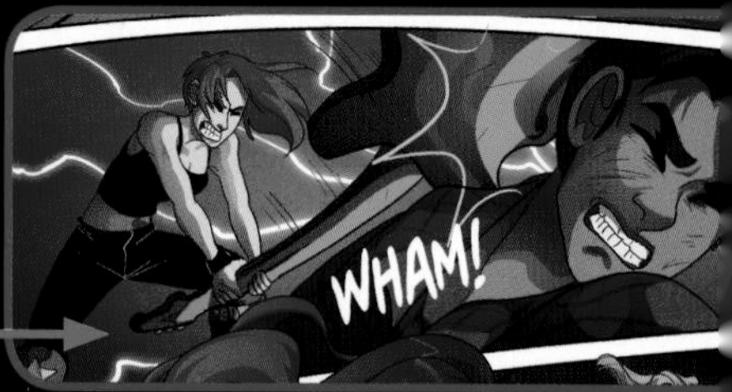
WHAM!

Kim Q. and Saar have a complicated relatio

ISSUE 2: With fugitive Tom Quilt in tow, the Fighting Kims go off in search of the mysterious Lady Babylon, o come up short. Turning to necromancy to help find her, things go about as badly as they possibly can.

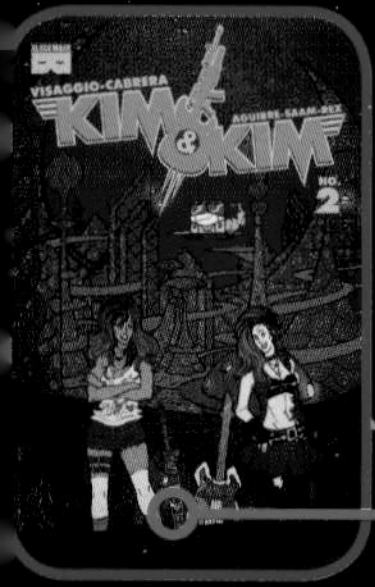
VISAGGIO-CABRERA
KIM & KIM
NO. 2

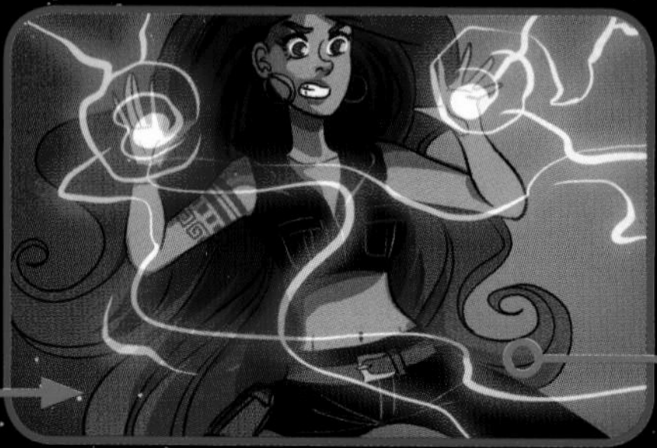

Kim D. has magic. That is her deal.

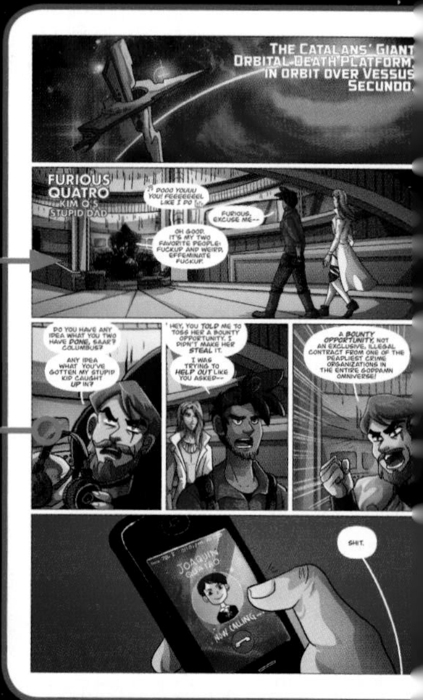
THE CATALANS' GIANT ORBITAL DEATH PLATFORM, IN ORBIT OVER VESSUS SECUNDO.
FURIOUS QUATRO
KIM Q.'S STUPID DAD
DOOO YOUUU YOU! FEEEEEEL LIKE I DO
FURIOUS, EXCUSE ME--
OH GOOD. IT'S MY TWO FAVORITE PEOPLE: FUCKUP AND WEIRD, EFFEMINATE FUCKUP.
DO YOU HAVE ANY IDEA WHAT YOU TWO HAVE DONE, SAAR? COLUMBUS?
ANY IDEA WHAT YOU'VE GOTTEN MY STUPID KID CAUGHT UP IN?
HEY, YOU TOLD ME TO TOSS HER A BOUNTY OPPORTUNITY. I DIDN'T MAKE HER STEAL IT.
I WAS TRYING TO HELP OUT LIKE YOU ASKED--
A BOUNTY OPPORTUNITY, NOT AN EXCLUSIVE, ILLEGAL CONTRACT FROM ONE OF THE DEADLIEST CRIME ORGANIZATIONS IN THE ENTIRE GODDAMN OMNIVERSE!
SHIT.

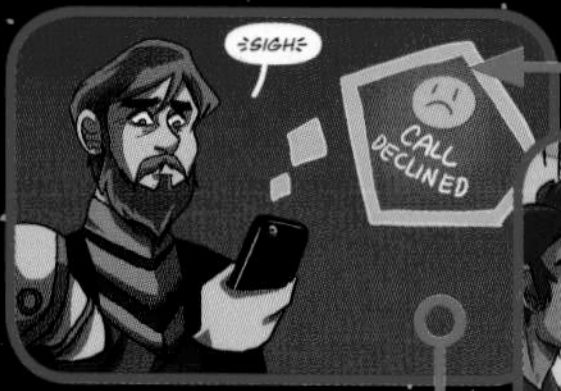
SIGH
CALL DECLINED

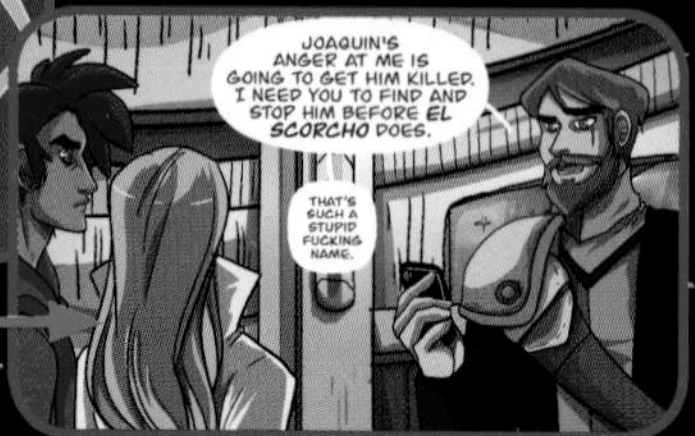
JOAQUIN'S ANGER AT ME IS GOING TO GET HIM KILLED. I NEED YOU TO FIND AND STOP HIM BEFORE EL SCORCHO DOES.
THAT'S SUCH A STUPID FUCKING NAME.

Kim Q. declines the call and Furious is concerned about El Scorcho.

This introduced The Catalan's Orbit Death Platform. Here we met Furio and Kim Q. called him.

ISSUE 3: Interstellar-cowboy life just keeps getting worse for our badass besties. On the hunt for Lady Babylon, Kim & Kim get shot out the sky by an unknown enemy and end up stranded on the frozen world of Never-Look-Back. But what they find there might be the breakthrough they've been looking for.

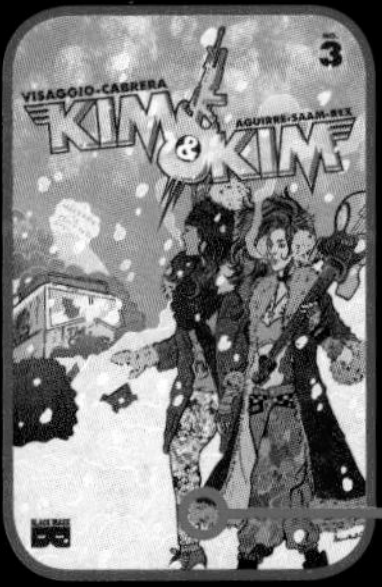

VISAGGIO·CABRERA
AGUIRRE-SAAM·REX
KIM & KIM
3

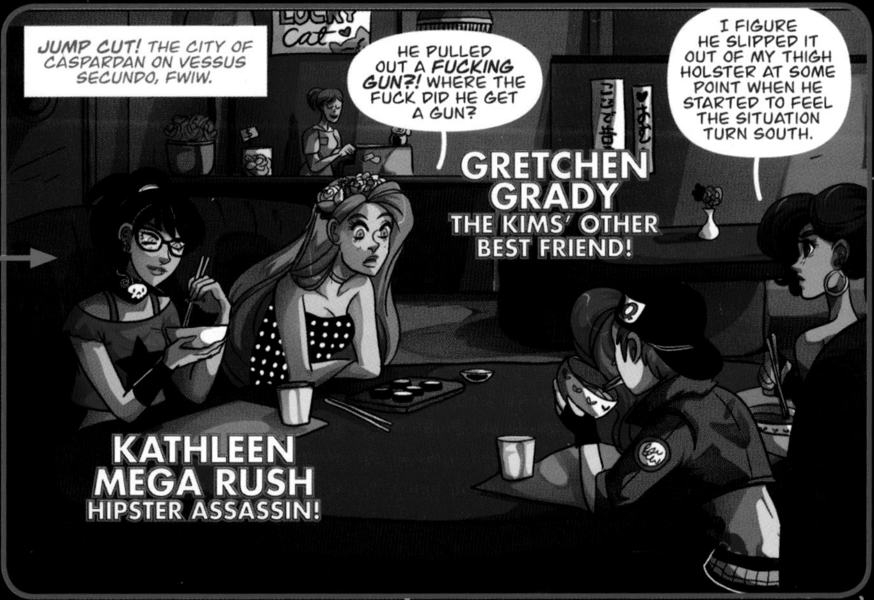

JUMP CUT! THE CITY OF CASPARDAN ON VESSUS SECUNDO, FWIW.
HE PULLED OUT A FUCKING GUN?! WHERE THE FUCK DID HE GET A GUN?
I FIGURE HE SLIPPED IT OUT OF MY THIGH HOLSTER AT SOME POINT WHEN HE STARTED TO FEEL THE SITUATION TURN SOUTH.
GRETCHEN GRADY
THE KIMS' OTHER BEST FRIEND!
KATHLEEN MEGA RUSH
HIPSTER ASSASSIN!

In this issue we also met Kathleen and Gretchen.

ISSUE 4: The Kims return home to find the very same messes they left behind -- and a bunch more they brought back with them. Unable to make rent after their recent adventure, the Kims take an easy bounty to make some quick cash. But nothing's ever easy.

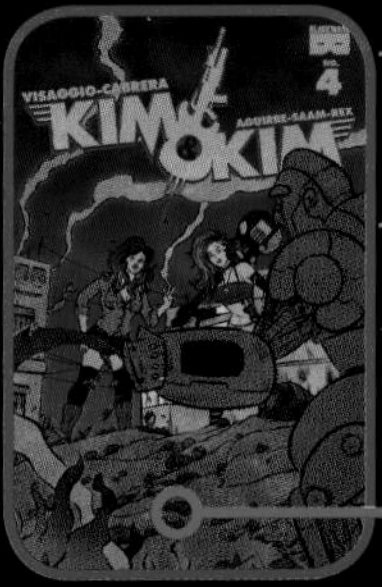

VISAGGIO·CABRERA
AGUIRRE-SAAM·REX
KIM & KIM
4

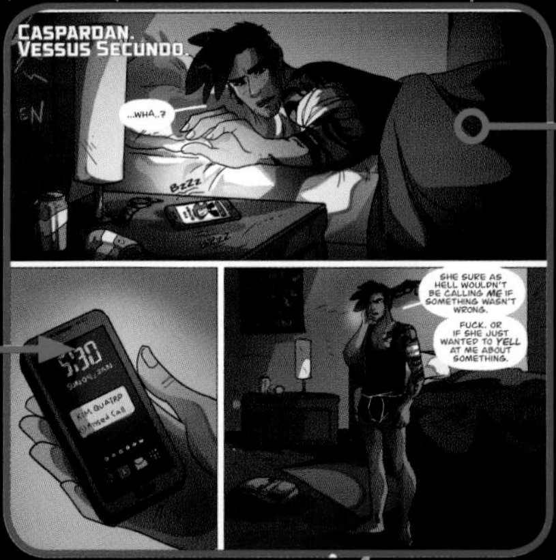

CASPARDAN. VESSUS SECUNDO.
...WHA..?
BzZz
SHE SURE AS HELL WOULDN'T BE CALLING ME IF SOMETHING WASN'T WRONG.
FUCK. OR IF SHE JUST WANTED TO YELL AT ME ABOUT SOMETHING.

Saar and Kim Q.'s relationship. Still Complicated

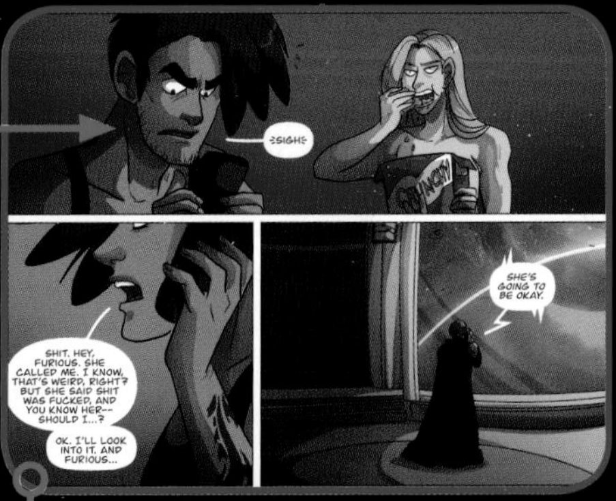

≷SIGH≷
SHIT. HEY, FURIOUS. SHE CALLED ME. I KNOW, THAT'S WEIRD, RIGHT? BUT SHE SAID SHIT WAS FUCKED, AND YOU KNOW HER-- SHOULD I...?
OK. I'LL LOOK INTO IT. AND FURIOUS...
SHE'S GOING TO BE OKAY.

Saar and Furious both worrying about Kim Q.

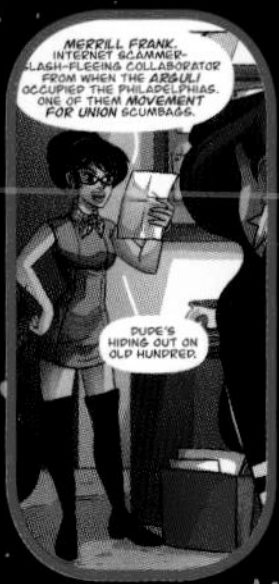

MERRILL FRANK. INTERNET SCAMMER-SLASH-FLEEING COLLABORATOR FROM WHEN THE ARGULI OCCUPIED THE PHILADELPHIAS. ONE OF THEM MOVEMENT FOR UNION SCUMBAGS.
DUDE'S HIDING OUT ON OLD HUNDRED.

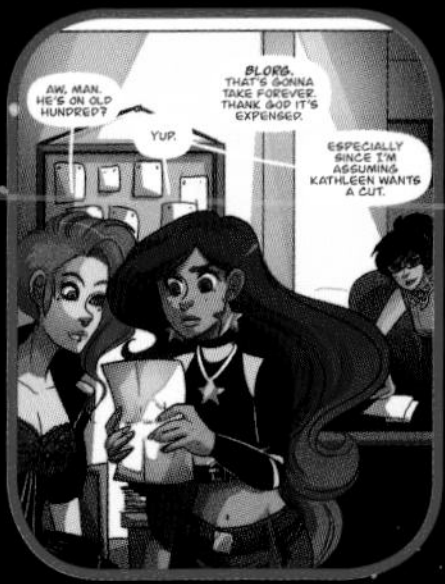

AW, MAN. HE'S ON OLD HUNDRED?
BLORG. THAT'S GONNA TAKE FOREVER. THANK GOD IT'S EXPENSED.
YUP.
ESPECIALLY SINCE I'M ASSUMING KATHLEEN WANTS A CUT.

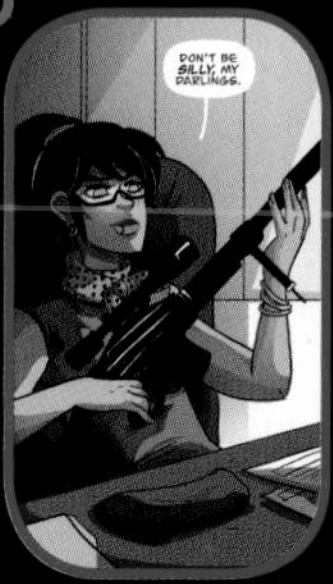

DON'T BE SILLY, MY DARLINGS.

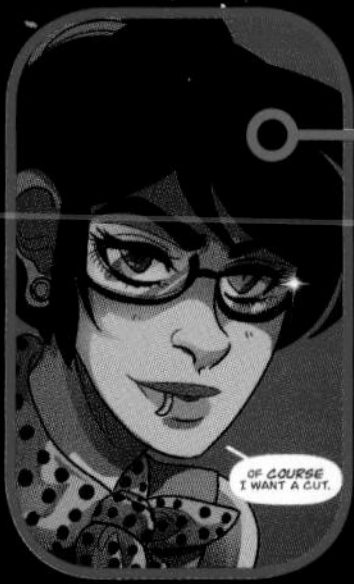

OF COURSE I WANT A CUT.

The Kims and Kathleen have a good working relationship.

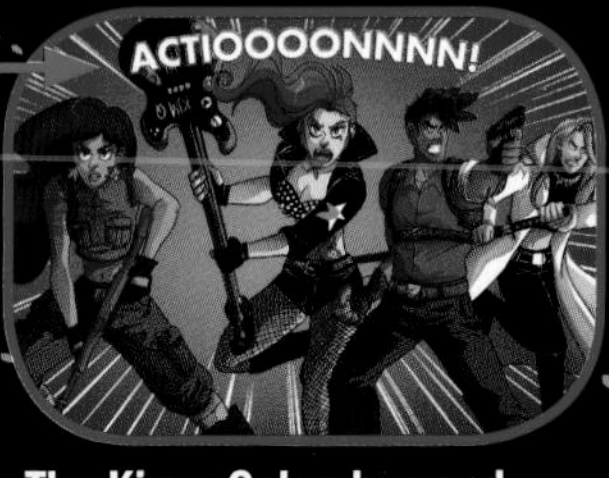

ACTIOOOONNNN!

The Kims, Columbus and Saar all work together.

PREVIOUSLY IN: *KIM AND KIM* VOLUME 2
"LOVE IS A BATTLEFIELD"

ISSUE 1: The Fighting Kims finally get the bounty of their lives and Kim D. re-connects with an ex-girlfriend, so of course everything immediately goes catastrophically wrong. This high-flying, rad AF tale of exes and woes.

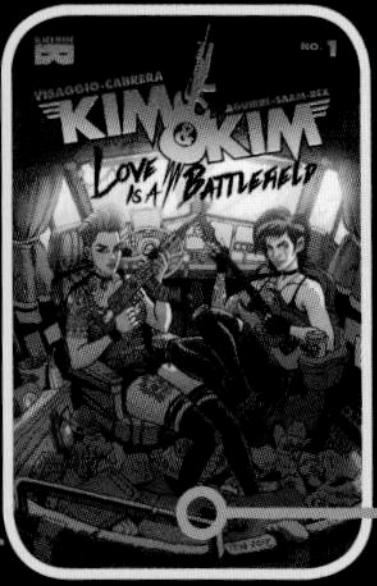
NO. 1
VISAGGIO-CABRERA
KIM & KIM
LOVE IS A BATTLEFIELD

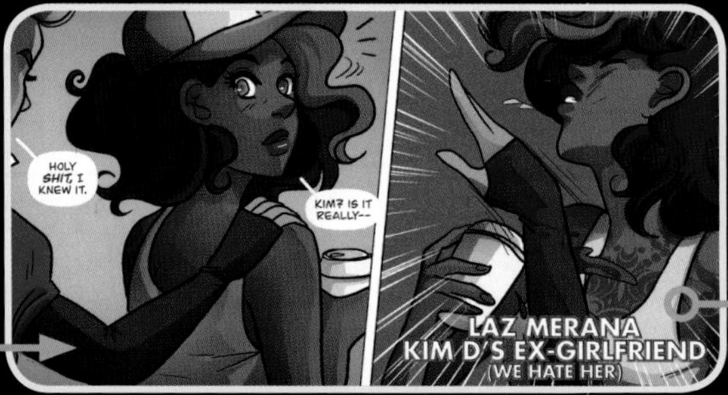
HOLY SHIT, I KNEW IT.
KIM? IS IT REALLY--
LAZ MERANA
KIM D'S EX-GIRLFRIEND
(WE HATE HER)

Meet Laz.

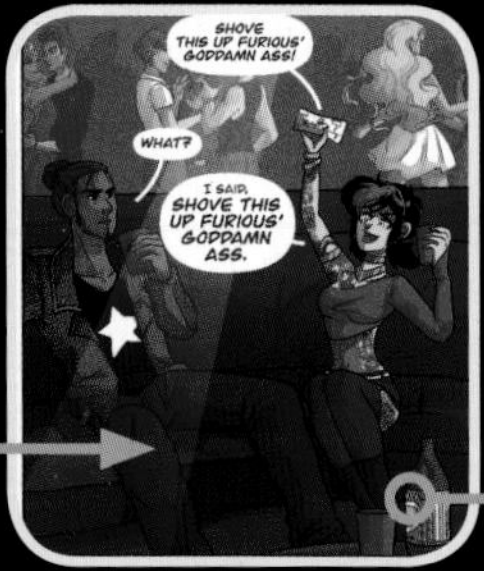
SHOVE THIS UP FURIOUS' GODDAMN ASS!
WHAT?
I SAID, SHOVE THIS UP FURIOUS' GODDAMN ASS.

Saar and Kim Q. Complicated.

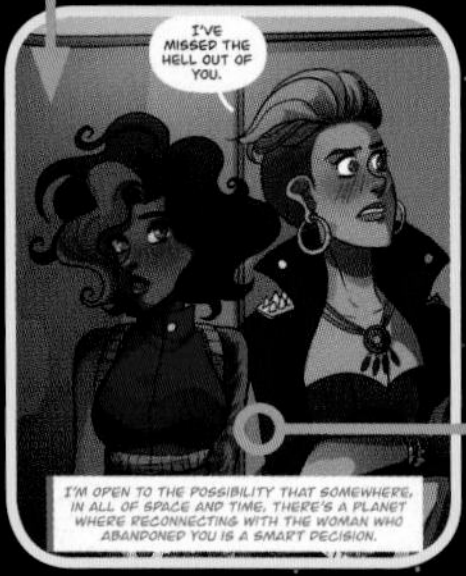
I'VE MISSED THE HELL OUT OF YOU.
I'M OPEN TO THE POSSIBILITY THAT SOMEWHERE, IN ALL OF SPACE AND TIME, THERE'S A PLANET WHERE RECONNECTING WITH THE WOMAN WHO ABANDONED YOU IS A SMART DECISION.

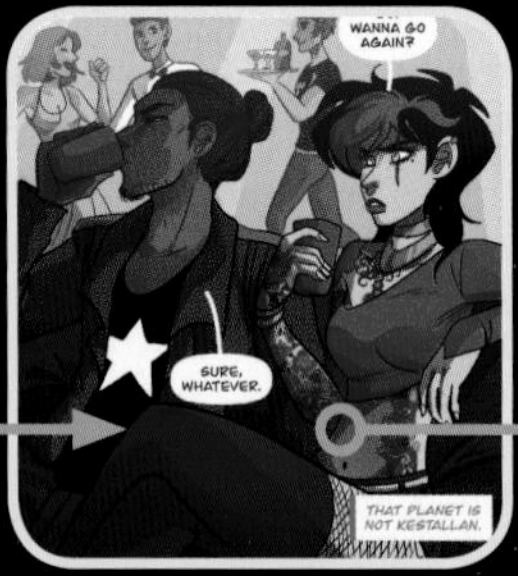
WANNA GO AGAIN?
SURE, WHATEVER.
THAT PLANET IS NOT KESTALLAN.

The Kims make bad love life choices.

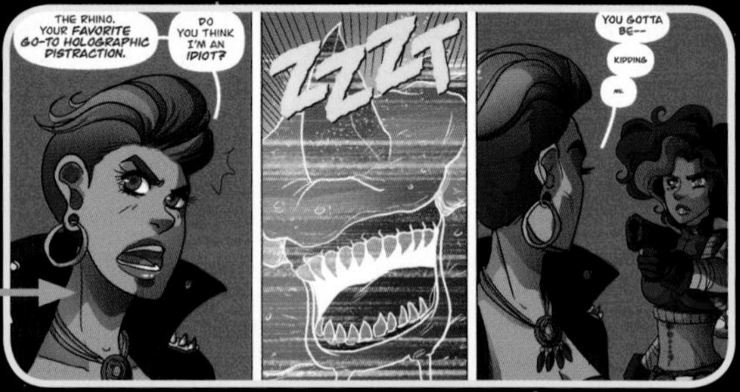
THE RHINO. YOUR FAVORITE GO-TO HOLOGRAPHIC DISTRACTION.
DO YOU THINK I'M AN IDIOT?
ZZZT
YOU GOTTA BE--
KIDDING
ME.

Laz betrays Kim D.

ISSUE 2: The Fighting Kims are broke and stranded. So what do they do about it? The answer, as usual, is "nothing helpful." Featuring a journey into the afterlife and an action scene in a fruit stand and also some legit relationship stuff.

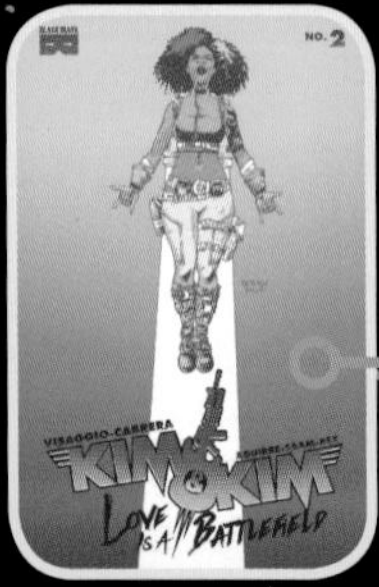
NO. 2
VISAGGIO-CABRERA
KIM & KIM
LOVE IS A BATTLEFIELD

The Kims pretty much literally in Hell.

Kathleen! And there is a bounty on Laz.

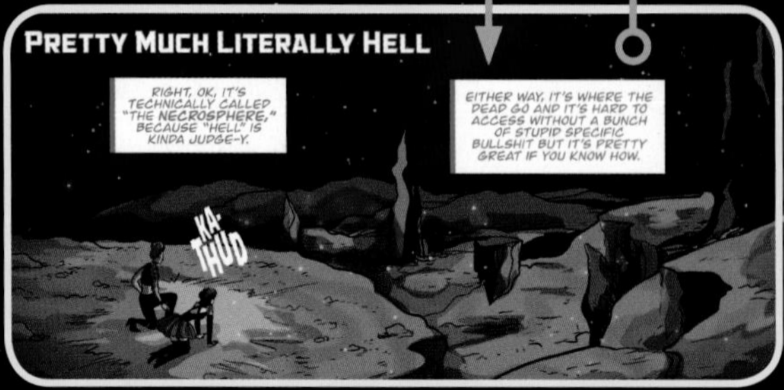
PRETTY MUCH LITERALLY HELL
RIGHT, OK, IT'S TECHNICALLY CALLED "THE NECROSPHERE," BECAUSE "HELL" IS KINDA JUDGE-Y.
EITHER WAY, IT'S WHERE THE DEAD GO AND IT'S HARD TO ACCESS WITHOUT A BUNCH OF STUPID SPECIFIC BULLSHIT BUT IT'S PRETTY GREAT IF YOU KNOW HOW.
KA-THUD

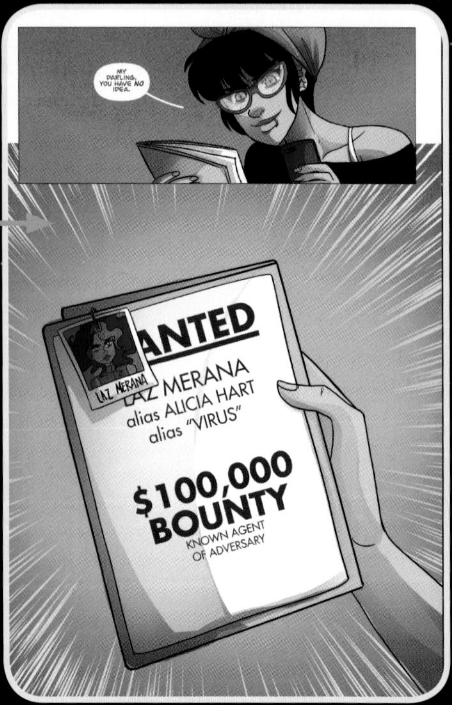
MY DARLING, YOU HAVE NO IDEA.
WANTED
LAZ MERANA
LAZ MERANA
alias ALICIA HART
alias "VIRUS"
$100,000
BOUNTY
KNOWN AGENT OF ADVERSARY

ISSUE 3: The Kims' old friend Kathleen shows up with some startling news: Kim D's ex-girlfriend has a bounty on her head the size of Texas -- and the criminal resources to justify it. So this is the part where stuff gets kinda serious. It does have a giant robot, though.

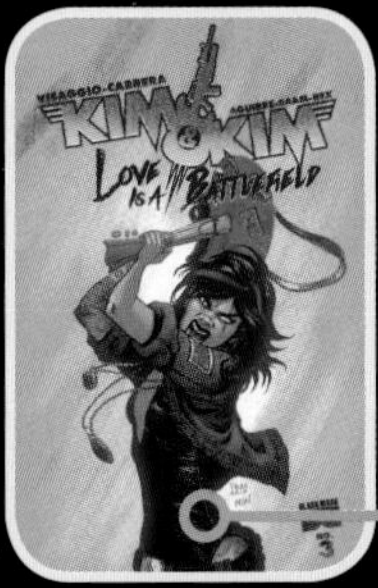
Love is a Battlefield
3

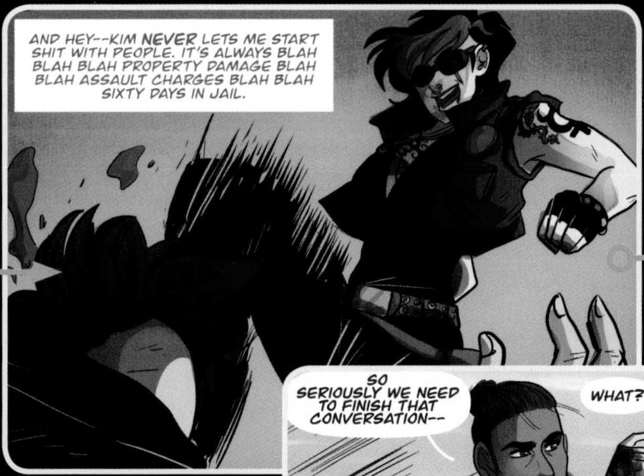
AND HEY--KIM NEVER LETS ME START SHIT WITH PEOPLE. IT'S ALWAYS BLAH BLAH BLAH PROPERTY DAMAGE BLAH BLAH ASSAULT CHARGES BLAH BLAH SIXTY DAYS IN JAIL.

Kim Q. is getting more violent.

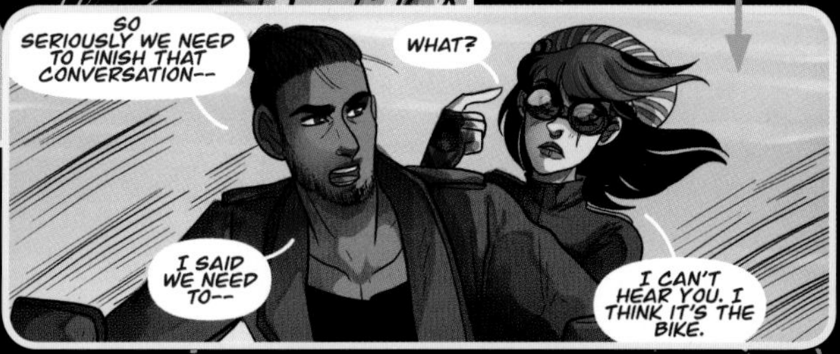
SO SERIOUSLY WE NEED TO FINISH THAT CONVERSATION--
WHAT?
I SAID WE NEED TO--
I CAN'T HEAR YOU. I THINK IT'S THE BIKE.

Saar and Kim Q. Still complicated.

ISSUE 4: Breakups aren't usually quite this violent. The fighting Kims square off against Kim D's ex-girlfriend in the final act of a messy affair that will only end with someone lying bloody on the ground. Dramatic? You bet!

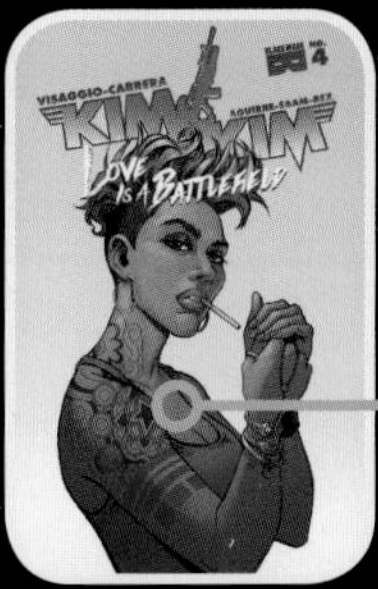
Love is a Battlefield
4

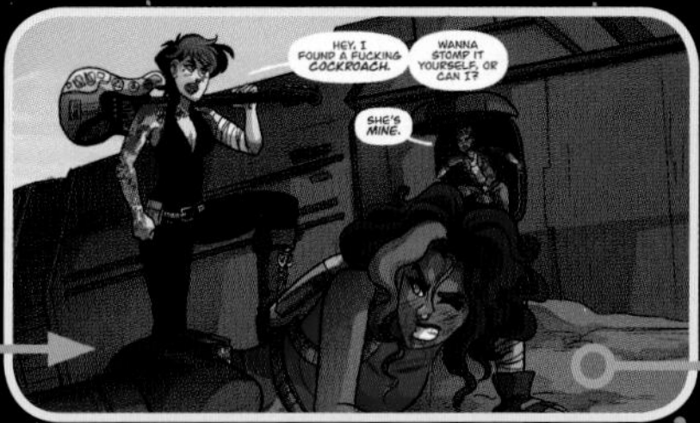
HEY, I FOUND A FUCKING COCKROACH.
WANNA STOMP IT YOURSELF, OR CAN I?
SHE'S MINE.

The Kims defeat Laz.

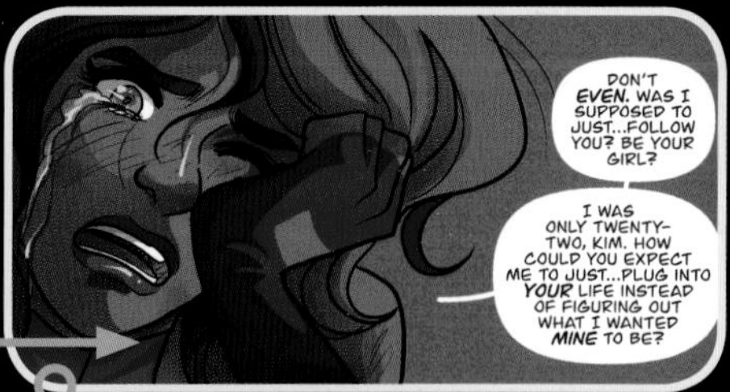
DON'T EVEN. WAS I SUPPOSED TO JUST...FOLLOW YOU? BE YOUR GIRL?
I WAS ONLY TWENTY-TWO, KIM. HOW COULD YOU EXPECT ME TO JUST...PLUG INTO YOUR LIFE INSTEAD OF FIGURING OUT WHAT I WANTED MINE TO BE?

Laz and Kim D. Their relationship was more complicated than we thought.

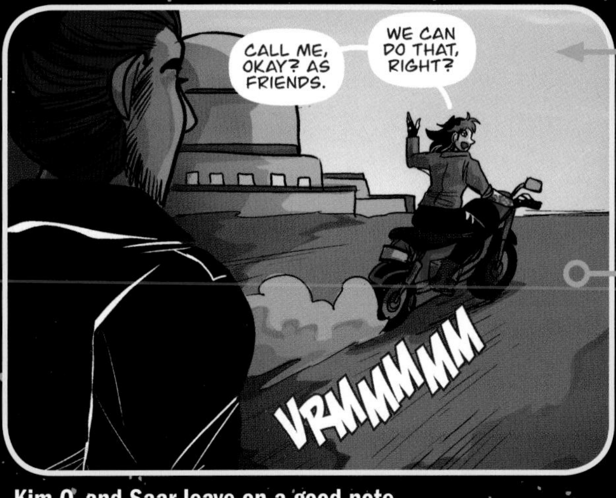
CALL ME, OKAY? AS FRIENDS.
WE CAN DO THAT, RIGHT?
VRMMMMM

Kim Q. and Saar leave on a good note...

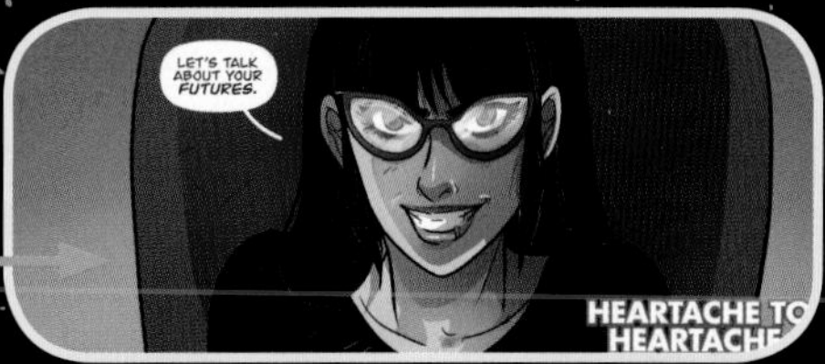
LET'S TALK ABOUT YOUR FUTURES.
HEARTACHE TO HEARTACHE

...Kathleen has plans for them.

All caught up.

OH S#!T IT'S KIM & KIM

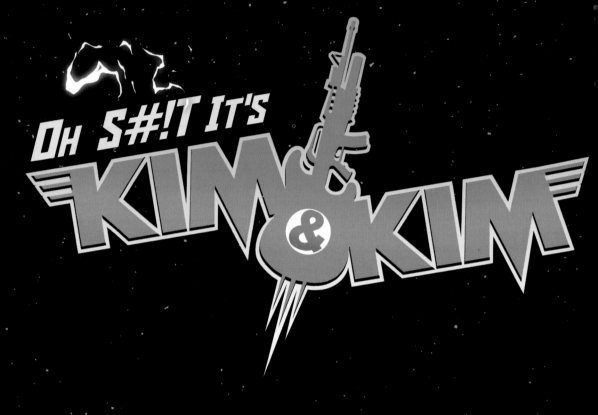

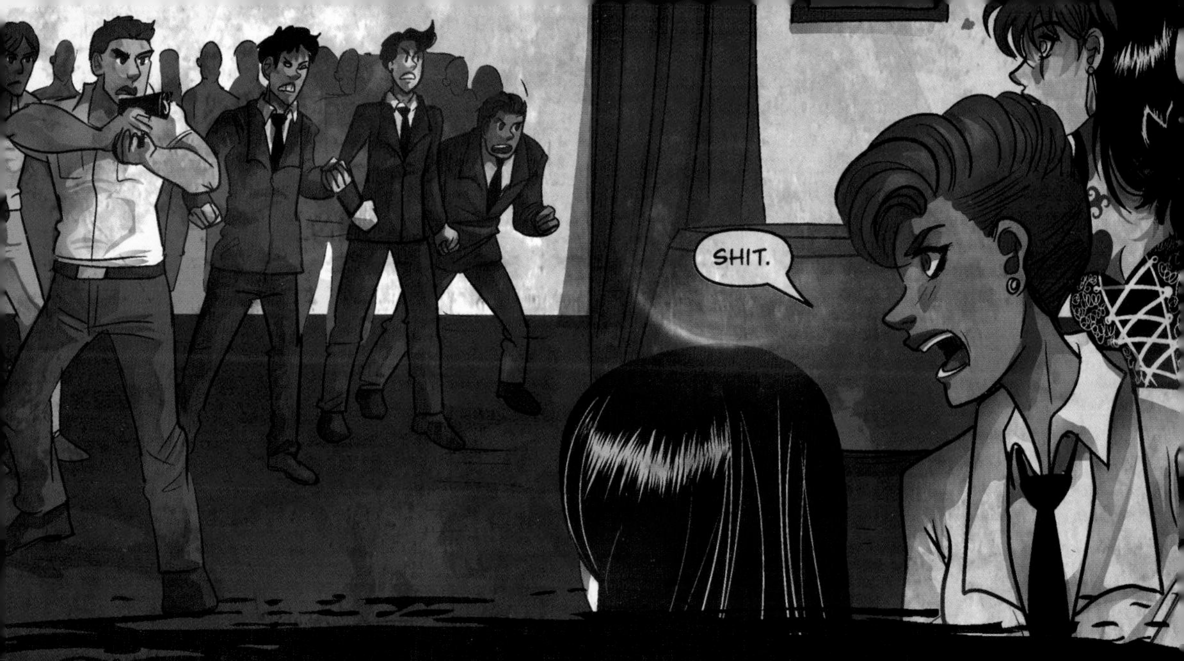
SHIT.

1

"OH S#IT! IT'S KIM AND KIM!"

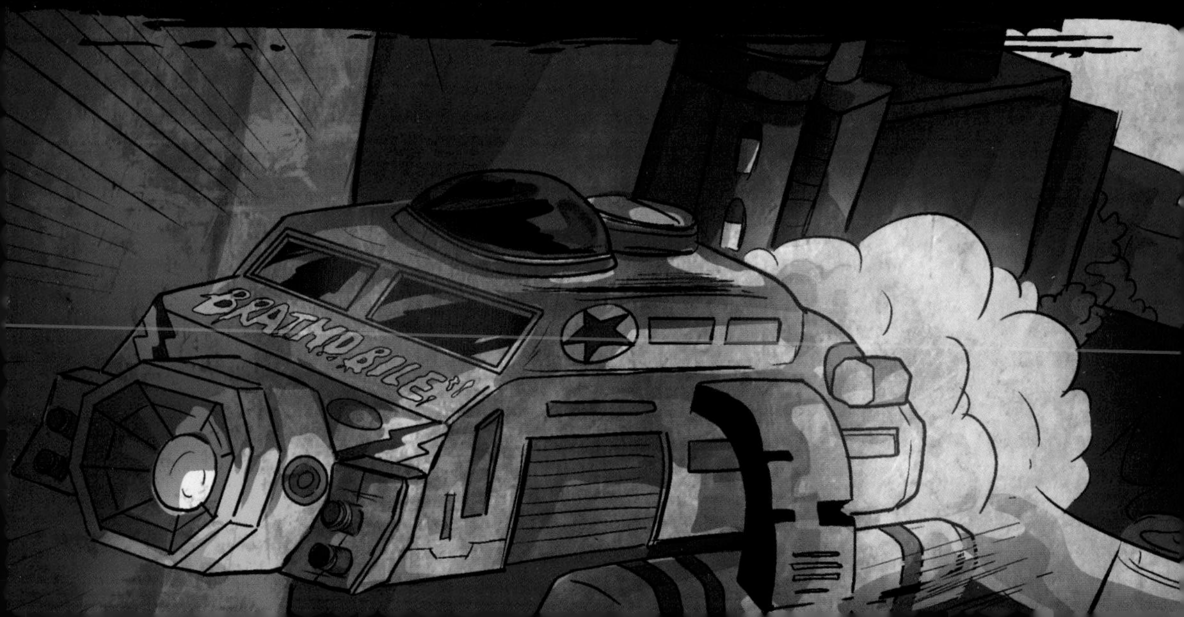
BRATMOBILE

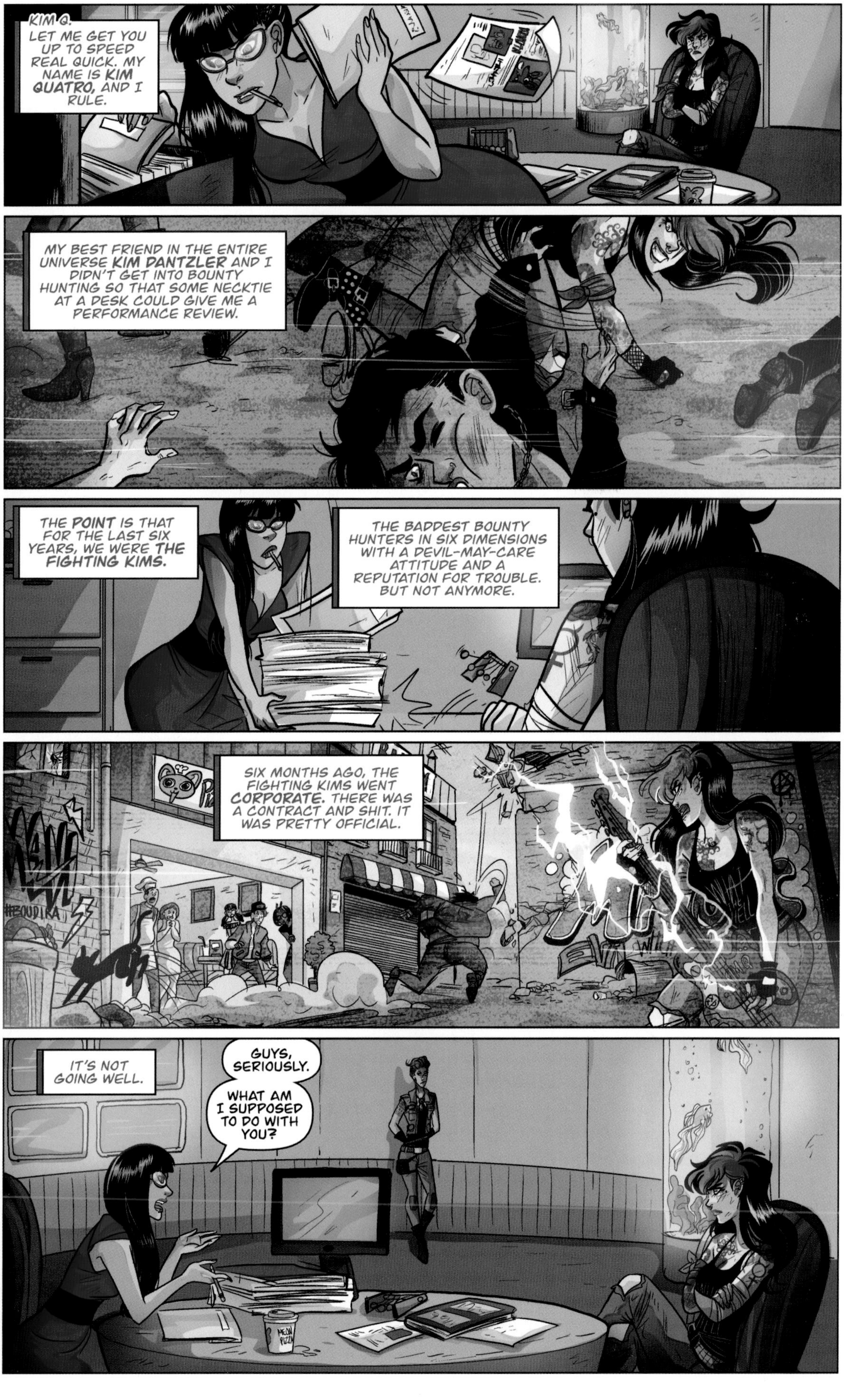
KIM Q.
LET ME GET YOU UP TO SPEED REAL QUICK. MY NAME IS **KIM QUATRO,** AND I RULE.
MY BEST FRIEND IN THE ENTIRE UNIVERSE **KIM DANTZLER** AND I DIDN'T GET INTO BOUNTY HUNTING SO THAT SOME NECKTIE AT A DESK COULD GIVE ME A PERFORMANCE REVIEW.
THE **POINT** IS THAT FOR THE LAST SIX YEARS, WE WERE **THE FIGHTING KIMS.**
THE BADDEST BOUNTY HUNTERS IN SIX DIMENSIONS WITH A DEVIL-MAY-CARE ATTITUDE AND A REPUTATION FOR TROUBLE. BUT NOT ANYMORE.
SIX MONTHS AGO, THE FIGHTING KIMS WENT **CORPORATE.** THERE WAS A CONTRACT AND SHIT. IT WAS PRETTY OFFICIAL.
IT'S NOT GOING WELL.
GUYS, SERIOUSLY.
WHAT AM I SUPPOSED TO DO WITH YOU?

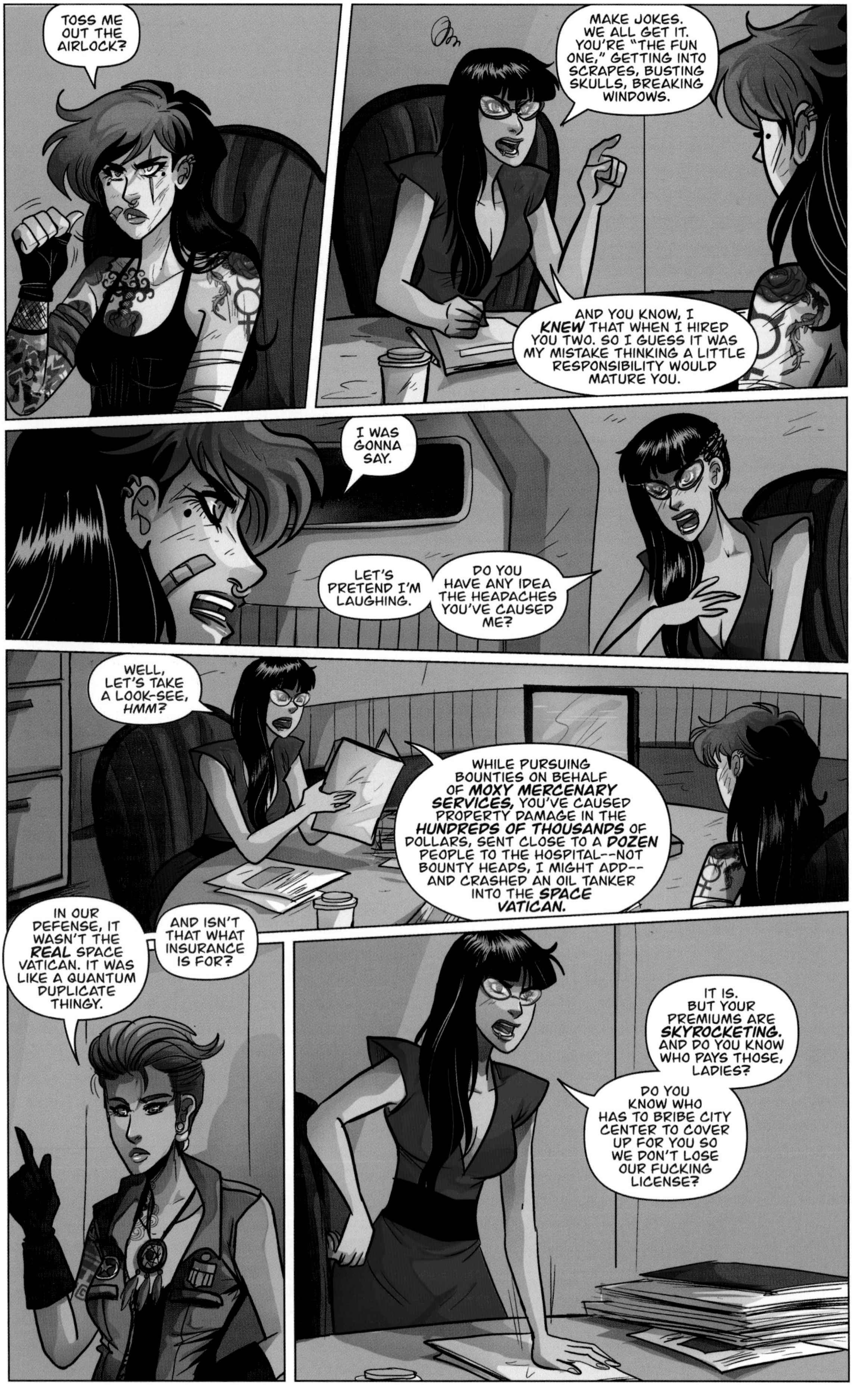
TOSS ME OUT THE AIRLOCK?
MAKE JOKES. WE ALL GET IT. YOU'RE "THE FUN ONE," GETTING INTO SCRAPES, BUSTING SKULLS, BREAKING WINDOWS.
AND YOU KNOW, I KNEW THAT WHEN I HIRED YOU TWO. SO I GUESS IT WAS MY MISTAKE THINKING A LITTLE RESPONSIBILITY WOULD MATURE YOU.
I WAS GONNA SAY.
LET'S PRETEND I'M LAUGHING.
DO YOU HAVE ANY IDEA THE HEADACHES YOU'VE CAUSED ME?
WELL, LET'S TAKE A LOOK-SEE, HMM?
WHILE PURSUING BOUNTIES ON BEHALF OF MOXY MERCENARY SERVICES, YOU'VE CAUSED PROPERTY DAMAGE IN THE HUNDREDS OF THOUSANDS OF DOLLARS, SENT CLOSE TO A DOZEN PEOPLE TO THE HOSPITAL--NOT BOUNTY HEADS, I MIGHT ADD--AND CRASHED AN OIL TANKER INTO THE SPACE VATICAN.
IN OUR DEFENSE, IT WASN'T THE REAL SPACE VATICAN. IT WAS LIKE A QUANTUM DUPLICATE THINGY.
AND ISN'T THAT WHAT INSURANCE IS FOR?
IT IS. BUT YOUR PREMIUMS ARE SKYROCKETING. AND DO YOU KNOW WHO PAYS THOSE, LADIES?
DO YOU KNOW WHO HAS TO BRIBE CITY CENTER TO COVER UP FOR YOU SO WE DON'T LOSE OUR FUCKING LICENSE?

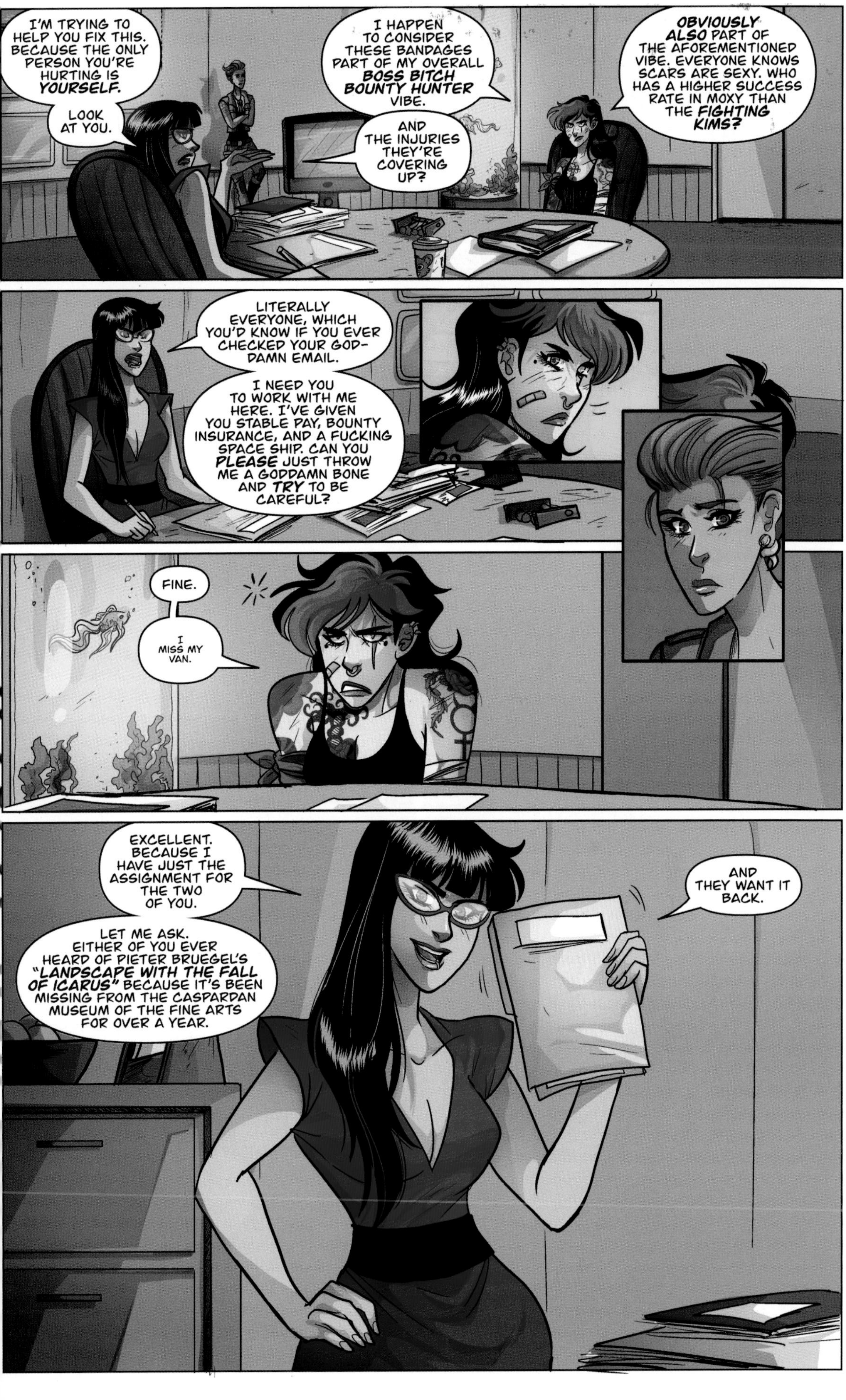
I'M TRYING TO HELP YOU FIX THIS. BECAUSE THE ONLY PERSON YOU'RE HURTING IS YOURSELF.
LOOK AT YOU.
I HAPPEN TO CONSIDER THESE BANDAGES PART OF MY OVERALL BOSS BITCH BOUNTY HUNTER VIBE.
AND THE INJURIES THEY'RE COVERING UP?
OBVIOUSLY ALSO PART OF THE AFOREMENTIONED VIBE. EVERYONE KNOWS SCARS ARE SEXY. WHO HAS A HIGHER SUCCESS RATE IN MOXY THAN THE FIGHTING KIMS?
LITERALLY EVERYONE, WHICH YOU'D KNOW IF YOU EVER CHECKED YOUR GOD-DAMN EMAIL.
I NEED YOU TO WORK WITH ME HERE. I'VE GIVEN YOU STABLE PAY, BOUNTY INSURANCE, AND A FUCKING SPACE SHIP. CAN YOU PLEASE JUST THROW ME A GODDAMN BONE AND TRY TO BE CAREFUL?
FINE.
I MISS MY VAN.
EXCELLENT. BECAUSE I HAVE JUST THE ASSIGNMENT FOR THE TWO OF YOU.
LET ME ASK. EITHER OF YOU EVER HEARD OF PIETER BRUEGEL'S "LANDSCAPE WITH THE FALL OF ICARUS" BECAUSE IT'S BEEN MISSING FROM THE CASPARDAN MUSEUM OF THE FINE ARTS FOR OVER A YEAR.
AND THEY WANT IT BACK.

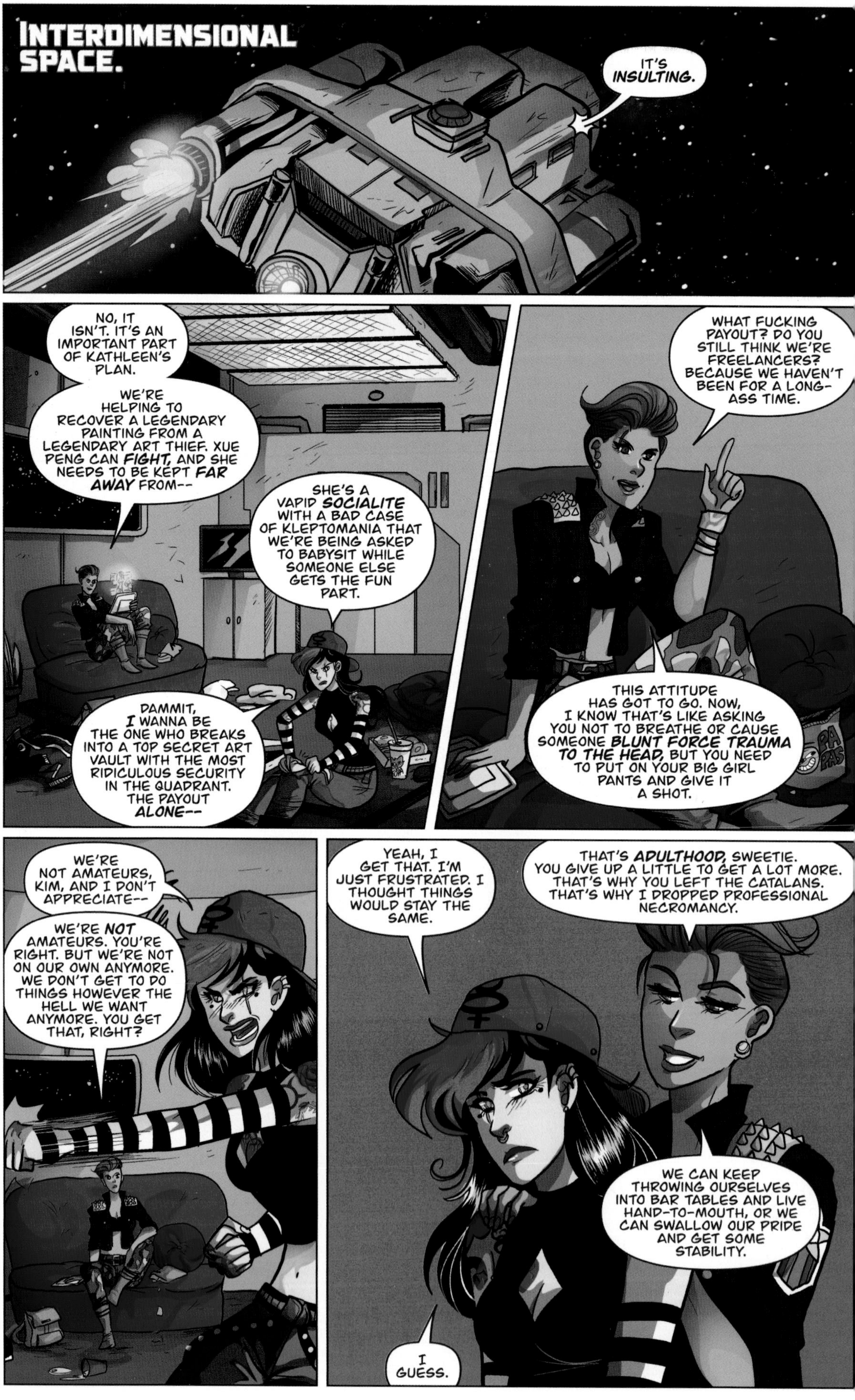
INTERDIMENSIONAL SPACE.
IT'S INSULTING.
NO, IT ISN'T. IT'S AN IMPORTANT PART OF KATHLEEN'S PLAN.
WE'RE HELPING TO RECOVER A LEGENDARY PAINTING FROM A LEGENDARY ART THIEF. XUE PENG CAN FIGHT, AND SHE NEEDS TO BE KEPT FAR AWAY FROM--
SHE'S A VAPID SOCIALITE WITH A BAD CASE OF KLEPTOMANIA THAT WE'RE BEING ASKED TO BABYSIT WHILE SOMEONE ELSE GETS THE FUN PART.
DAMMIT, I WANNA BE THE ONE WHO BREAKS INTO A TOP SECRET ART VAULT WITH THE MOST RIDICULOUS SECURITY IN THE QUADRANT. THE PAYOUT ALONE--
WHAT FUCKING PAYOUT? DO YOU STILL THINK WE'RE FREELANCERS? BECAUSE WE HAVEN'T BEEN FOR A LONG-ASS TIME.
THIS ATTITUDE HAS GOT TO GO. NOW, I KNOW THAT'S LIKE ASKING YOU NOT TO BREATHE OR CAUSE SOMEONE BLUNT FORCE TRAUMA TO THE HEAD, BUT YOU NEED TO PUT ON YOUR BIG GIRL PANTS AND GIVE IT A SHOT.
PAPAS
WE'RE NOT AMATEURS, KIM, AND I DON'T APPRECIATE--
WE'RE NOT AMATEURS. YOU'RE RIGHT. BUT WE'RE NOT ON OUR OWN ANYMORE. WE DON'T GET TO DO THINGS HOWEVER THE HELL WE WANT ANYMORE. YOU GET THAT, RIGHT?
YEAH, I GET THAT. I'M JUST FRUSTRATED. I THOUGHT THINGS WOULD STAY THE SAME.
THAT'S ADULTHOOD, SWEETIE. YOU GIVE UP A LITTLE TO GET A LOT MORE. THAT'S WHY YOU LEFT THE CATALANS. THAT'S WHY I DROPPED PROFESSIONAL NECROMANCY.
WE CAN KEEP THROWING OURSELVES INTO BAR TABLES AND LIVE HAND-TO-MOUTH, OR WE CAN SWALLOW OUR PRIDE AND GET SOME STABILITY.
I GUESS.

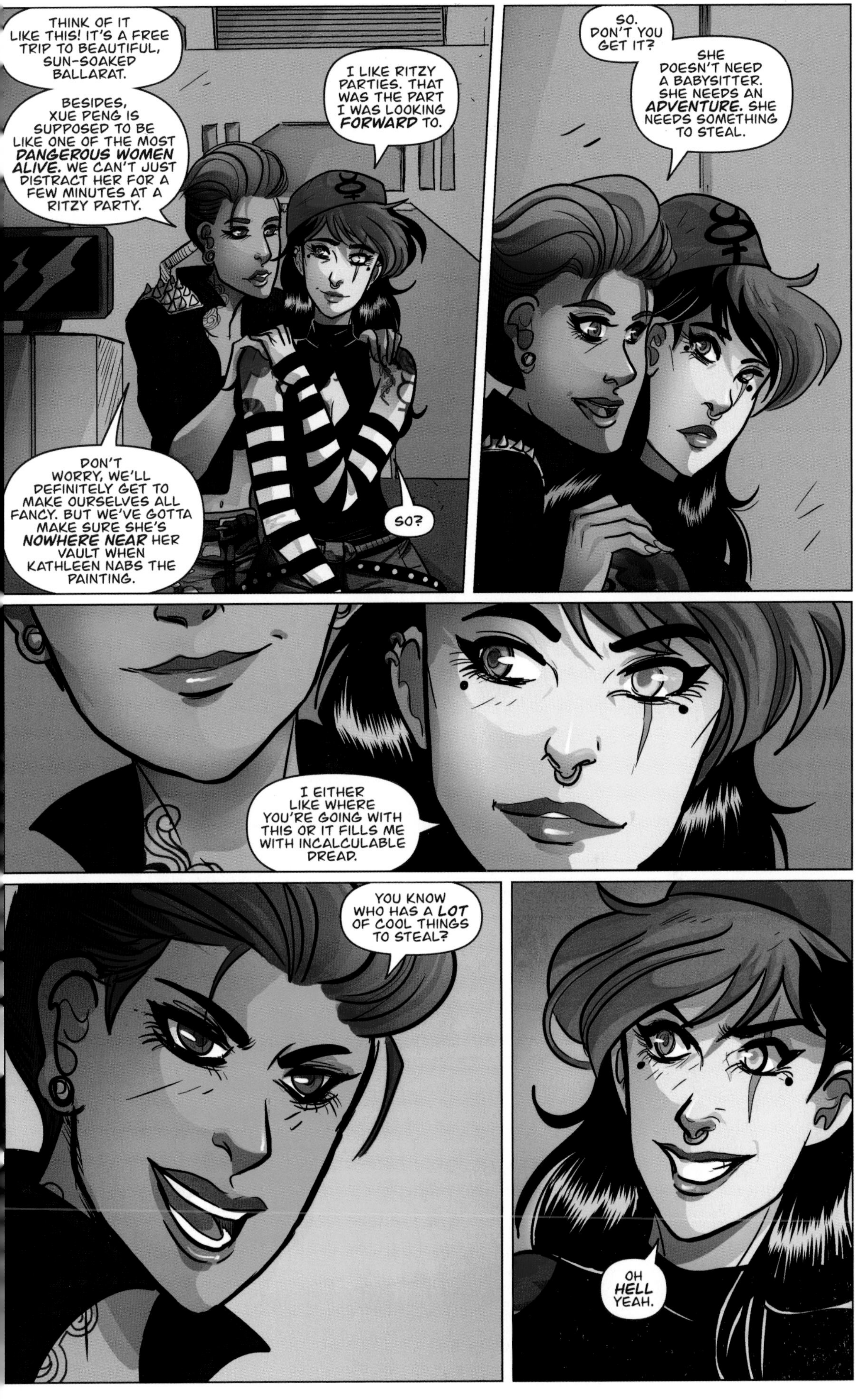

THINK OF IT LIKE THIS! IT'S A FREE TRIP TO BEAUTIFUL, SUN-SOAKED BALLARAT.
BESIDES, XUE PENG IS SUPPOSED TO BE LIKE ONE OF THE MOST DANGEROUS WOMEN ALIVE. WE CAN'T JUST DISTRACT HER FOR A FEW MINUTES AT A RITZY PARTY.
I LIKE RITZY PARTIES. THAT WAS THE PART I WAS LOOKING FORWARD TO.
DON'T WORRY, WE'LL DEFINITELY GET TO MAKE OURSELVES ALL FANCY. BUT WE'VE GOTTA MAKE SURE SHE'S NOWHERE NEAR HER VAULT WHEN KATHLEEN NABS THE PAINTING.
SO?
SO. DON'T YOU GET IT?
SHE DOESN'T NEED A BABYSITTER. SHE NEEDS AN ADVENTURE. SHE NEEDS SOMETHING TO STEAL.
I EITHER LIKE WHERE YOU'RE GOING WITH THIS OR IT FILLS ME WITH INCALCULABLE DREAD.
YOU KNOW WHO HAS A LOT OF COOL THINGS TO STEAL?
OH HELL YEAH.

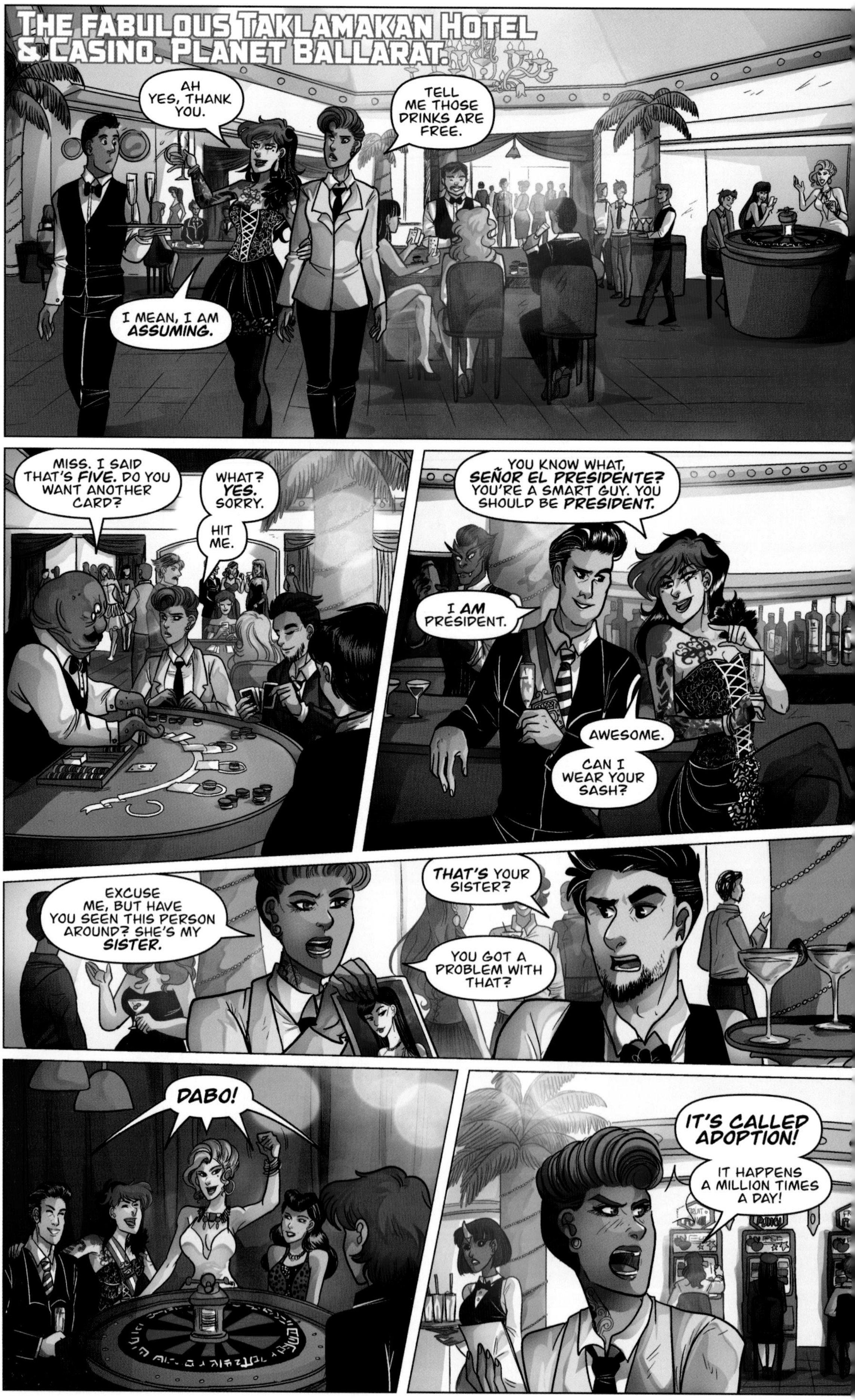
THE FABULOUS TAKLAMAKAN HOTEL & CASINO. PLANET BALLARAT.
AH YES, THANK YOU.
TELL ME THOSE DRINKS ARE FREE.
I MEAN, I AM ASSUMING.
MISS. I SAID THAT'S FIVE. DO YOU WANT ANOTHER CARD?
WHAT? YES. SORRY.
HIT ME.
YOU KNOW WHAT, SEÑOR EL PRESIDENTE? YOU'RE A SMART GUY. YOU SHOULD BE PRESIDENT.
I AM PRESIDENT.
AWESOME.
CAN I WEAR YOUR SASH?
EXCUSE ME, BUT HAVE YOU SEEN THIS PERSON AROUND? SHE'S MY SISTER.
THAT'S YOUR SISTER?
YOU GOT A PROBLEM WITH THAT?
DABO!
IT'S CALLED ADOPTION!
IT HAPPENS A MILLION TIMES A DAY!

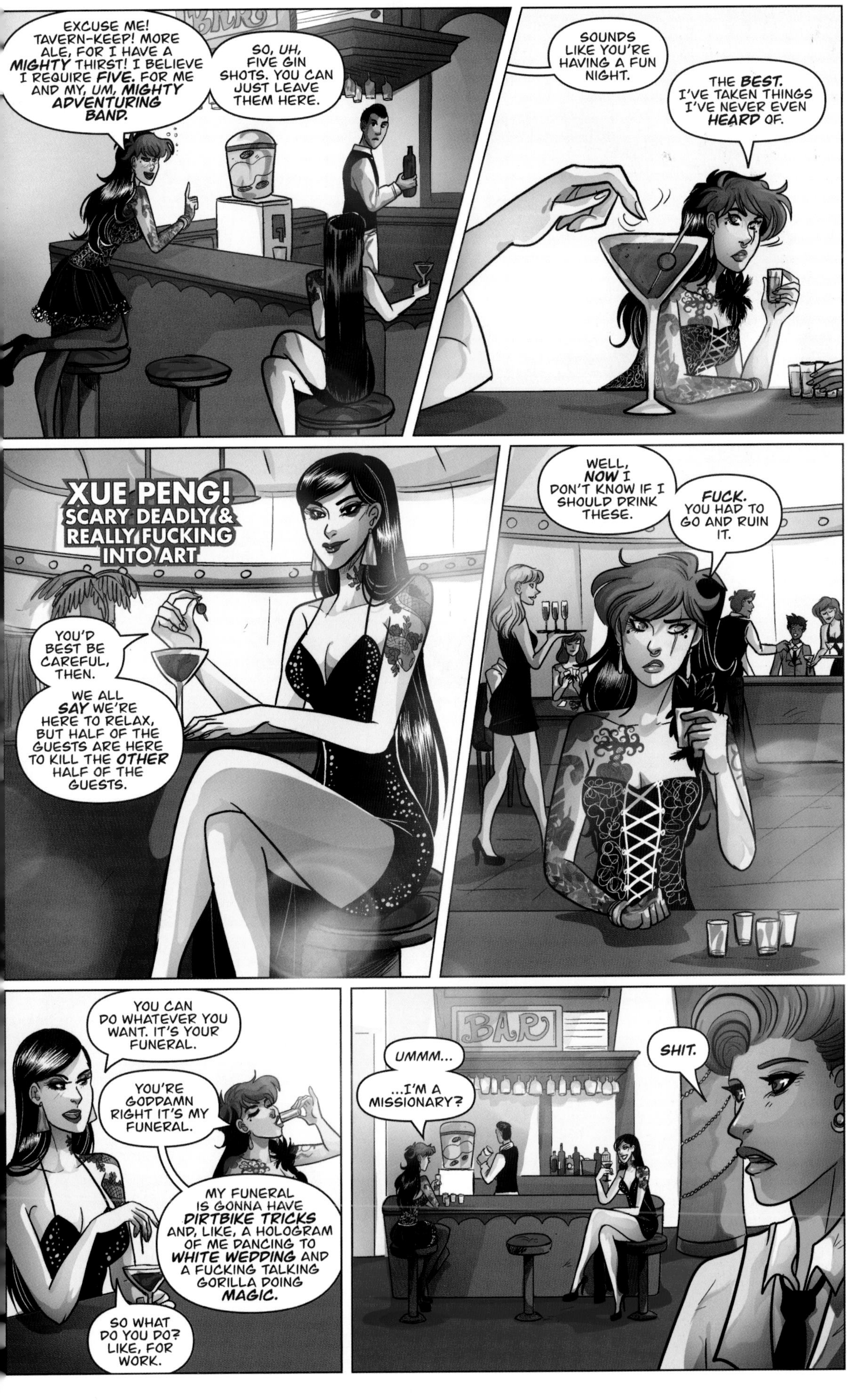

EXCUSE ME! TAVERN-KEEP! MORE ALE, FOR I HAVE A MIGHTY THIRST! I BELIEVE I REQUIRE FIVE. FOR ME AND MY, UM, MIGHTY ADVENTURING BAND.
SO, UH, FIVE GIN SHOTS. YOU CAN JUST LEAVE THEM HERE.
SOUNDS LIKE YOU'RE HAVING A FUN NIGHT.
THE BEST. I'VE TAKEN THINGS I'VE NEVER EVEN HEARD OF.
XUE PENG! SCARY DEADLY & REALLY FUCKING INTO ART
YOU'D BEST BE CAREFUL, THEN.
WE ALL SAY WE'RE HERE TO RELAX, BUT HALF OF THE GUESTS ARE HERE TO KILL THE OTHER HALF OF THE GUESTS.
WELL, NOW I DON'T KNOW IF I SHOULD DRINK THESE.
FUCK. YOU HAD TO GO AND RUIN IT.
YOU CAN DO WHATEVER YOU WANT. IT'S YOUR FUNERAL.
YOU'RE GODDAMN RIGHT IT'S MY FUNERAL.
MY FUNERAL IS GONNA HAVE DIRTBIKE TRICKS AND, LIKE, A HOLOGRAM OF ME DANCING TO WHITE WEDDING AND A FUCKING TALKING GORILLA DOING MAGIC.
SO WHAT DO YOU DO? LIKE, FOR WORK.
BAR
UMMM...
...I'M A MISSIONARY?
SHIT.

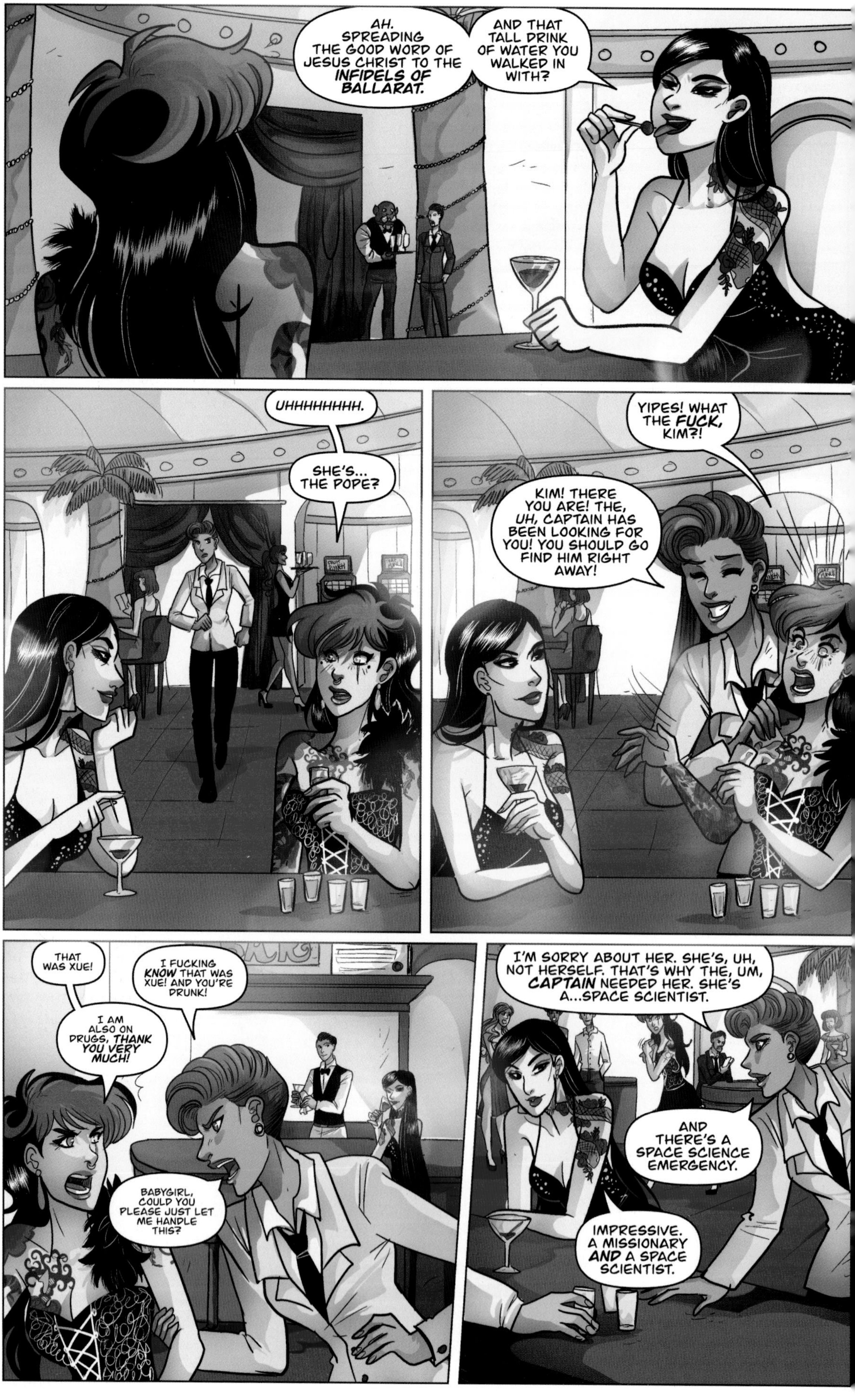
AH. SPREADING THE GOOD WORD OF JESUS CHRIST TO THE INFIDELS OF BALLARAT.
AND THAT TALL DRINK OF WATER YOU WALKED IN WITH?
UHHHHHHHH.
SHE'S... THE POPE?
YIPES! WHAT THE FUCK, KIM?!
KIM! THERE YOU ARE! THE, UH, CAPTAIN HAS BEEN LOOKING FOR YOU! YOU SHOULD GO FIND HIM RIGHT AWAY!
THAT WAS XUE!
I FUCKING KNOW THAT WAS XUE! AND YOU'RE DRUNK!
I AM ALSO ON DRUGS, THANK YOU VERY MUCH!
BABYGIRL, COULD YOU PLEASE JUST LET ME HANDLE THIS?
I'M SORRY ABOUT HER. SHE'S, UH, NOT HERSELF. THAT'S WHY THE, UM, CAPTAIN NEEDED HER. SHE'S A...SPACE SCIENTIST.
AND THERE'S A SPACE SCIENCE EMERGENCY.
IMPRESSIVE. A MISSIONARY AND A SPACE SCIENTIST.

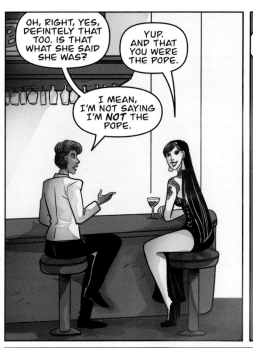

OH, RIGHT, YES, DEFINTELY THAT TOO. IS THAT WHAT SHE SAID SHE WAS?

YUP. AND THAT YOU WERE THE POPE.

I MEAN, I'M NOT SAYING I'M **NOT** THE POPE.

ALRIGHT, COME ON. LEVEL WITH ME. YOU GUYS HAVE BEEN ABOUT AS INCONSPICUOUS AS A BULL PERFORMING HEART SURGERY ON AN ELEPHANT IN THE MIDDLE OF TRAFFIC.

I MEAN, COLOR ME FLATTERED THAT A GORGEOUS LADY LIKE YOU MIGHT LAND HER ROVING EYE ON LITTLE OLD ME, BUT LET'S BE STRAIGHT WITH EACH OTHER, FIGURATIVELY SPEAKING.

WHY ARE YOU TWO LOOKING SO HARD FOR ME?

OH MAN. WAS IT THAT OBVIOUS? I THOUGHT WE WERE BEING REALLY SUBTLE.

LISTEN. I'M GOOD AT WHAT I DO, AND THAT MEANS I PAY ATTENTION. IF YOU ASKED ME HOW MANY CLORRIANS WERE IN THIS ROOM RIGHT NOW, I'D TELL YOU THERE WERE TWENTY-TWO, AND THAT WOULD BE CORRECT. TWENTY-TWO AND A HALF IF YOU WANNA PUSH IT.

AND THEY'RE NOT EVEN BEING OBVIOUS. BUT YOU? YOU'VE BEEN FLASHING MY HEADSHOT TO HALF THE WAITSTAFF AND YOU'RE THE ONLY PERSON HERE NOT HAVING ANY FUN.

HAND. THIGH.

OTHER THAN **THAT** GUY, ANYWAY.

BUT HE HASN'T MOVED ALL NIGHT.

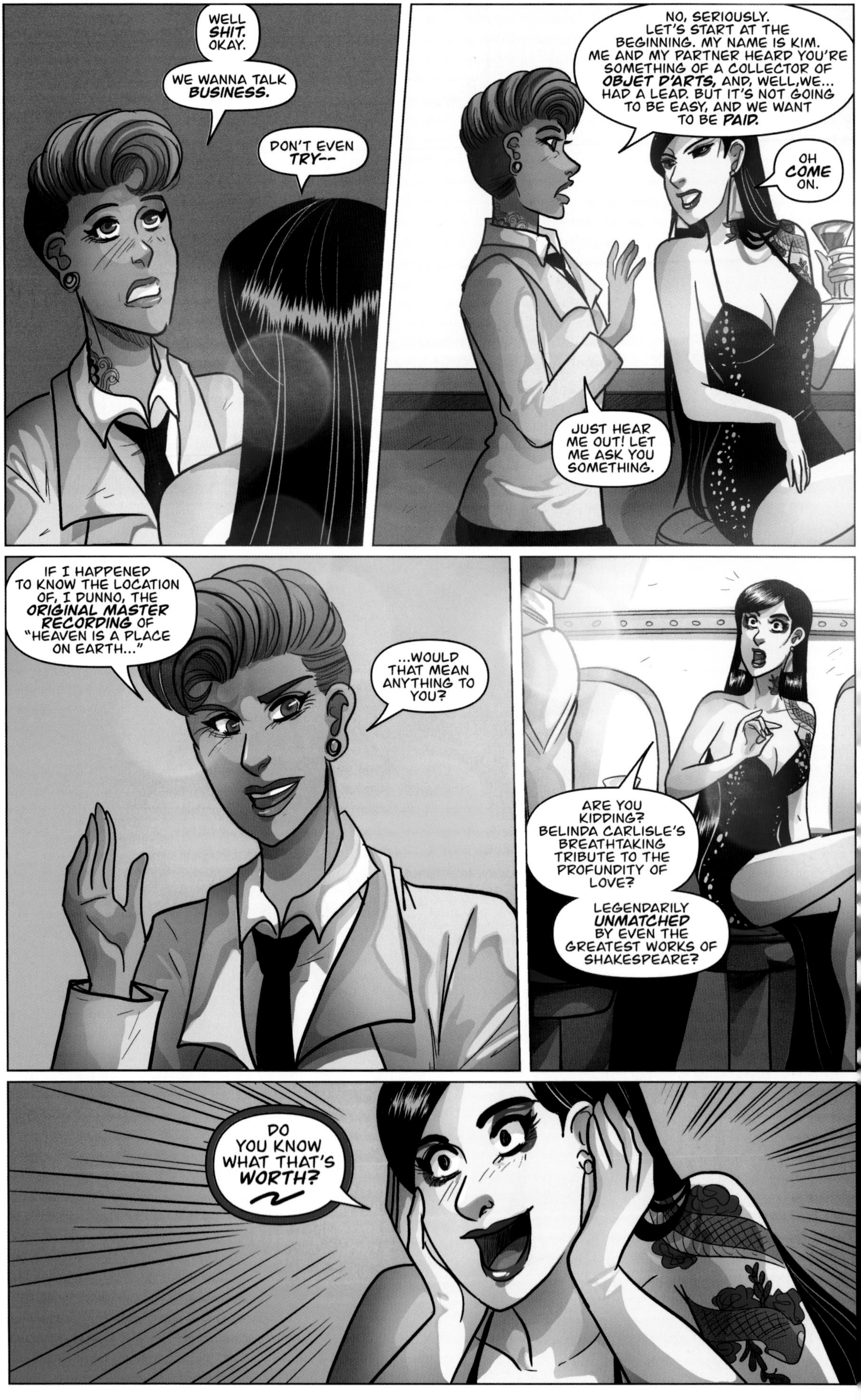
WELL SHIT. OKAY.
WE WANNA TALK BUSINESS.
DON'T EVEN TRY--
NO, SERIOUSLY. LET'S START AT THE BEGINNING. MY NAME IS KIM. ME AND MY PARTNER HEARD YOU'RE SOMETHING OF A COLLECTOR OF OBJET D'ARTS, AND, WELL, WE... HAD A LEAD. BUT IT'S NOT GOING TO BE EASY, AND WE WANT TO BE PAID.
OH COME ON.
JUST HEAR ME OUT! LET ME ASK YOU SOMETHING.
IF I HAPPENED TO KNOW THE LOCATION OF, I DUNNO, THE ORIGINAL MASTER RECORDING OF "HEAVEN IS A PLACE ON EARTH..."
...WOULD THAT MEAN ANYTHING TO YOU?
ARE YOU KIDDING? BELINDA CARLISLE'S BREATHTAKING TRIBUTE TO THE PROFUNDITY OF LOVE?
LEGENDARILY UNMATCHED BY EVEN THE GREATEST WORKS OF SHAKESPEARE?
DO YOU KNOW WHAT THAT'S WORTH?

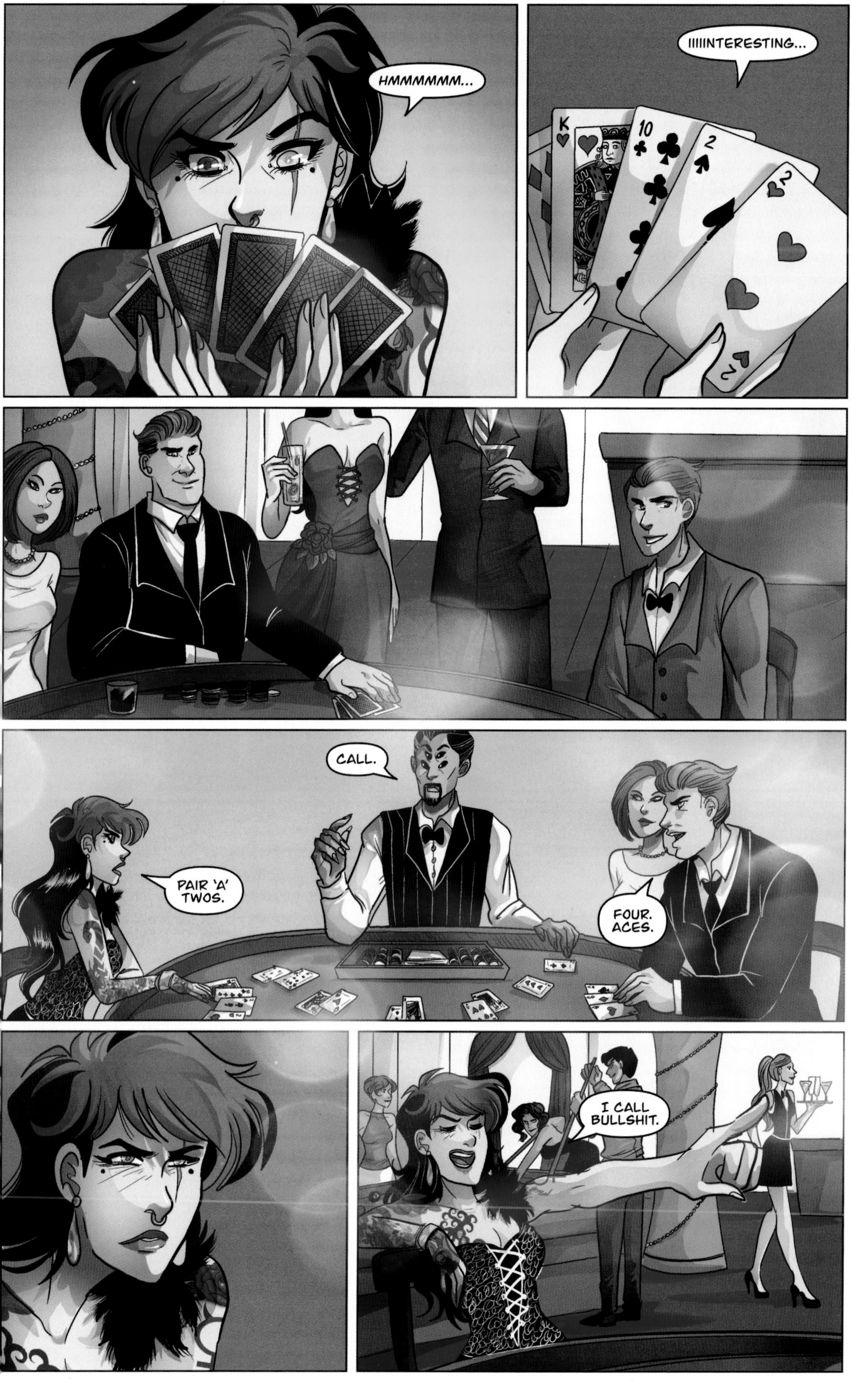
HMMMMMM...
IIIIINTERESTING...
CALL.
PAIR 'A' TWOS.
FOUR. ACES.
I CALL BULLSHIT.

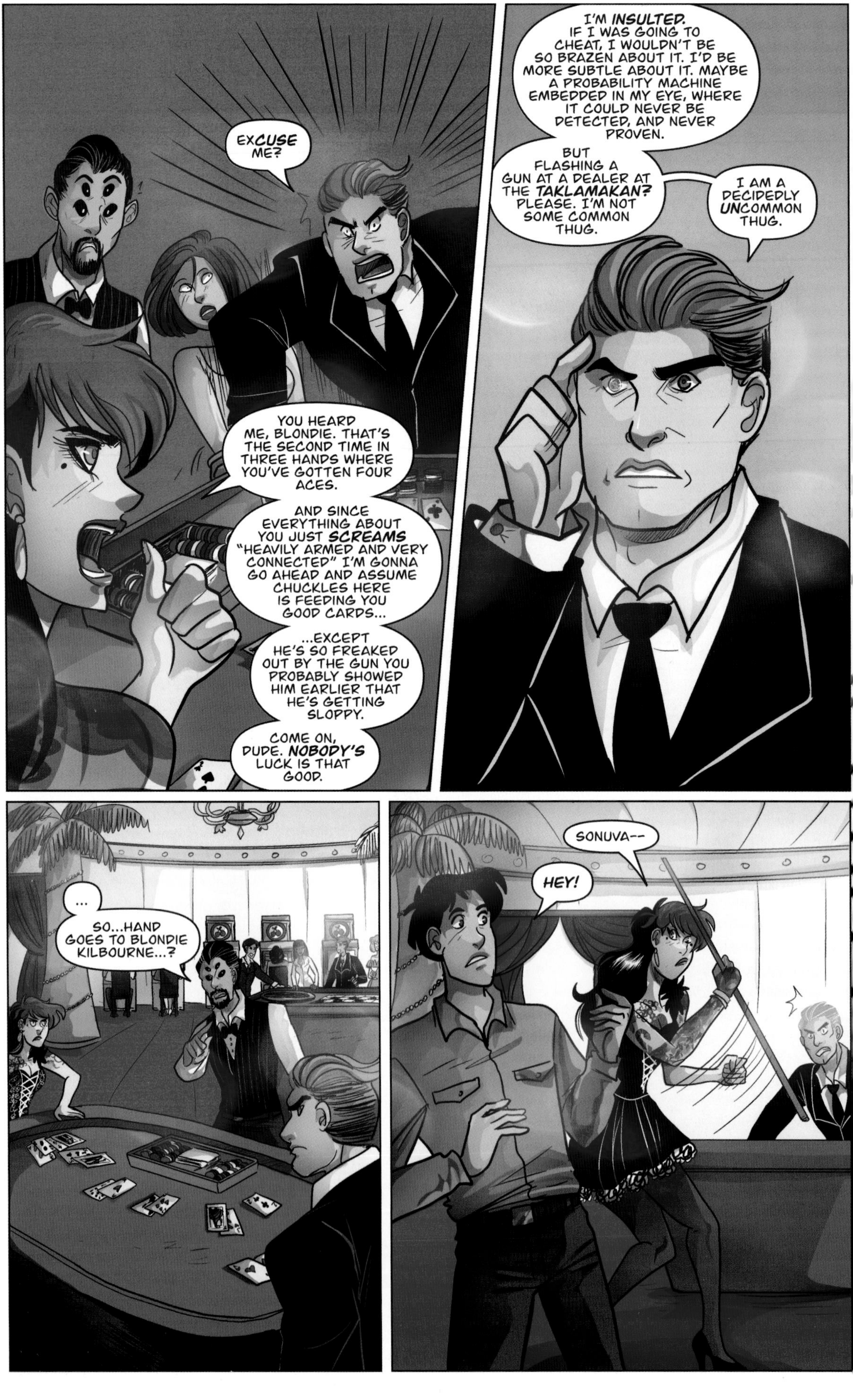
EXCUSE ME?
YOU HEARD ME, BLONDIE. THAT'S THE SECOND TIME IN THREE HANDS WHERE YOU'VE GOTTEN FOUR ACES.
AND SINCE EVERYTHING ABOUT YOU JUST SCREAMS "HEAVILY ARMED AND VERY CONNECTED" I'M GONNA GO AHEAD AND ASSUME CHUCKLES HERE IS FEEDING YOU GOOD CARDS...
...EXCEPT HE'S SO FREAKED OUT BY THE GUN YOU PROBABLY SHOWED HIM EARLIER THAT HE'S GETTING SLOPPY.
COME ON, DUDE. NOBODY'S LUCK IS THAT GOOD.
I'M INSULTED. IF I WAS GOING TO CHEAT, I WOULDN'T BE SO BRAZEN ABOUT IT. I'D BE MORE SUBTLE ABOUT IT. MAYBE A PROBABILITY MACHINE EMBEDDED IN MY EYE, WHERE IT COULD NEVER BE DETECTED, AND NEVER PROVEN.
BUT FLASHING A GUN AT A DEALER AT THE TAKLAMAKAN? PLEASE. I'M NOT SOME COMMON THUG.
I AM A DECIDEDLY UNCOMMON THUG.
...
SO...HAND GOES TO BLONDIE KILBOURNE...?
SONUVA--
HEY!

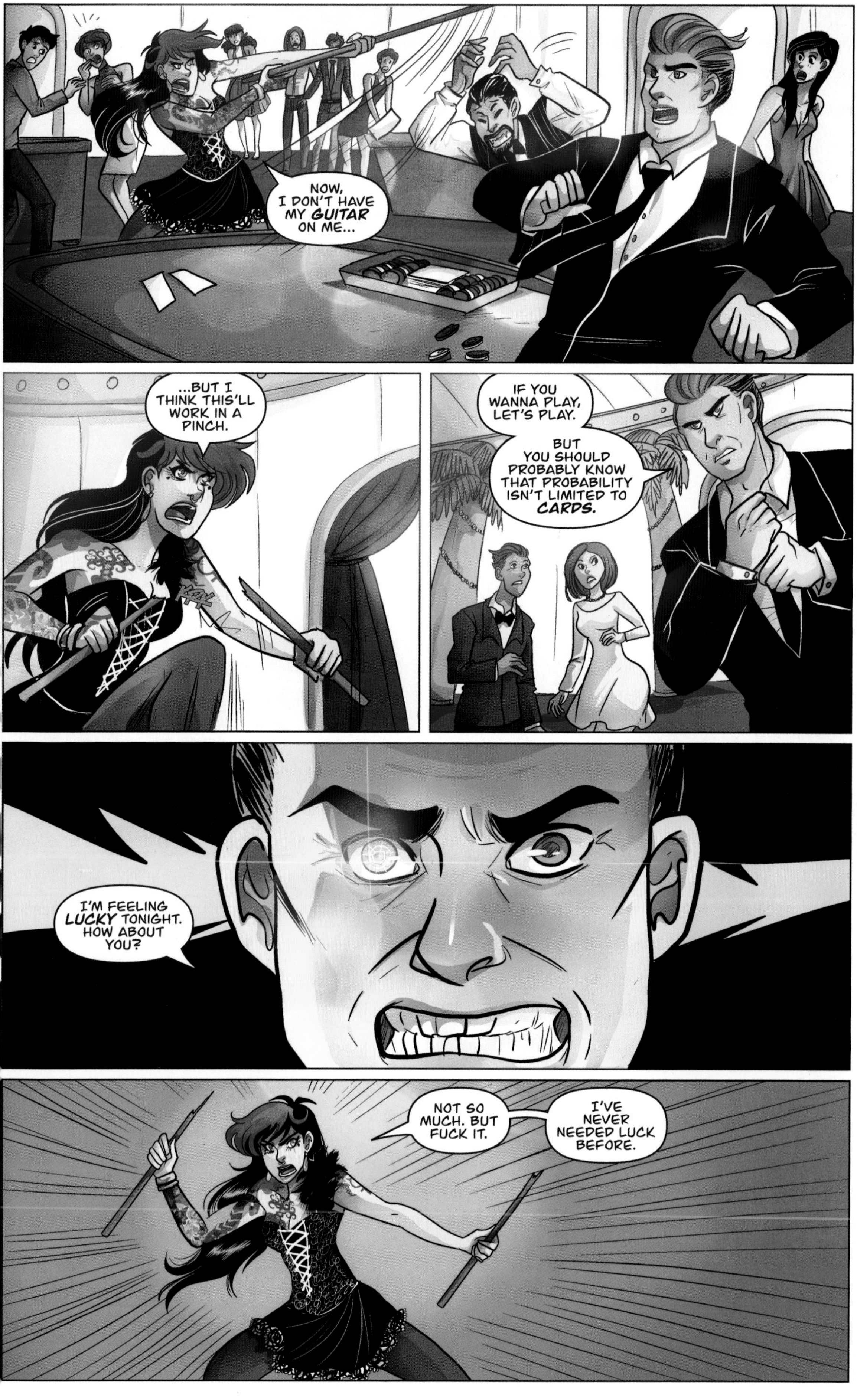
NOW, I DON'T HAVE MY GUITAR ON ME...
...BUT I THINK THIS'LL WORK IN A PINCH.
IF YOU WANNA PLAY, LET'S PLAY.
BUT YOU SHOULD PROBABLY KNOW THAT PROBABILITY ISN'T LIMITED TO CARDS.
I'M FEELING LUCKY TONIGHT. HOW ABOUT YOU?
NOT SO MUCH. BUT FUCK IT.
I'VE NEVER NEEDED LUCK BEFORE.

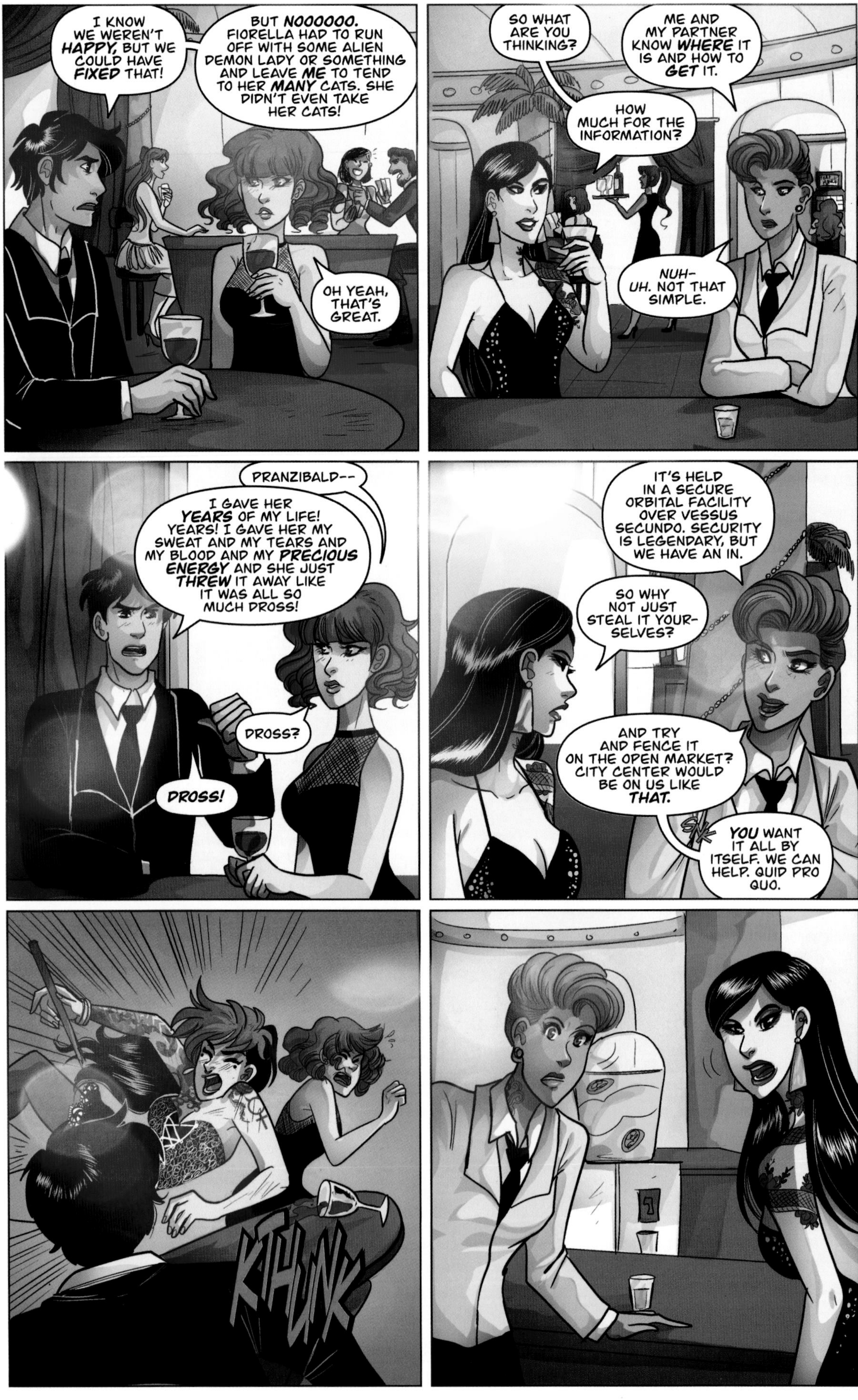
I KNOW WE WEREN'T HAPPY, BUT WE COULD HAVE FIXED THAT!
BUT NOOOOOO. FIORELLA HAD TO RUN OFF WITH SOME ALIEN DEMON LADY OR SOMETHING AND LEAVE ME TO TEND TO HER MANY CATS. SHE DIDN'T EVEN TAKE HER CATS!
OH YEAH, THAT'S GREAT.
SO WHAT ARE YOU THINKING?
ME AND MY PARTNER KNOW WHERE IT IS AND HOW TO GET IT.
HOW MUCH FOR THE INFORMATION?
NUH-UH. NOT THAT SIMPLE.
PRANZIBALD--
I GAVE HER YEARS OF MY LIFE! YEARS! I GAVE HER MY SWEAT AND MY TEARS AND MY BLOOD AND MY PRECIOUS ENERGY AND SHE JUST THREW IT AWAY LIKE IT WAS ALL SO MUCH DROSS!
DROSS?
DROSS!
IT'S HELD IN A SECURE ORBITAL FACILITY OVER VESSUS SECUNDO. SECURITY IS LEGENDARY, BUT WE HAVE AN IN.
SO WHY NOT JUST STEAL IT YOUR-SELVES?
AND TRY AND FENCE IT ON THE OPEN MARKET? CITY CENTER WOULD BE ON US LIKE THAT.
SNK
YOU WANT IT ALL BY ITSELF. WE CAN HELP. QUID PRO QUO.
KTHUNK

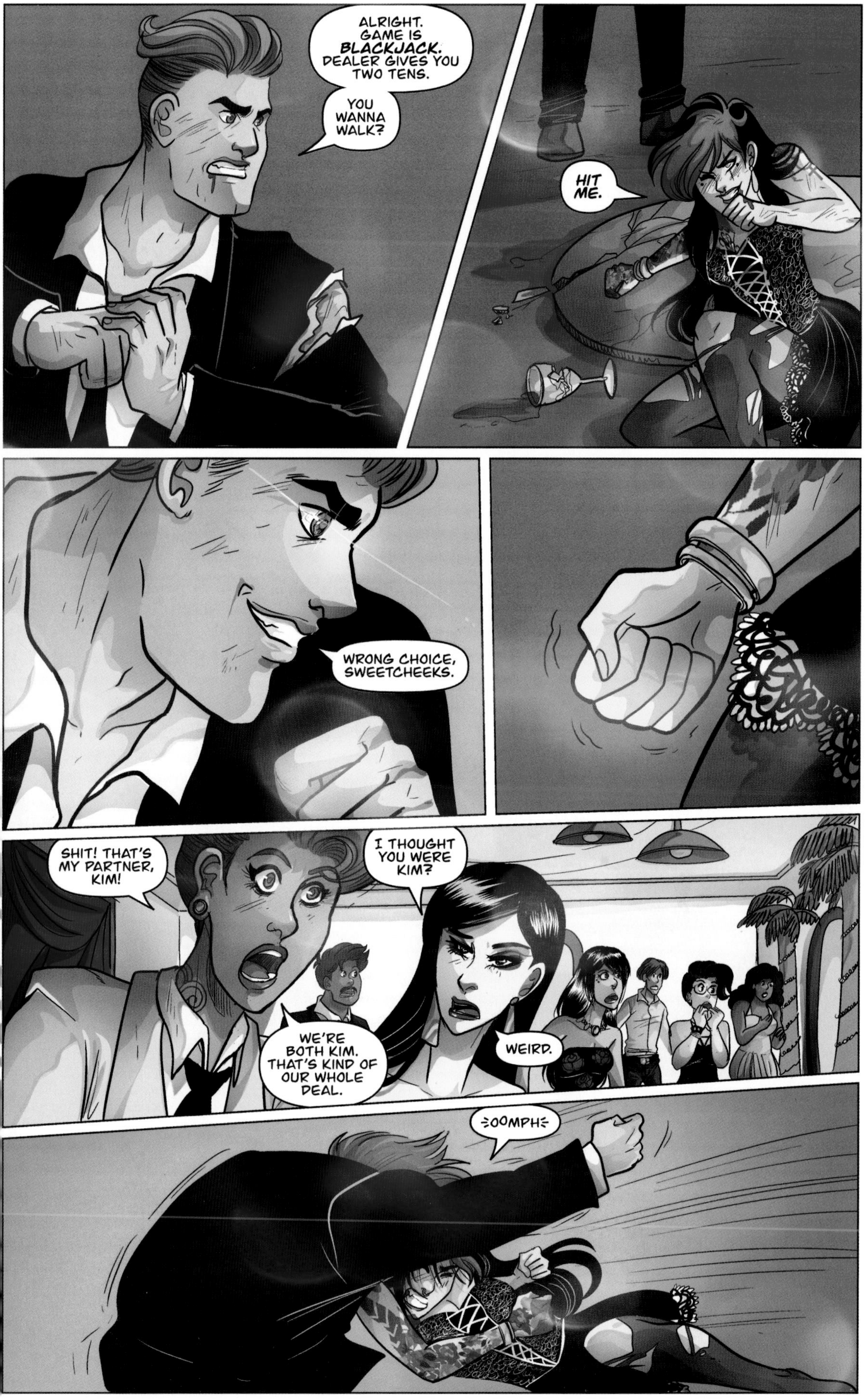
ALRIGHT. GAME IS BLACKJACK. DEALER GIVES YOU TWO TENS.
YOU WANNA WALK?
HIT ME.
WRONG CHOICE, SWEETCHEEKS.
SHIT! THAT'S MY PARTNER, KIM!
I THOUGHT YOU WERE KIM?
WE'RE BOTH KIM. THAT'S KIND OF OUR WHOLE DEAL.
WEIRD.
OOMPH

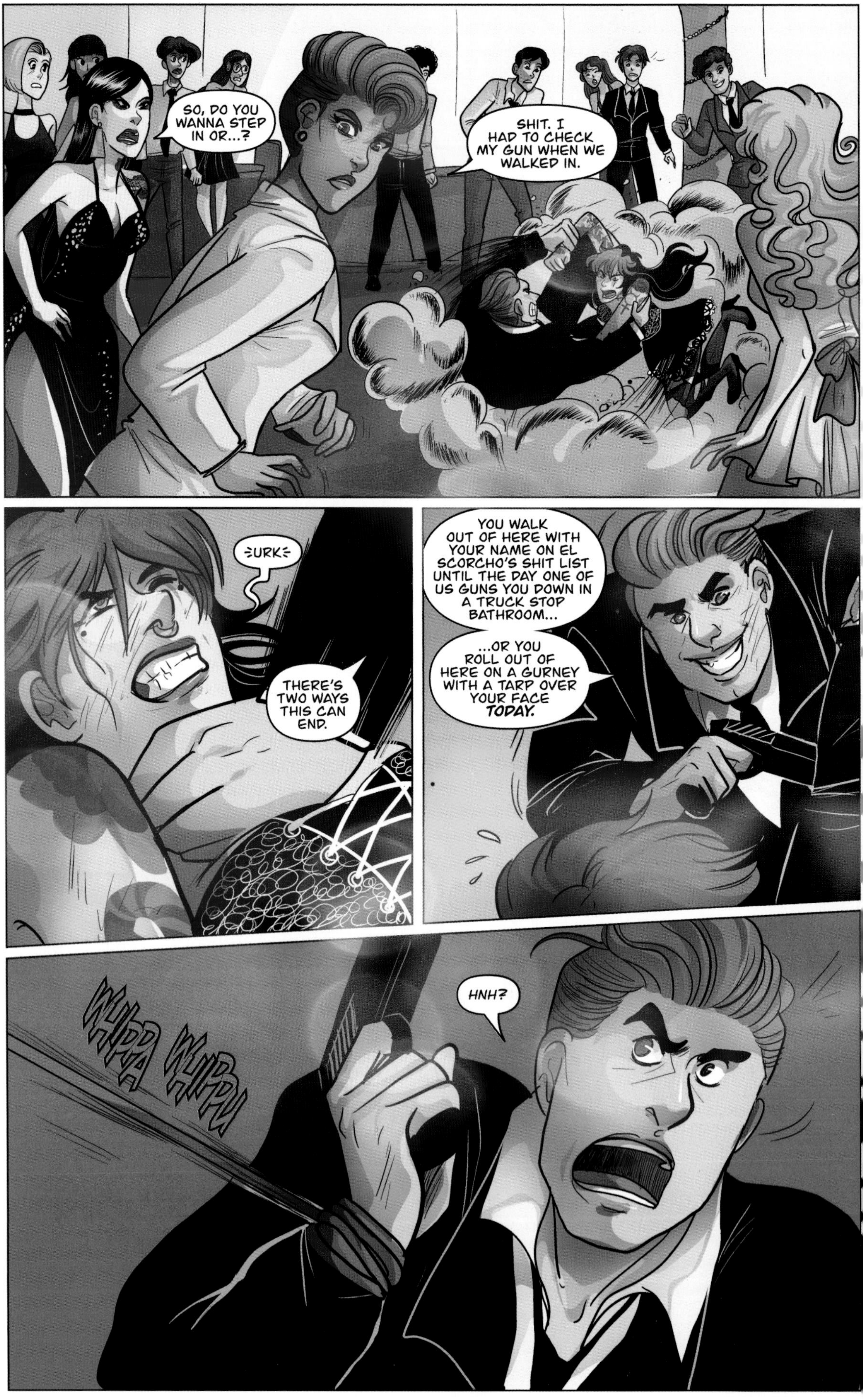
SO, DO YOU WANNA STEP IN OR...?
SHIT. I HAD TO CHECK MY GUN WHEN WE WALKED IN.
URK
THERE'S TWO WAYS THIS CAN END.
YOU WALK OUT OF HERE WITH YOUR NAME ON EL SCORCHO'S SHIT LIST UNTIL THE DAY ONE OF US GUNS YOU DOWN IN A TRUCK STOP BATHROOM...
...OR YOU ROLL OUT OF HERE ON A GURNEY WITH A TARP OVER YOUR FACE ***TODAY.***
WHPPA WHPPU
HNH?

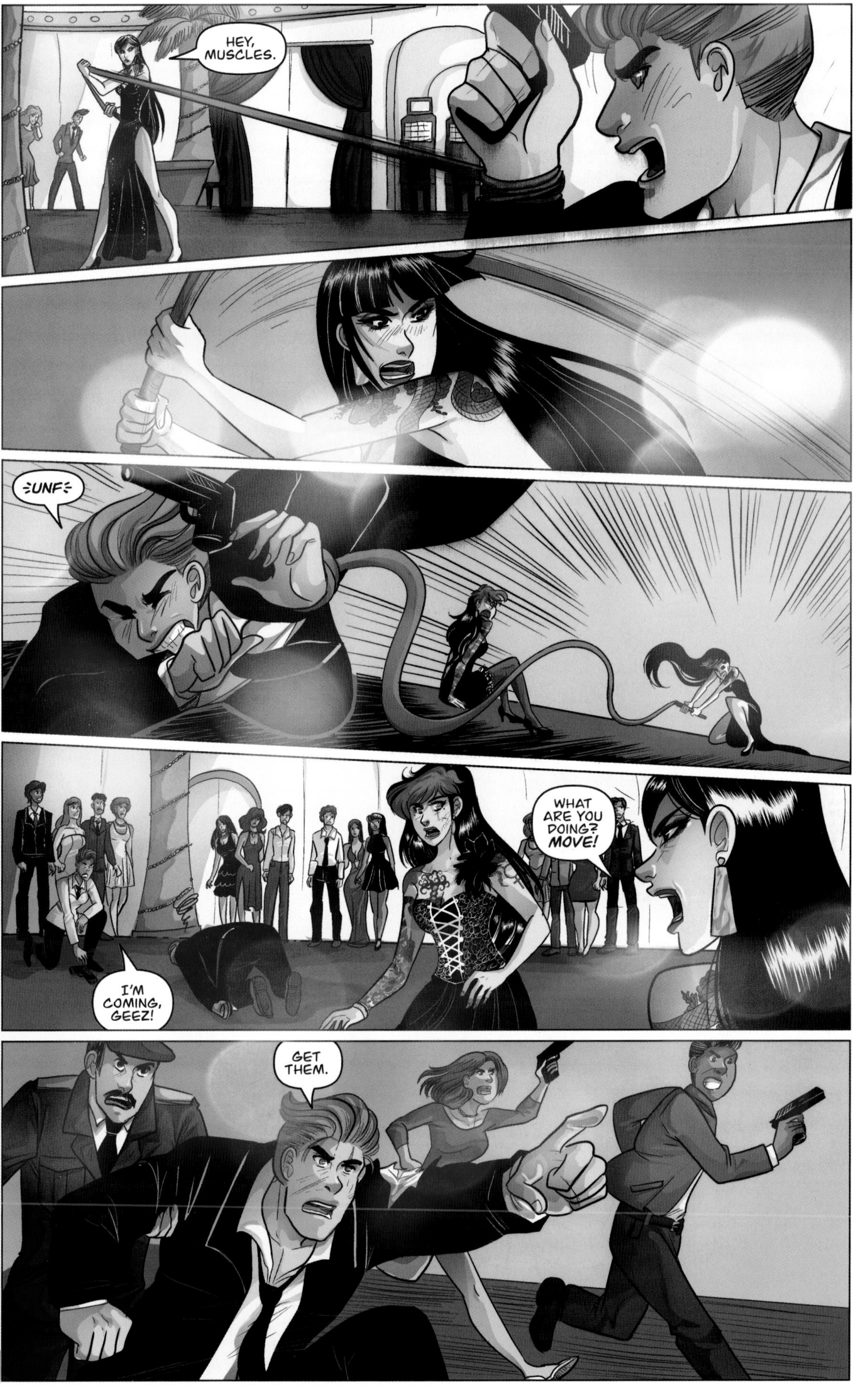
HEY, MUSCLES.
UNF
WHAT ARE YOU DOING? MOVE!
I'M COMING, GEEZ!
GET THEM.

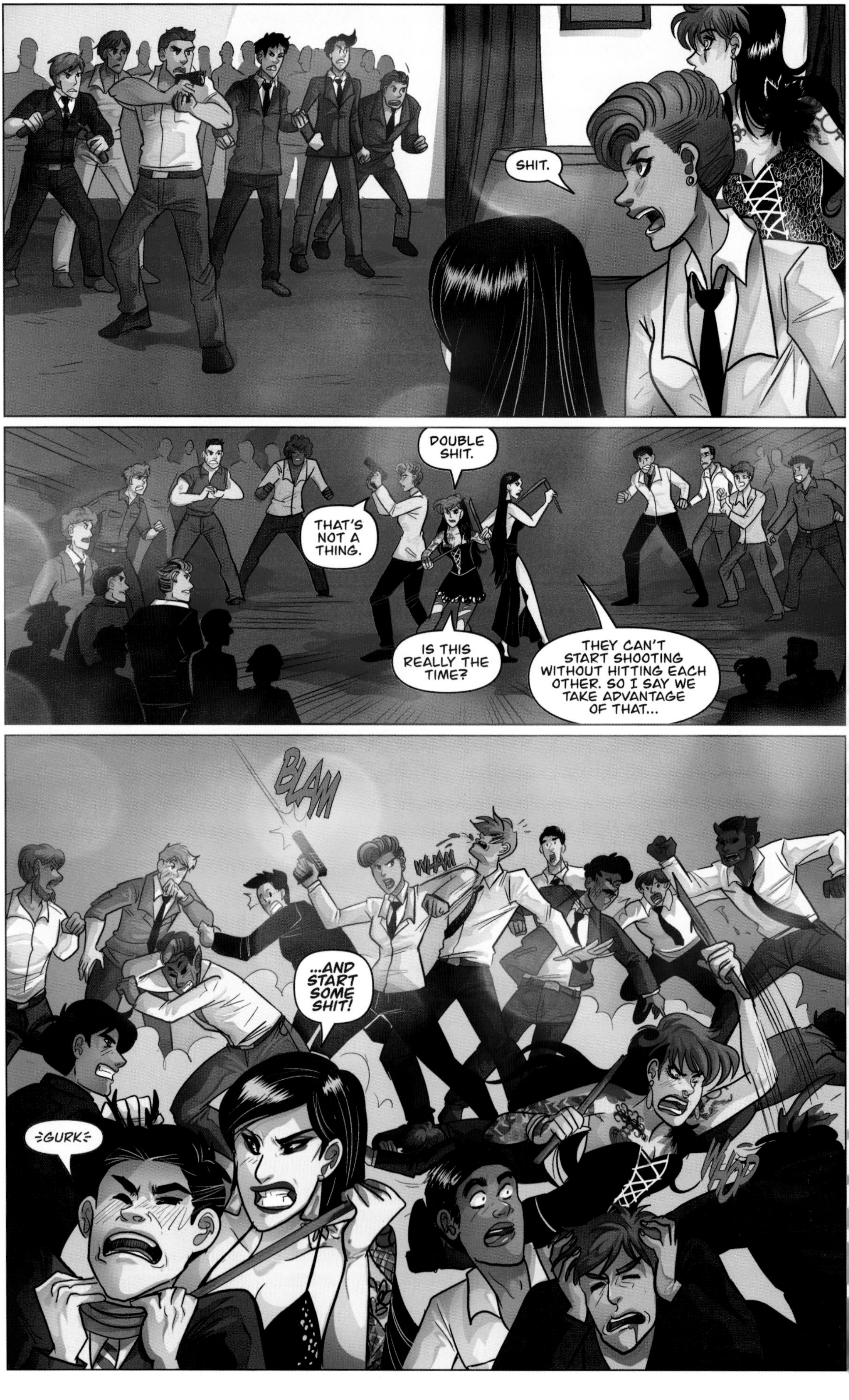
SHIT.
DOUBLE SHIT.
THAT'S NOT A THING.
IS THIS REALLY THE TIME?
THEY CAN'T START SHOOTING WITHOUT HITTING EACH OTHER. SO I SAY WE TAKE ADVANTAGE OF THAT...
BLAM
WHAM
...AND START SOME SHIT!
GURK

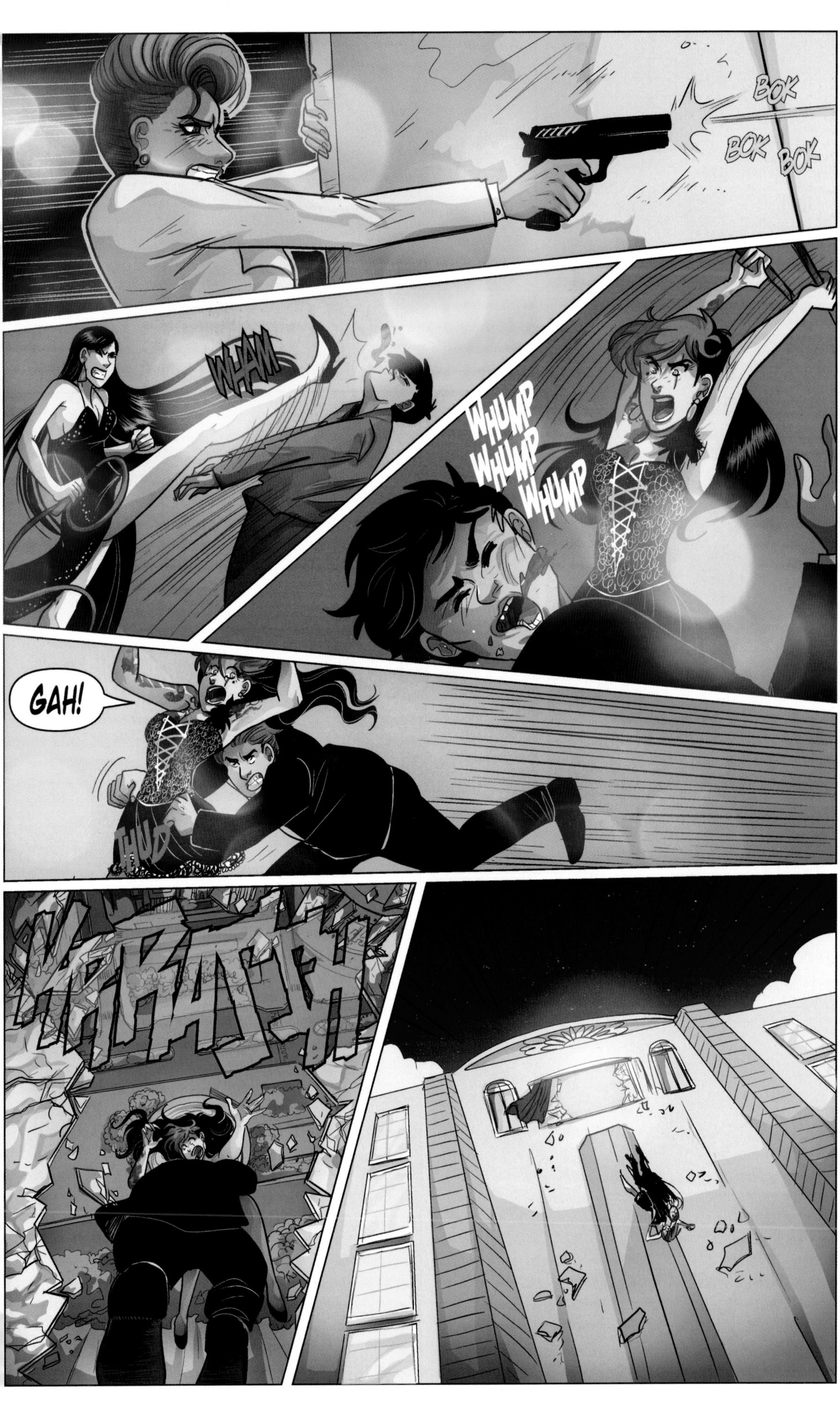
BOK
BOK
BOK
WHAM
WHUMP
WHUMP
WHUMP
GAH!
THUD

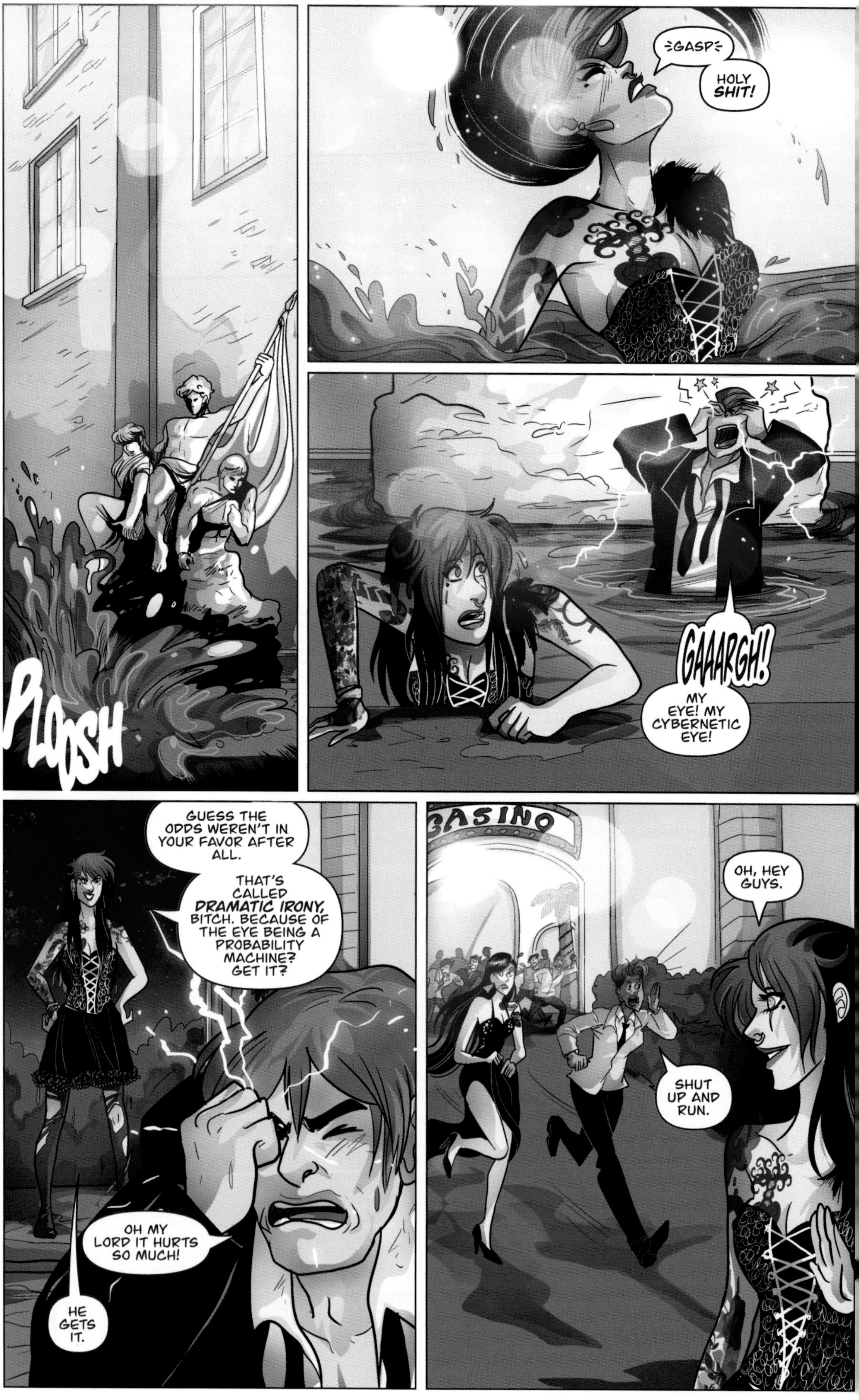
PLOSH
GASP
HOLY SHIT!
GAAARGH!
MY EYE! MY CYBERNETIC EYE!
GUESS THE ODDS WEREN'T IN YOUR FAVOR AFTER ALL.
THAT'S CALLED DRAMATIC IRONY, BITCH. BECAUSE OF THE EYE BEING A PROBABILITY MACHINE? GET IT?
OH MY LORD IT HURTS SO MUCH!
HE GETS IT.
CASINO
OH, HEY GUYS.
SHUT UP AND RUN.

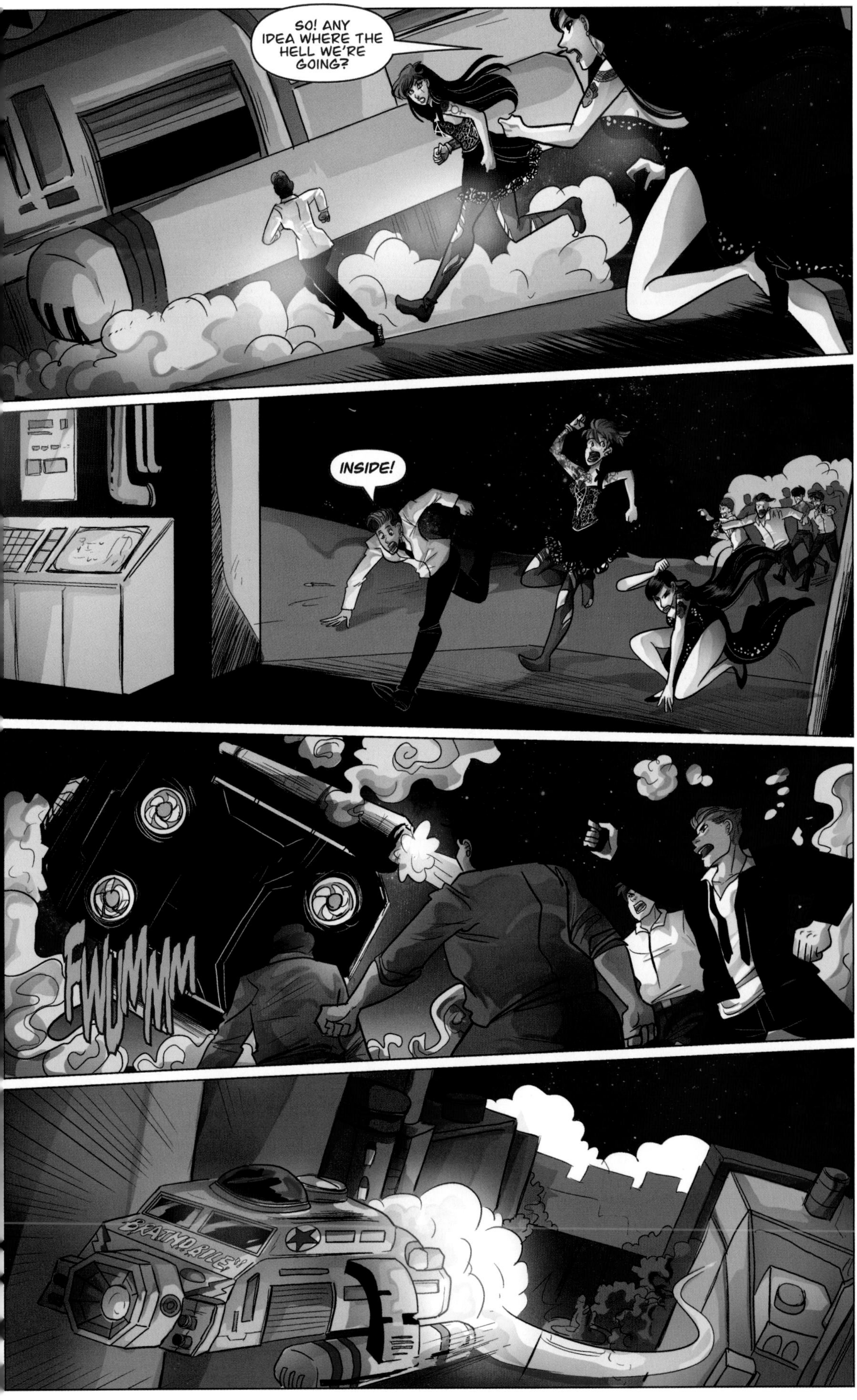
SO! ANY IDEA WHERE THE HELL WE'RE GOING?
INSIDE!
FWUMMM
BRATMOBILE!

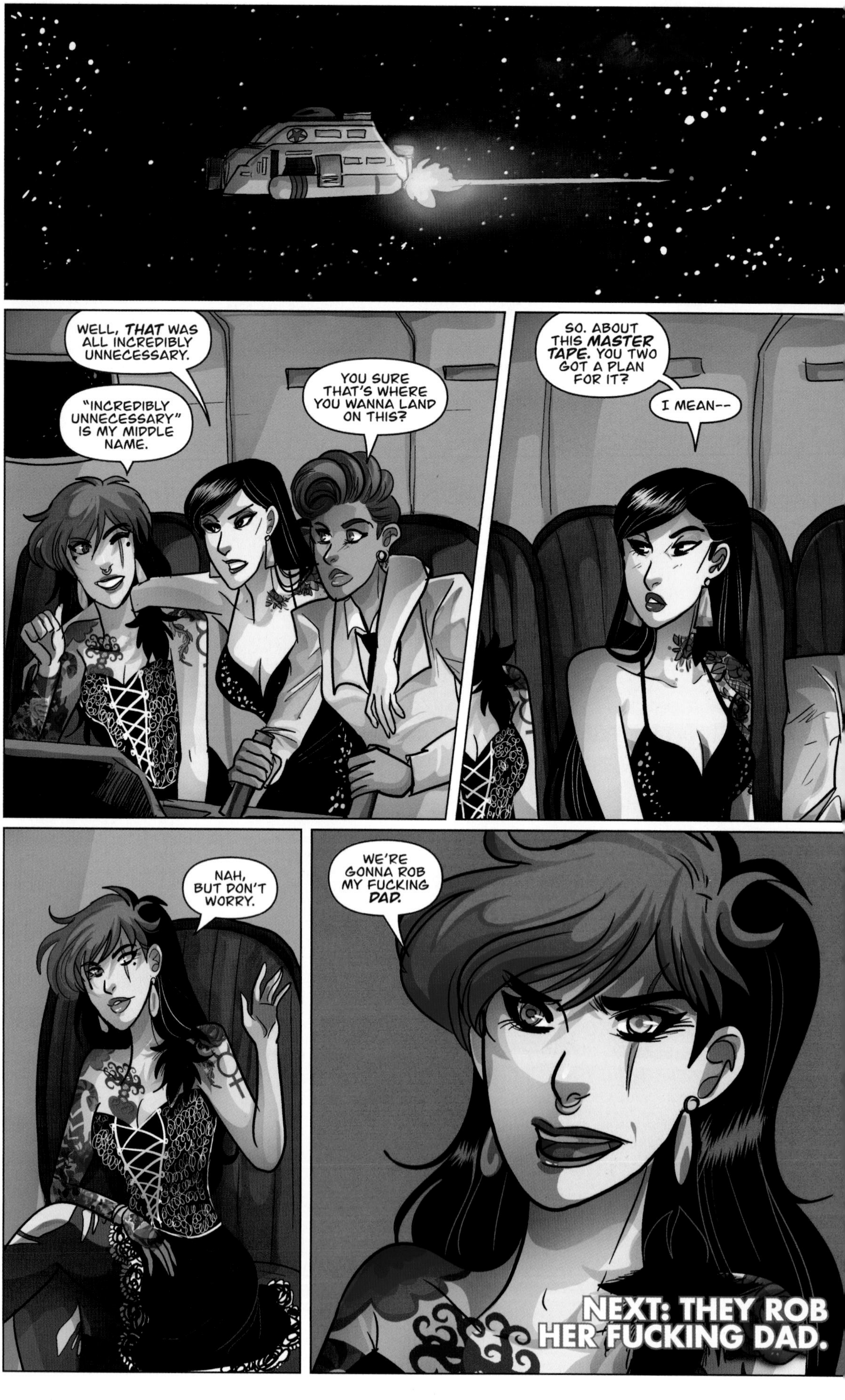
WELL, THAT WAS ALL INCREDIBLY UNNECESSARY.
"INCREDIBLY UNNECESSARY" IS MY MIDDLE NAME.
YOU SURE THAT'S WHERE YOU WANNA LAND ON THIS?
SO. ABOUT THIS MASTER TAPE. YOU TWO GOT A PLAN FOR IT?
I MEAN--
NAH, BUT DON'T WORRY.
WE'RE GONNA ROB MY FUCKING DAD.
NEXT: THEY ROB HER FUCKING DAD.

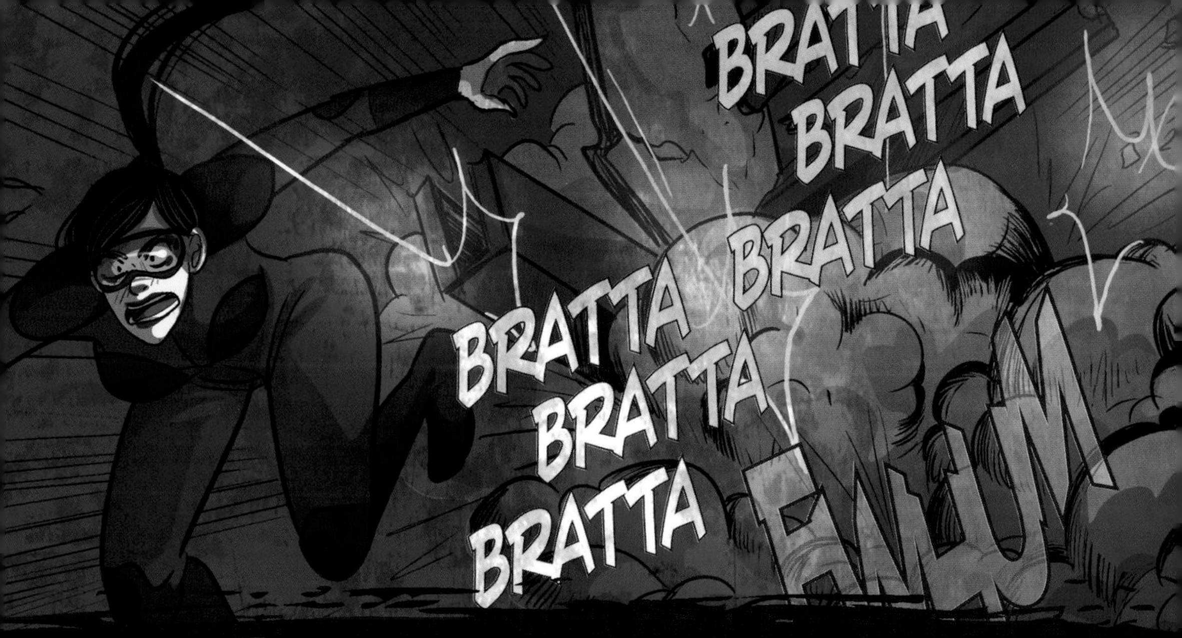
BRATTA
BRATTA
BRATTA
BRATTA
BRATTA
BRATTA
BRATTA

2

“THEY ROB HER FUCKING DAD!”

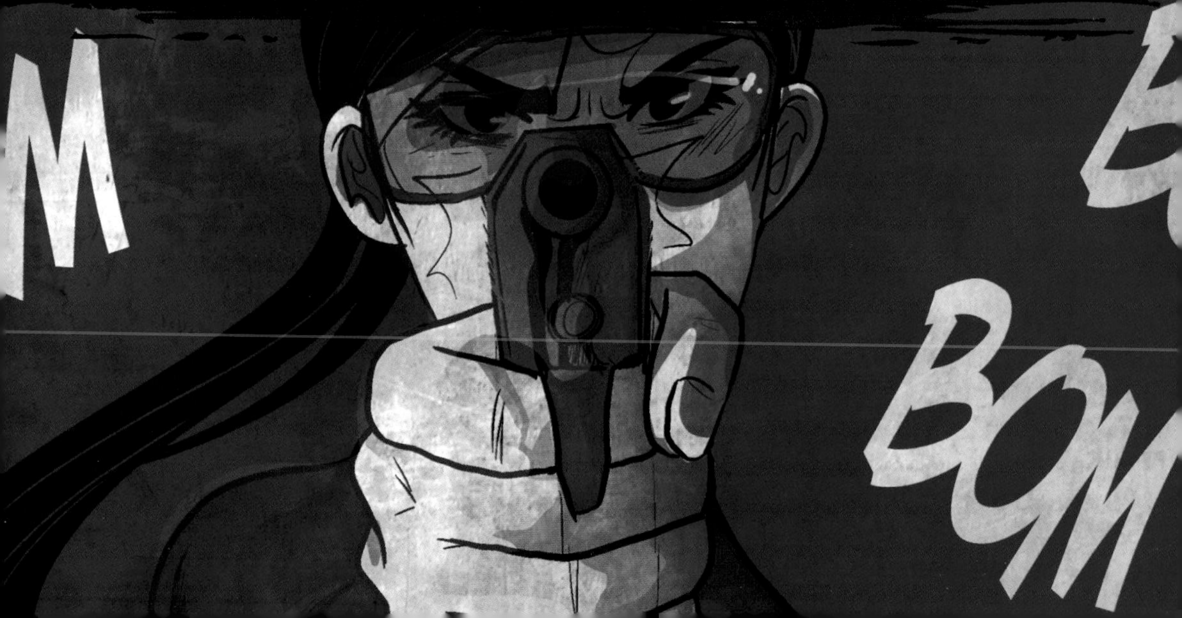

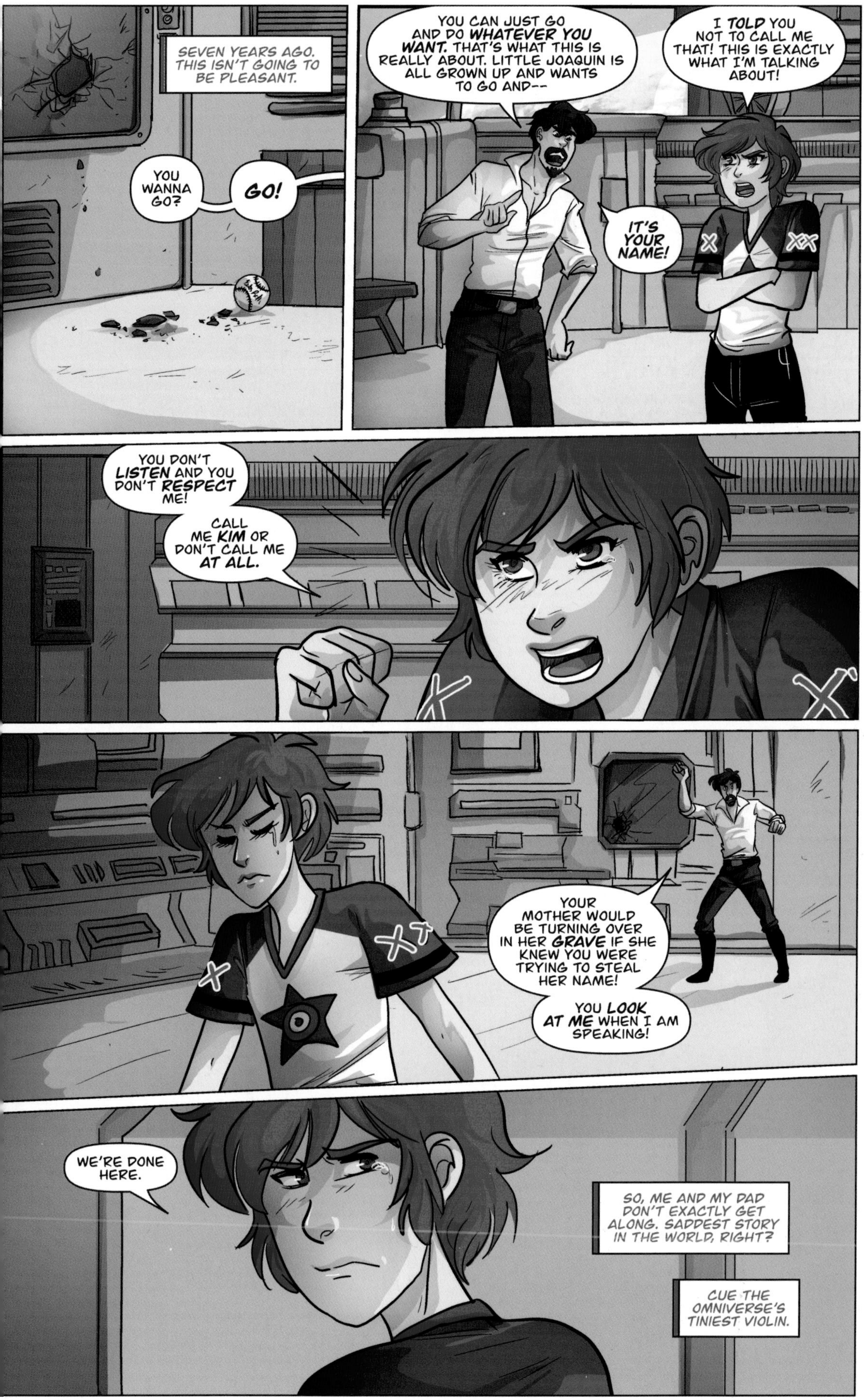
SEVEN YEARS AGO. THIS ISN'T GOING TO BE PLEASANT.
YOU WANNA GO?
GO!
YOU CAN JUST GO AND DO WHATEVER YOU WANT. THAT'S WHAT THIS IS REALLY ABOUT. LITTLE JOAQUIN IS ALL GROWN UP AND WANTS TO GO AND--
I TOLD YOU NOT TO CALL ME THAT! THIS IS EXACTLY WHAT I'M TALKING ABOUT!
IT'S YOUR NAME!
YOU DON'T LISTEN AND YOU DON'T RESPECT ME!
CALL ME KIM OR DON'T CALL ME AT ALL.
YOUR MOTHER WOULD BE TURNING OVER IN HER GRAVE IF SHE KNEW YOU WERE TRYING TO STEAL HER NAME!
YOU LOOK AT ME WHEN I AM SPEAKING!
WE'RE DONE HERE.
SO, ME AND MY DAD DON'T EXACTLY GET ALONG. SADDEST STORY IN THE WORLD, RIGHT?
CUE THE OMNIVERSE'S TINIEST VIOLIN.

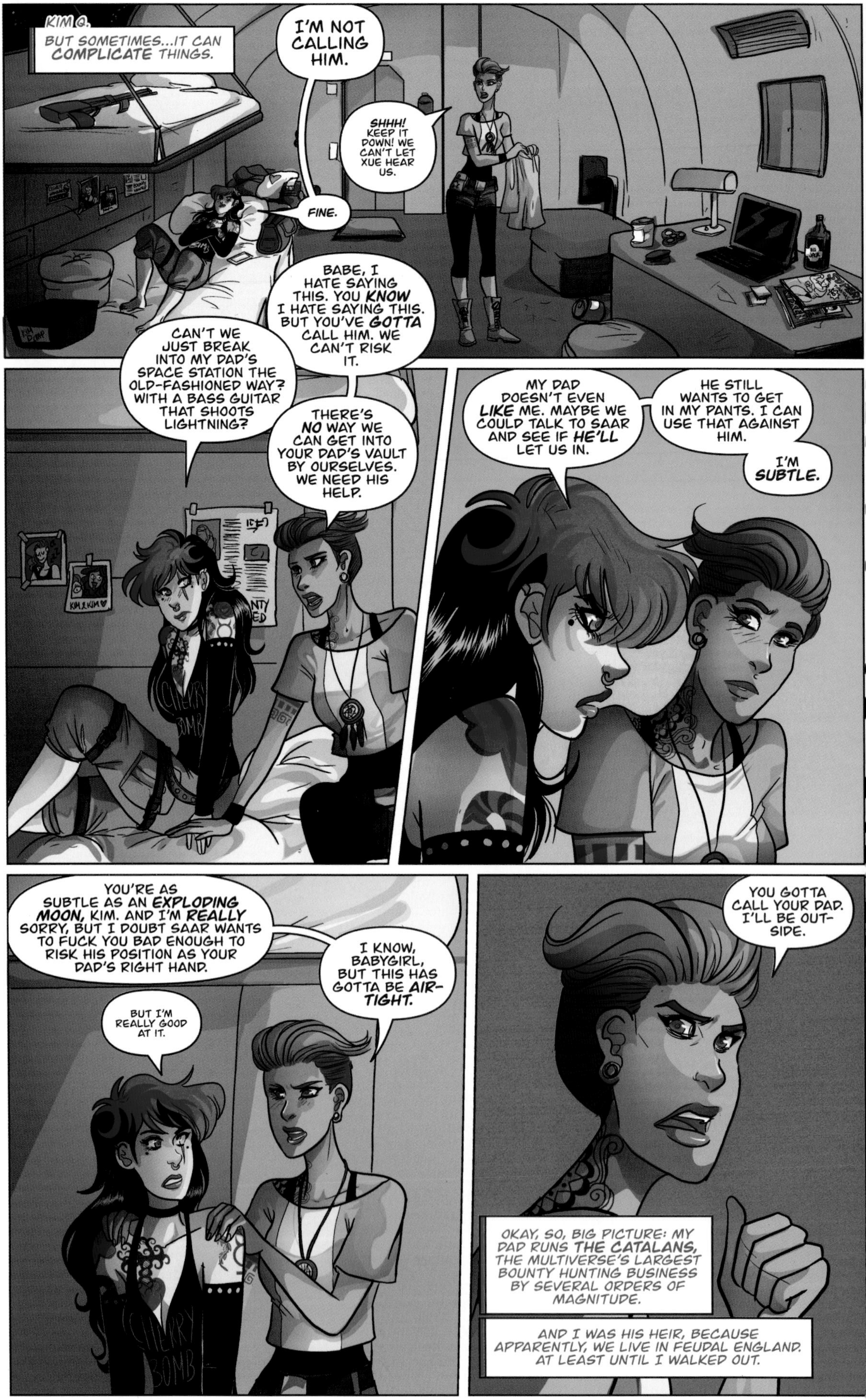
KIM Q.
BUT SOMETIMES...IT CAN COMPLICATE THINGS.
I'M NOT CALLING HIM.
SHHH! KEEP IT DOWN! WE CAN'T LET XUE HEAR US.
FINE.
BABE, I HATE SAYING THIS. YOU KNOW I HATE SAYING THIS. BUT YOU'VE GOTTA CALL HIM. WE CAN'T RISK IT.
CAN'T WE JUST BREAK INTO MY DAD'S SPACE STATION THE OLD-FASHIONED WAY? WITH A BASS GUITAR THAT SHOOTS LIGHTNING?
THERE'S NO WAY WE CAN GET INTO YOUR DAD'S VAULT BY OURSELVES. WE NEED HIS HELP.
MY DAD DOESN'T EVEN LIKE ME. MAYBE WE COULD TALK TO SAAR AND SEE IF HE'LL LET US IN.
HE STILL WANTS TO GET IN MY PANTS. I CAN USE THAT AGAINST HIM.
I'M SUBTLE.
YOU'RE AS SUBTLE AS AN EXPLODING MOON, KIM. AND I'M REALLY SORRY, BUT I DOUBT SAAR WANTS TO FUCK YOU BAD ENOUGH TO RISK HIS POSITION AS YOUR DAD'S RIGHT HAND.
BUT I'M REALLY GOOD AT IT.
I KNOW, BABYGIRL, BUT THIS HAS GOTTA BE AIR-TIGHT.
YOU GOTTA CALL YOUR DAD. I'LL BE OUT-SIDE.
OKAY, SO, BIG PICTURE: MY DAD RUNS THE CATALANS, THE MULTIVERSE'S LARGEST BOUNTY HUNTING BUSINESS BY SEVERAL ORDERS OF MAGNITUDE.
AND I WAS HIS HEIR, BECAUSE APPARENTLY, WE LIVE IN FEUDAL ENGLAND. AT LEAST UNTIL I WALKED OUT.

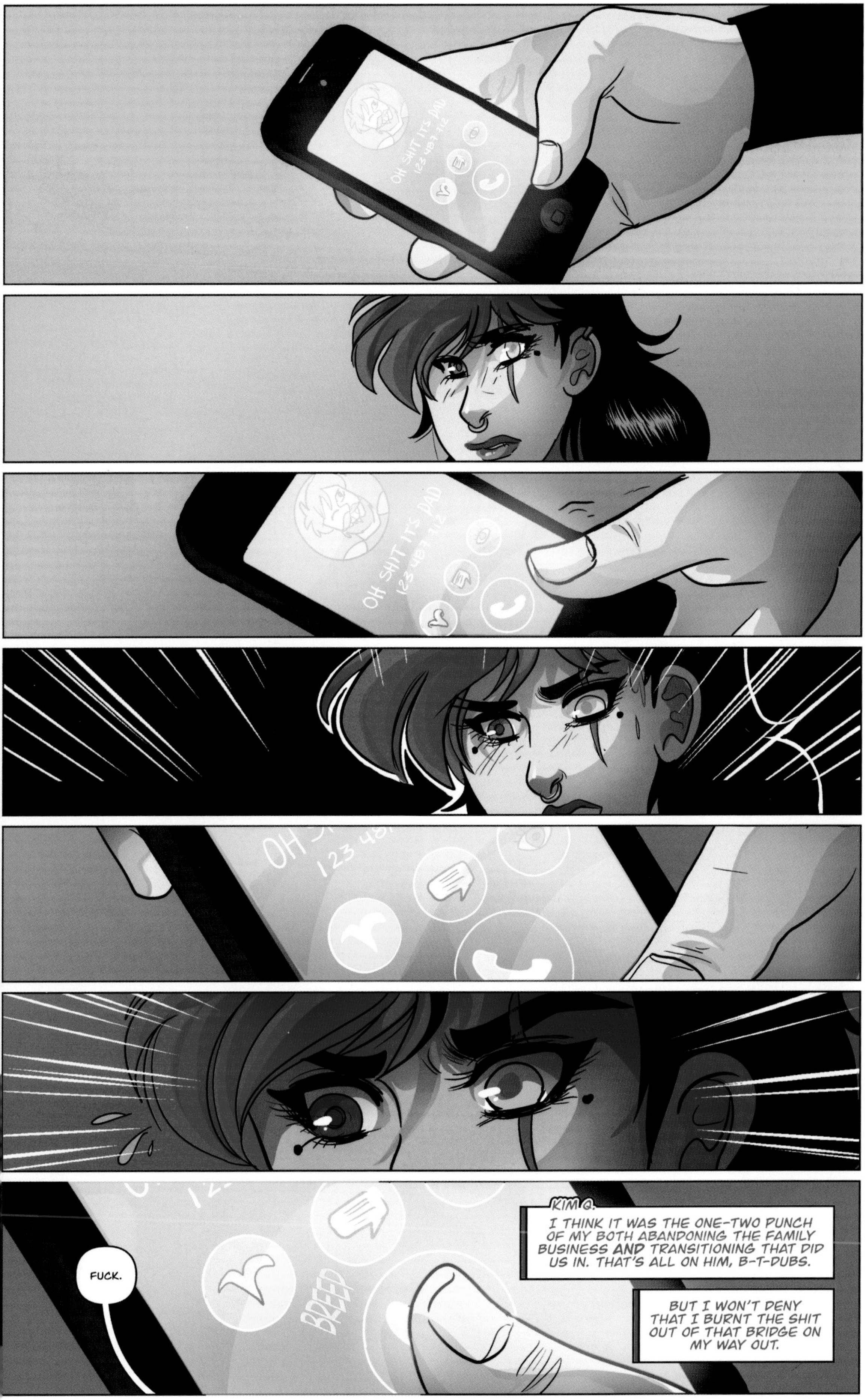
OH SHIT IT'S DAD
123 487 412
FUCK.
KIM Q.
I THINK IT WAS THE ONE-TWO PUNCH OF MY BOTH ABANDONING THE FAMILY BUSINESS **AND** TRANSITIONING THAT DID US IN. THAT'S ALL ON HIM, B-T-DUBS.
BUT I WON'T DENY THAT I BURNT THE SHIT OUT OF THAT BRIDGE ON MY WAY OUT.
BREEP

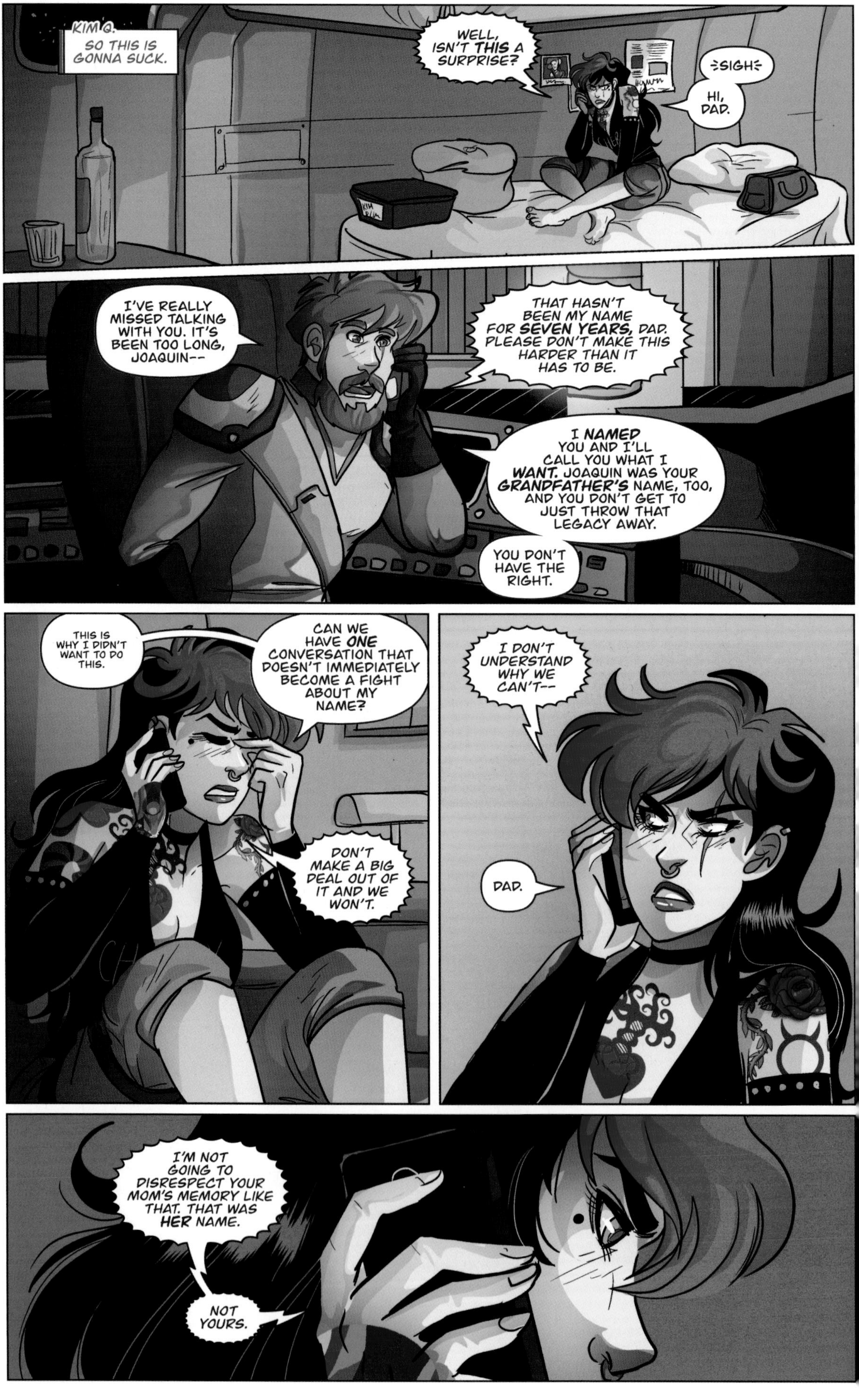
KIM Q.
SO THIS IS GONNA SUCK.
WELL, ISN'T THIS A SURPRISE?
=SIGH=
HI, DAD.
I'VE REALLY MISSED TALKING WITH YOU. IT'S BEEN TOO LONG, JOAQUIN--
THAT HASN'T BEEN MY NAME FOR SEVEN YEARS, DAD. PLEASE DON'T MAKE THIS HARDER THAN IT HAS TO BE.
I NAMED YOU AND I'LL CALL YOU WHAT I WANT. JOAQUIN WAS YOUR GRANDFATHER'S NAME, TOO, AND YOU DON'T GET TO JUST THROW THAT LEGACY AWAY.
YOU DON'T HAVE THE RIGHT.
THIS IS WHY I DIDN'T WANT TO DO THIS.
CAN WE HAVE ONE CONVERSATION THAT DOESN'T IMMEDIATELY BECOME A FIGHT ABOUT MY NAME?
DON'T MAKE A BIG DEAL OUT OF IT AND WE WON'T.
I DON'T UNDERSTAND WHY WE CAN'T--
DAD.
I'M NOT GOING TO DISRESPECT YOUR MOM'S MEMORY LIKE THAT. THAT WAS HER NAME.
NOT YOURS.

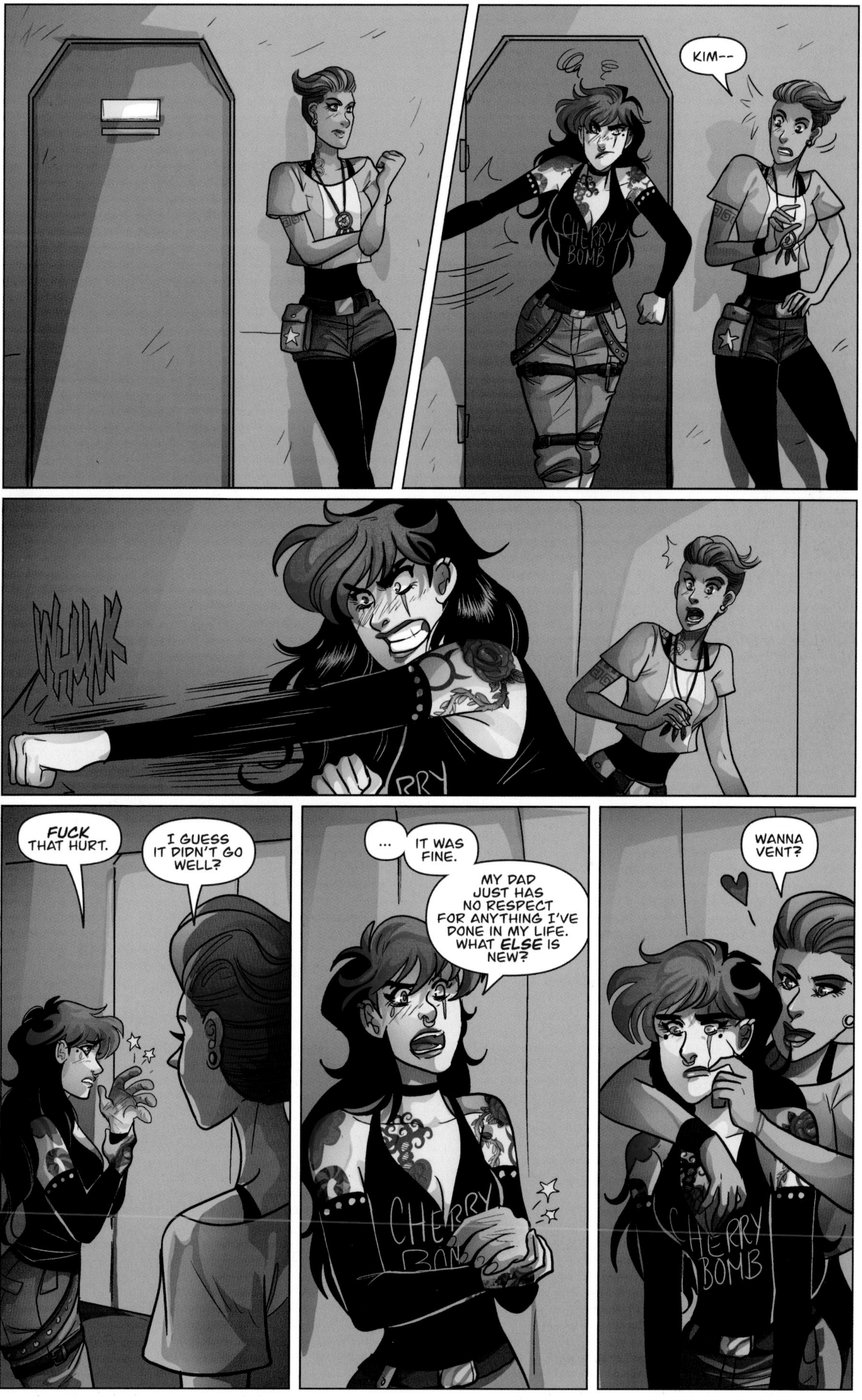
KIM--
WHUNK
FUCK THAT HURT.
I GUESS IT DIDN'T GO WELL?
...
IT WAS FINE.
MY DAD JUST HAS NO RESPECT FOR ANYTHING I'VE DONE IN MY LIFE. WHAT ELSE IS NEW?
WANNA VENT?

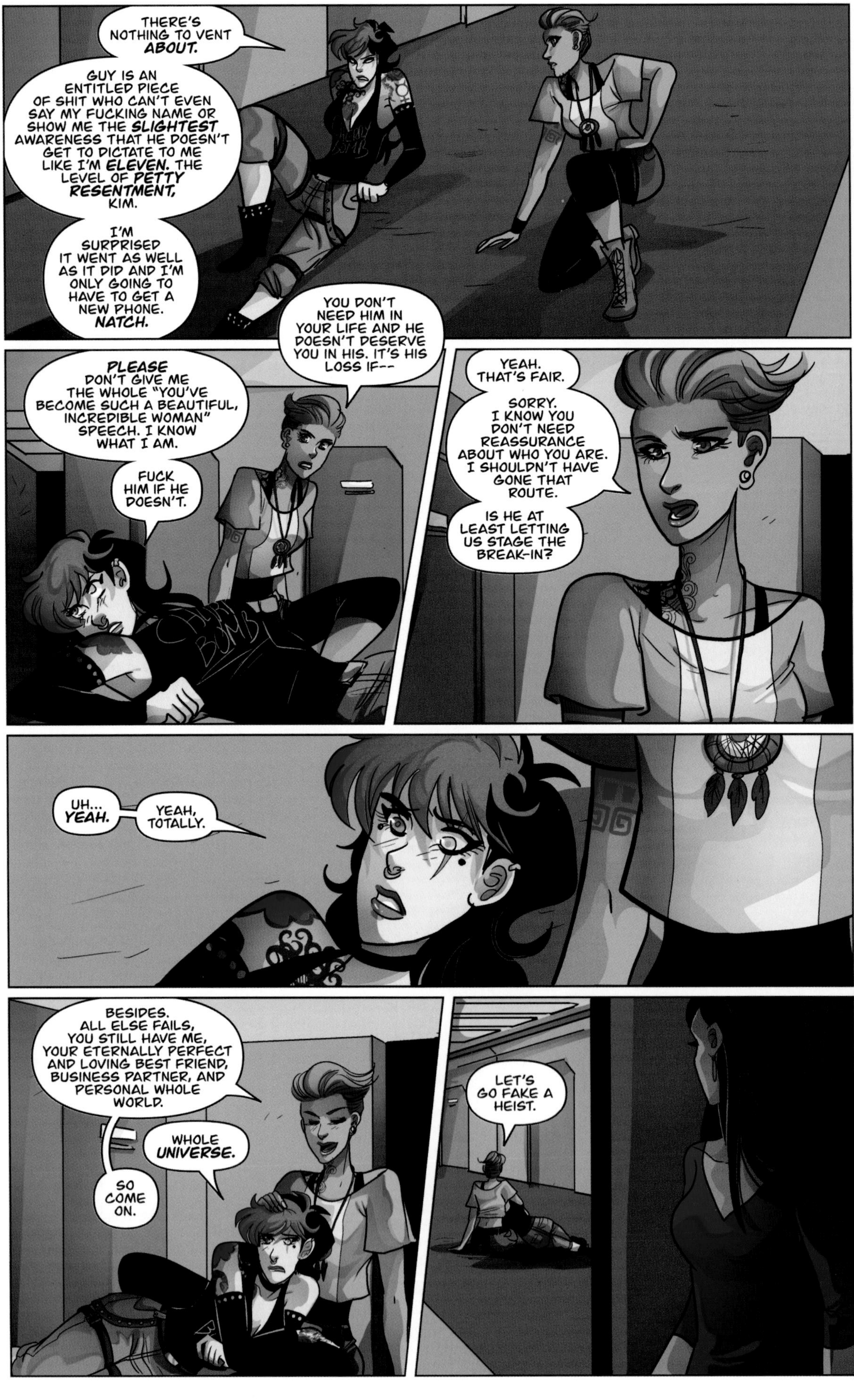
THERE'S NOTHING TO VENT ABOUT.
GUY IS AN ENTITLED PIECE OF SHIT WHO CAN'T EVEN SAY MY FUCKING NAME OR SHOW ME THE SLIGHTEST AWARENESS THAT HE DOESN'T GET TO DICTATE TO ME LIKE I'M ELEVEN. THE LEVEL OF PETTY RESENTMENT, KIM.
I'M SURPRISED IT WENT AS WELL AS IT DID AND I'M ONLY GOING TO HAVE TO GET A NEW PHONE. NATCH.
YOU DON'T NEED HIM IN YOUR LIFE AND HE DOESN'T DESERVE YOU IN HIS. IT'S HIS LOSS IF--
PLEASE DON'T GIVE ME THE WHOLE "YOU'VE BECOME SUCH A BEAUTIFUL, INCREDIBLE WOMAN" SPEECH. I KNOW WHAT I AM.
FUCK HIM IF HE DOESN'T.
YEAH. THAT'S FAIR.
SORRY. I KNOW YOU DON'T NEED REASSURANCE ABOUT WHO YOU ARE. I SHOULDN'T HAVE GONE THAT ROUTE.
IS HE AT LEAST LETTING US STAGE THE BREAK-IN?
UH... YEAH.
YEAH, TOTALLY.
BESIDES. ALL ELSE FAILS, YOU STILL HAVE ME, YOUR ETERNALLY PERFECT AND LOVING BEST FRIEND, BUSINESS PARTNER, AND PERSONAL WHOLE WORLD.
WHOLE UNIVERSE.
SO COME ON.
LET'S GO FAKE A HEIST.

FURIOUS QUATRO'S GIANT ORBITAL DEATH PLATFORM, IN ORBIT OVER VESSUS SECUNDO.

YUP.

YOUR DAD IS *FURIOUS QUATRO*? OF THE CATALANS?

UNFORTUNATELY.

SO. PINK HAIR. YOU SAY THIS IS YOUR *DAD'S* ORBITAL DEATH PLATFORM?

WOULDN'T HE RECOGNIZE YOUR SHIP? MIGHT MAKE SNEAKING IN A LITTLE IFFY.

PSHAW.

THE *BRATMOBILE* HERE IS *BRAND NEW* RELATIVELY SPEAKING, WHICH I GUESS IS TRUE ABOUT *EVERYTHING*, BUT EITHER WAY FURIOUS WON'T EVER SEE US COMING.

HE'LL BE EXPECTING A SPACE VAN. WELL, NOT *EXPECTING*, BUT YOU KNOW.

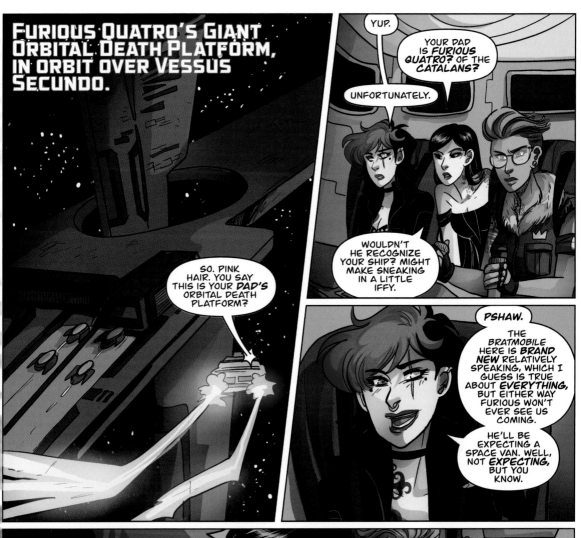

GREAT! SO, WHAT'S THE PLAN?

ASSUMING WE HAVE ONE.

UH.

WE HAVE SOME FAKE MUSTACHES IN THE BACK--

YEAH, NO.

HERE'S THE PLAN.

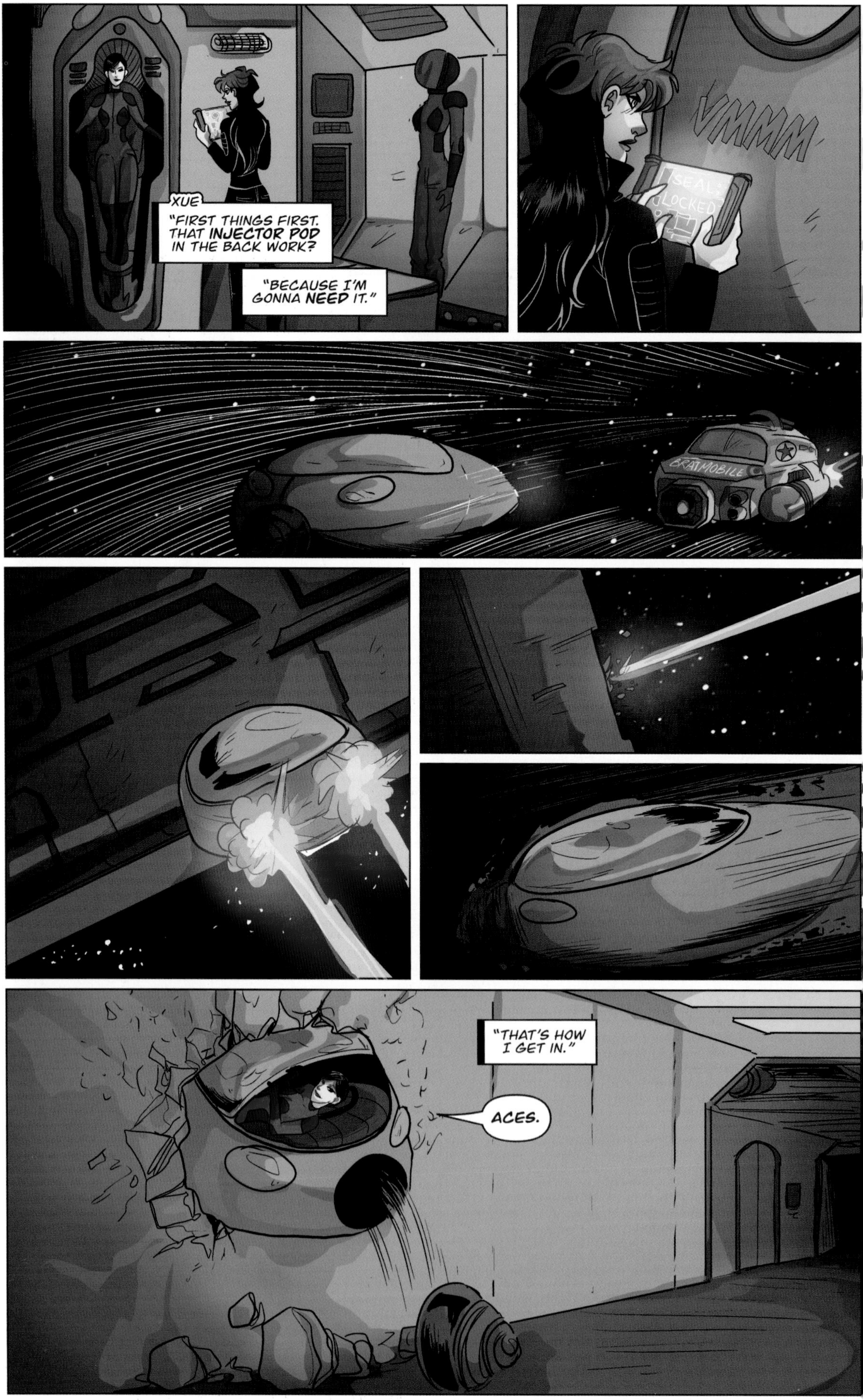
XUE
"FIRST THINGS FIRST. THAT INJECTOR POD IN THE BACK WORK?
"BECAUSE I'M GONNA NEED IT."
VMMM
SEAL: LOCKED
BRATMOBILE
"THAT'S HOW I GET IN."
ACES.

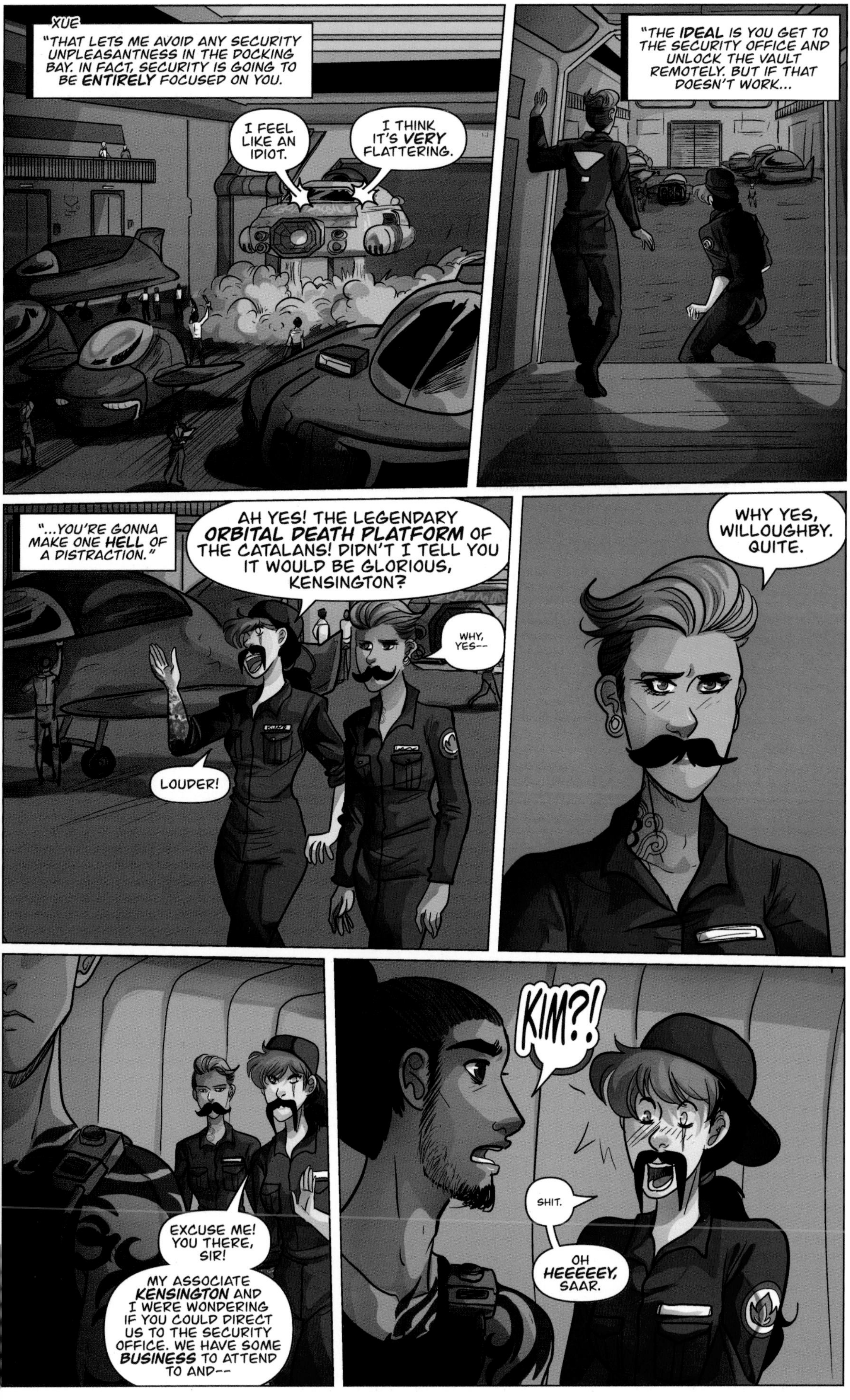
XUE
"THAT LETS ME AVOID ANY SECURITY UNPLEASANTNESS IN THE DOCKING BAY. IN FACT, SECURITY IS GOING TO BE ENTIRELY FOCUSED ON YOU.
I FEEL LIKE AN IDIOT.
I THINK IT'S VERY FLATTERING.
"THE IDEAL IS YOU GET TO THE SECURITY OFFICE AND UNLOCK THE VAULT REMOTELY. BUT IF THAT DOESN'T WORK...
"...YOU'RE GONNA MAKE ONE HELL OF A DISTRACTION."
AH YES! THE LEGENDARY ORBITAL DEATH PLATFORM OF THE CATALANS! DIDN'T I TELL YOU IT WOULD BE GLORIOUS, KENSINGTON?
WHY, YES--
LOUDER!
WHY YES, WILLOUGHBY. QUITE.
EXCUSE ME! YOU THERE, SIR!
MY ASSOCIATE KENSINGTON AND I WERE WONDERING IF YOU COULD DIRECT US TO THE SECURITY OFFICE. WE HAVE SOME BUSINESS TO ATTEND TO AND--
KIM?!
SHIT.
OH HEEEEEY, SAAR.

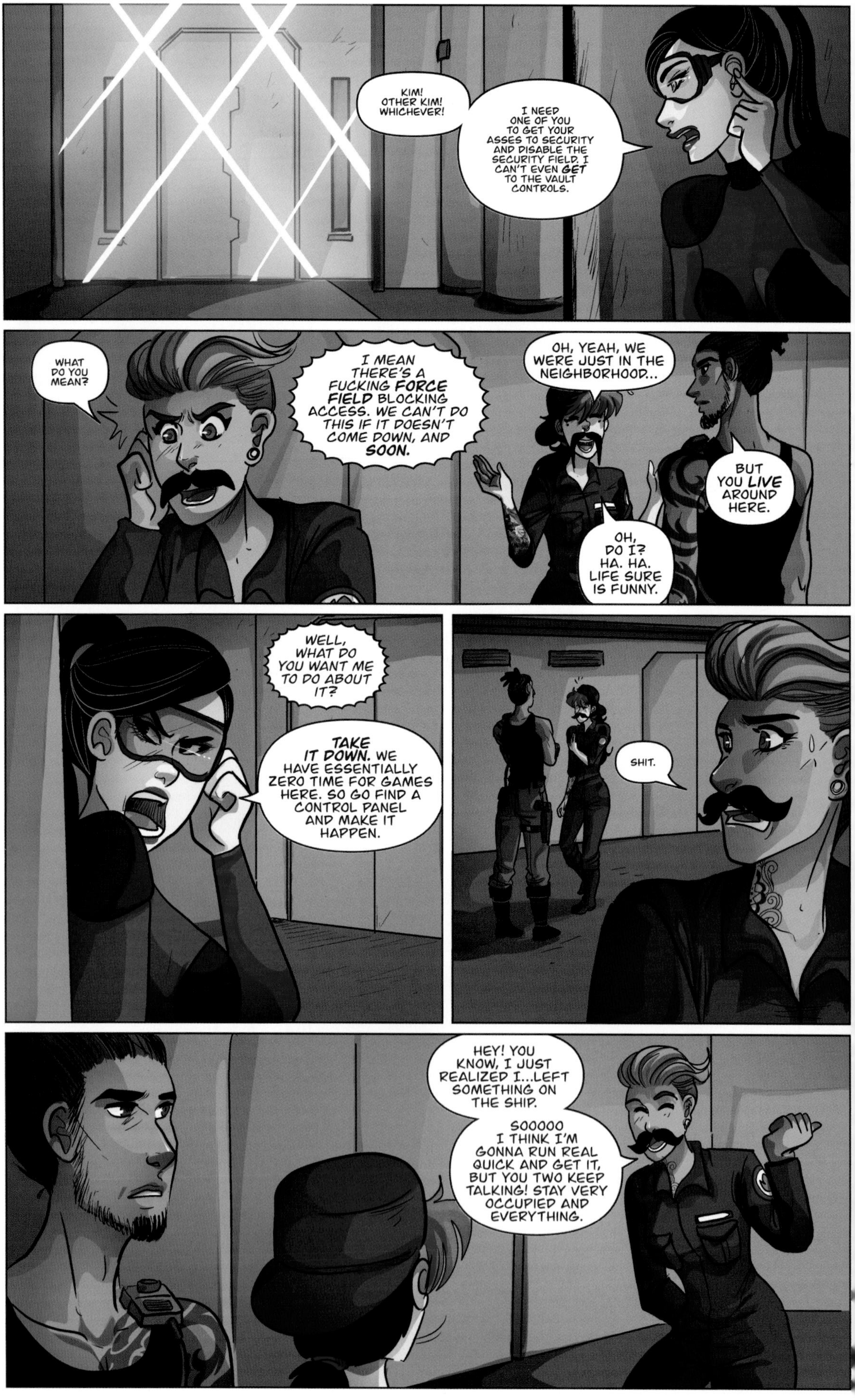
KIM! OTHER KIM! WHICHEVER!
I NEED ONE OF YOU TO GET YOUR ASSES TO SECURITY AND DISABLE THE SECURITY FIELD. I CAN'T EVEN **GET** TO THE VAULT CONTROLS.
WHAT DO YOU MEAN?
I MEAN THERE'S A FUCKING **FORCE FIELD** BLOCKING ACCESS. WE CAN'T DO THIS IF IT DOESN'T COME DOWN, AND **SOON.**
OH, YEAH, WE WERE JUST IN THE NEIGHBORHOOD...
BUT YOU **LIVE** AROUND HERE.
OH, DO I? HA. HA. LIFE SURE IS FUNNY.
WELL, WHAT DO YOU WANT ME TO DO ABOUT IT?
TAKE IT DOWN. WE HAVE ESSENTIALLY ZERO TIME FOR GAMES HERE. SO GO FIND A CONTROL PANEL AND MAKE IT HAPPEN.
SHIT.
HEY! YOU KNOW, I JUST REALIZED I...LEFT SOMETHING ON THE SHIP.
SOOOOO I THINK I'M GONNA RUN REAL QUICK AND GET IT, BUT YOU TWO KEEP TALKING! STAY VERY OCCUPIED AND EVERYTHING.

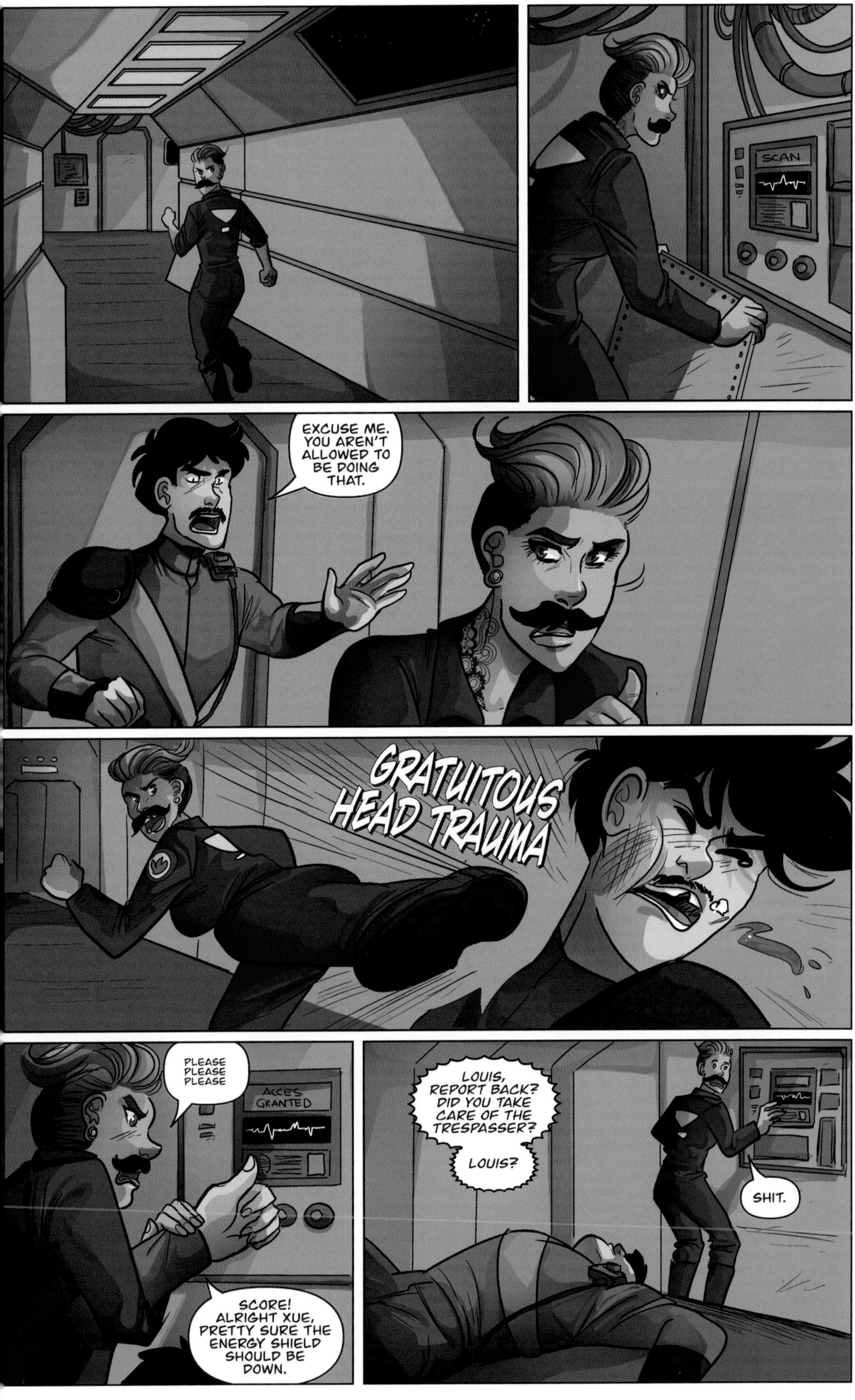
SCAN
EXCUSE ME. YOU AREN'T ALLOWED TO BE DOING THAT.
GRATUITOUS HEAD TRAUMA
PLEASE PLEASE PLEASE
ACCES GRANTED
SCORE! ALRIGHT XUE, PRETTY SURE THE ENERGY SHIELD SHOULD BE DOWN.
LOUIS, REPORT BACK? DID YOU TAKE CARE OF THE TRESPASSER?
LOUIS?
SHIT.

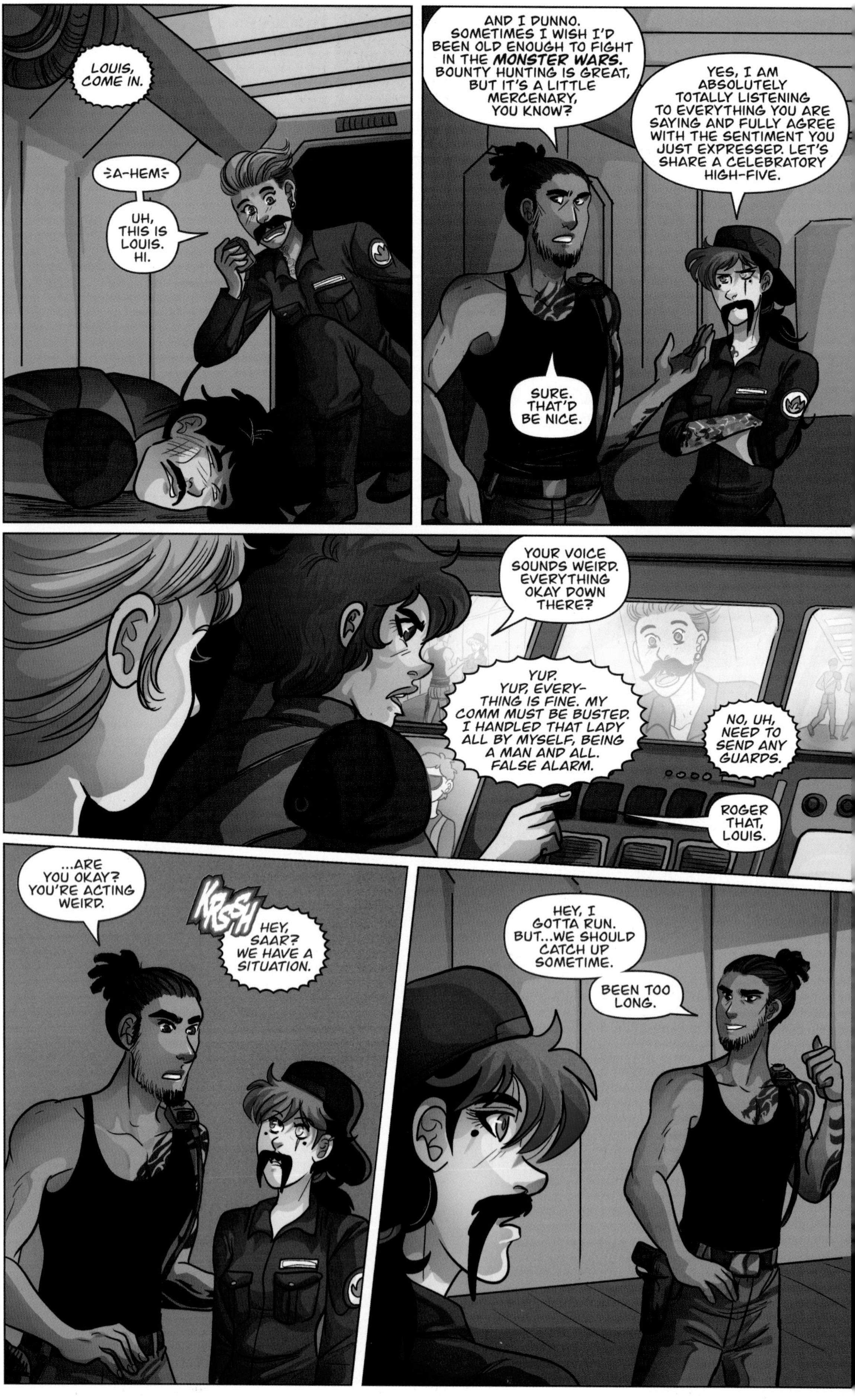
LOUIS, COME IN.
A-HEM
UH, THIS IS LOUIS. HI.
AND I DUNNO. SOMETIMES I WISH I'D BEEN OLD ENOUGH TO FIGHT IN THE MONSTER WARS. BOUNTY HUNTING IS GREAT, BUT IT'S A LITTLE MERCENARY, YOU KNOW?
YES, I AM ABSOLUTELY TOTALLY LISTENING TO EVERYTHING YOU ARE SAYING AND FULLY AGREE WITH THE SENTIMENT YOU JUST EXPRESSED. LET'S SHARE A CELEBRATORY HIGH-FIVE.
SURE. THAT'D BE NICE.
YOUR VOICE SOUNDS WEIRD. EVERYTHING OKAY DOWN THERE?
YUP. YUP, EVERY-THING IS FINE. MY COMM MUST BE BUSTED. I HANDLED THAT LADY ALL BY MYSELF, BEING A MAN AND ALL. FALSE ALARM.
NO, UH, NEED TO SEND ANY GUARDS.
ROGER THAT, LOUIS.
...ARE YOU OKAY? YOU'RE ACTING WEIRD.
KRSSH
HEY, SAAR? WE HAVE A SITUATION.
HEY, I GOTTA RUN. BUT...WE SHOULD CATCH UP SOMETIME.
BEEN TOO LONG.

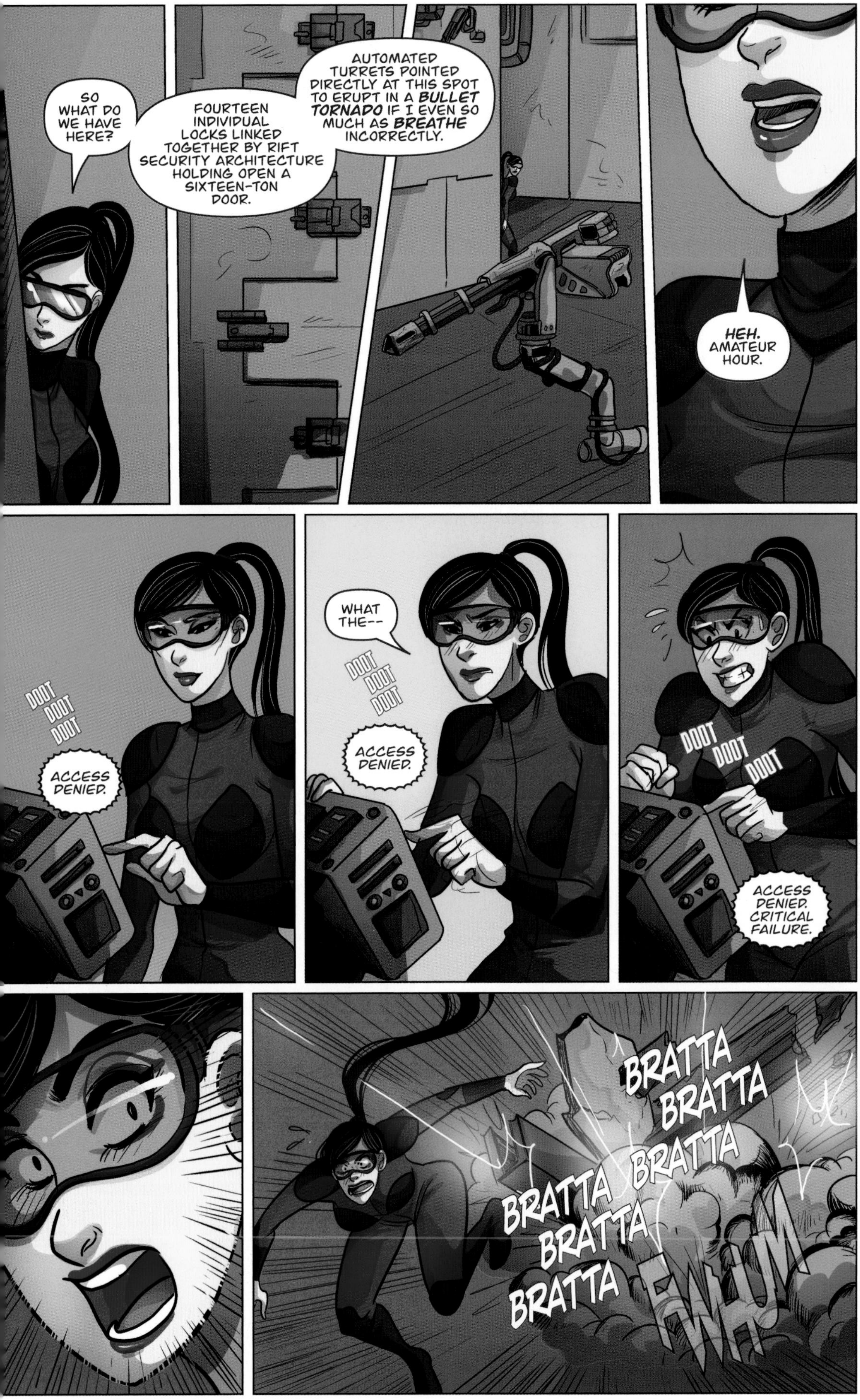
SO WHAT DO WE HAVE HERE?
FOURTEEN INDIVIDUAL LOCKS LINKED TOGETHER BY RIFT SECURITY ARCHITECTURE HOLDING OPEN A SIXTEEN-TON DOOR.
AUTOMATED TURRETS POINTED DIRECTLY AT THIS SPOT TO ERUPT IN A **BULLET TORNADO** IF I EVEN SO MUCH AS **BREATHE** INCORRECTLY.
HEH. AMATEUR HOUR.
DOOT DOOT DOOT
ACCESS DENIED.
WHAT THE--
DOOT DOOT DOOT
ACCESS DENIED.
DOOT DOOT DOOT
ACCESS DENIED. CRITICAL FAILURE.
BRATTA BRATTA BRATTA BRATTA BRATTA BRATTA
FWUM

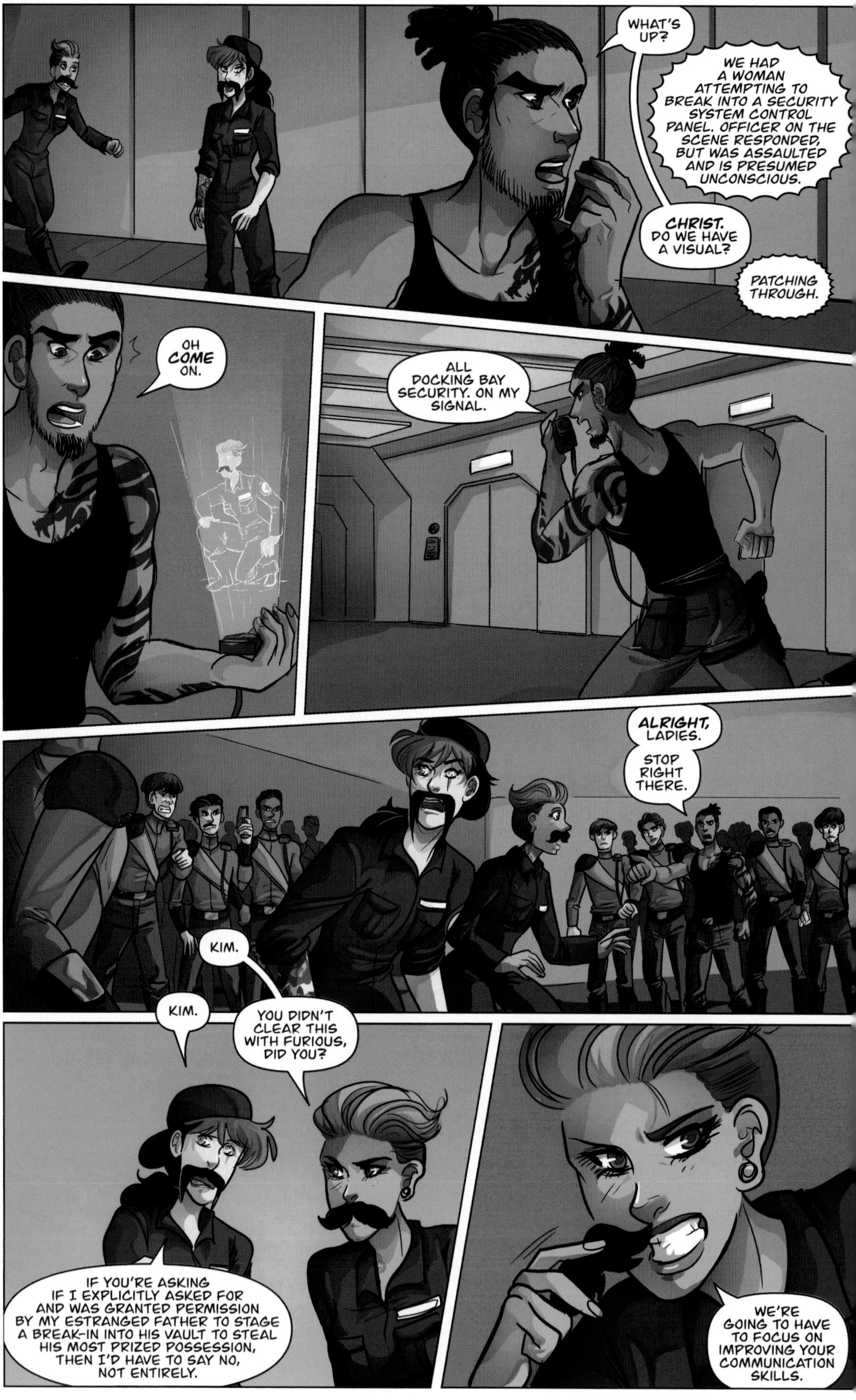
WHAT'S UP?
WE HAD A WOMAN ATTEMPTING TO BREAK INTO A SECURITY SYSTEM CONTROL PANEL. OFFICER ON THE SCENE RESPONDED, BUT WAS ASSAULTED AND IS PRESUMED UNCONSCIOUS.
CHRIST. DO WE HAVE A VISUAL?
PATCHING THROUGH.
OH COME ON.
ALL DOCKING BAY SECURITY. ON MY SIGNAL.
ALRIGHT, LADIES.
STOP RIGHT THERE.
KIM.
KIM.
YOU DIDN'T CLEAR THIS WITH FURIOUS, DID YOU?
IF YOU'RE ASKING IF I EXPLICITLY ASKED FOR AND WAS GRANTED PERMISSION BY MY ESTRANGED FATHER TO STAGE A BREAK-IN INTO HIS VAULT TO STEAL HIS MOST PRIZED POSSESSION, THEN I'D HAVE TO SAY NO, NOT ENTIRELY.
WE'RE GOING TO HAVE TO FOCUS ON IMPROVING YOUR COMMUNICATION SKILLS.

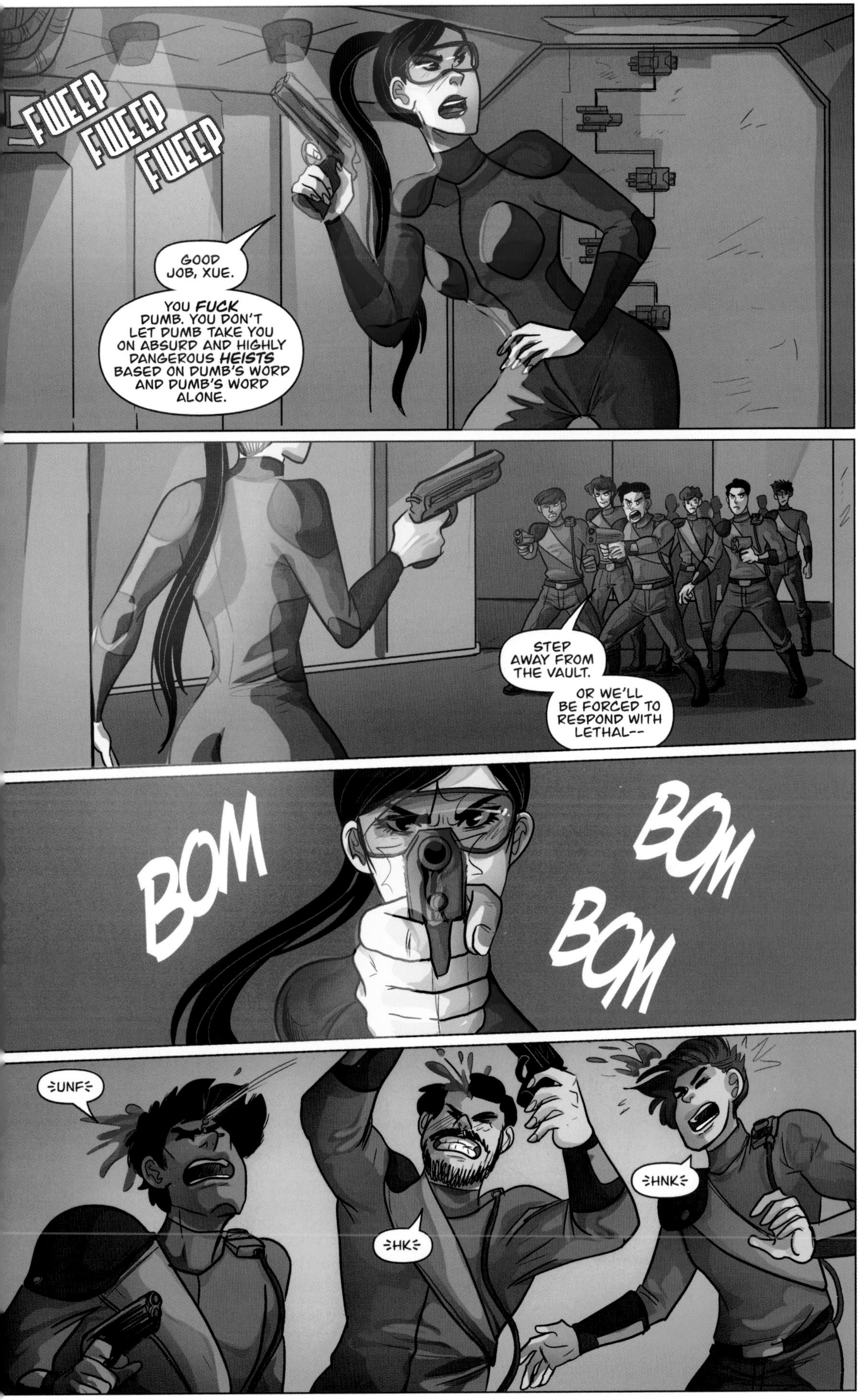
FWEEP FWEEP FWEEP
GOOD JOB, XUE.
YOU FUCK DUMB. YOU DON'T LET DUMB TAKE YOU ON ABSURD AND HIGHLY DANGEROUS HEISTS BASED ON DUMB'S WORD AND DUMB'S WORD ALONE.
STEP AWAY FROM THE VAULT.
OR WE'LL BE FORCED TO RESPOND WITH LETHAL--
BOM
BOM
BOM
UNF
HK
HNK

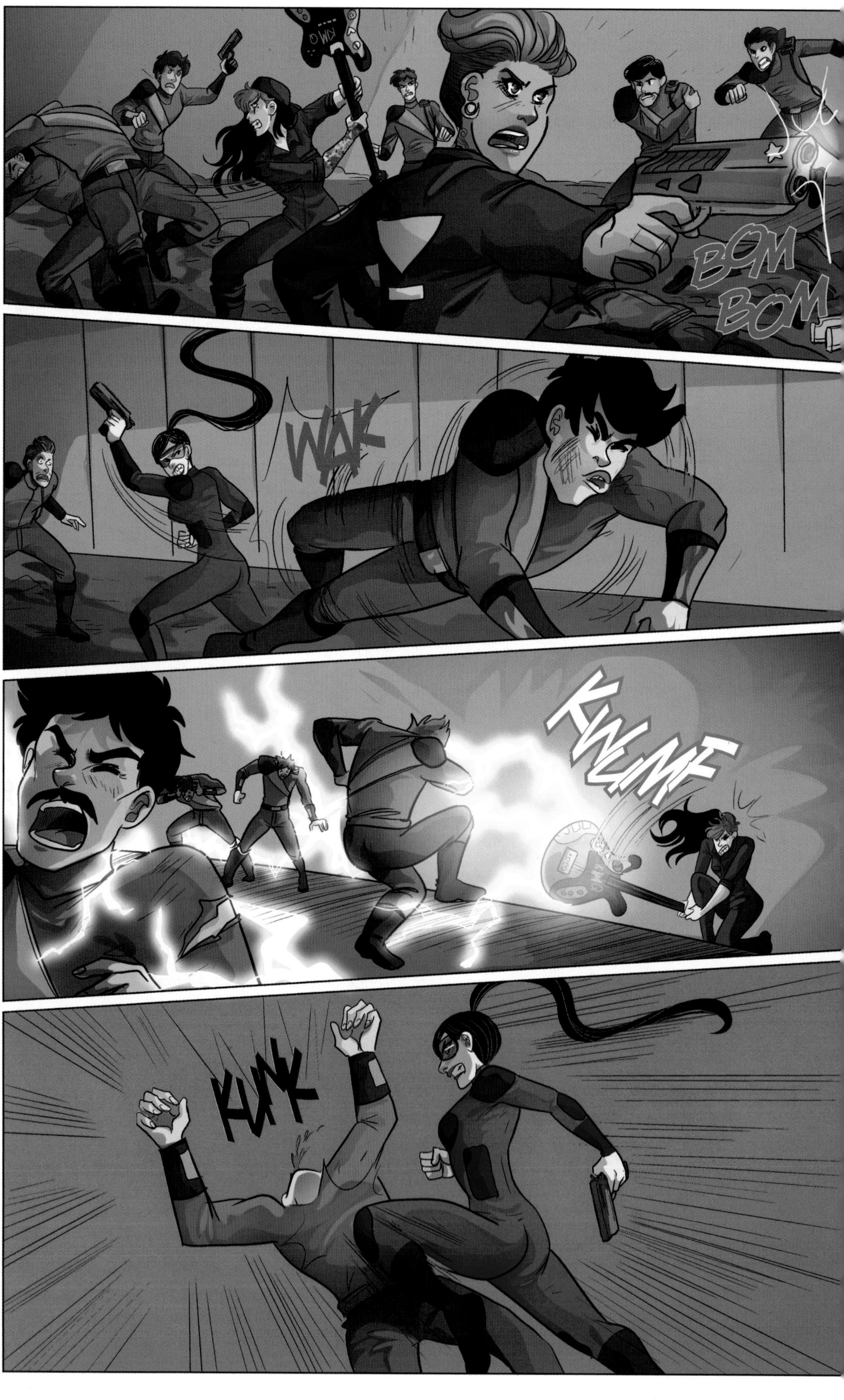

BOM
BOM
WAK
KWUMF
KUNK

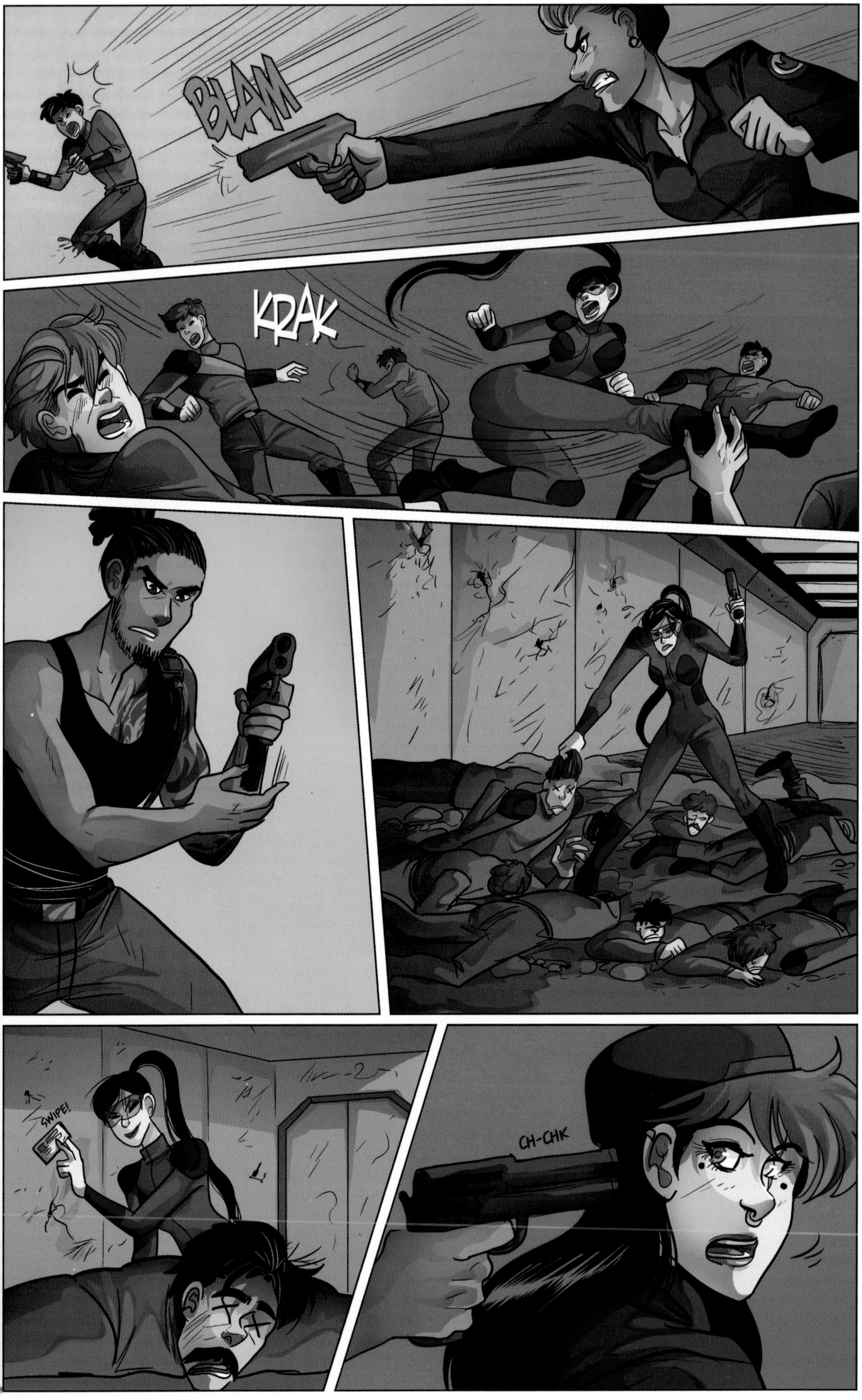
BLAM
KRAK
SWIPE!
CH-CHK

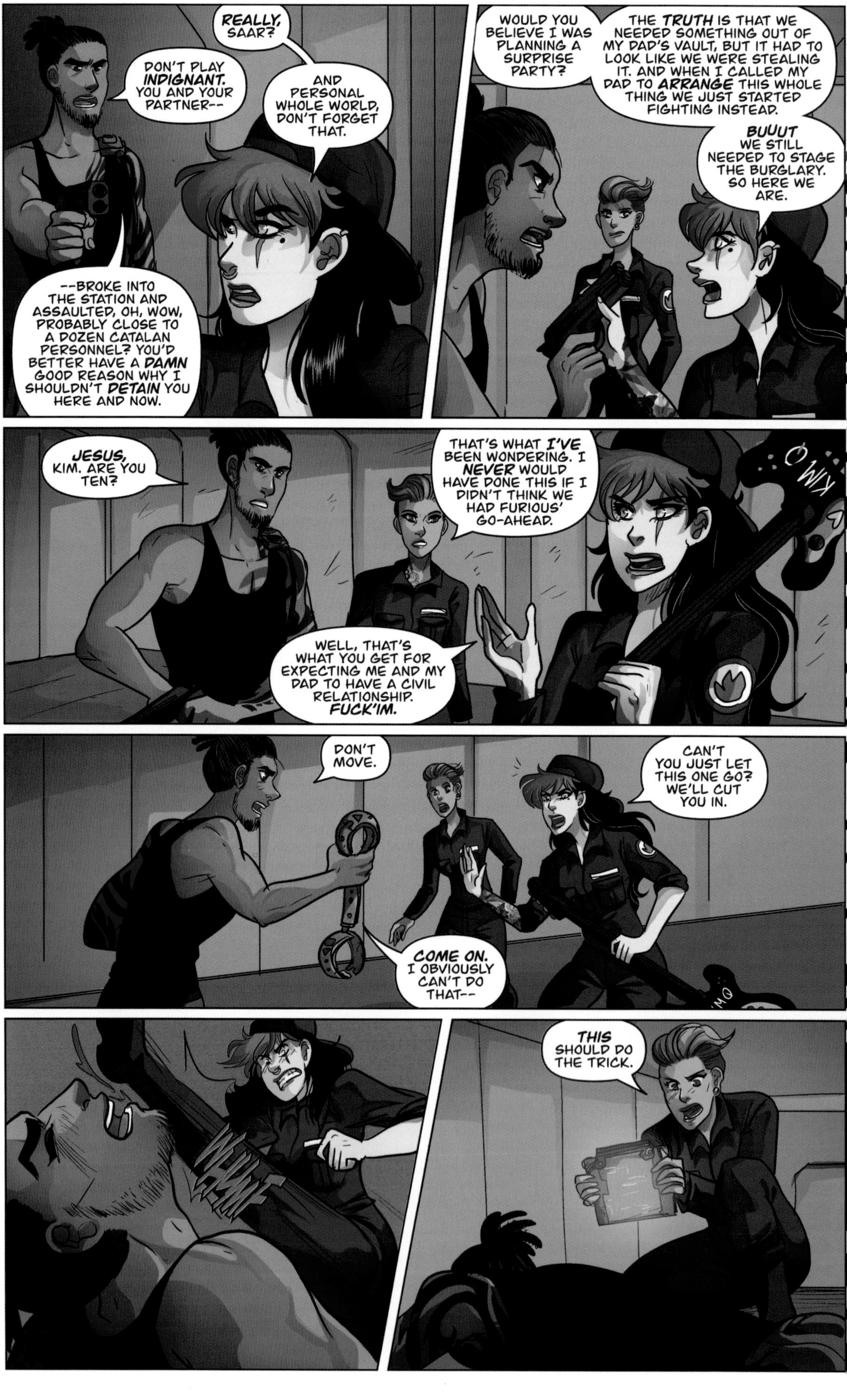
DON'T PLAY INDIGNANT. YOU AND YOUR PARTNER--
REALLY, SAAR?
AND PERSONAL WHOLE WORLD, DON'T FORGET THAT.
--BROKE INTO THE STATION AND ASSAULTED, OH, WOW, PROBABLY CLOSE TO A DOZEN CATALAN PERSONNEL? YOU'D BETTER HAVE A DAMN GOOD REASON WHY I SHOULDN'T DETAIN YOU HERE AND NOW.
WOULD YOU BELIEVE I WAS PLANNING A SURPRISE PARTY?
THE TRUTH IS THAT WE NEEDED SOMETHING OUT OF MY DAD'S VAULT, BUT IT HAD TO LOOK LIKE WE WERE STEALING IT. AND WHEN I CALLED MY DAD TO ARRANGE THIS WHOLE THING WE JUST STARTED FIGHTING INSTEAD.
BUUUT WE STILL NEEDED TO STAGE THE BURGLARY. SO HERE WE ARE.
JESUS, KIM. ARE YOU TEN?
THAT'S WHAT I'VE BEEN WONDERING. I NEVER WOULD HAVE DONE THIS IF I DIDN'T THINK WE HAD FURIOUS' GO-AHEAD.
WELL, THAT'S WHAT YOU GET FOR EXPECTING ME AND MY DAD TO HAVE A CIVIL RELATIONSHIP. FUCK'IM.
DON'T MOVE.
CAN'T YOU JUST LET THIS ONE GO? WE'LL CUT YOU IN.
COME ON. I OBVIOUSLY CAN'T DO THAT--
THIS SHOULD DO THE TRICK.

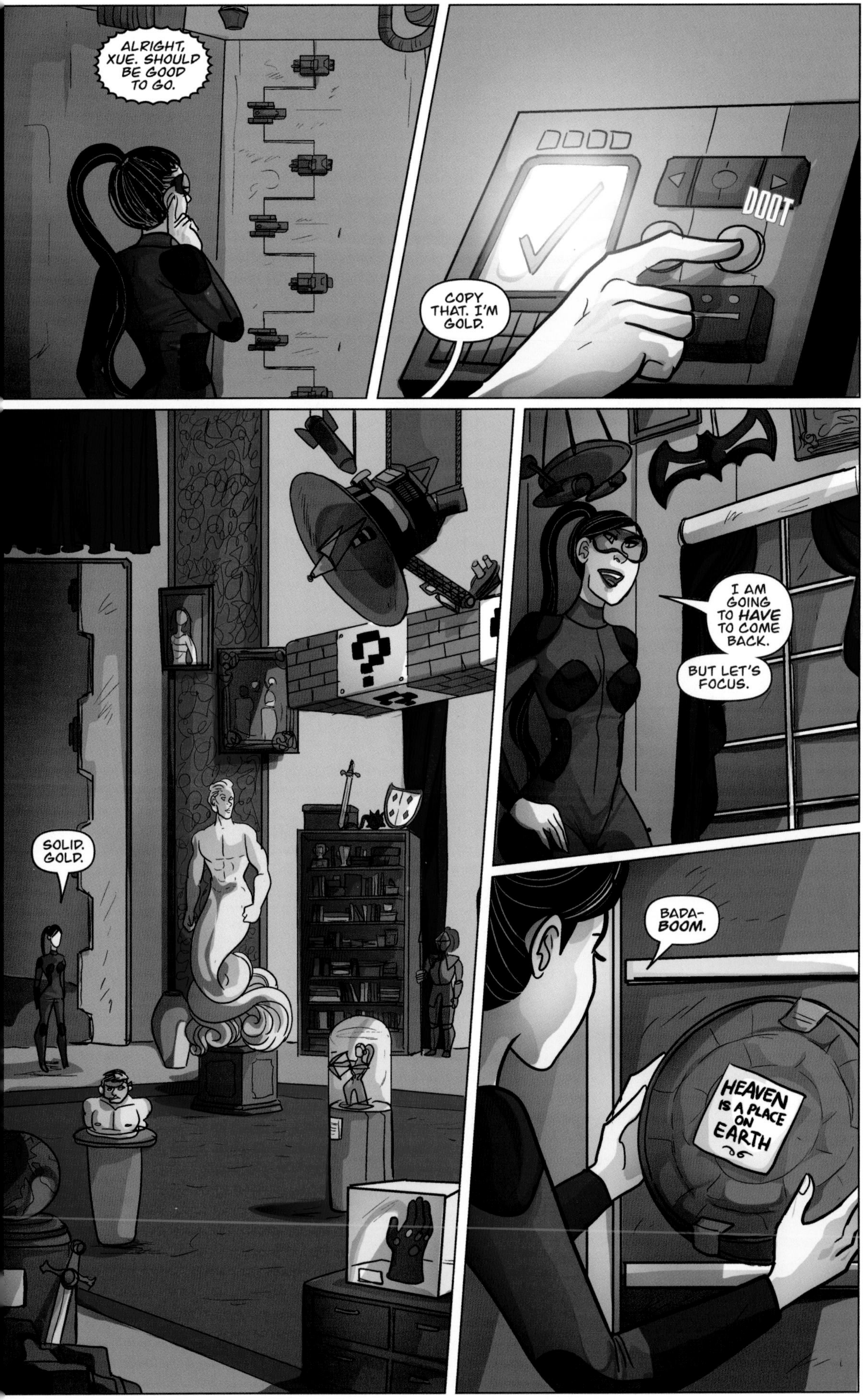
ALRIGHT, XUE. SHOULD BE GOOD TO GO.
DOOT
COPY THAT. I'M GOLD.
SOLID. GOLD.
I AM GOING TO HAVE TO COME BACK.
BUT LET'S FOCUS.
BADA-BOOM.
HEAVEN IS A PLACE ON EARTH

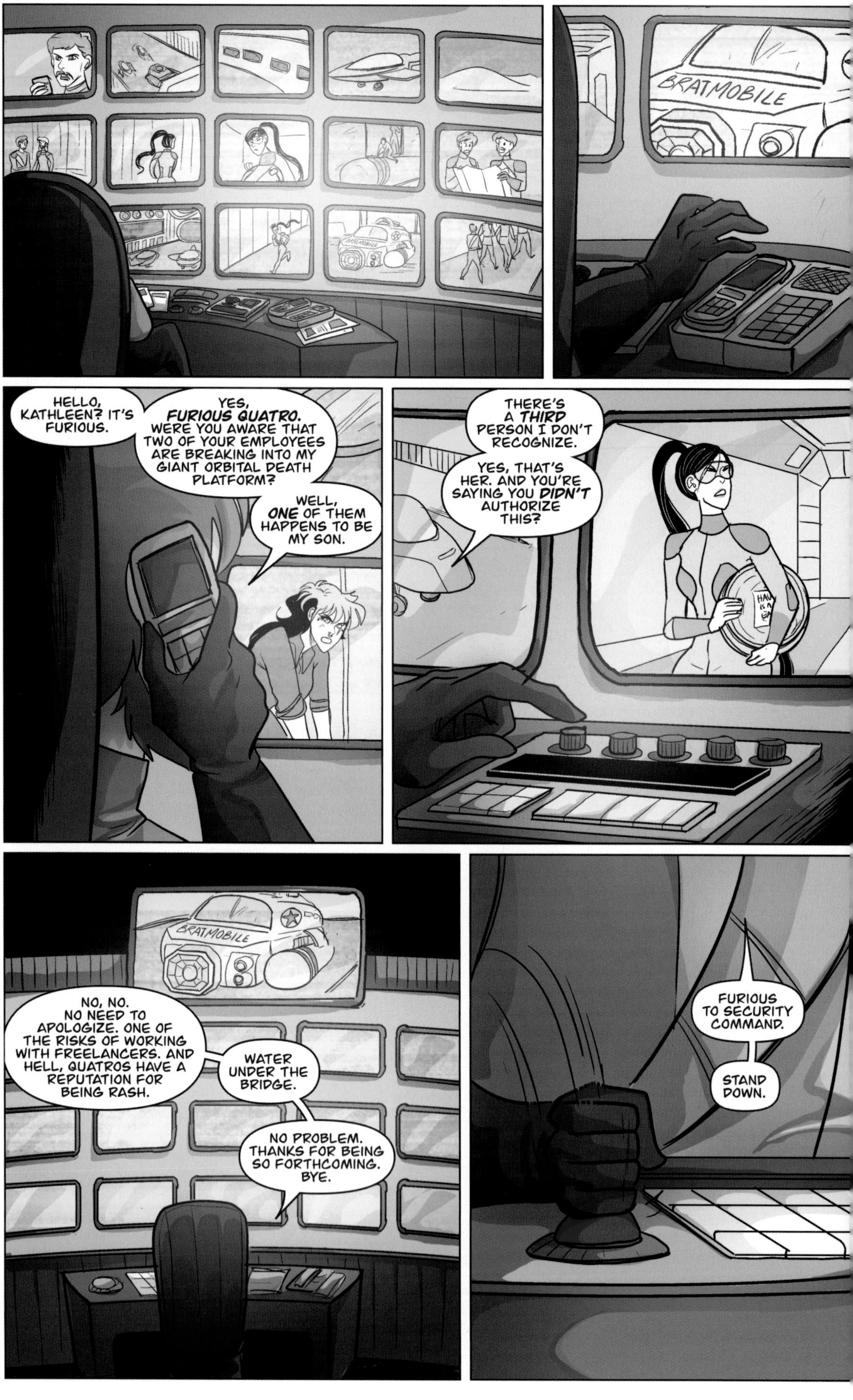
BRATMOBILE
HELLO, KATHLEEN? IT'S FURIOUS.
YES, *FURIOUS QUATRO.* WERE YOU AWARE THAT TWO OF YOUR EMPLOYEES ARE BREAKING INTO MY GIANT ORBITAL DEATH PLATFORM?
WELL, *ONE* OF THEM HAPPENS TO BE MY SON.
THERE'S A *THIRD* PERSON I DON'T RECOGNIZE.
YES, THAT'S HER. AND YOU'RE SAYING YOU *DIDN'T* AUTHORIZE THIS?
BRATMOBILE
NO, NO. NO NEED TO APOLOGIZE. ONE OF THE RISKS OF WORKING WITH FREELANCERS. AND HELL, QUATROS HAVE A REPUTATION FOR BEING RASH.
WATER UNDER THE BRIDGE.
NO PROBLEM. THANKS FOR BEING SO FORTHCOMING. BYE.
FURIOUS TO SECURITY COMMAND.
STAND DOWN.

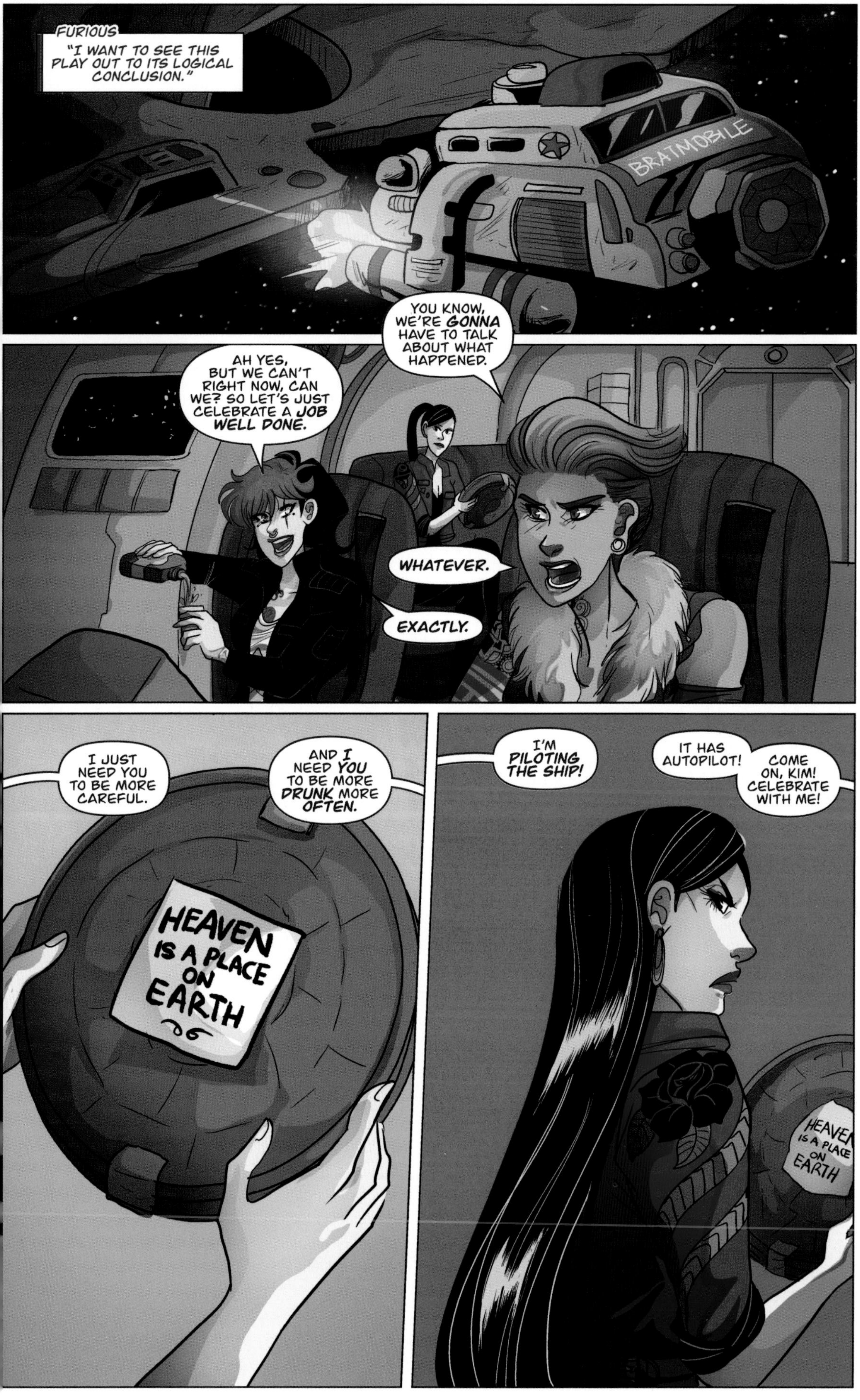
FURIOUS
"I WANT TO SEE THIS PLAY OUT TO ITS LOGICAL CONCLUSION."
BRATMOBILE
YOU KNOW, WE'RE GONNA HAVE TO TALK ABOUT WHAT HAPPENED.
AH YES, BUT WE CAN'T RIGHT NOW, CAN WE? SO LET'S JUST CELEBRATE A JOB WELL DONE.
WHATEVER.
EXACTLY.
I JUST NEED YOU TO BE MORE CAREFUL.
AND I NEED YOU TO BE MORE DRUNK MORE OFTEN.
HEAVEN IS A PLACE ON EARTH
I'M PILOTING THE SHIP!
IT HAS AUTOPILOT!
COME ON, KIM! CELEBRATE WITH ME!
HEAVEN IS A PLACE ON EARTH

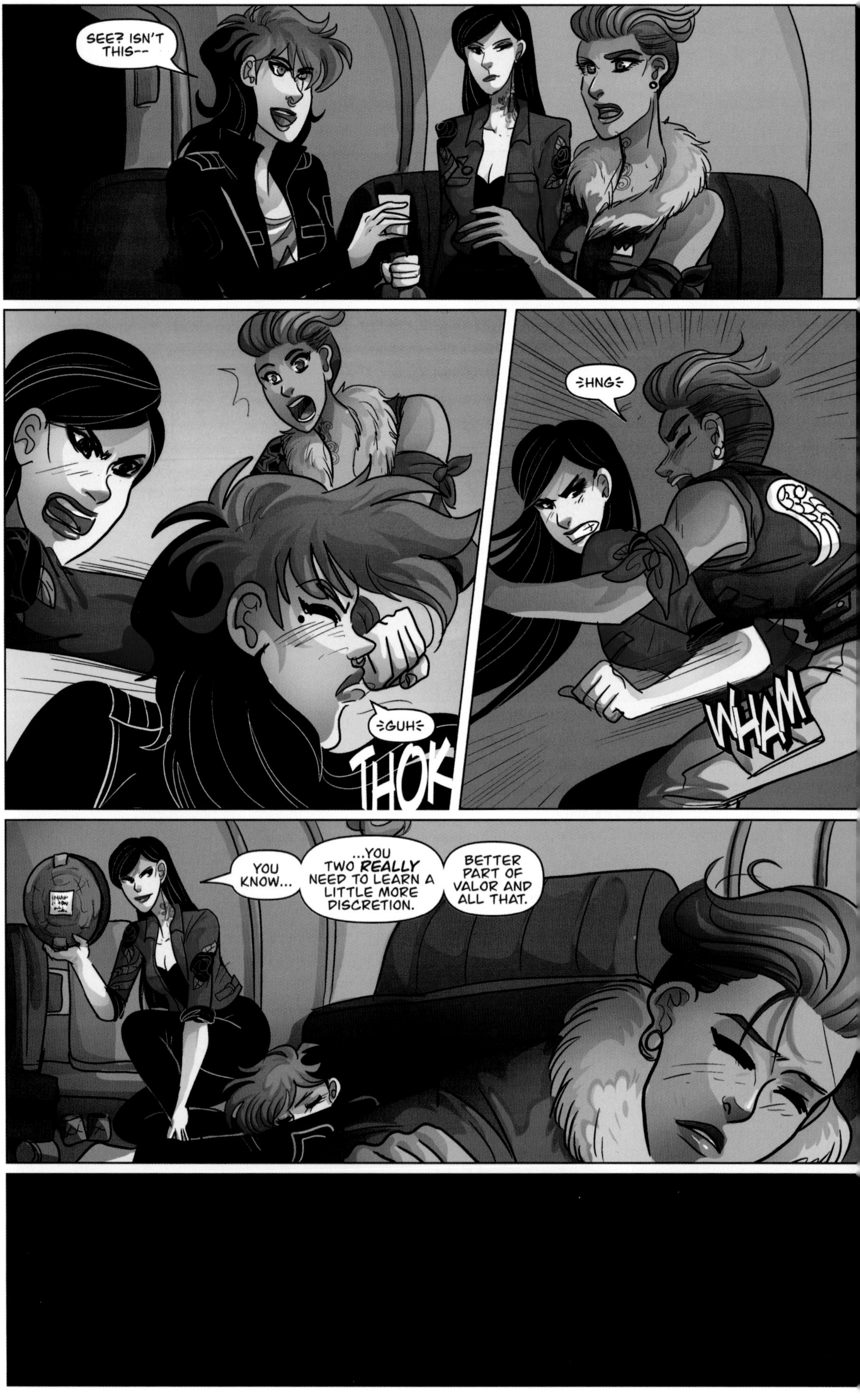
SEE? ISN'T THIS--
GUH
THOK
HNG
WHAM
YOU KNOW...
...YOU TWO REALLY NEED TO LEARN A LITTLE MORE DISCRETION.
BETTER PART OF VALOR AND ALL THAT.

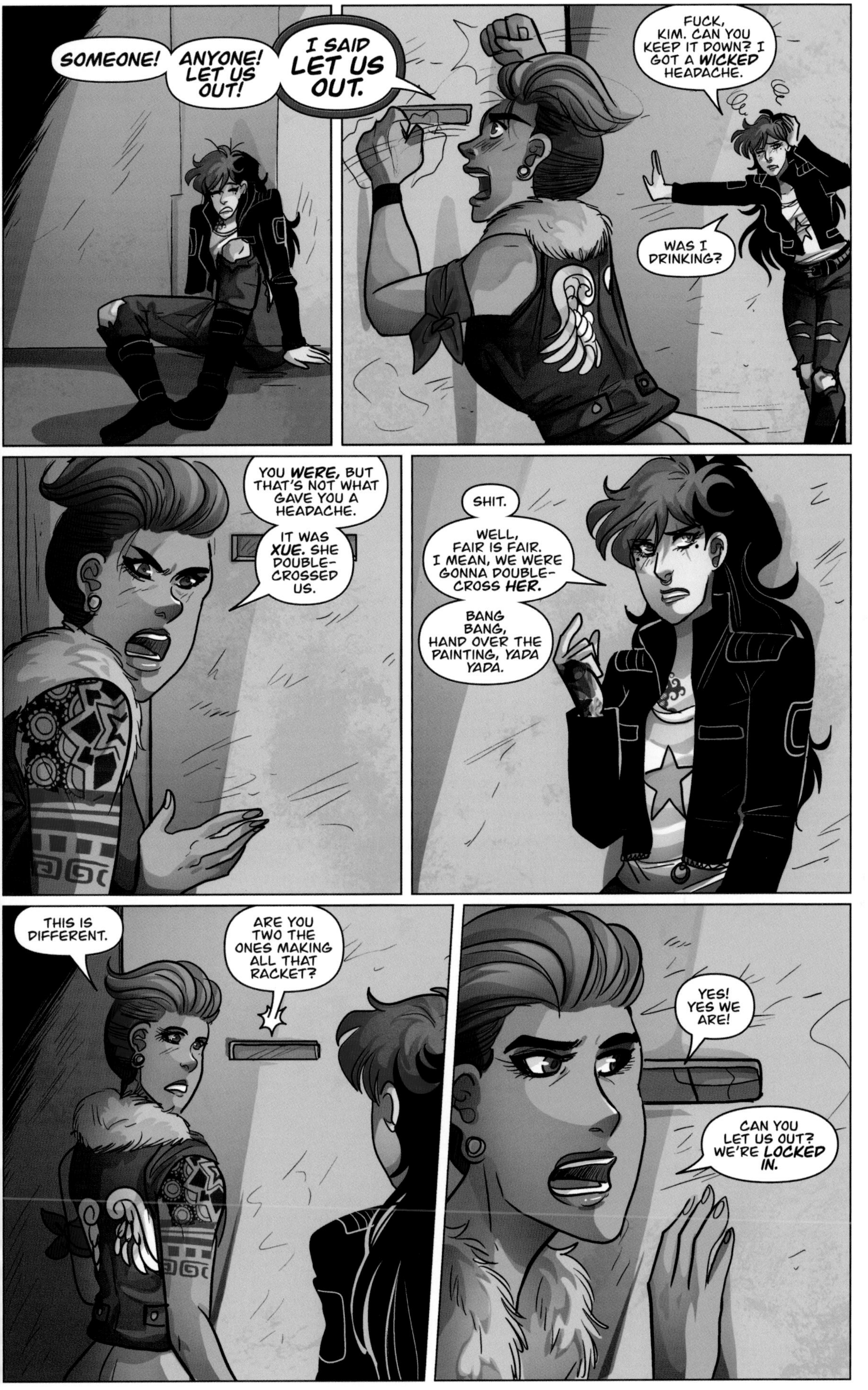
SOMEONE!
ANYONE! LET US OUT!
I SAID LET US OUT.
FUCK, KIM. CAN YOU KEEP IT DOWN? I GOT A WICKED HEADACHE.
WAS I DRINKING?
YOU WERE, BUT THAT'S NOT WHAT GAVE YOU A HEADACHE.
IT WAS XUE. SHE DOUBLE-CROSSED US.
SHIT.
WELL, FAIR IS FAIR. I MEAN, WE WERE GONNA DOUBLE-CROSS HER.
BANG BANG, HAND OVER THE PAINTING, YADA YADA.
THIS IS DIFFERENT.
ARE YOU TWO THE ONES MAKING ALL THAT RACKET?
YES! YES WE ARE!
CAN YOU LET US OUT? WE'RE LOCKED IN.

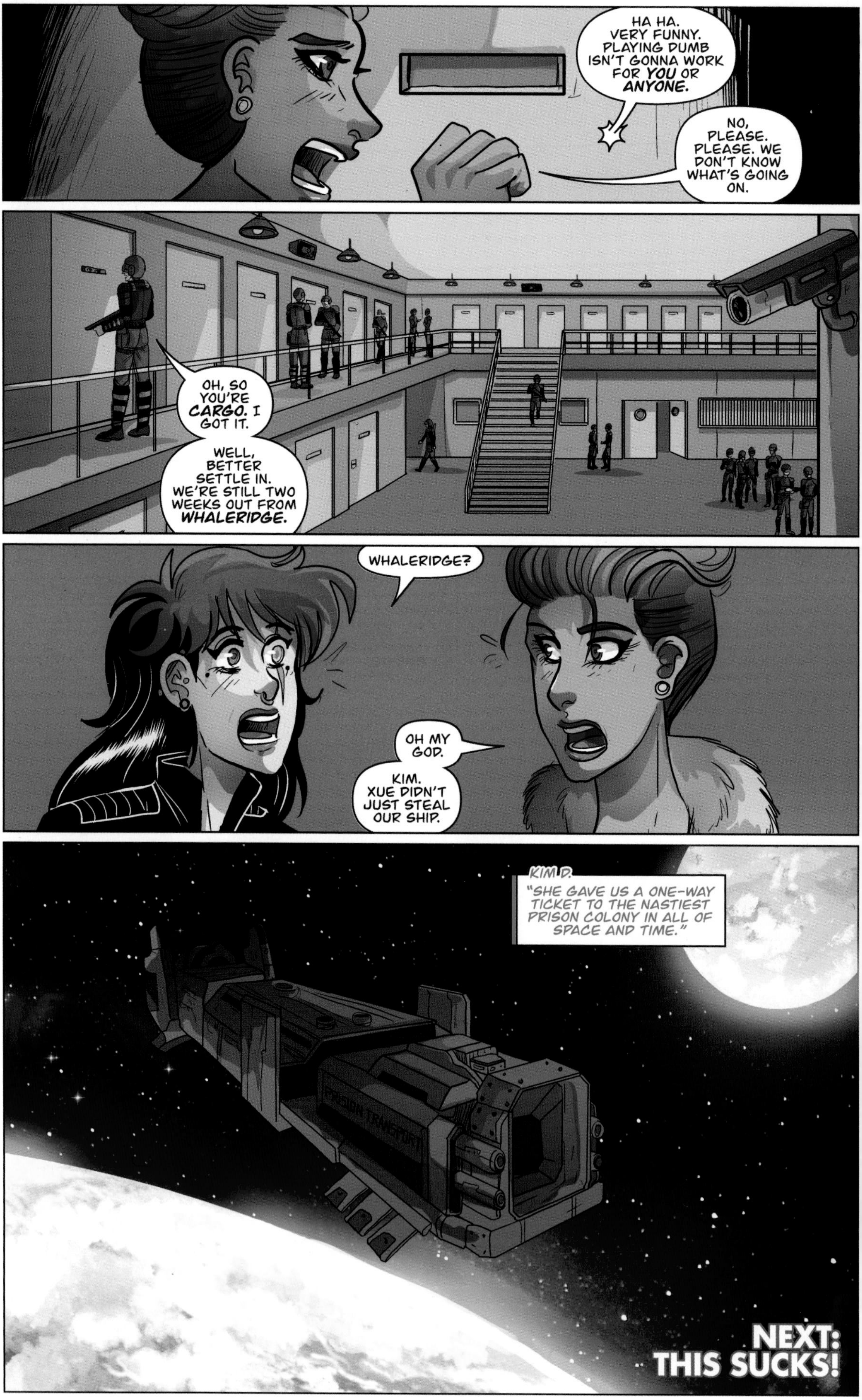
HA HA. VERY FUNNY. PLAYING DUMB ISN'T GONNA WORK FOR YOU OR ANYONE.
NO, PLEASE. PLEASE. WE DON'T KNOW WHAT'S GOING ON.
OH, SO YOU'RE CARGO. I GOT IT.
WELL, BETTER SETTLE IN. WE'RE STILL TWO WEEKS OUT FROM WHALERIDGE.
WHALERIDGE?
OH MY GOD.
KIM. XUE DIDN'T JUST STEAL OUR SHIP.
KIM D.
"SHE GAVE US A ONE-WAY TICKET TO THE NASTIEST PRISON COLONY IN ALL OF SPACE AND TIME."
PRISON TRANSPORT
NEXT: THIS SUCKS!

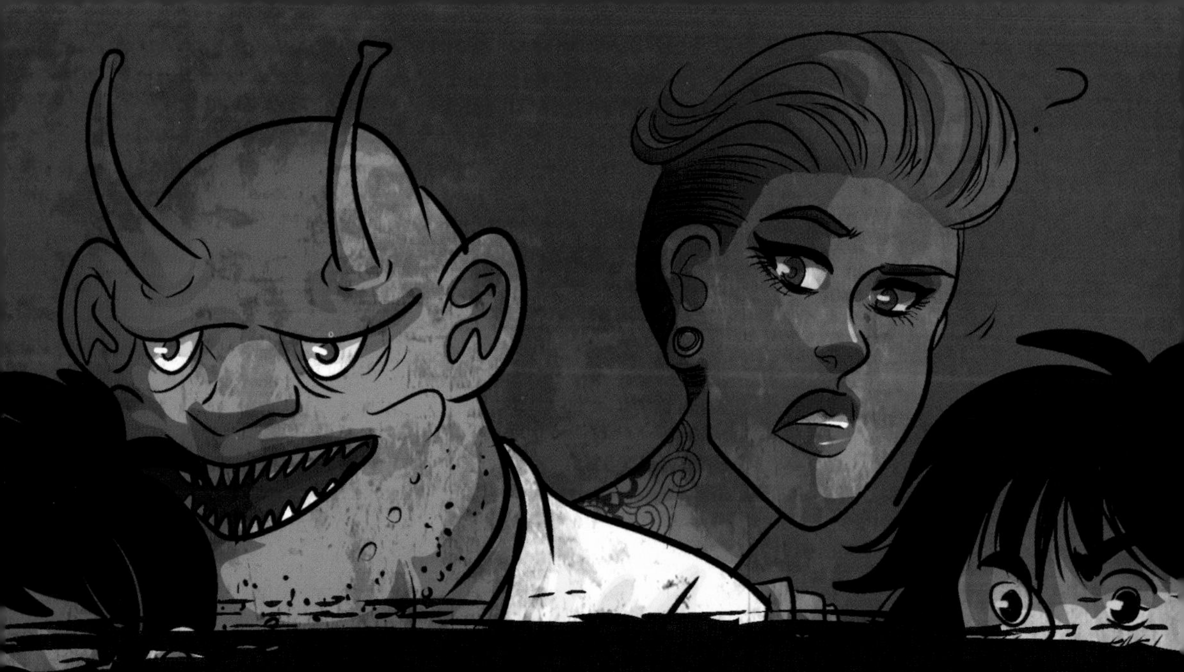

3

"THIS SUCKS!"

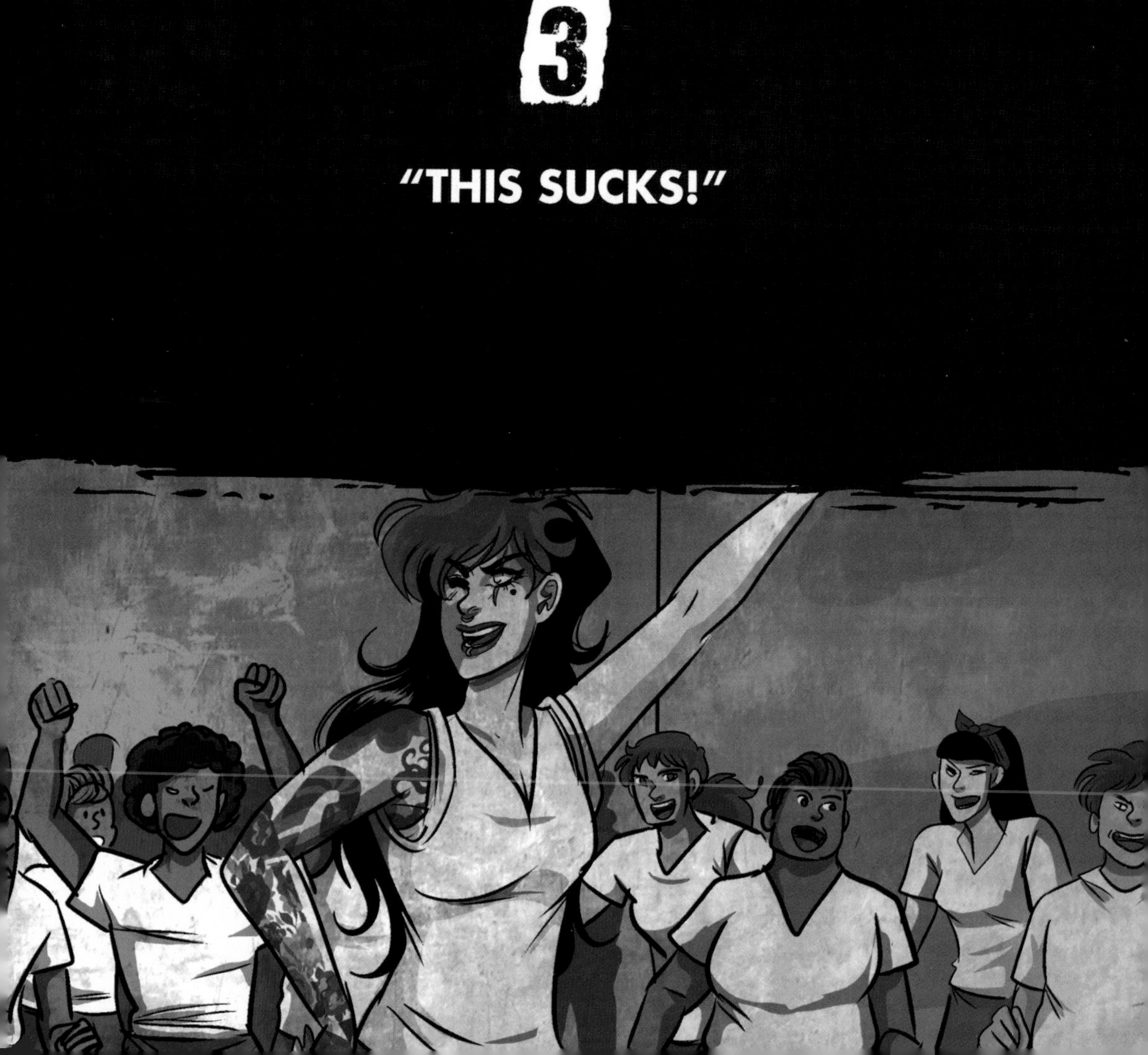

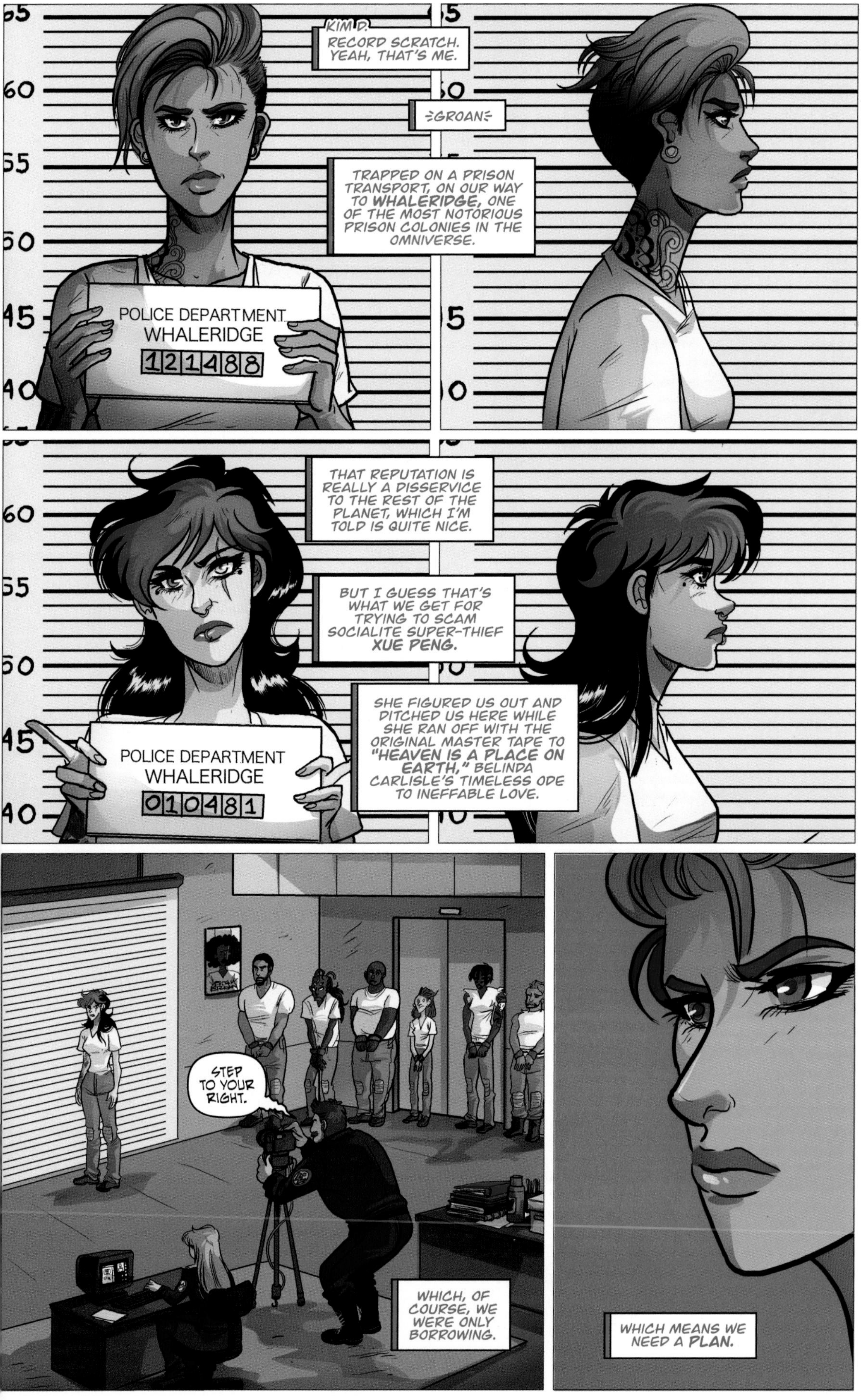
KIM D.
RECORD SCRATCH. YEAH, THAT'S ME.
≈GROAN≈
TRAPPED ON A PRISON TRANSPORT, ON OUR WAY TO WHALERIDGE, ONE OF THE MOST NOTORIOUS PRISON COLONIES IN THE OMNIVERSE.
POLICE DEPARTMENT
WHALERIDGE
121488
THAT REPUTATION IS REALLY A DISSERVICE TO THE REST OF THE PLANET, WHICH I'M TOLD IS QUITE NICE.
BUT I GUESS THAT'S WHAT WE GET FOR TRYING TO SCAM SOCIALITE SUPER-THIEF XUE PENG.
SHE FIGURED US OUT AND DITCHED US HERE WHILE SHE RAN OFF WITH THE ORIGINAL MASTER TAPE TO "HEAVEN IS A PLACE ON EARTH," BELINDA CARLISLE'S TIMELESS ODE TO INEFFABLE LOVE.
POLICE DEPARTMENT
WHALERIDGE
010481
STEP TO YOUR RIGHT.
WHICH, OF COURSE, WE WERE ONLY BORROWING.
WHICH MEANS WE NEED A PLAN.

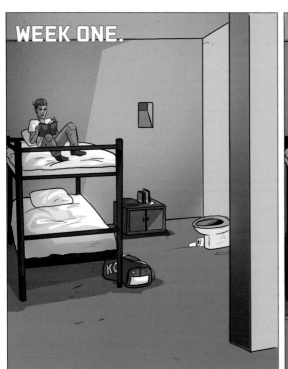

KIM!

WHO THE FUCK DO YOU THINK YOU ARE?

THERE'S A *PECKING ORDER*, LITTLE GIRL. AND YOU'RE ON THE WRONG SIDE OF IT RIGHT NOW.

PECKING ORDERS DON'T REALLY *HAVE* SIDES, *BIG, DUMB, AND UGLY.*

YOU WANNA BACK THAT UP?

I--

LADIES!

IGNORE HER. SHE'S NEW AND STUPID AND SHE'S, AH, *STILL FEELING OUT THE PLACE.* IT WON'T HAPPEN AGAIN.

YOUR FRIEND NEEDS TO LEARN NOT TO START WHAT SHE CAN'T FINISH.

MY FRIEND NEEDS TO LEARN A LOT OF THINGS. SADLY...

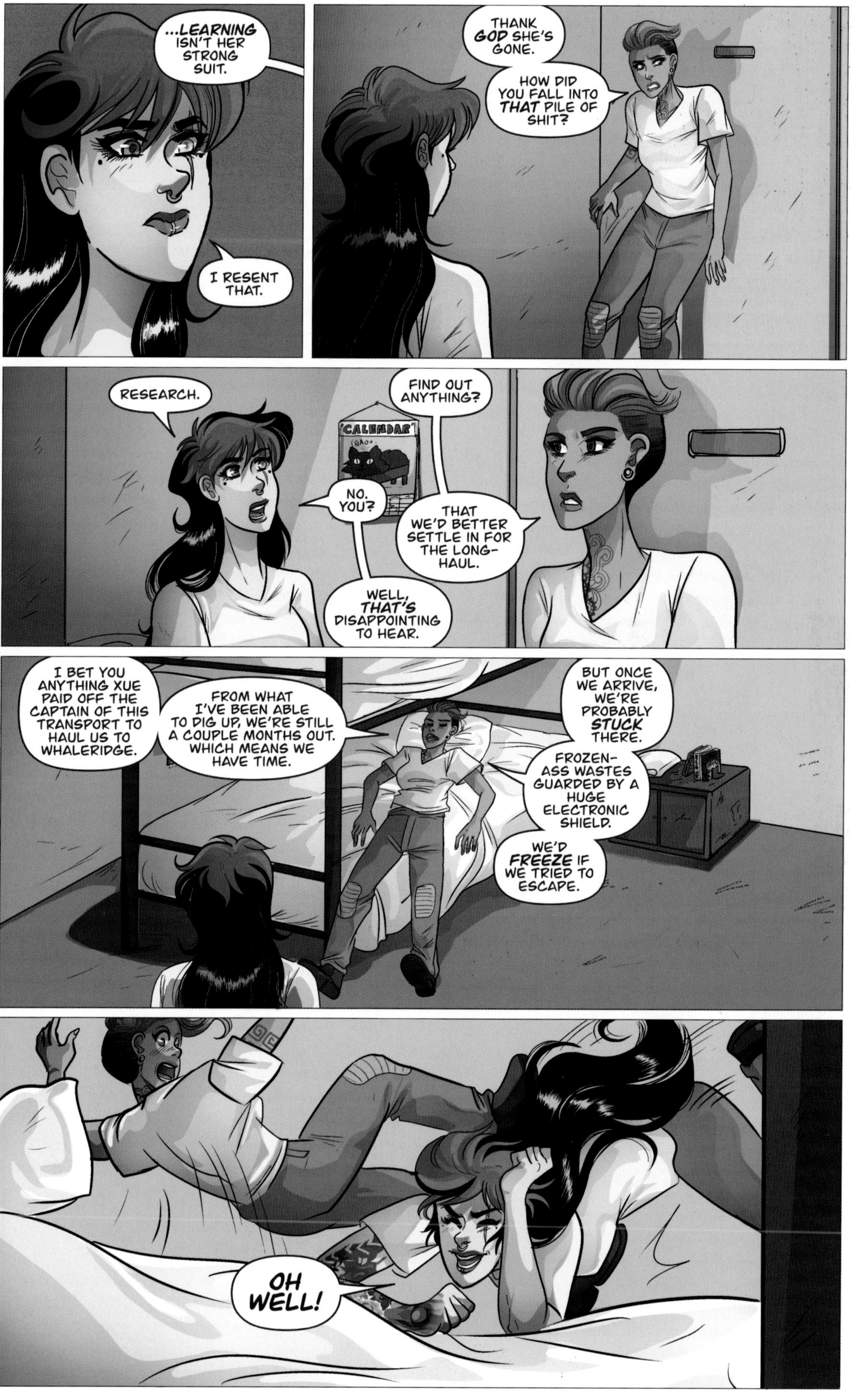

...LEARNING ISN'T HER STRONG SUIT.
I RESENT THAT.
THANK GOD SHE'S GONE.
HOW DID YOU FALL INTO THAT PILE OF SHIT?
RESEARCH.
FIND OUT ANYTHING?
CALENDAR
NO. YOU?
THAT WE'D BETTER SETTLE IN FOR THE LONG-HAUL.
WELL, THAT'S DISAPPOINTING TO HEAR.
I BET YOU ANYTHING XUE PAID OFF THE CAPTAIN OF THIS TRANSPORT TO HAUL US TO WHALERIDGE.
FROM WHAT I'VE BEEN ABLE TO DIG UP, WE'RE STILL A COUPLE MONTHS OUT. WHICH MEANS WE HAVE TIME.
BUT ONCE WE ARRIVE, WE'RE PROBABLY STUCK THERE.
FROZEN-ASS WASTES GUARDED BY A HUGE ELECTRONIC SHIELD.
WE'D FREEZE IF WE TRIED TO ESCAPE.
OH WELL!

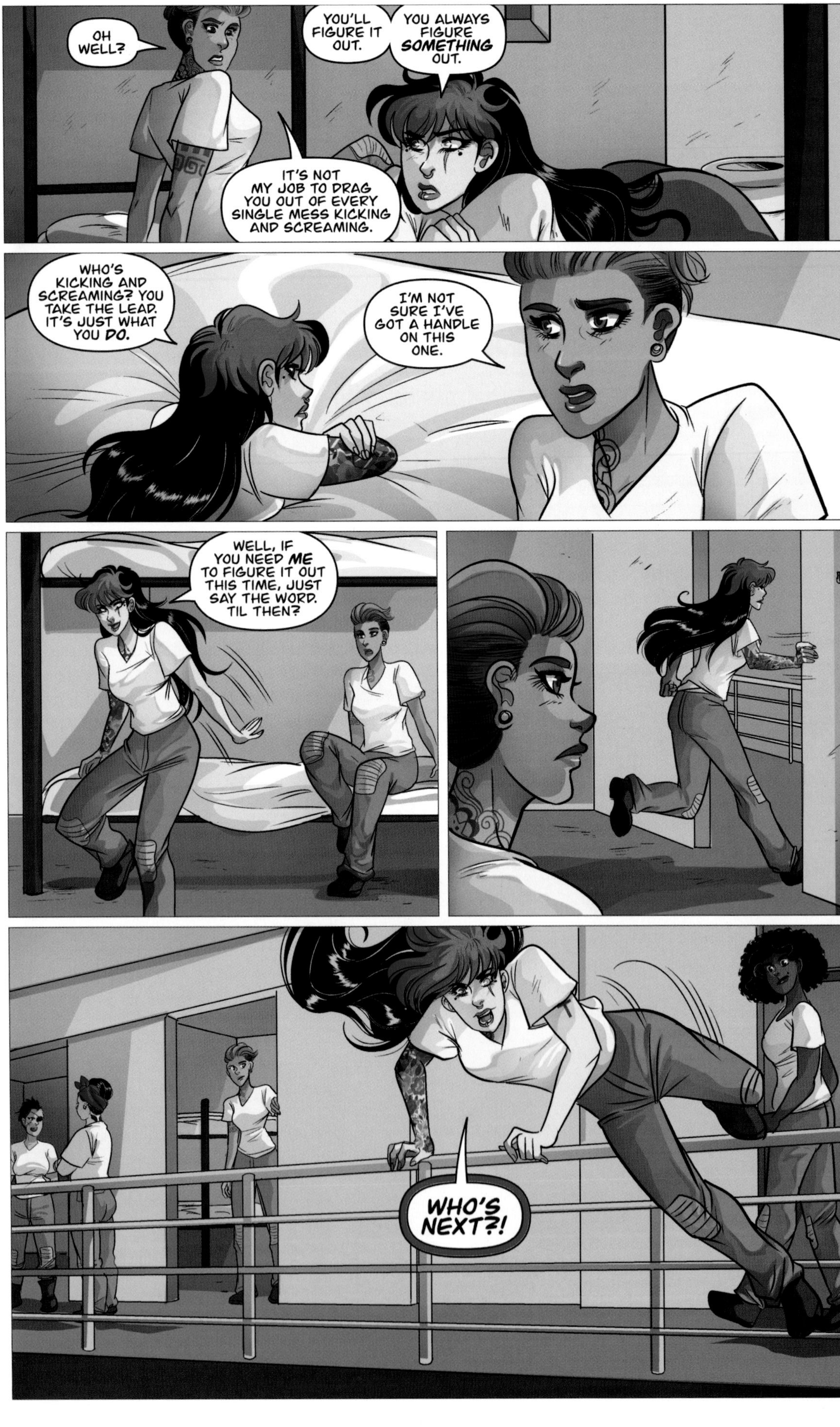
OH WELL?
YOU'LL FIGURE IT OUT.
YOU ALWAYS FIGURE **SOMETHING** OUT.
IT'S NOT MY JOB TO DRAG YOU OUT OF EVERY SINGLE MESS KICKING AND SCREAMING.
WHO'S KICKING AND SCREAMING? YOU TAKE THE LEAD. IT'S JUST WHAT YOU **DO.**
I'M NOT SURE I'VE GOT A HANDLE ON THIS ONE.
WELL, IF YOU NEED **ME** TO FIGURE IT OUT THIS TIME, JUST SAY THE WORD. TIL THEN?
WHO'S NEXT?!

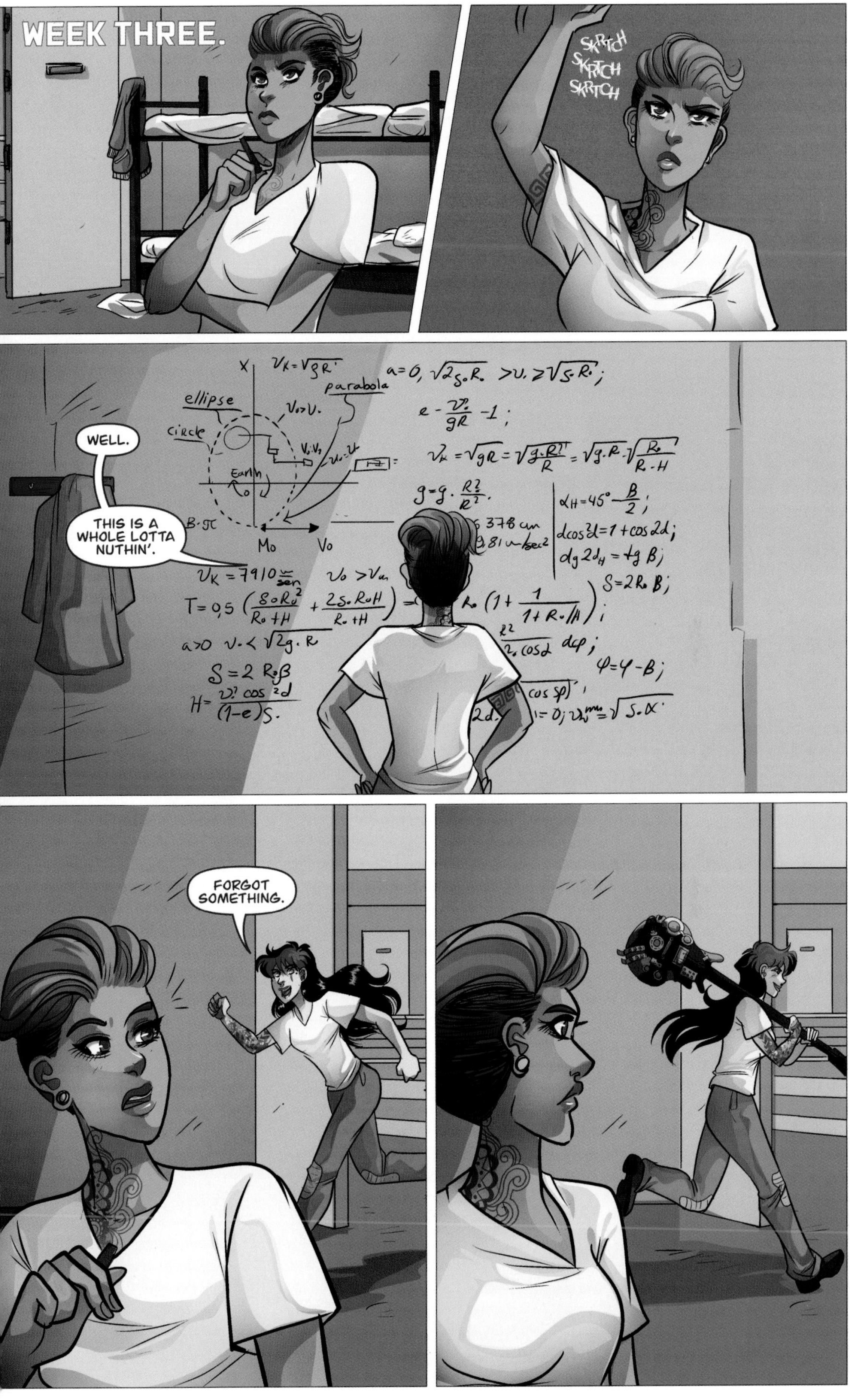
WEEK THREE.
SKRTCH
SKRTCH
SKRTCH
parabola
ellipse
circle
WELL.
THIS IS A WHOLE LOTTA NUTHIN'.
FORGOT SOMETHING.

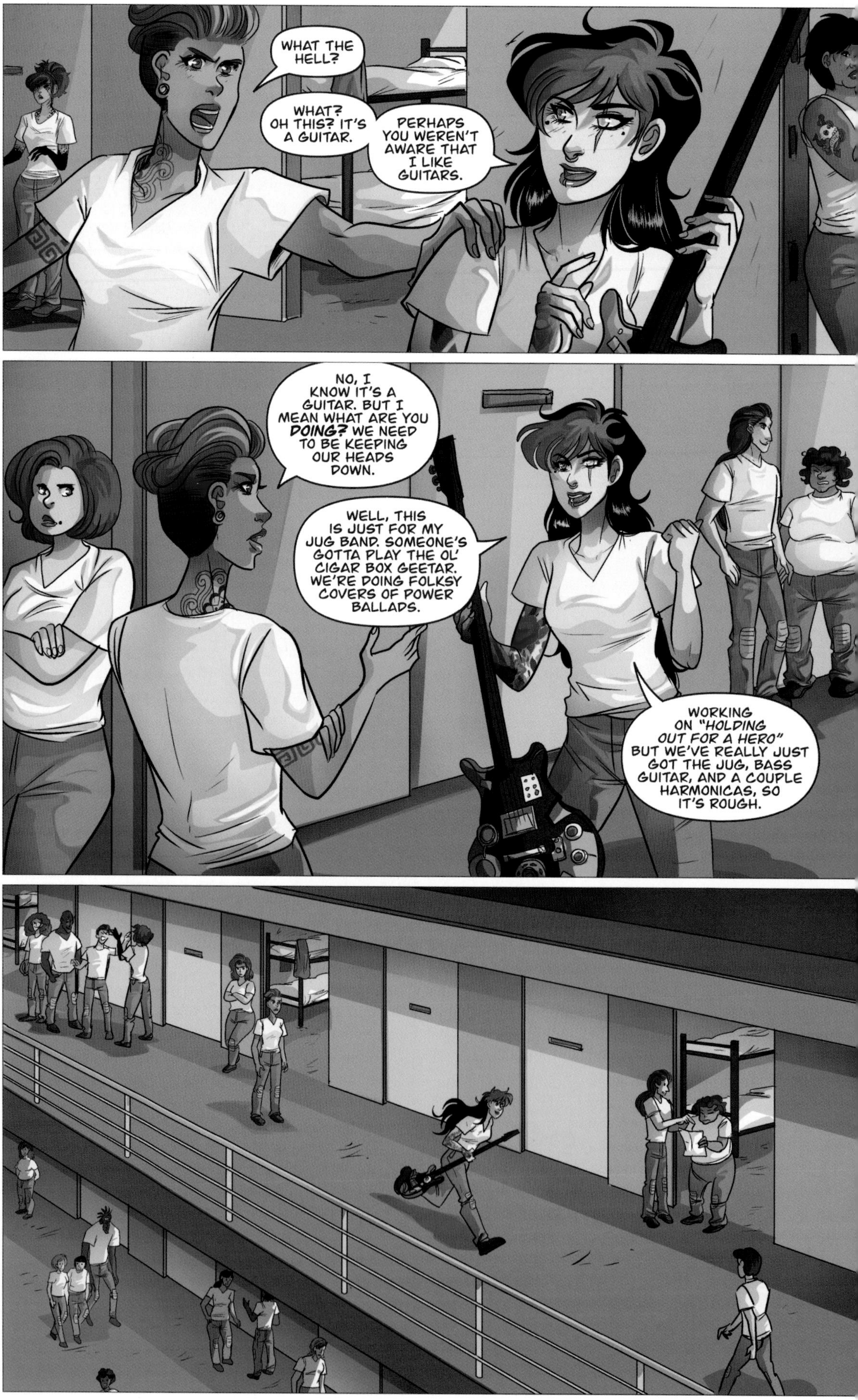
WHAT THE HELL?
WHAT? OH THIS? IT'S A GUITAR.
PERHAPS YOU WEREN'T AWARE THAT I LIKE GUITARS.
NO, I KNOW IT'S A GUITAR. BUT I MEAN WHAT ARE YOU DOING? WE NEED TO BE KEEPING OUR HEADS DOWN.
WELL, THIS IS JUST FOR MY JUG BAND. SOMEONE'S GOTTA PLAY THE OL' CIGAR BOX GEETAR. WE'RE DOING FOLKSY COVERS OF POWER BALLADS.
WORKING ON "HOLDING OUT FOR A HERO" BUT WE'VE REALLY JUST GOT THE JUG, BASS GUITAR, AND A COUPLE HARMONICAS, SO IT'S ROUGH.

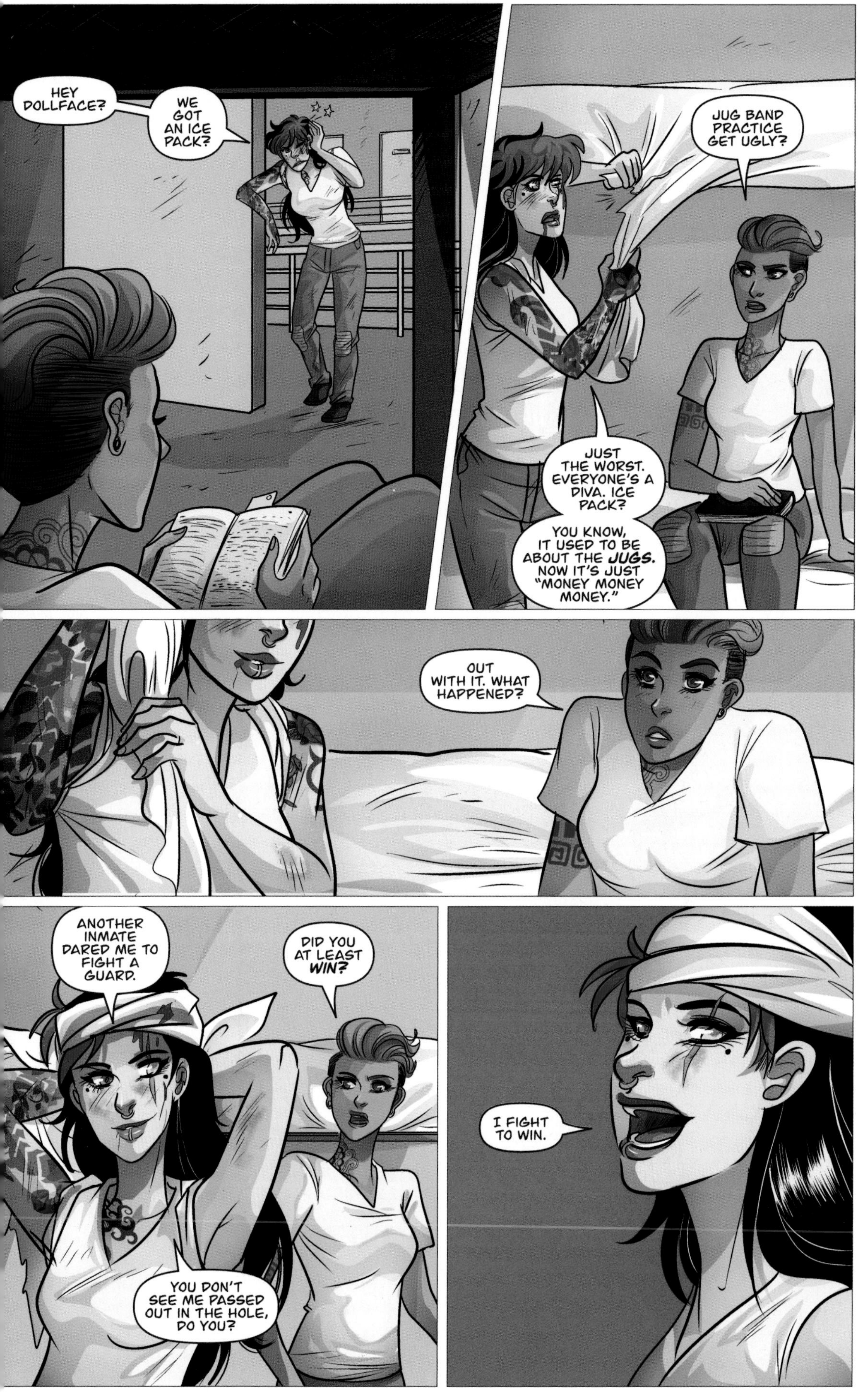
HEY DOLLFACE?
WE GOT AN ICE PACK?
JUG BAND PRACTICE GET UGLY?
JUST THE WORST. EVERYONE'S A DIVA. ICE PACK?
YOU KNOW, IT USED TO BE ABOUT THE JUGS. NOW IT'S JUST "MONEY MONEY MONEY."
OUT WITH IT. WHAT HAPPENED?
ANOTHER INMATE DARED ME TO FIGHT A GUARD.
DID YOU AT LEAST WIN?
YOU DON'T SEE ME PASSED OUT IN THE HOLE, DO YOU?
I FIGHT TO WIN.

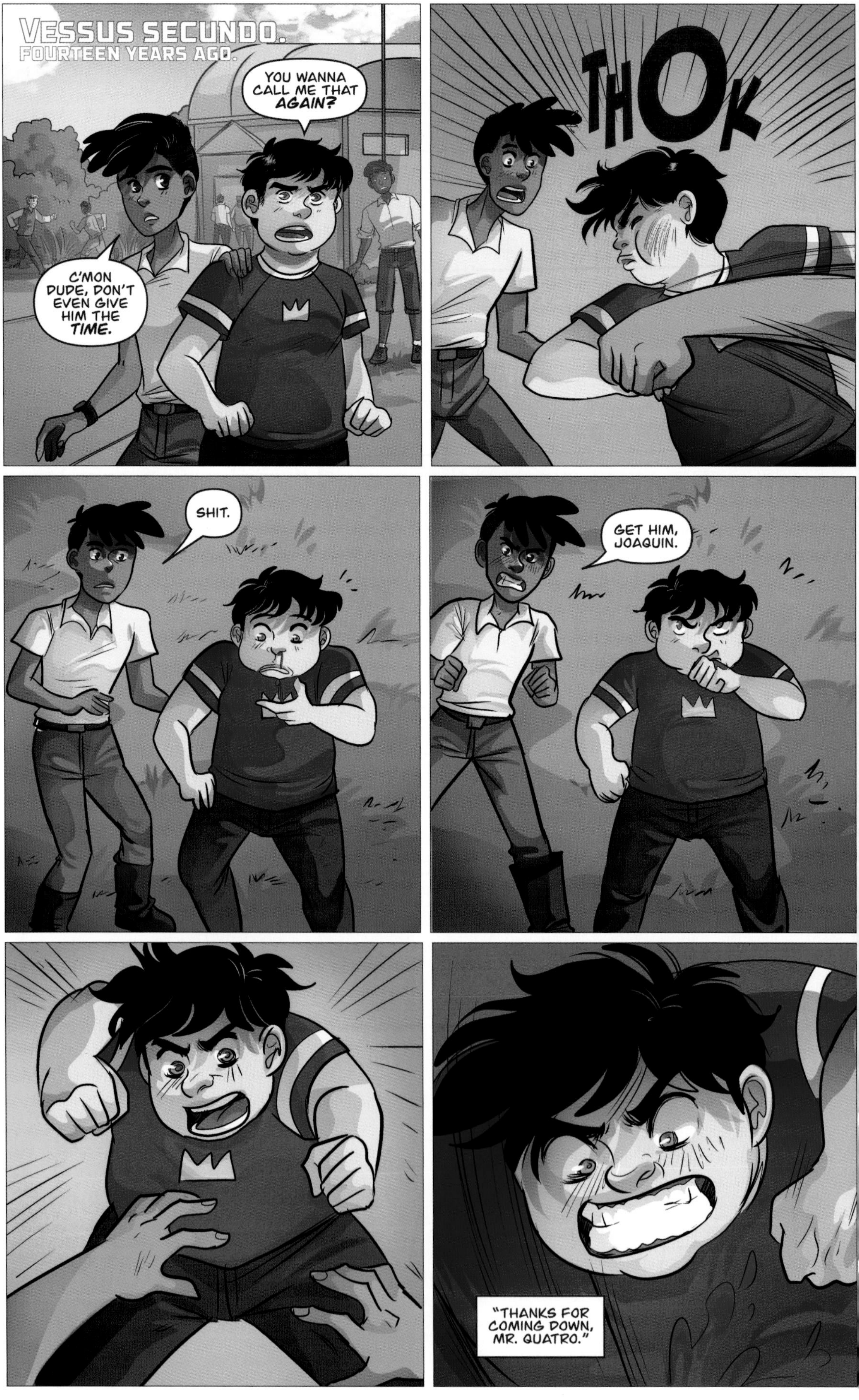
VESSUS SECUNDO.
FOURTEEN YEARS AGO.
YOU WANNA CALL ME THAT AGAIN?
C'MON DUDE, DON'T EVEN GIVE HIM THE TIME.
THOK
SHIT.
GET HIM, JOAQUIN.
"THANKS FOR COMING DOWN, MR. QUATRO."

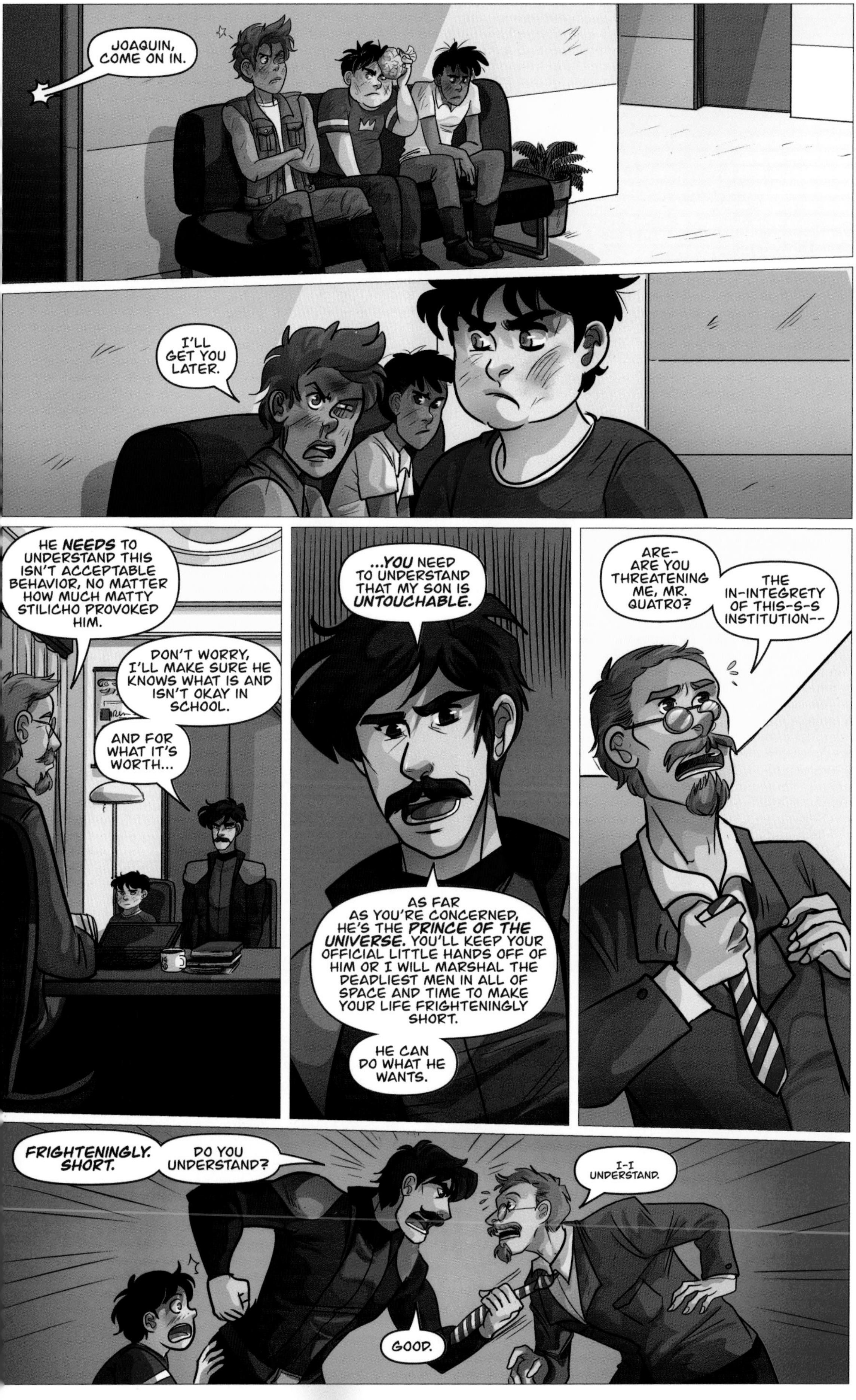

JOAQUIN, COME ON IN.
I'LL GET YOU LATER.
HE NEEDS TO UNDERSTAND THIS ISN'T ACCEPTABLE BEHAVIOR, NO MATTER HOW MUCH MATTY STILICHO PROVOKED HIM.
DON'T WORRY, I'LL MAKE SURE HE KNOWS WHAT IS AND ISN'T OKAY IN SCHOOL.
AND FOR WHAT IT'S WORTH...
...YOU NEED TO UNDERSTAND THAT MY SON IS UNTOUCHABLE.
AS FAR AS YOU'RE CONCERNED, HE'S THE PRINCE OF THE UNIVERSE. YOU'LL KEEP YOUR OFFICIAL LITTLE HANDS OFF OF HIM OR I WILL MARSHAL THE DEADLIEST MEN IN ALL OF SPACE AND TIME TO MAKE YOUR LIFE FRIGHTENINGLY SHORT.
HE CAN DO WHAT HE WANTS.
ARE- ARE YOU THREATENING ME, MR. QUATRO?
THE IN-INTEGRETY OF THIS-S-S INSTITUTION--
FRIGHTENINGLY. SHORT.
DO YOU UNDERSTAND?
I-I UNDERSTAND.
GOOD.

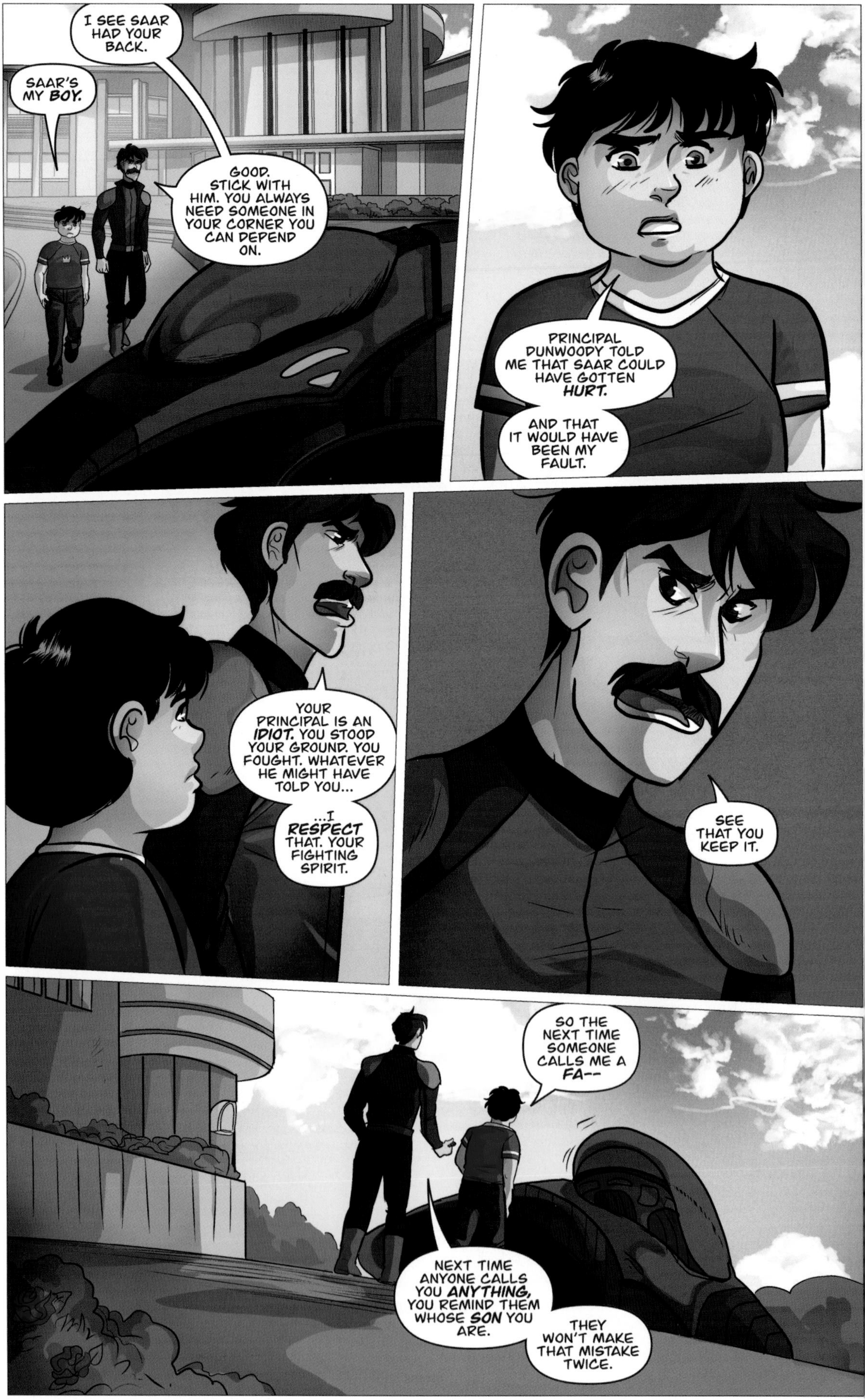
SAAR'S MY BOY.
I SEE SAAR HAD YOUR BACK.
GOOD. STICK WITH HIM. YOU ALWAYS NEED SOMEONE IN YOUR CORNER YOU CAN DEPEND ON.
PRINCIPAL DUNWOODY TOLD ME THAT SAAR COULD HAVE GOTTEN HURT.
AND THAT IT WOULD HAVE BEEN MY FAULT.
YOUR PRINCIPAL IS AN IDIOT. YOU STOOD YOUR GROUND. YOU FOUGHT. WHATEVER HE MIGHT HAVE TOLD YOU...
...I RESPECT THAT. YOUR FIGHTING SPIRIT.
SEE THAT YOU KEEP IT.
SO THE NEXT TIME SOMEONE CALLS ME A FA--
NEXT TIME ANYONE CALLS YOU ANYTHING, YOU REMIND THEM WHOSE SON YOU ARE.
THEY WON'T MAKE THAT MISTAKE TWICE.

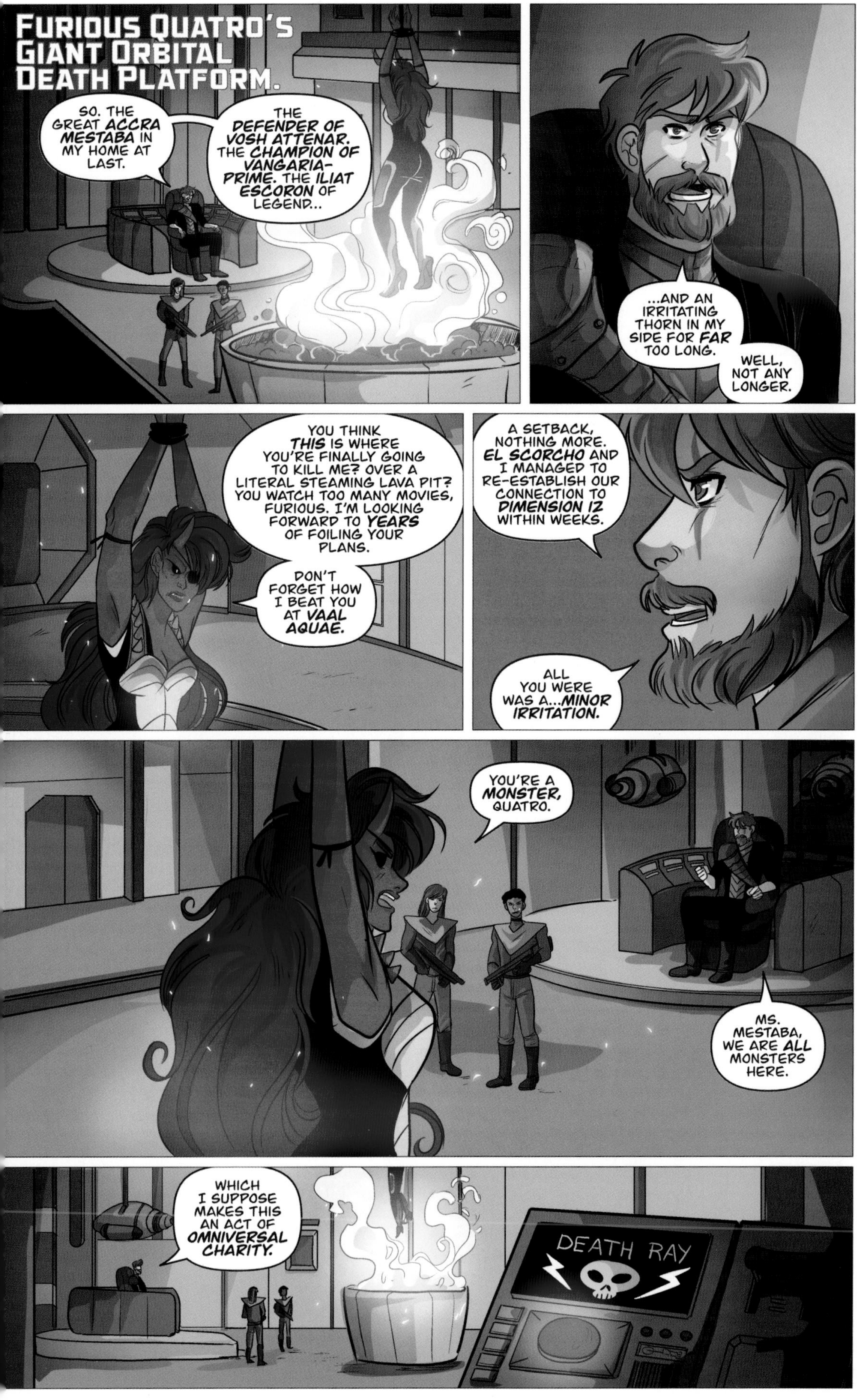

FURIOUS QUATRO'S GIANT ORBITAL DEATH PLATFORM.
SO. THE GREAT ACCRA MESTABA IN MY HOME AT LAST.
THE DEFENDER OF VOSH ATTENAR. THE CHAMPION OF VANGARIA-PRIME. THE ILIAT ESCORON OF LEGEND...
...AND AN IRRITATING THORN IN MY SIDE FOR FAR TOO LONG.
WELL, NOT ANY LONGER.
YOU THINK THIS IS WHERE YOU'RE FINALLY GOING TO KILL ME? OVER A LITERAL STEAMING LAVA PIT? YOU WATCH TOO MANY MOVIES, FURIOUS. I'M LOOKING FORWARD TO YEARS OF FOILING YOUR PLANS.
DON'T FORGET HOW I BEAT YOU AT VAAL AQUAE.
A SETBACK, NOTHING MORE. EL SCORCHO AND I MANAGED TO RE-ESTABLISH OUR CONNECTION TO DIMENSION IZ WITHIN WEEKS.
ALL YOU WERE WAS A...MINOR IRRITATION.
YOU'RE A MONSTER, QUATRO.
MS. MESTABA, WE ARE ALL MONSTERS HERE.
WHICH I SUPPOSE MAKES THIS AN ACT OF OMNIVERSAL CHARITY.
DEATH RAY

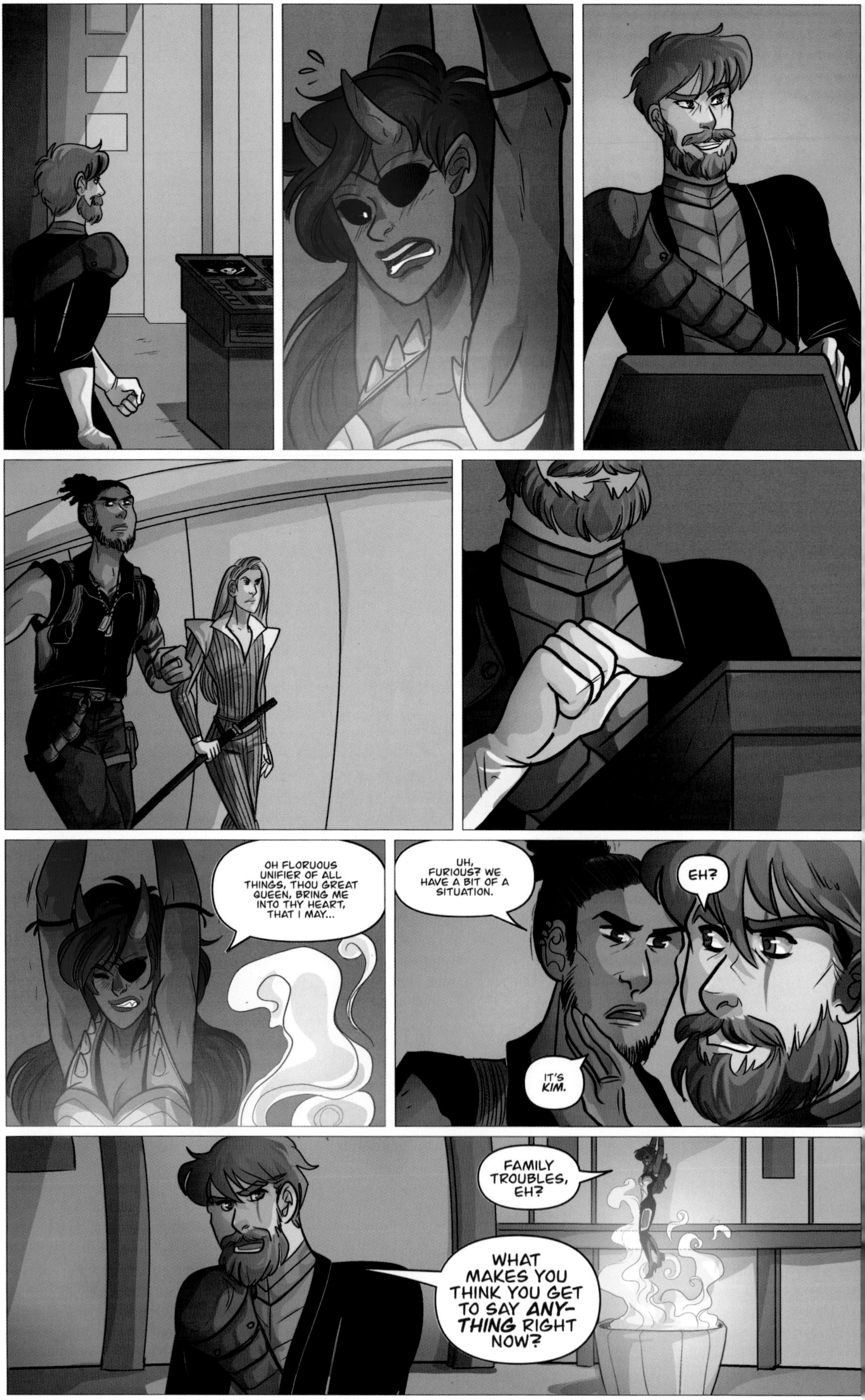

OH FLORUOUS UNIFIER OF ALL THINGS, THOU GREAT QUEEN, BRING ME INTO THY HEART, THAT I MAY...
UH, FURIOUS? WE HAVE A BIT OF A SITUATION.
EH?
IT'S KIM.
FAMILY TROUBLES, EH?
WHAT MAKES YOU THINK YOU GET TO SAY ANY-THING RIGHT NOW?

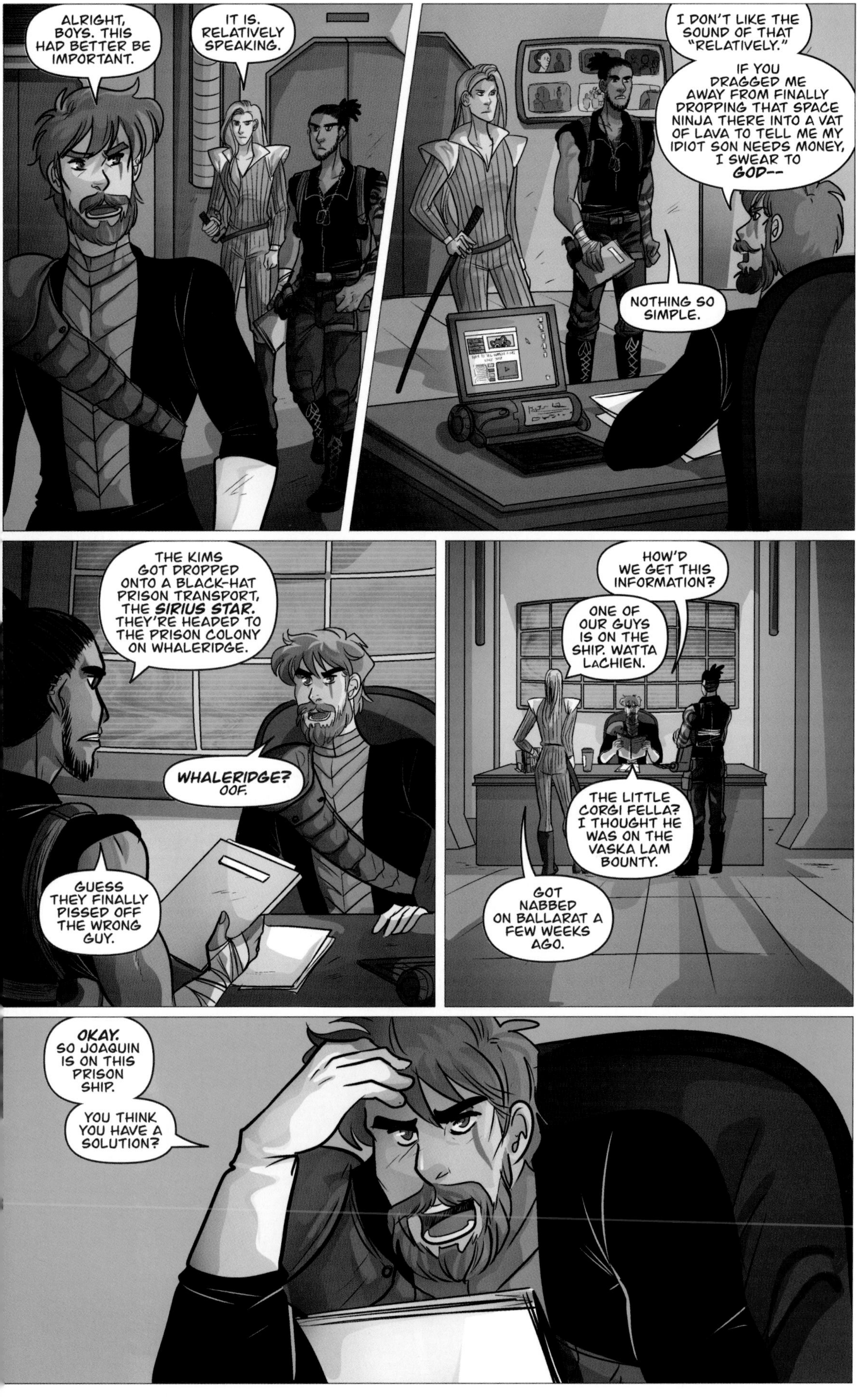

ALRIGHT, BOYS. THIS HAD BETTER BE IMPORTANT.
IT IS. RELATIVELY SPEAKING.
I DON'T LIKE THE SOUND OF THAT "RELATIVELY."
IF YOU DRAGGED ME AWAY FROM FINALLY DROPPING THAT SPACE NINJA THERE INTO A VAT OF LAVA TO TELL ME MY IDIOT SON NEEDS MONEY, I SWEAR TO GOD--
NOTHING SO SIMPLE.
THE KIMS GOT DROPPED ONTO A BLACK-HAT PRISON TRANSPORT, THE SIRIUS STAR. THEY'RE HEADED TO THE PRISON COLONY ON WHALERIDGE.
WHALERIDGE? OOF.
GUESS THEY FINALLY PISSED OFF THE WRONG GUY.
HOW'D WE GET THIS INFORMATION?
ONE OF OUR GUYS IS ON THE SHIP. WATTA LACHIEN.
THE LITTLE CORGI FELLA? I THOUGHT HE WAS ON THE VASKA LAM BOUNTY.
GOT NABBED ON BALLARAT A FEW WEEKS AGO.
OKAY. SO JOAQUIN IS ON THIS PRISON SHIP.
YOU THINK YOU HAVE A SOLUTION?

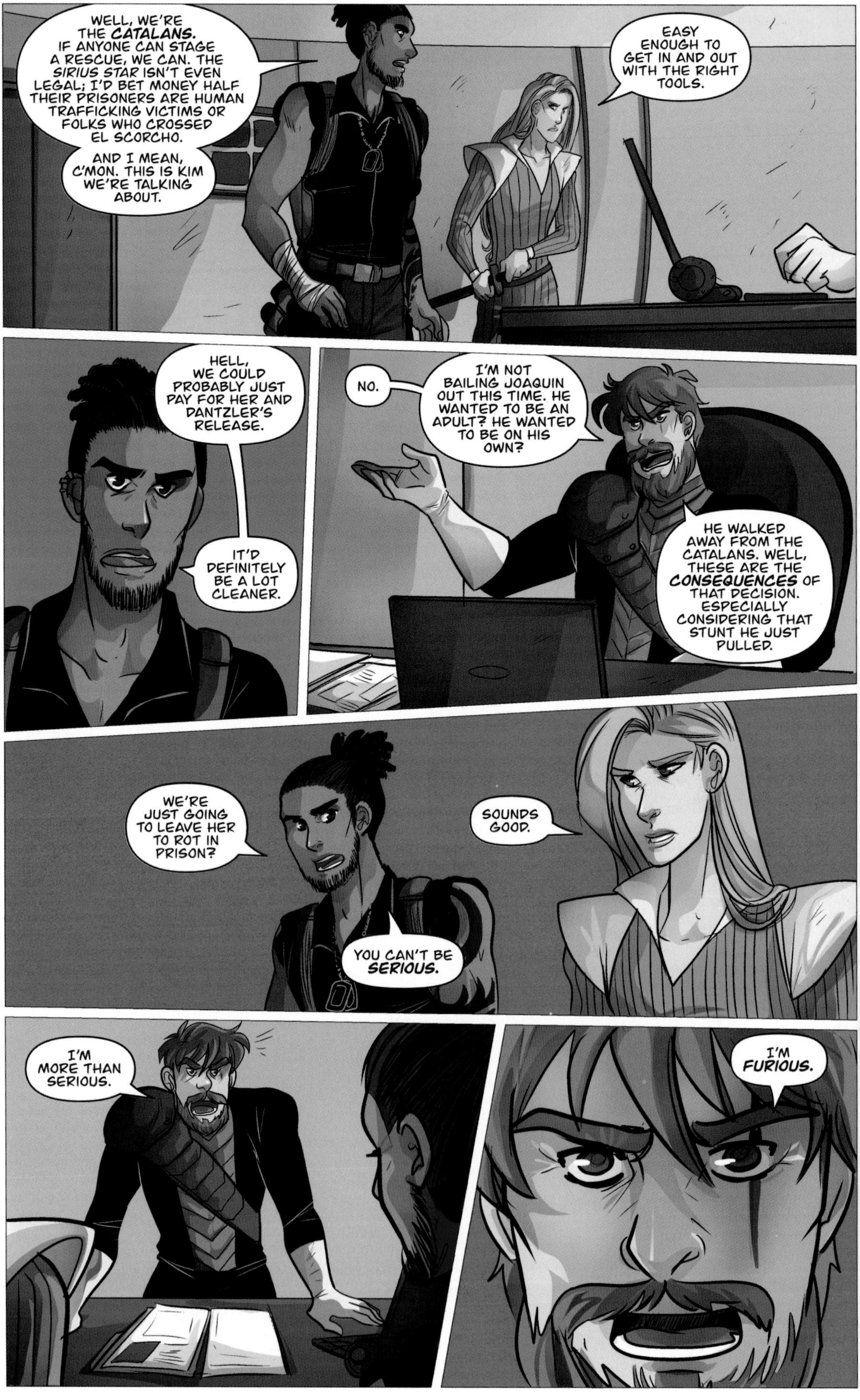
WELL, WE'RE THE **CATALANS.** IF ANYONE CAN STAGE A RESCUE, WE CAN. THE *SIRIUS STAR* ISN'T EVEN LEGAL; I'D BET MONEY HALF THEIR PRISONERS ARE HUMAN TRAFFICKING VICTIMS OR FOLKS WHO CROSSED EL SCORCHO.
AND I MEAN, C'MON. THIS IS KIM WE'RE TALKING ABOUT.
EASY ENOUGH TO GET IN AND OUT WITH THE RIGHT TOOLS.
HELL, WE COULD PROBABLY JUST PAY FOR HER AND DANTZLER'S RELEASE.
IT'D DEFINITELY BE A LOT CLEANER.
NO.
I'M NOT BAILING JOAQUIN OUT THIS TIME. HE WANTED TO BE AN ADULT? HE WANTED TO BE ON HIS OWN?
HE WALKED AWAY FROM THE CATALANS. WELL, THESE ARE THE **CONSEQUENCES** OF THAT DECISION. ESPECIALLY CONSIDERING THAT STUNT HE JUST PULLED.
WE'RE JUST GOING TO LEAVE HER TO ROT IN PRISON?
SOUNDS GOOD.
YOU CAN'T BE **SERIOUS.**
I'M MORE THAN SERIOUS.
I'M ***FURIOUS.***

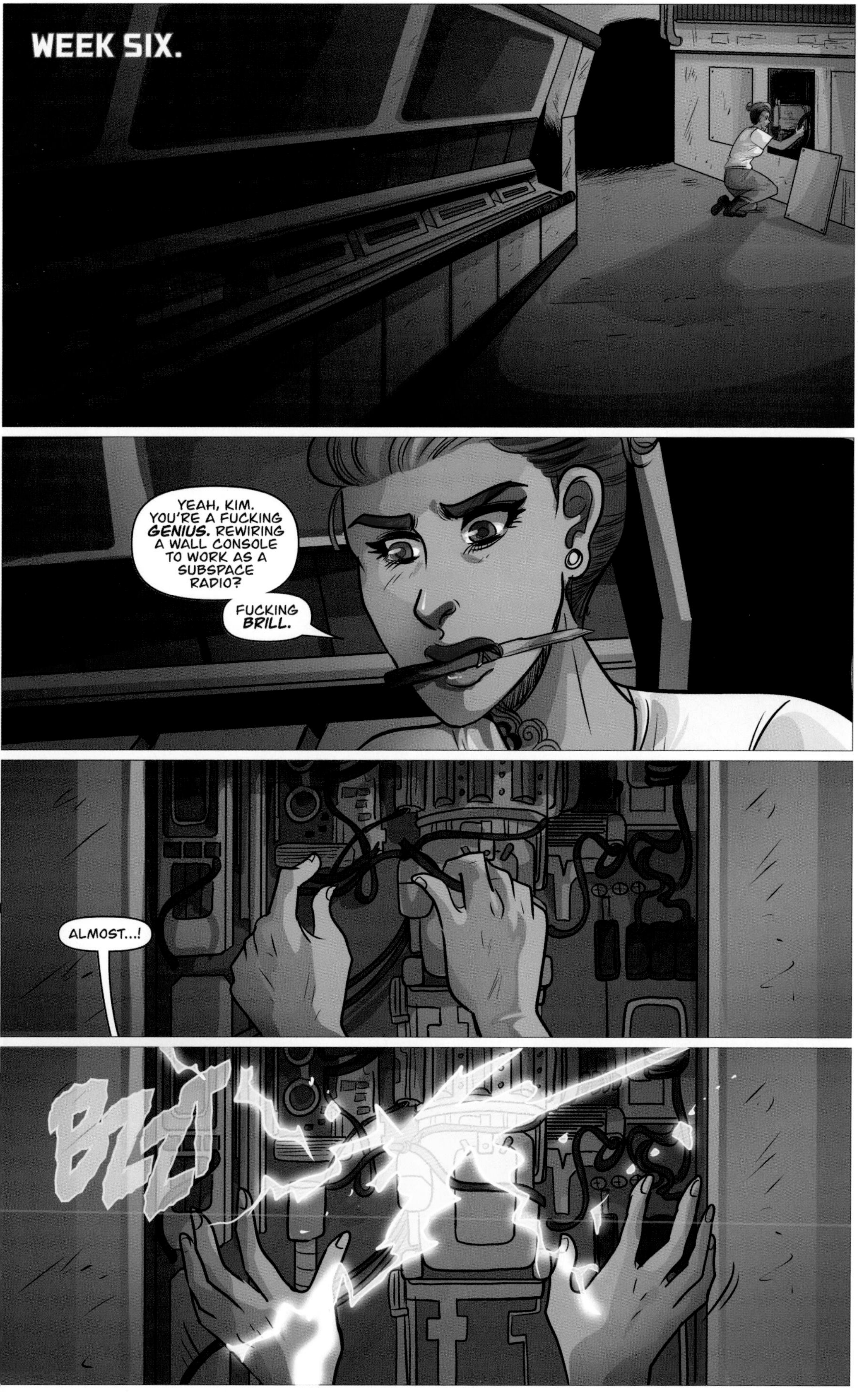
WEEK SIX.
YEAH, KIM. YOU'RE A FUCKING GENIUS. REWIRING A WALL CONSOLE TO WORK AS A SUBSPACE RADIO?
FUCKING BRILL.
ALMOST...!
BZZT

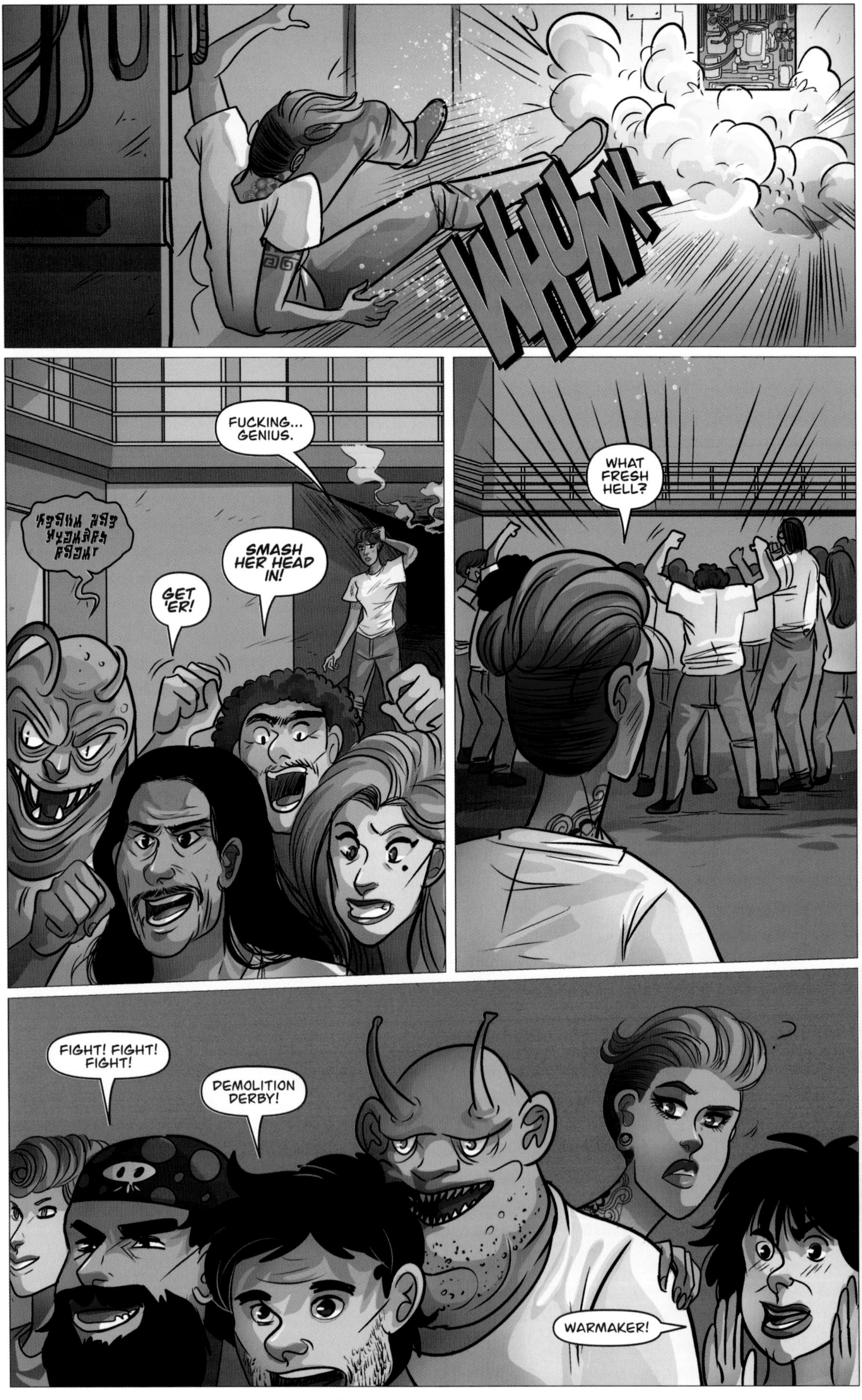
WHUNK
FUCKING... GENIUS.
GET 'ER!
SMASH HER HEAD IN!
WHAT FRESH HELL?
FIGHT! FIGHT! FIGHT!
DEMOLITION DERBY!
WARMAKER!

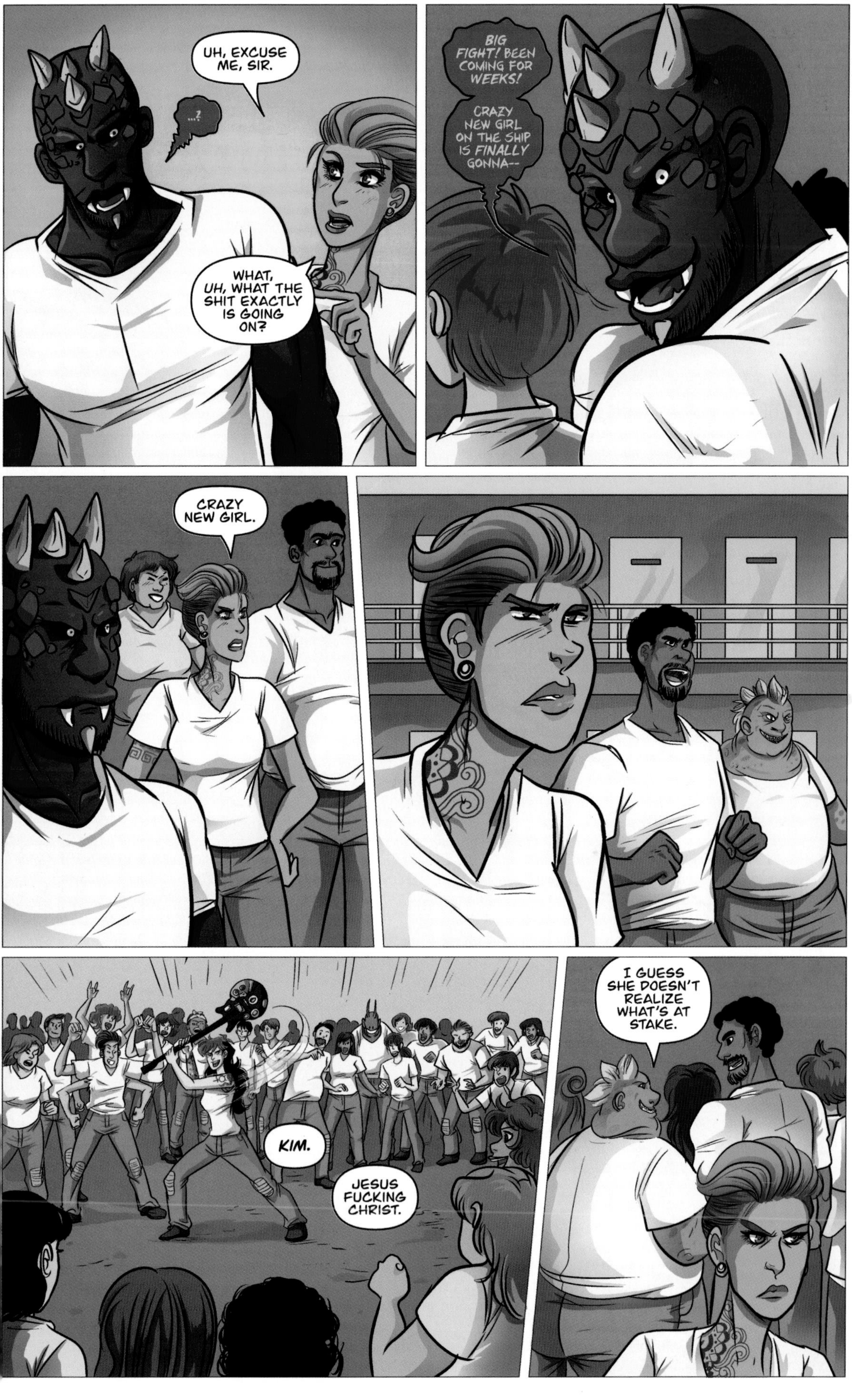
UH, EXCUSE ME, SIR.
...?
WHAT, UH, WHAT THE SHIT EXACTLY IS GOING ON?
BIG FIGHT! BEEN COMING FOR WEEKS!
CRAZY NEW GIRL ON THE SHIP IS FINALLY GONNA--
CRAZY NEW GIRL.
KIM.
JESUS FUCKING CHRIST.
I GUESS SHE DOESN'T REALIZE WHAT'S AT STAKE.

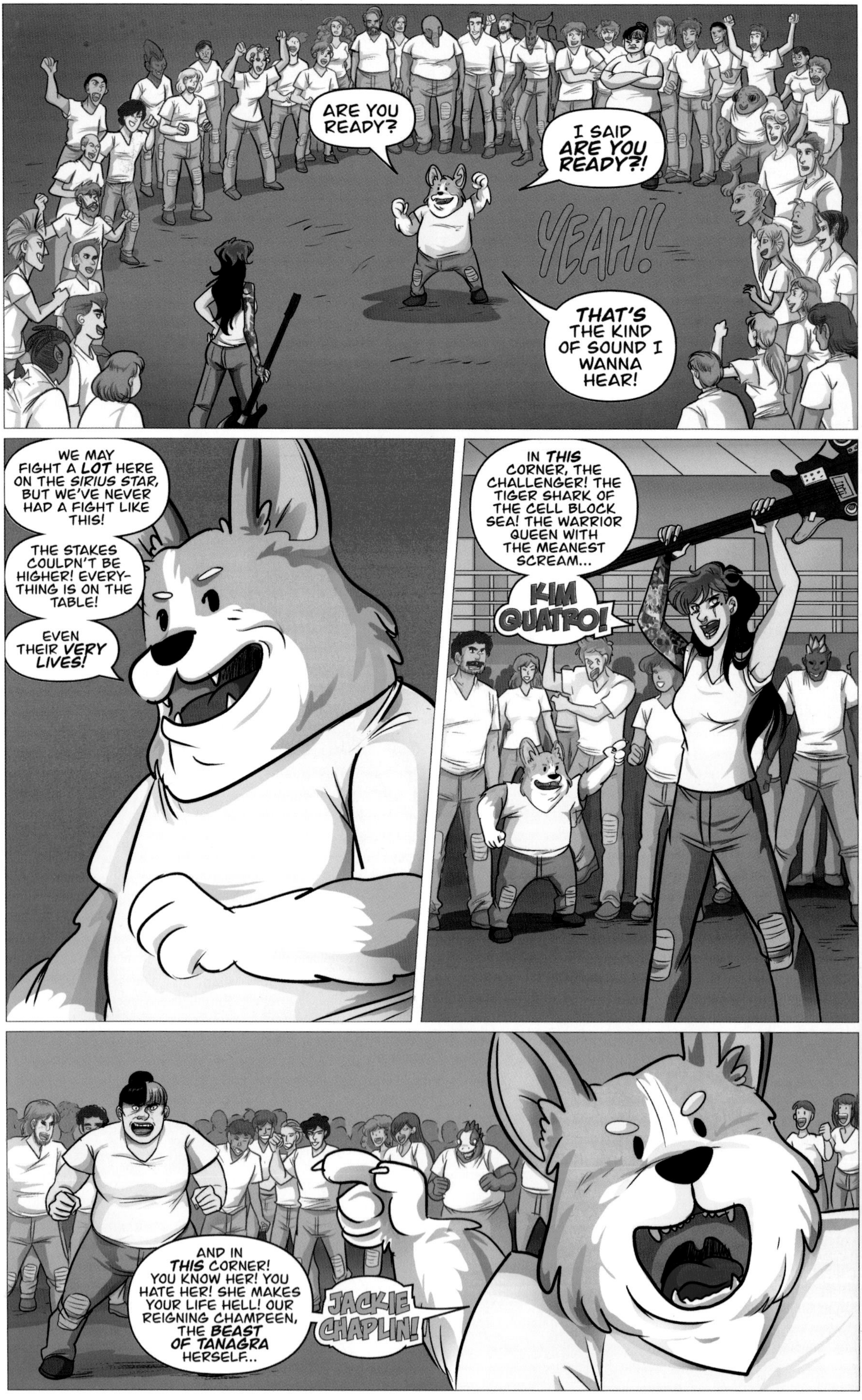
ARE YOU READY?
I SAID ARE YOU READY?!
YEAH!
THAT'S THE KIND OF SOUND I WANNA HEAR!
WE MAY FIGHT A LOT HERE ON THE SIRIUS STAR, BUT WE'VE NEVER HAD A FIGHT LIKE THIS!
THE STAKES COULDN'T BE HIGHER! EVERY-THING IS ON THE TABLE!
EVEN THEIR VERY LIVES!
IN THIS CORNER, THE CHALLENGER! THE TIGER SHARK OF THE CELL BLOCK SEA! THE WARRIOR QUEEN WITH THE MEANEST SCREAM...
KIM QUATRO!
AND IN THIS CORNER! YOU KNOW HER! YOU HATE HER! SHE MAKES YOUR LIFE HELL! OUR REIGNING CHAMPEEN, THE BEAST OF TANAGRA HERSELF...
JACKIE CHAPLIN!

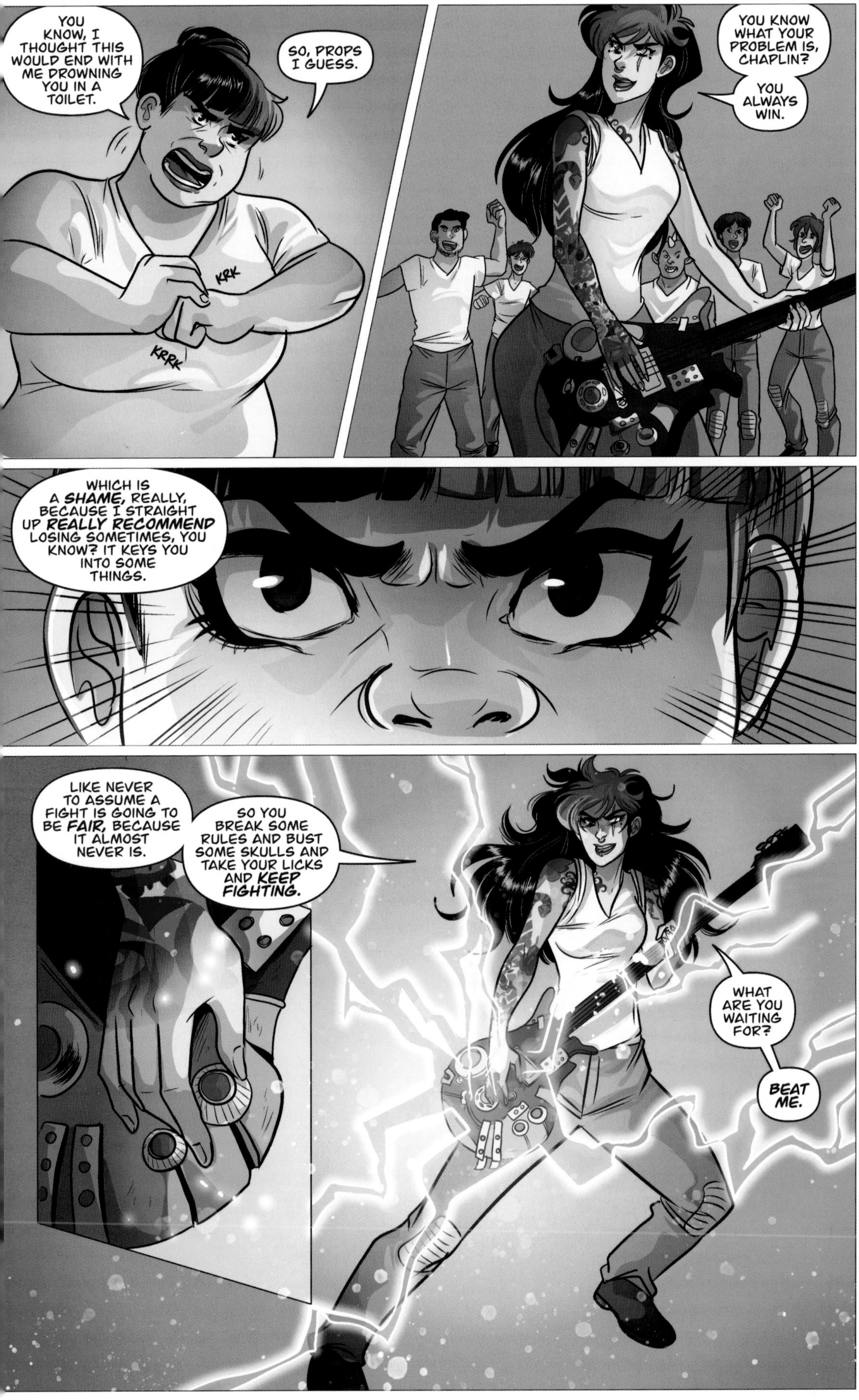
YOU KNOW, I THOUGHT THIS WOULD END WITH ME DROWNING YOU IN A TOILET.
SO, PROPS I GUESS.
KRK
KRRK
YOU KNOW WHAT YOUR PROBLEM IS, CHAPLIN?
YOU ALWAYS WIN.
WHICH IS A **SHAME,** REALLY, BECAUSE I STRAIGHT UP **REALLY RECOMMEND** LOSING SOMETIMES, YOU KNOW? IT KEYS YOU INTO SOME THINGS.
LIKE NEVER TO ASSUME A FIGHT IS GOING TO BE **FAIR,** BECAUSE IT ALMOST NEVER IS.
SO YOU BREAK SOME RULES AND BUST SOME SKULLS AND TAKE YOUR LICKS AND **KEEP FIGHTING.**
WHAT ARE YOU WAITING FOR?
BEAT ME.

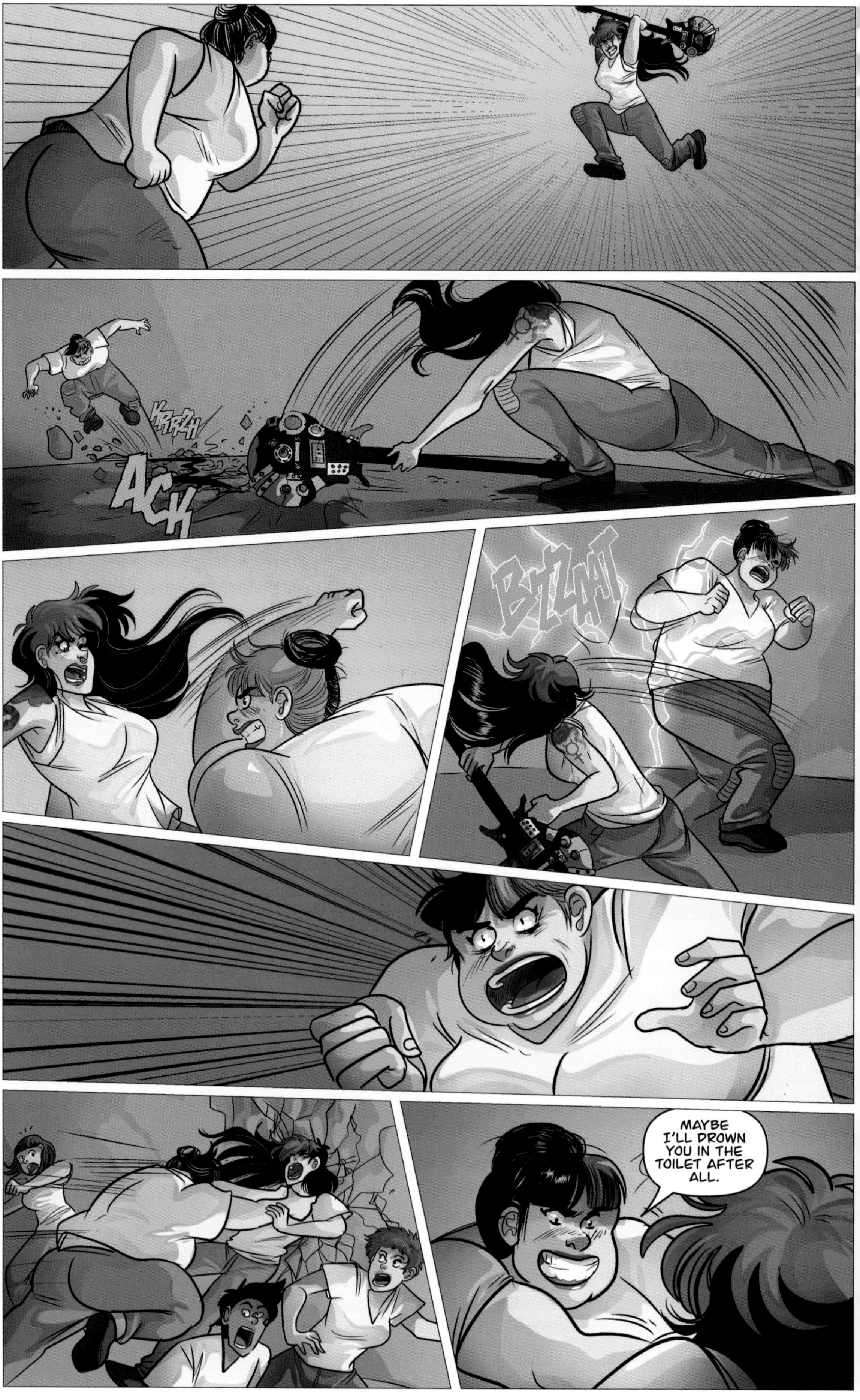
KRRZH
ACK
BZZAAT
MAYBE I'LL DROWN YOU IN THE TOILET AFTER ALL.

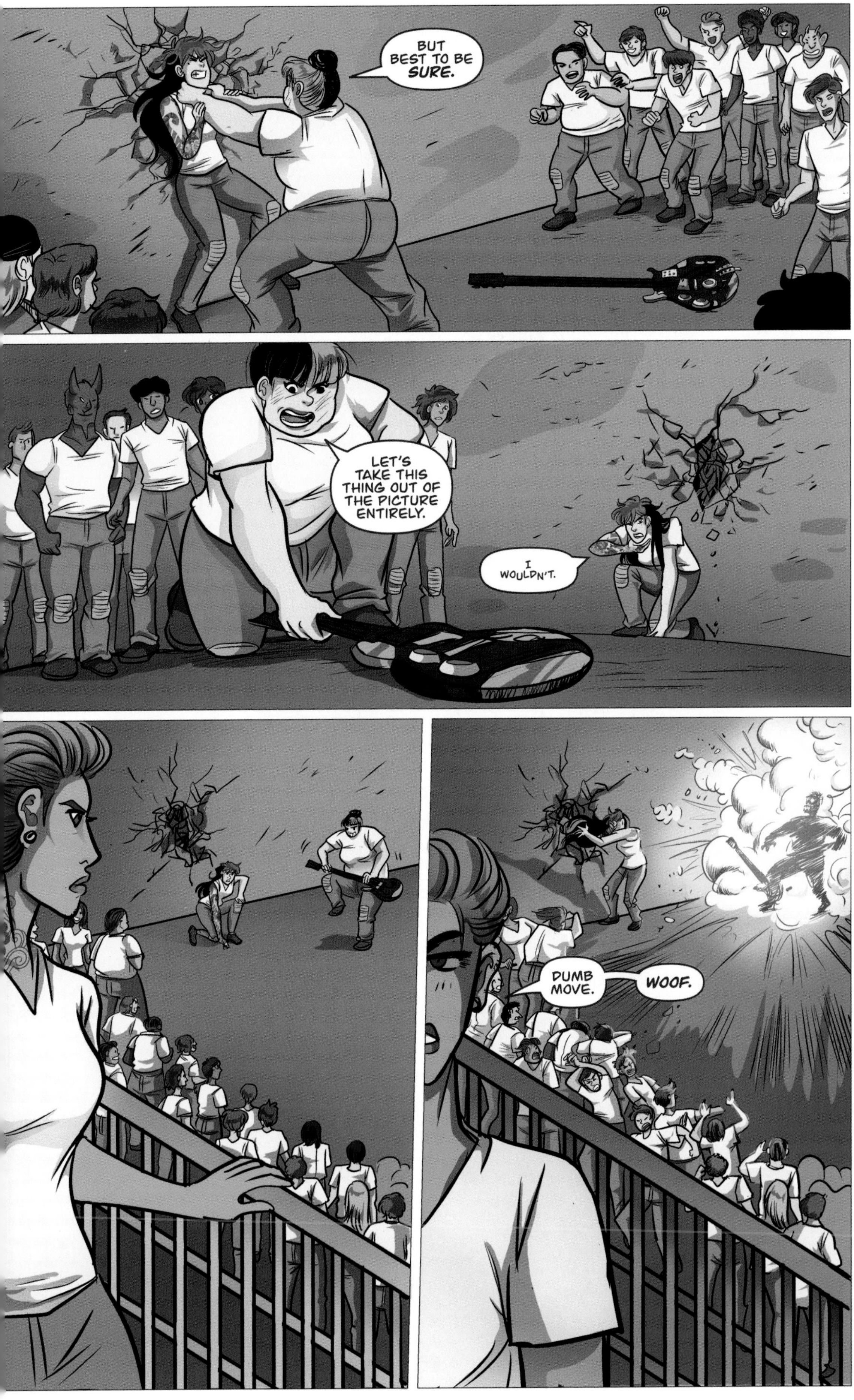
BUT BEST TO BE SURE.
LET'S TAKE THIS THING OUT OF THE PICTURE ENTIRELY.
I WOULDN'T.
DUMB MOVE.
WOOF.

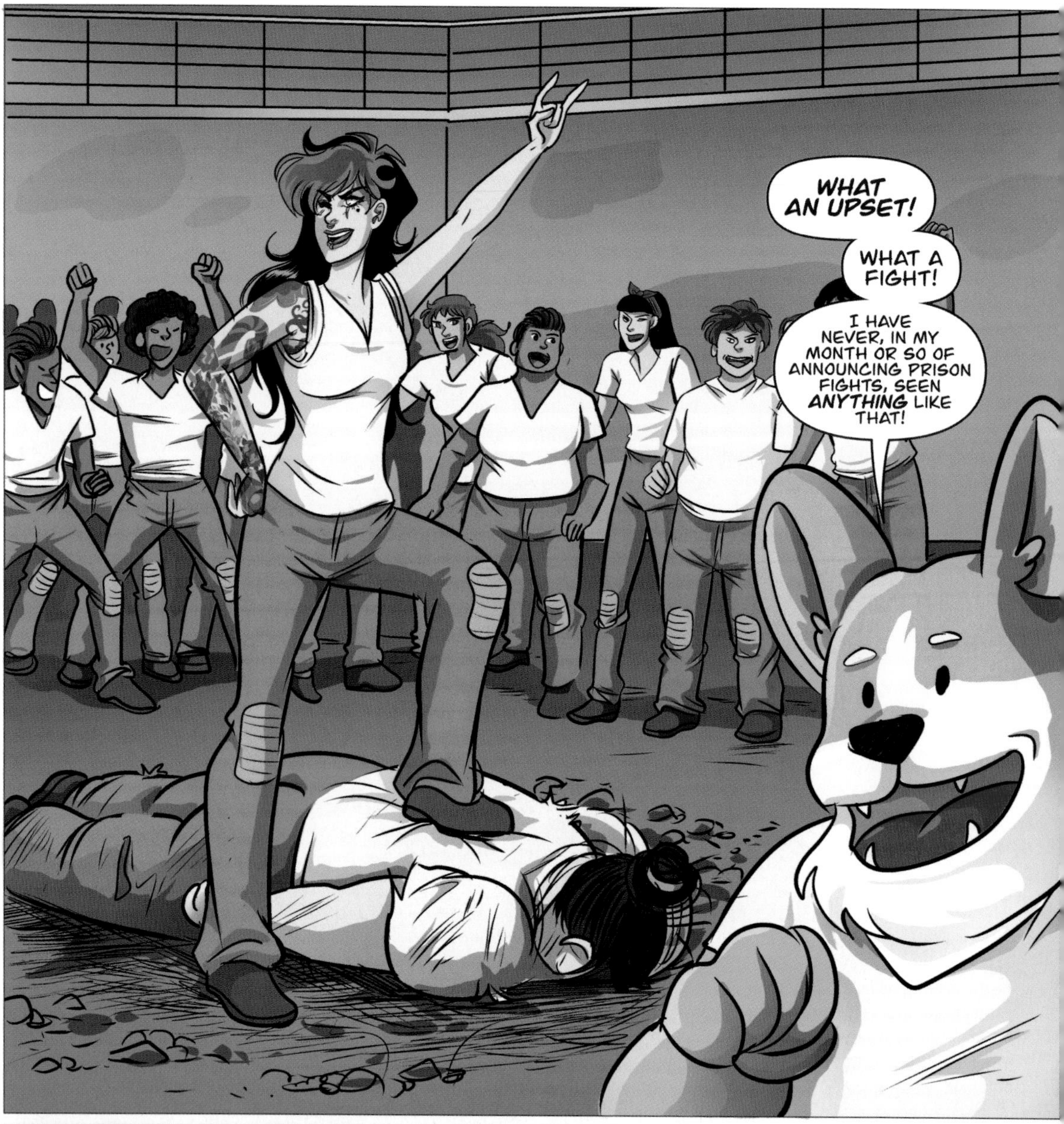
WHAT AN UPSET!
WHAT A FIGHT!
I HAVE NEVER, IN MY MONTH OR SO OF ANNOUNCING PRISON FIGHTS, SEEN ANYTHING LIKE THAT!

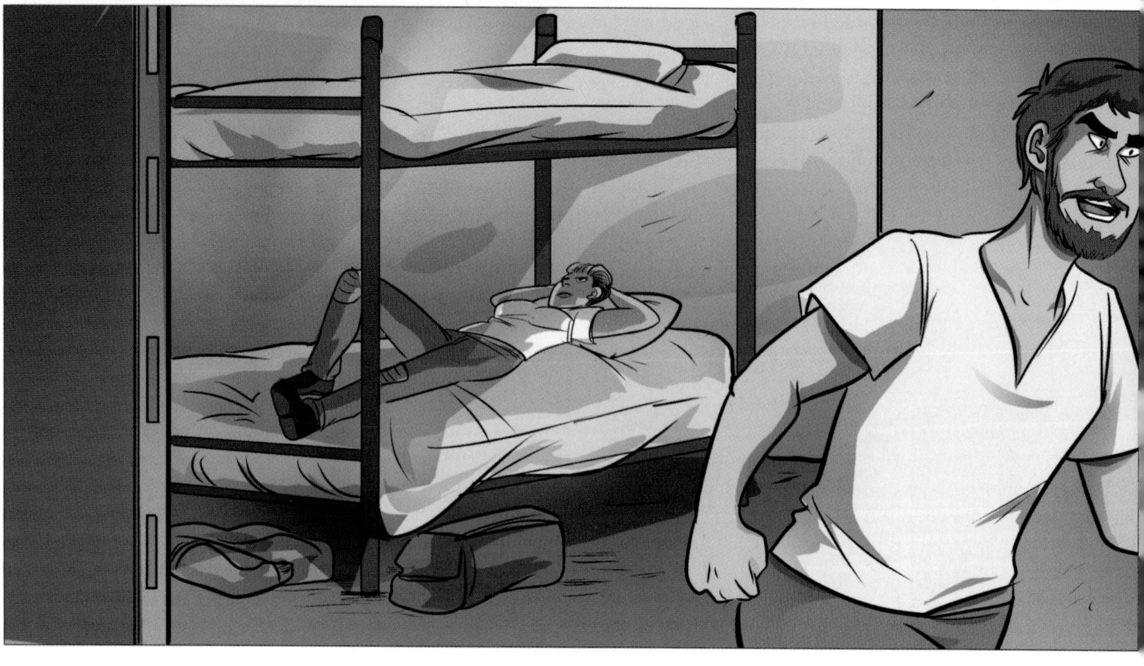

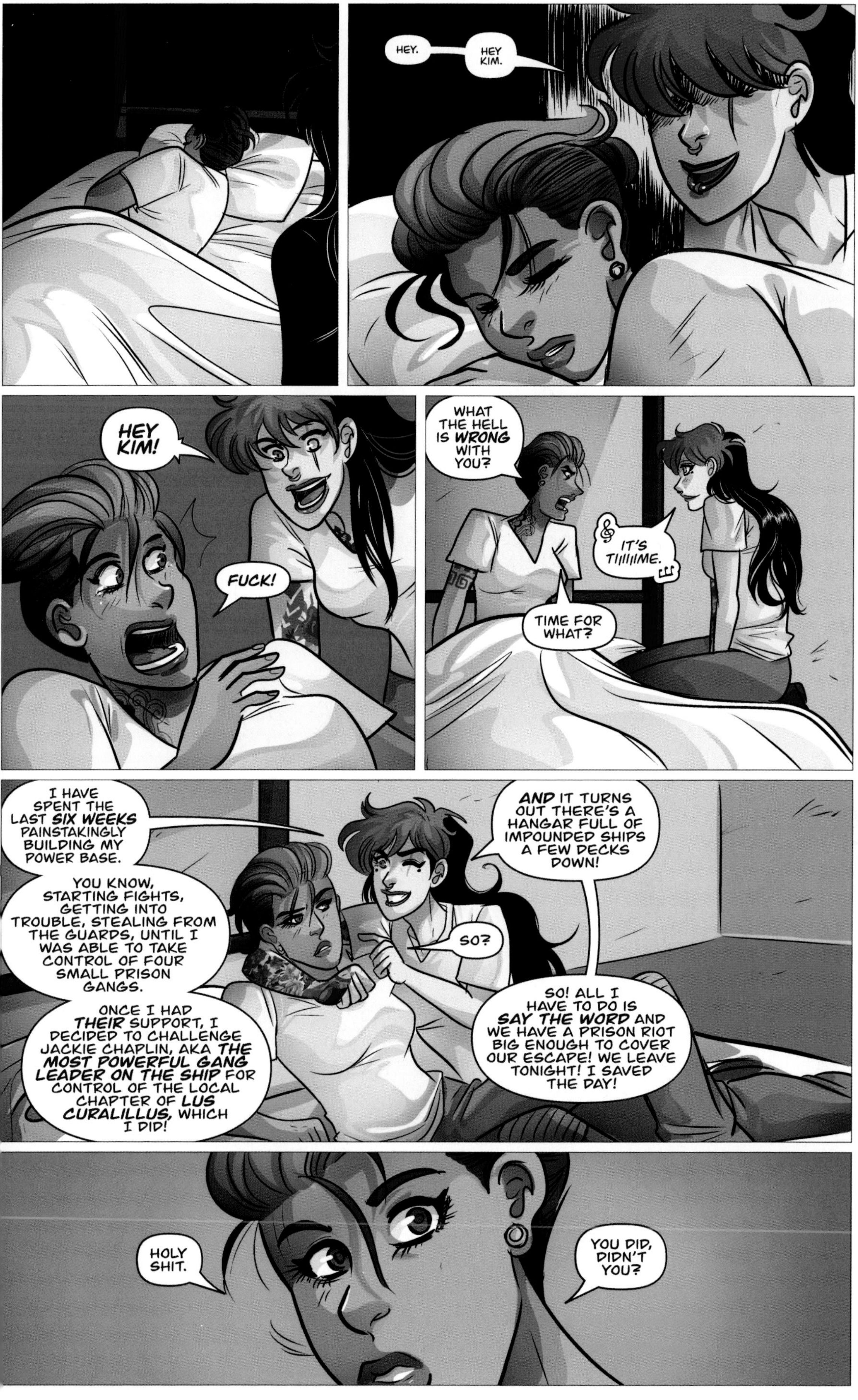
HEY.
HEY KIM.
HEY KIM!
FUCK!
WHAT THE HELL IS WRONG WITH YOU?
IT'S TIIIIIME.
TIME FOR WHAT?
I HAVE SPENT THE LAST SIX WEEKS PAINSTAKINGLY BUILDING MY POWER BASE.
YOU KNOW, STARTING FIGHTS, GETTING INTO TROUBLE, STEALING FROM THE GUARDS, UNTIL I WAS ABLE TO TAKE CONTROL OF FOUR SMALL PRISON GANGS.
ONCE I HAD THEIR SUPPORT, I DECIDED TO CHALLENGE JACKIE CHAPLIN, AKA THE MOST POWERFUL GANG LEADER ON THE SHIP FOR CONTROL OF THE LOCAL CHAPTER OF LUS CURALILLUS, WHICH I DID!
AND IT TURNS OUT THERE'S A HANGAR FULL OF IMPOUNDED SHIPS A FEW DECKS DOWN!
SO?
SO! ALL I HAVE TO DO IS SAY THE WORD AND WE HAVE A PRISON RIOT BIG ENOUGH TO COVER OUR ESCAPE! WE LEAVE TONIGHT! I SAVED THE DAY!
HOLY SHIT.
YOU DID, DIDN'T YOU?

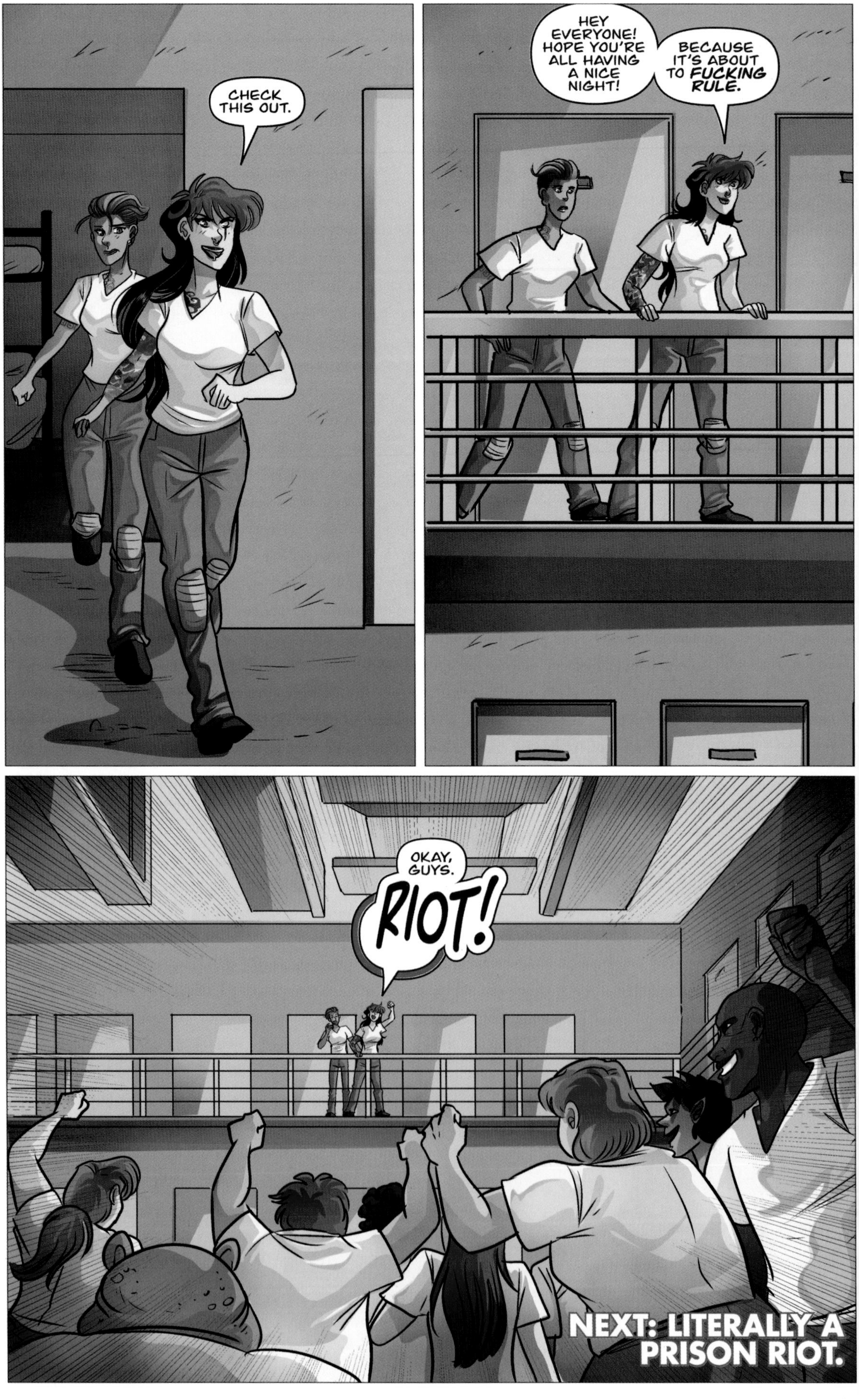
CHECK THIS OUT.
HEY EVERYONE! HOPE YOU'RE ALL HAVING A NICE NIGHT!
BECAUSE IT'S ABOUT TO FUCKING RULE.
OKAY, GUYS.
RIOT!
NEXT: LITERALLY A PRISON RIOT.

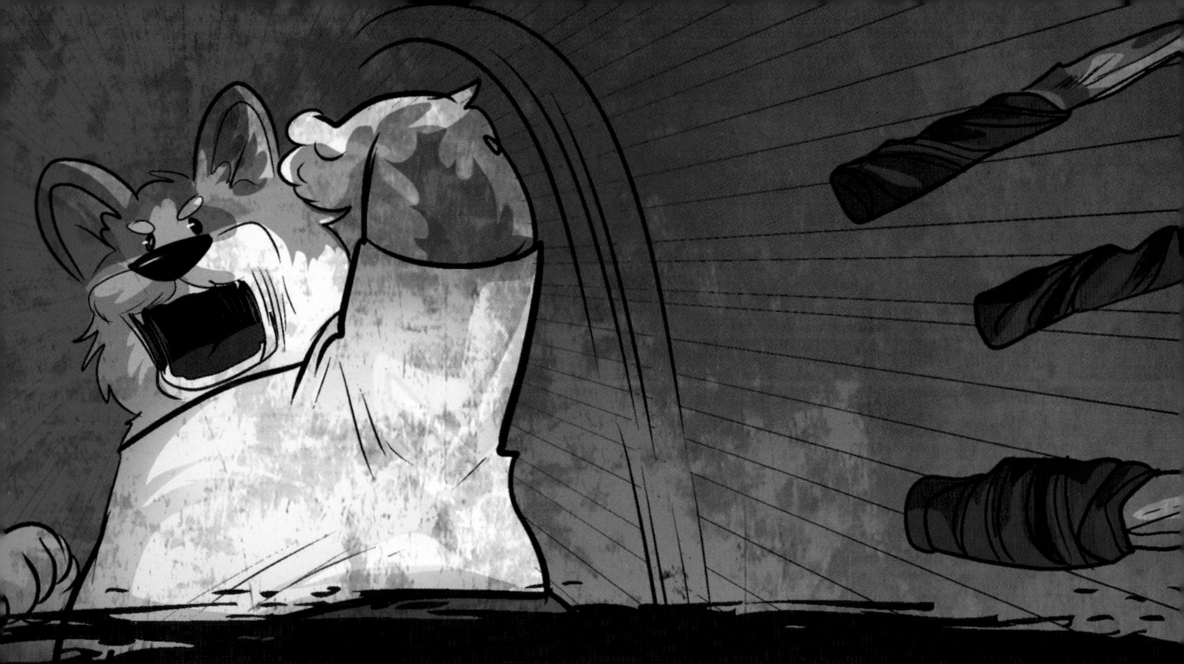

4

"LITERALLY A PRISON RIOT!"

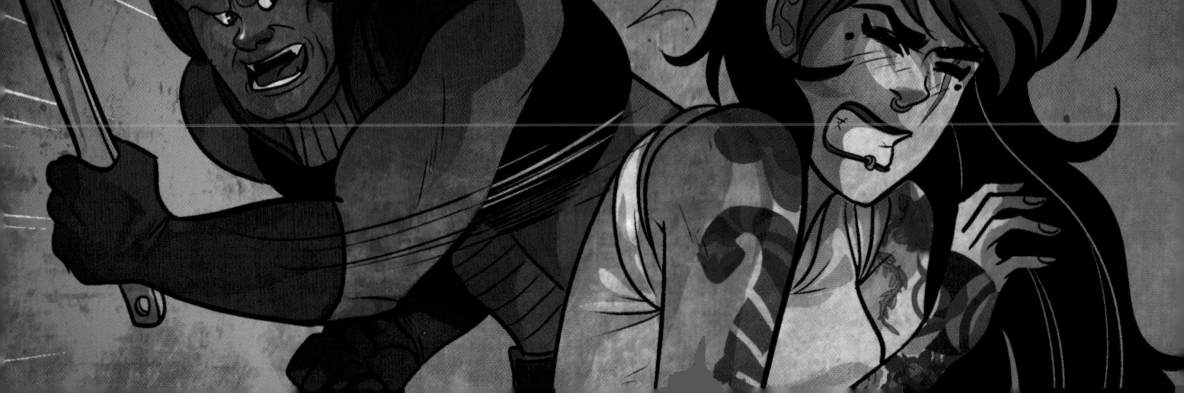
WHUNK

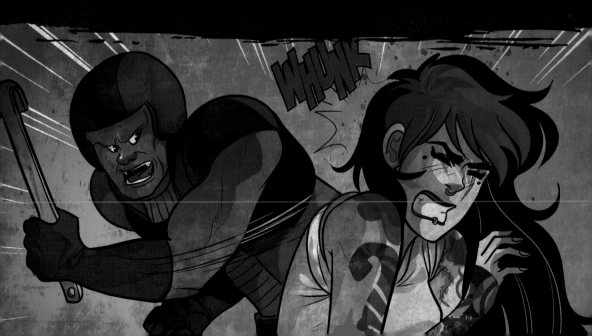

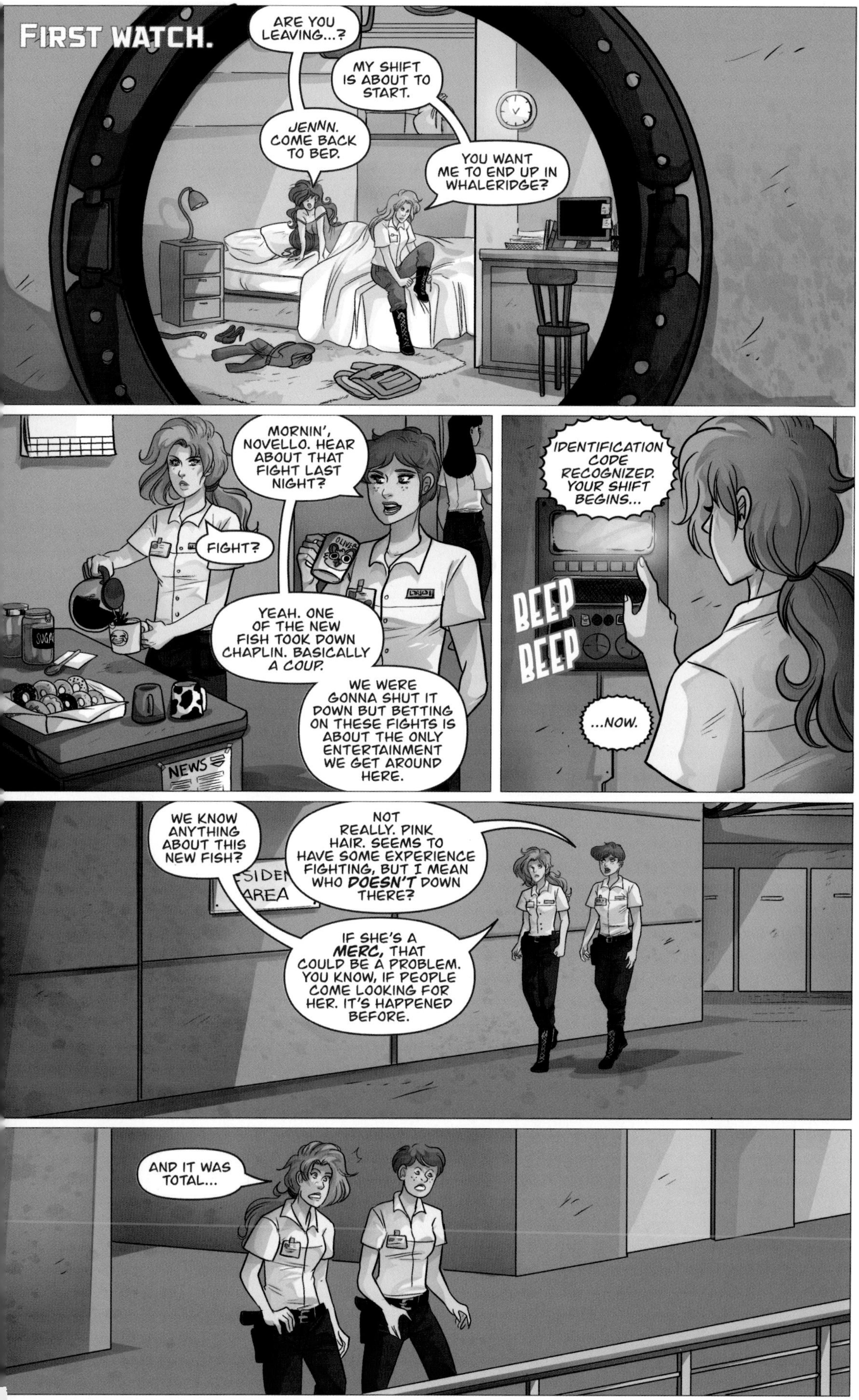
FIRST WATCH.
ARE YOU LEAVING...?
MY SHIFT IS ABOUT TO START.
JENNN. COME BACK TO BED.
YOU WANT ME TO END UP IN WHALERIDGE?
MORNIN', NOVELLO. HEAR ABOUT THAT FIGHT LAST NIGHT?
FIGHT?
YEAH. ONE OF THE NEW FISH TOOK DOWN CHAPLIN. BASICALLY A COUP.
WE WERE GONNA SHUT IT DOWN BUT BETTING ON THESE FIGHTS IS ABOUT THE ONLY ENTERTAINMENT WE GET AROUND HERE.
SUGAR
NEWS
IDENTIFICATION CODE RECOGNIZED. YOUR SHIFT BEGINS...
BEEP
BEEP
...NOW.
WE KNOW ANYTHING ABOUT THIS NEW FISH?
NOT REALLY. PINK HAIR. SEEMS TO HAVE SOME EXPERIENCE FIGHTING, BUT I MEAN WHO DOESN'T DOWN THERE?
IF SHE'S A MERC, THAT COULD BE A PROBLEM. YOU KNOW, IF PEOPLE COME LOOKING FOR HER. IT'S HAPPENED BEFORE.
AND IT WAS TOTAL...

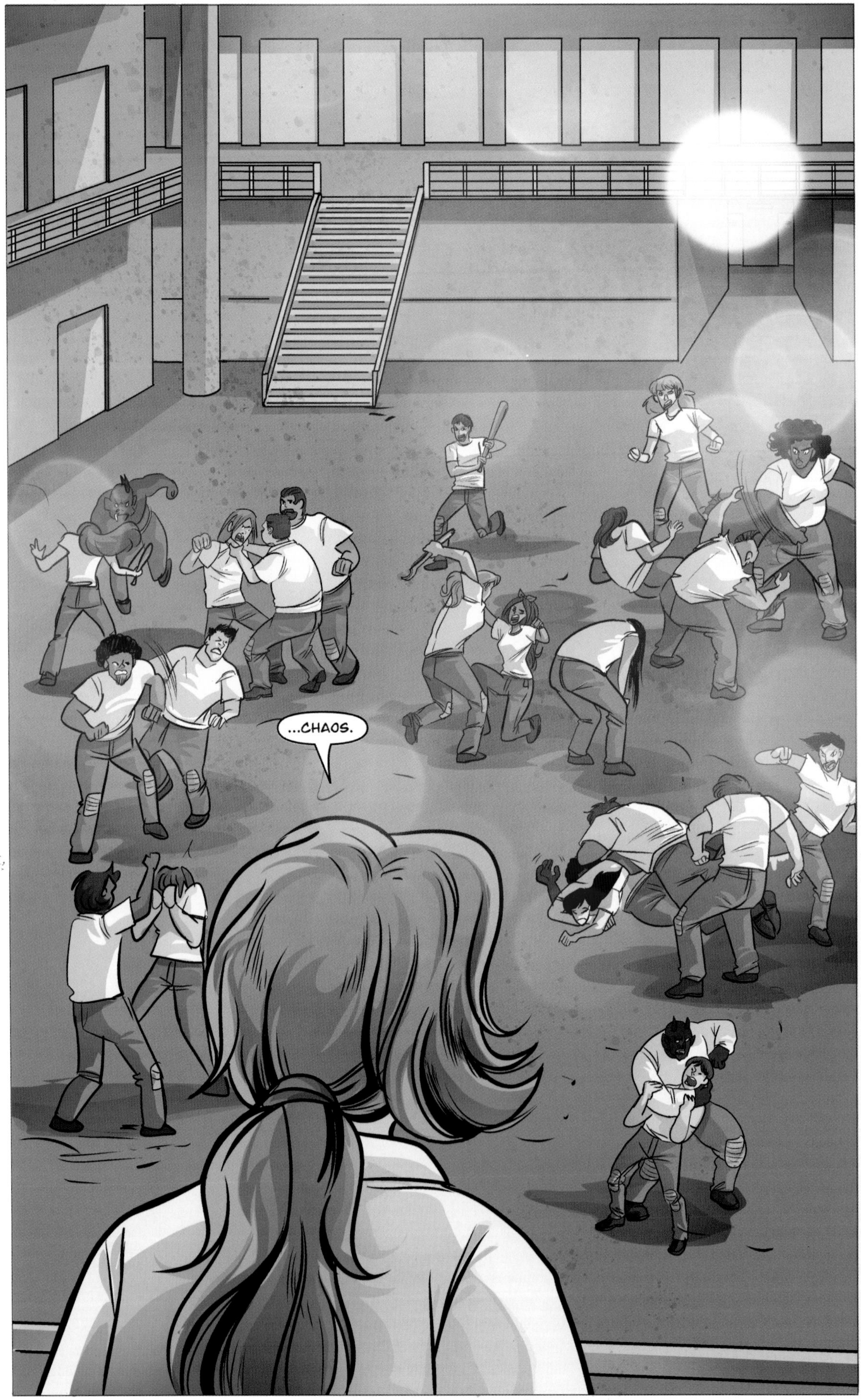
...CHAOS.

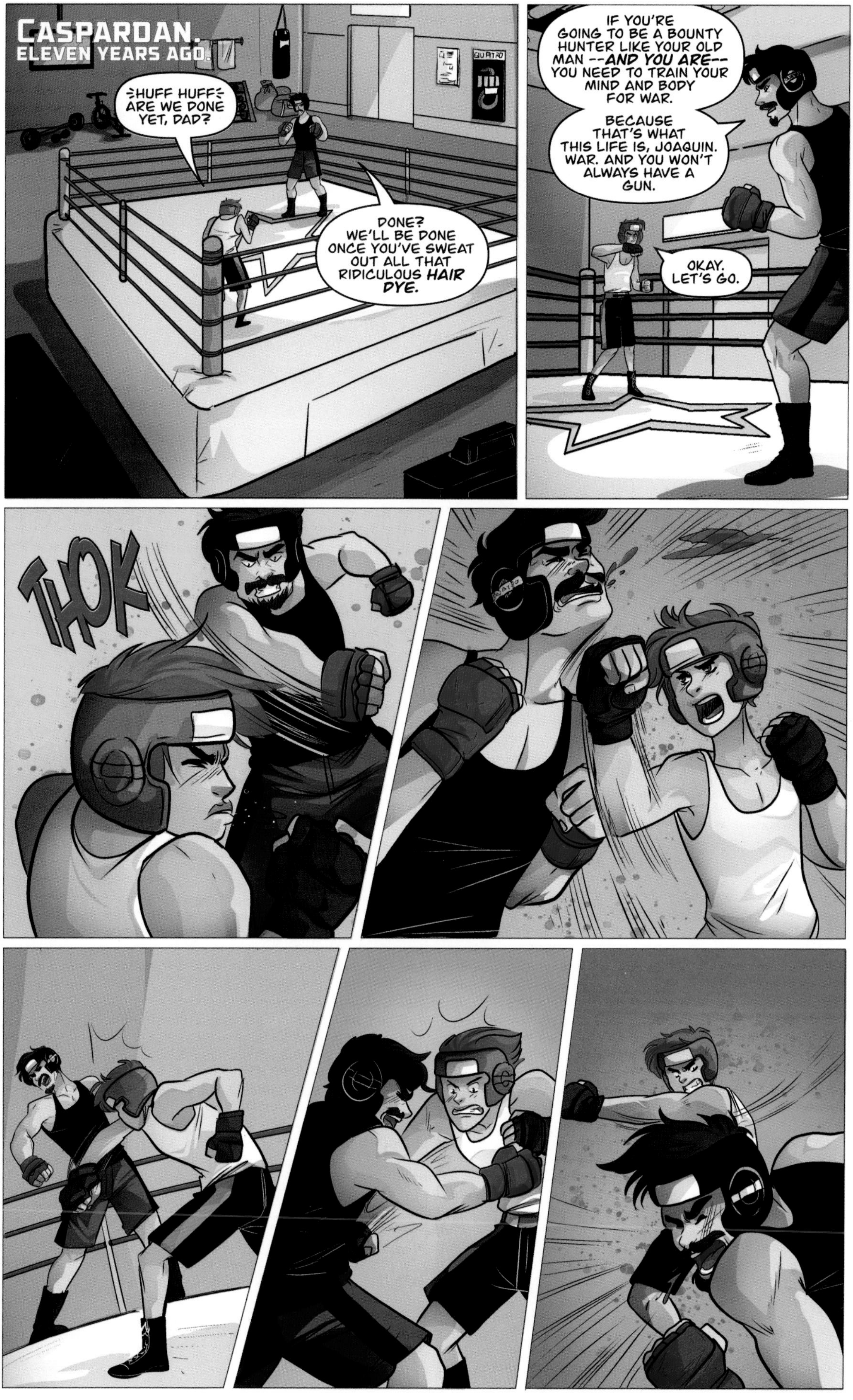
CASPARDAN.
ELEVEN YEARS AGO.
QUATRO
≈HUFF HUFF≈ ARE WE DONE YET, DAD?
DONE? WE'LL BE DONE ONCE YOU'VE SWEAT OUT ALL THAT RIDICULOUS **HAIR DYE.**
IF YOU'RE GOING TO BE A BOUNTY HUNTER LIKE YOUR OLD MAN --**AND YOU ARE**-- YOU NEED TO TRAIN YOUR MIND AND BODY FOR WAR.
BECAUSE THAT'S WHAT THIS LIFE IS, JOAQUIN. WAR. AND YOU WON'T ALWAYS HAVE A GUN.
OKAY. LET'S GO.
THOK

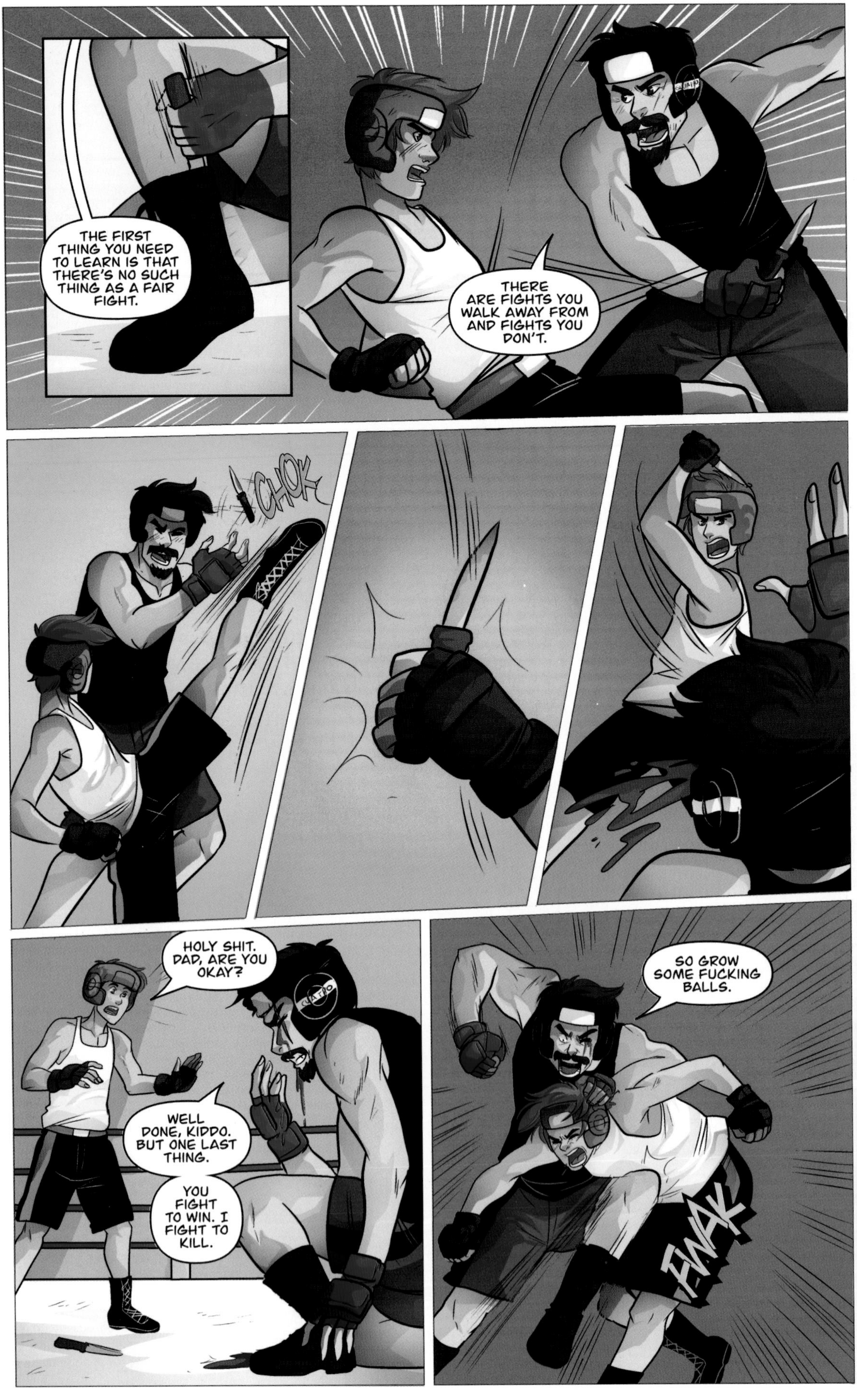
THE FIRST THING YOU NEED TO LEARN IS THAT THERE'S NO SUCH THING AS A FAIR FIGHT.
THERE ARE FIGHTS YOU WALK AWAY FROM AND FIGHTS YOU DON'T.
CHOK
HOLY SHIT. DAD, ARE YOU OKAY?
WELL DONE, KIDDO. BUT ONE LAST THING.
YOU FIGHT TO WIN. I FIGHT TO KILL.
SO GROW SOME FUCKING BALLS.
FWAK

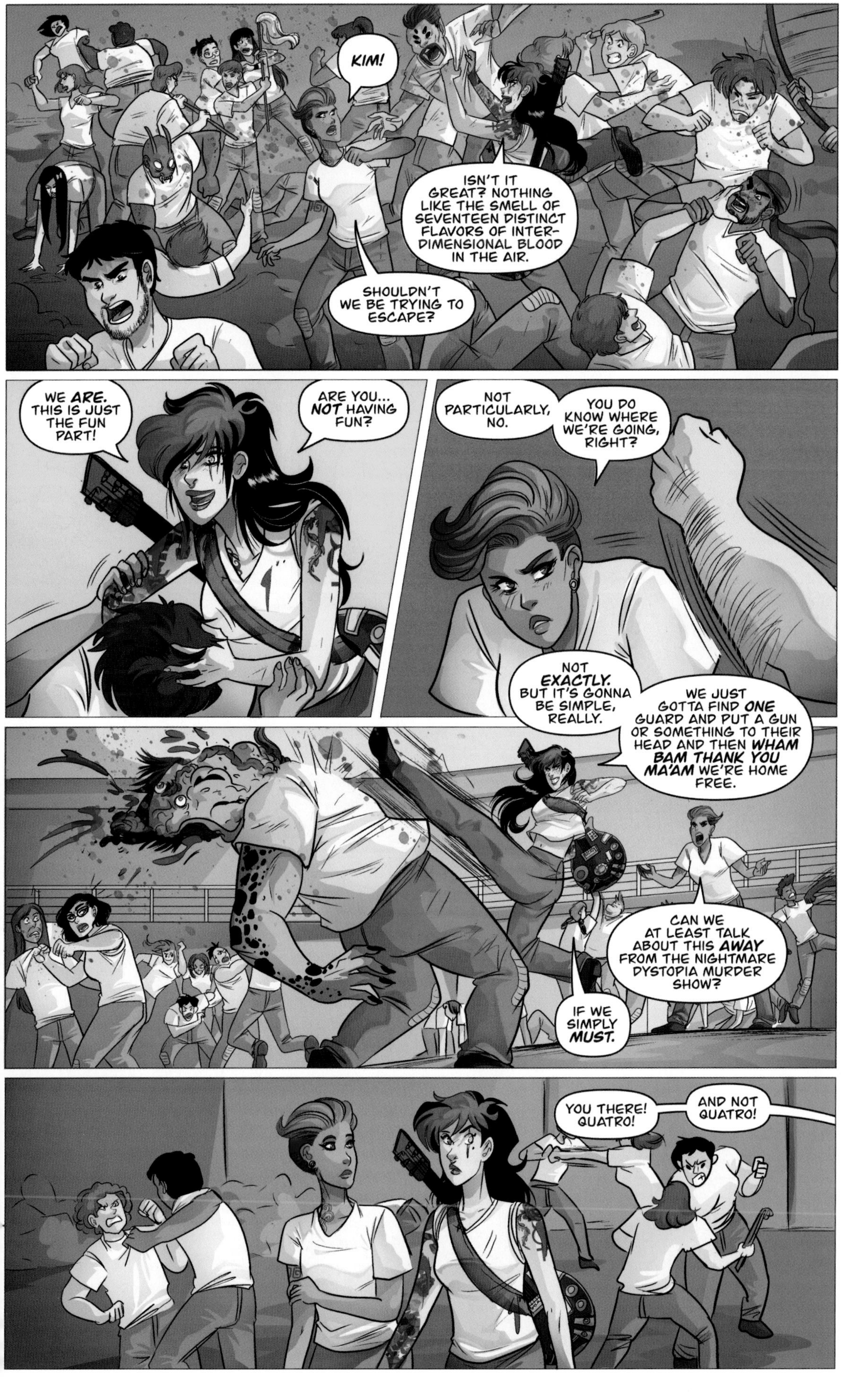
KIM!
ISN'T IT GREAT? NOTHING LIKE THE SMELL OF SEVENTEEN DISTINCT FLAVORS OF INTER-DIMENSIONAL BLOOD IN THE AIR.
SHOULDN'T WE BE TRYING TO ESCAPE?
WE **ARE.** THIS IS JUST THE FUN PART!
ARE YOU... **NOT** HAVING FUN?
NOT PARTICULARLY, NO.
YOU DO KNOW WHERE WE'RE GOING, RIGHT?
NOT **EXACTLY.** BUT IT'S GONNA BE SIMPLE, REALLY.
WE JUST GOTTA FIND **ONE** GUARD AND PUT A GUN OR SOMETHING TO THEIR HEAD AND THEN **WHAM BAM THANK YOU MA'AM** WE'RE HOME FREE.
CAN WE AT LEAST TALK ABOUT THIS **AWAY** FROM THE NIGHTMARE DYSTOPIA MURDER SHOW?
IF WE SIMPLY **MUST.**
YOU THERE! QUATRO!
AND NOT QUATRO!

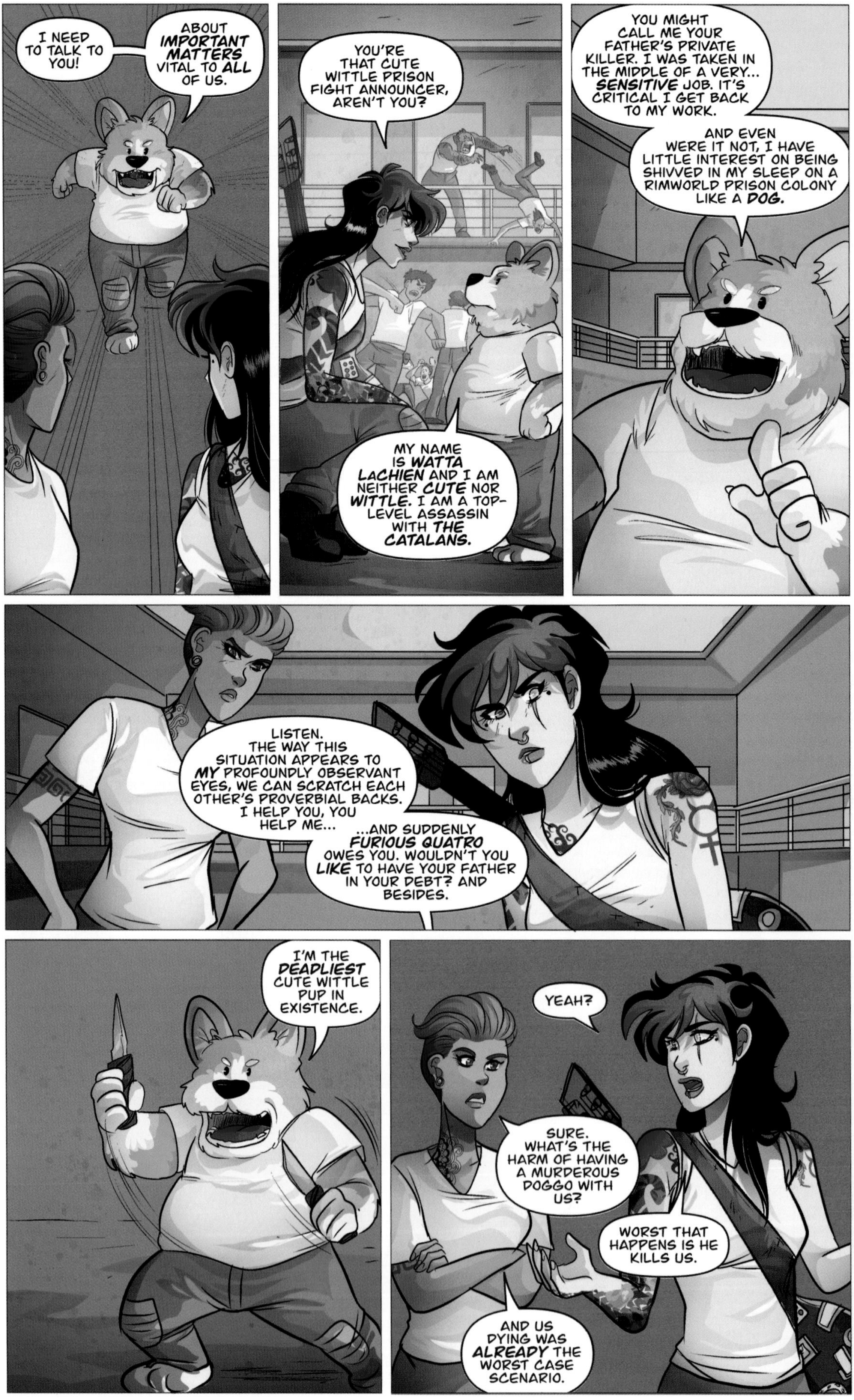
I NEED TO TALK TO YOU!
ABOUT IMPORTANT MATTERS VITAL TO ALL OF US.
YOU'RE THAT CUTE WITTLE PRISON FIGHT ANNOUNCER, AREN'T YOU?
MY NAME IS WATTA LACHIEN AND I AM NEITHER CUTE NOR WITTLE. I AM A TOP-LEVEL ASSASSIN WITH THE CATALANS.
YOU MIGHT CALL ME YOUR FATHER'S PRIVATE KILLER. I WAS TAKEN IN THE MIDDLE OF A VERY... SENSITIVE JOB. IT'S CRITICAL I GET BACK TO MY WORK.
AND EVEN WERE IT NOT, I HAVE LITTLE INTEREST ON BEING SHIVVED IN MY SLEEP ON A RIMWORLD PRISON COLONY LIKE A DOG.
LISTEN. THE WAY THIS SITUATION APPEARS TO MY PROFOUNDLY OBSERVANT EYES, WE CAN SCRATCH EACH OTHER'S PROVERBIAL BACKS. I HELP YOU, YOU HELP ME...
...AND SUDDENLY FURIOUS QUATRO OWES YOU. WOULDN'T YOU LIKE TO HAVE YOUR FATHER IN YOUR DEBT? AND BESIDES.
I'M THE DEADLIEST CUTE WITTLE PUP IN EXISTENCE.
YEAH?
SURE. WHAT'S THE HARM OF HAVING A MURDEROUS DOGGO WITH US?
WORST THAT HAPPENS IS HE KILLS US.
AND US DYING WAS ALREADY THE WORST CASE SCENARIO.

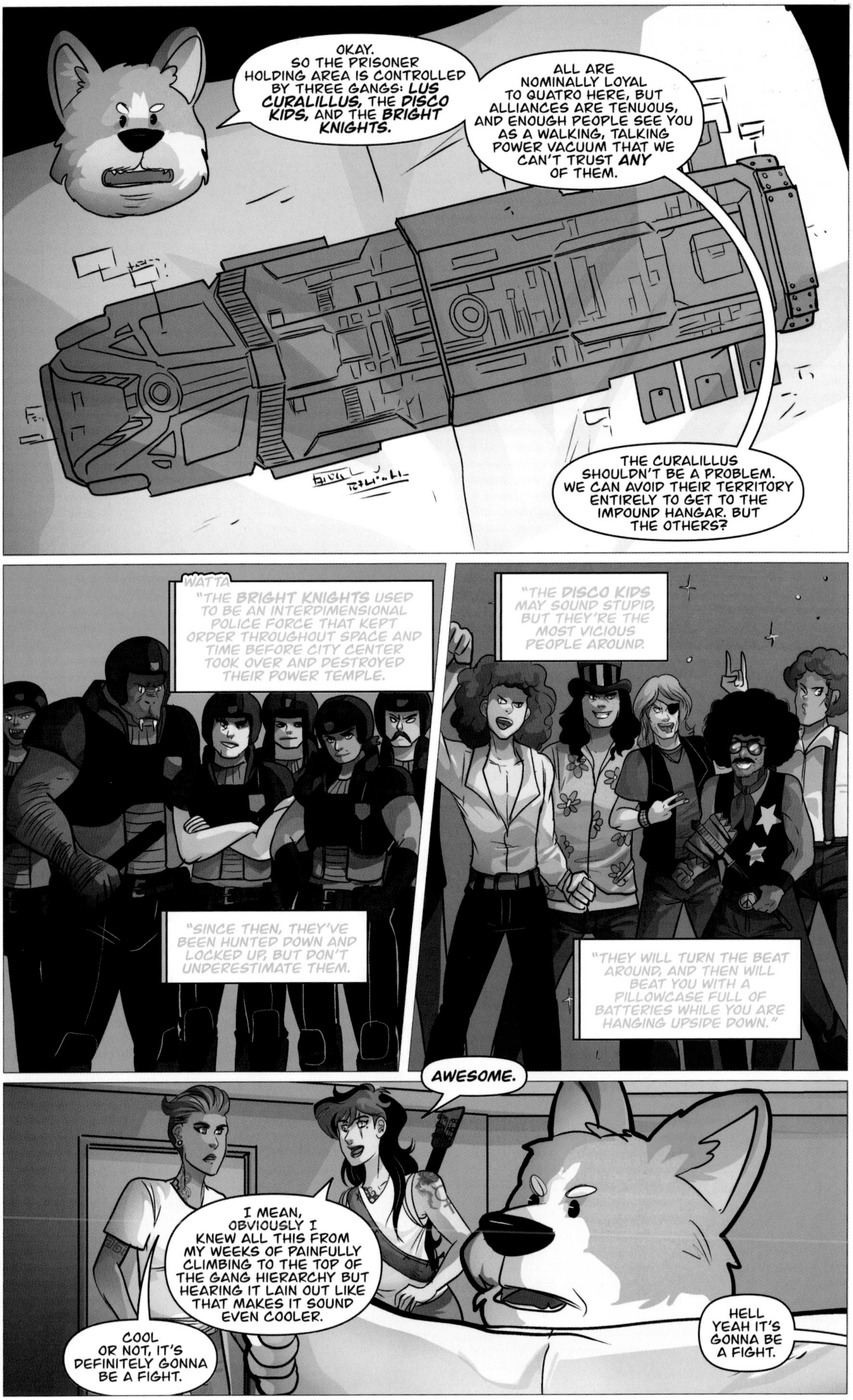
OKAY. SO THE PRISONER HOLDING AREA IS CONTROLLED BY THREE GANGS: LUS CURALILLUS, THE DISCO KIDS, AND THE BRIGHT KNIGHTS.
ALL ARE NOMINALLY LOYAL TO QUATRO HERE, BUT ALLIANCES ARE TENUOUS, AND ENOUGH PEOPLE SEE YOU AS A WALKING, TALKING POWER VACUUM THAT WE CAN'T TRUST ANY OF THEM.
THE CURALILLUS SHOULDN'T BE A PROBLEM. WE CAN AVOID THEIR TERRITORY ENTIRELY TO GET TO THE IMPOUND HANGAR. BUT THE OTHERS?
WATTA
"THE BRIGHT KNIGHTS USED TO BE AN INTERDIMENSIONAL POLICE FORCE THAT KEPT ORDER THROUGHOUT SPACE AND TIME BEFORE CITY CENTER TOOK OVER AND DESTROYED THEIR POWER TEMPLE.
"SINCE THEN, THEY'VE BEEN HUNTED DOWN AND LOCKED UP, BUT DON'T UNDERESTIMATE THEM.
"THE DISCO KIDS MAY SOUND STUPID, BUT THEY'RE THE MOST VICIOUS PEOPLE AROUND.
"THEY WILL TURN THE BEAT AROUND, AND THEN WILL BEAT YOU WITH A PILLOWCASE FULL OF BATTERIES WHILE YOU ARE HANGING UPSIDE DOWN."
AWESOME.
I MEAN, OBVIOUSLY I KNEW ALL THIS FROM MY WEEKS OF PAINFULLY CLIMBING TO THE TOP OF THE GANG HIERARCHY BUT HEARING IT LAIN OUT LIKE THAT MAKES IT SOUND EVEN COOLER.
COOL OR NOT, IT'S DEFINITELY GONNA BE A FIGHT.
HELL YEAH IT'S GONNA BE A FIGHT.

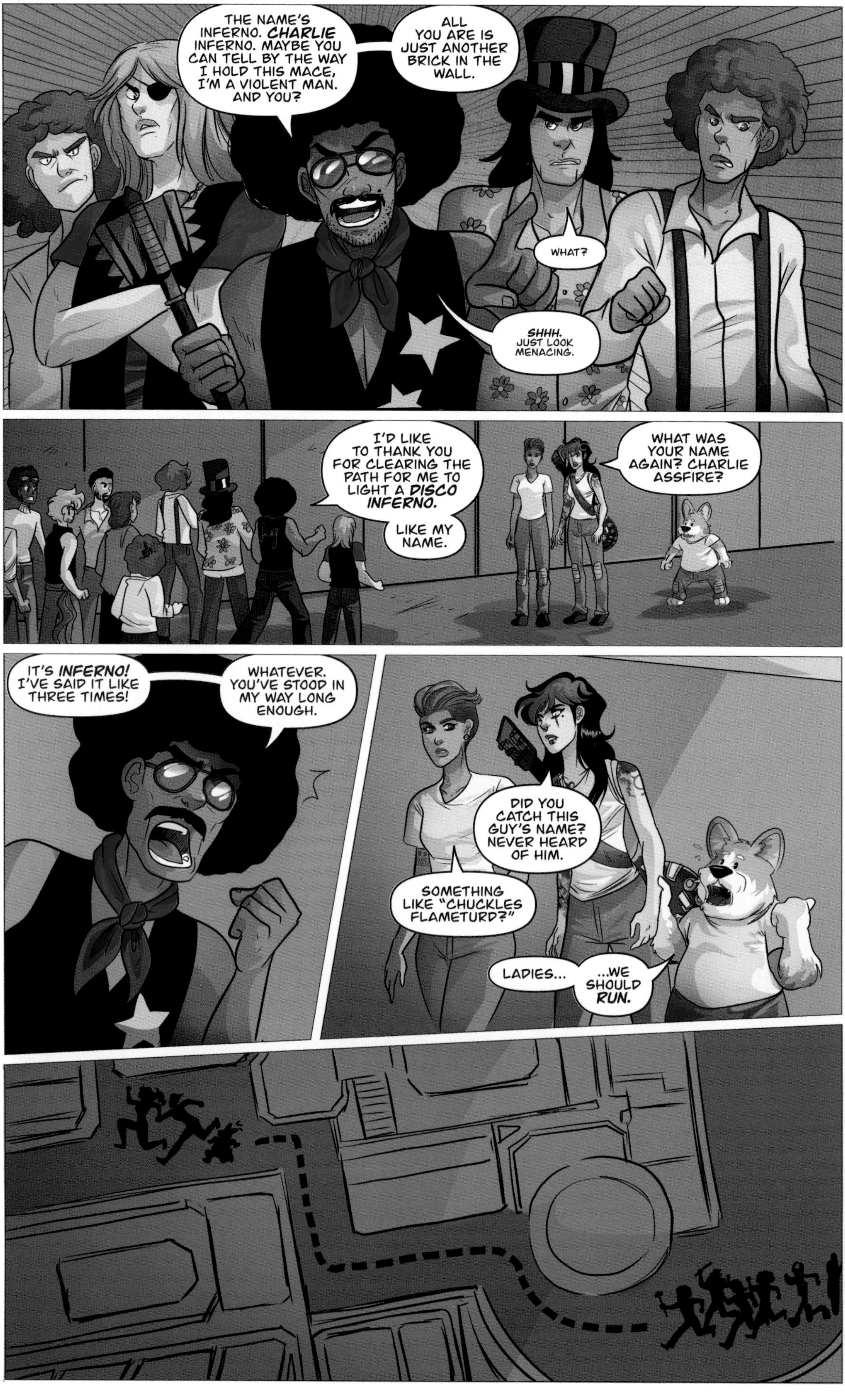
THE NAME'S INFERNO. CHARLIE INFERNO. MAYBE YOU CAN TELL BY THE WAY I HOLD THIS MACE, I'M A VIOLENT MAN. AND YOU?
ALL YOU ARE IS JUST ANOTHER BRICK IN THE WALL.
WHAT?
SHHH. JUST LOOK MENACING.
I'D LIKE TO THANK YOU FOR CLEARING THE PATH FOR ME TO LIGHT A DISCO INFERNO.
LIKE MY NAME.
WHAT WAS YOUR NAME AGAIN? CHARLIE ASSFIRE?
IT'S INFERNO! I'VE SAID IT LIKE THREE TIMES!
WHATEVER. YOU'VE STOOD IN MY WAY LONG ENOUGH.
DID YOU CATCH THIS GUY'S NAME? NEVER HEARD OF HIM.
SOMETHING LIKE "CHUCKLES FLAMETURD?"
LADIES...
...WE SHOULD RUN.

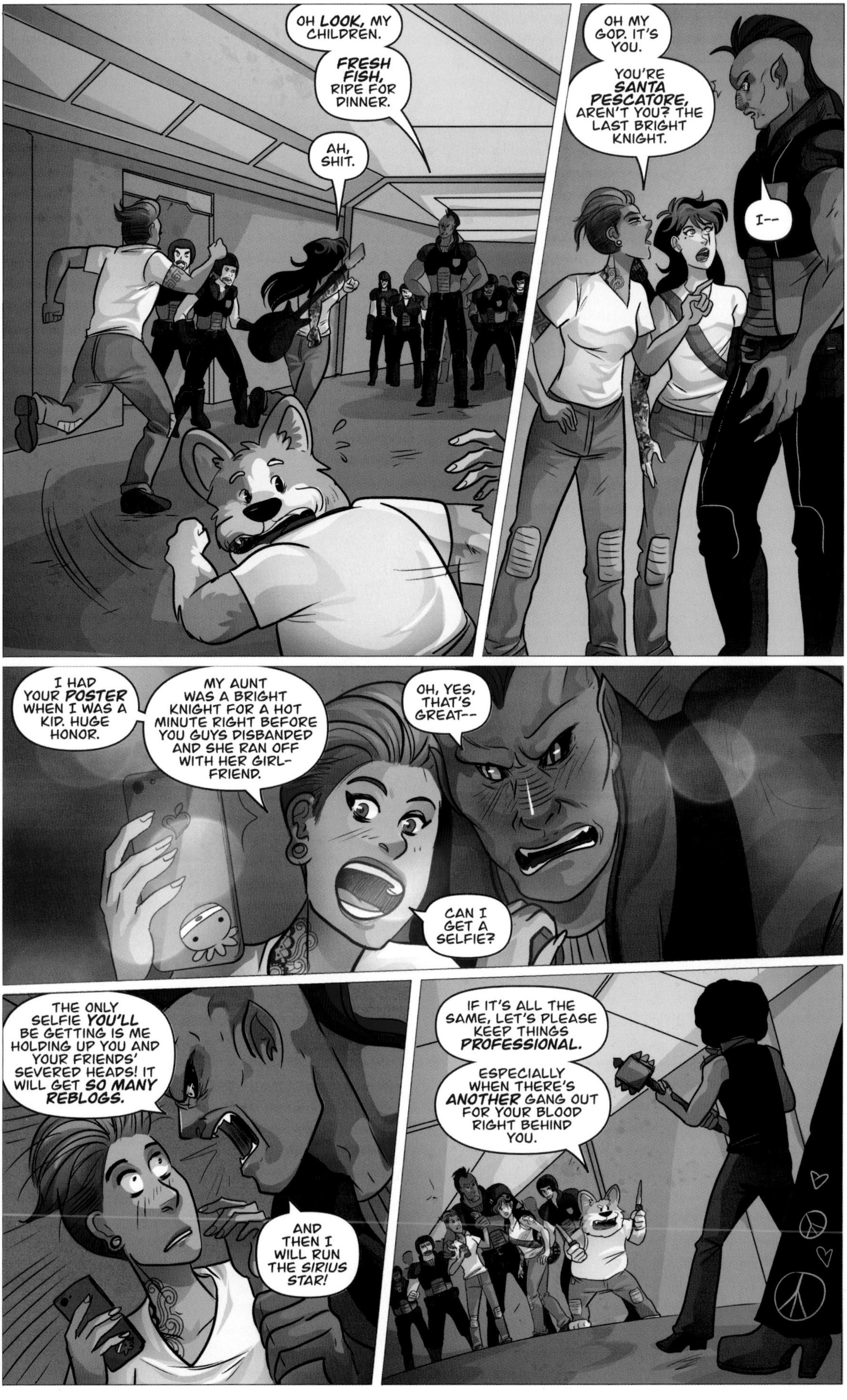
OH LOOK, MY CHILDREN.
FRESH FISH, RIPE FOR DINNER.
AH, SHIT.
OH MY GOD. IT'S YOU.
YOU'RE SANTA PESCATORE, AREN'T YOU? THE LAST BRIGHT KNIGHT.
I--
I HAD YOUR POSTER WHEN I WAS A KID. HUGE HONOR.
MY AUNT WAS A BRIGHT KNIGHT FOR A HOT MINUTE RIGHT BEFORE YOU GUYS DISBANDED AND SHE RAN OFF WITH HER GIRL-FRIEND.
OH, YES, THAT'S GREAT--
CAN I GET A SELFIE?
THE ONLY SELFIE YOU'LL BE GETTING IS ME HOLDING UP YOU AND YOUR FRIENDS' SEVERED HEADS! IT WILL GET SO MANY REBLOGS.
AND THEN I WILL RUN THE SIRIUS STAR!
IF IT'S ALL THE SAME, LET'S PLEASE KEEP THINGS PROFESSIONAL.
ESPECIALLY WHEN THERE'S ANOTHER GANG OUT FOR YOUR BLOOD RIGHT BEHIND YOU.

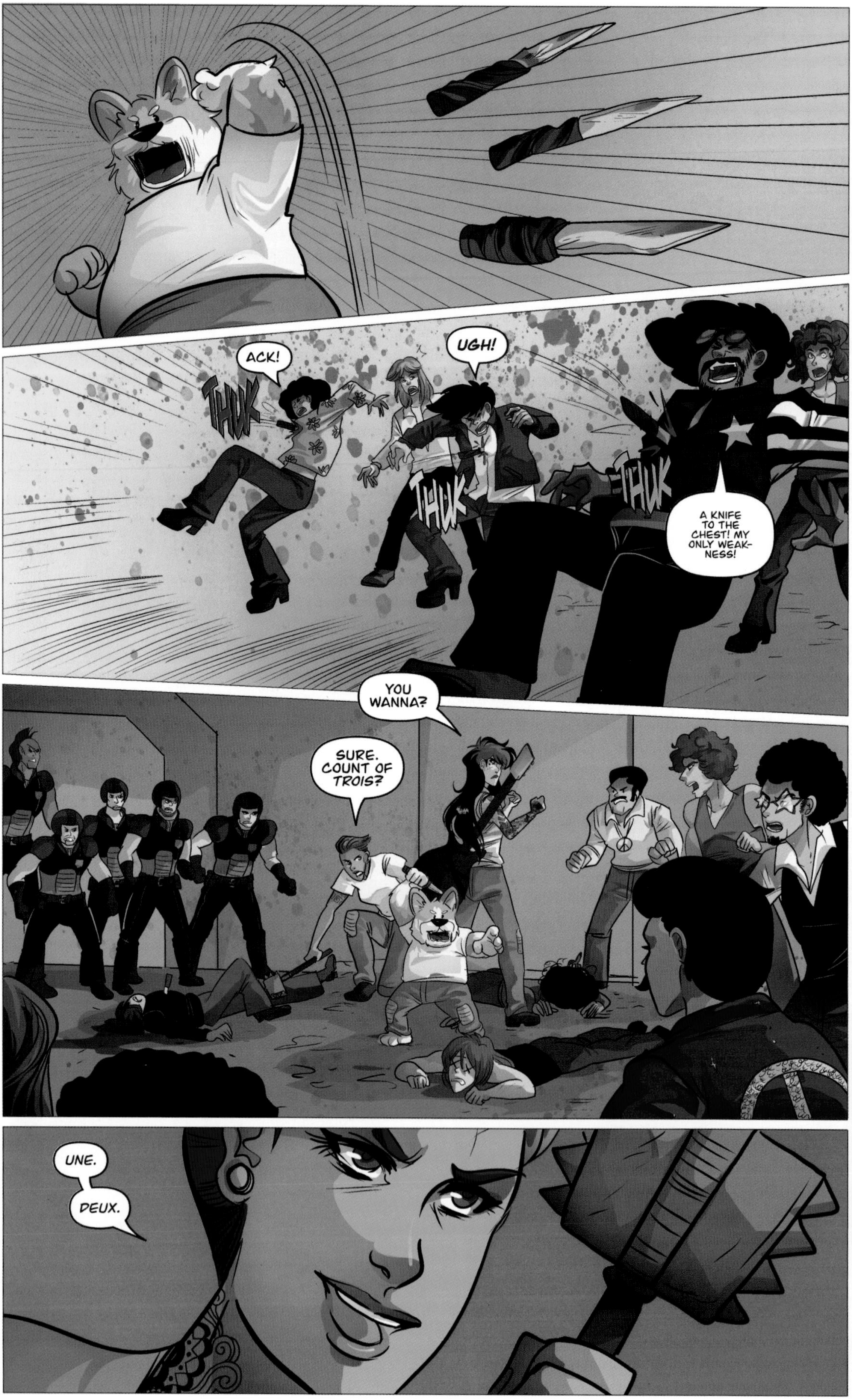
ACK!
THUK
UGH!
THUK
THUK
A KNIFE TO THE CHEST! MY ONLY WEAK- NESS!
YOU WANNA?
SURE. COUNT OF TROIS?
UNE.
DEUX.

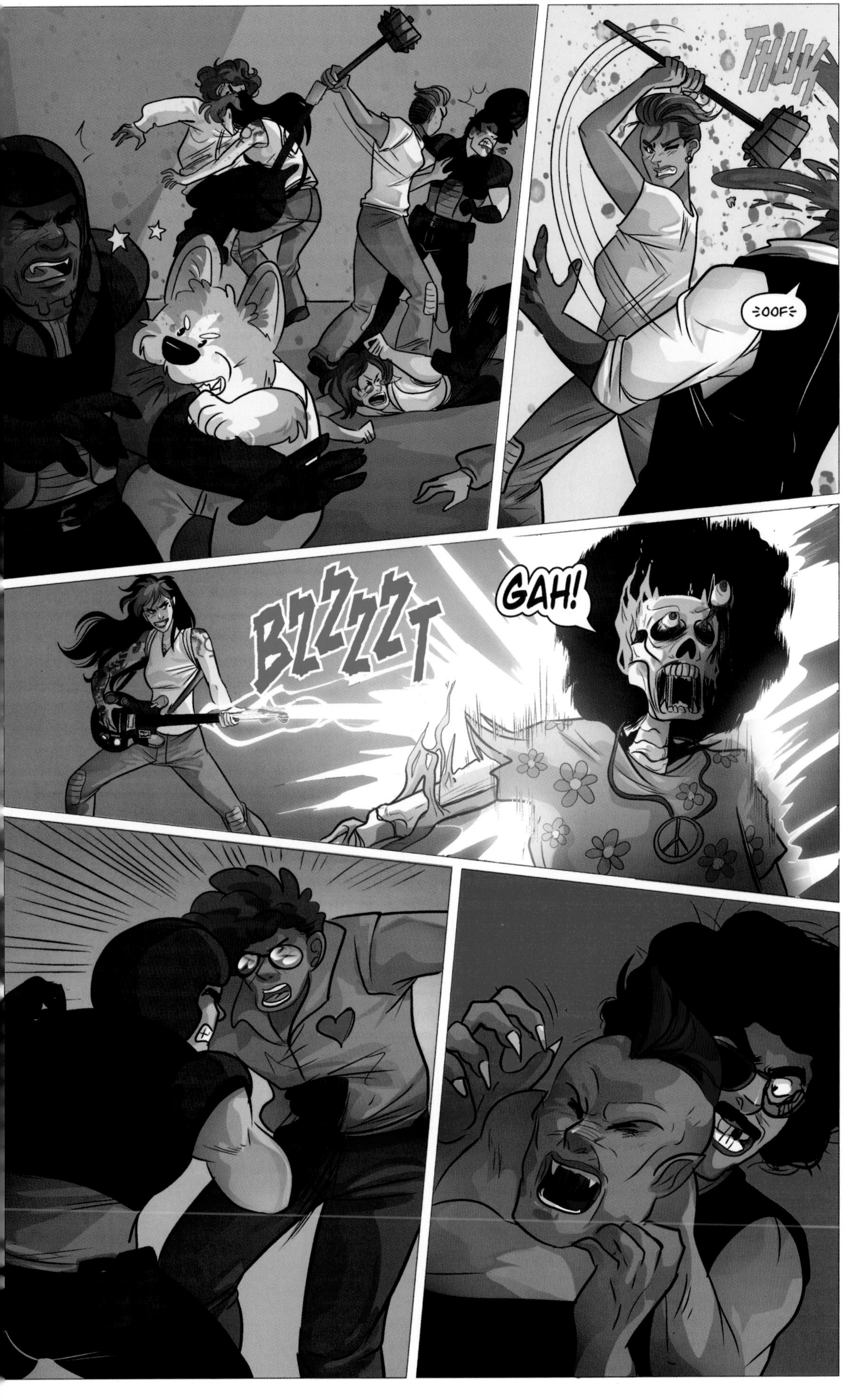
THUK
OOF
BZZZZT
GAH!

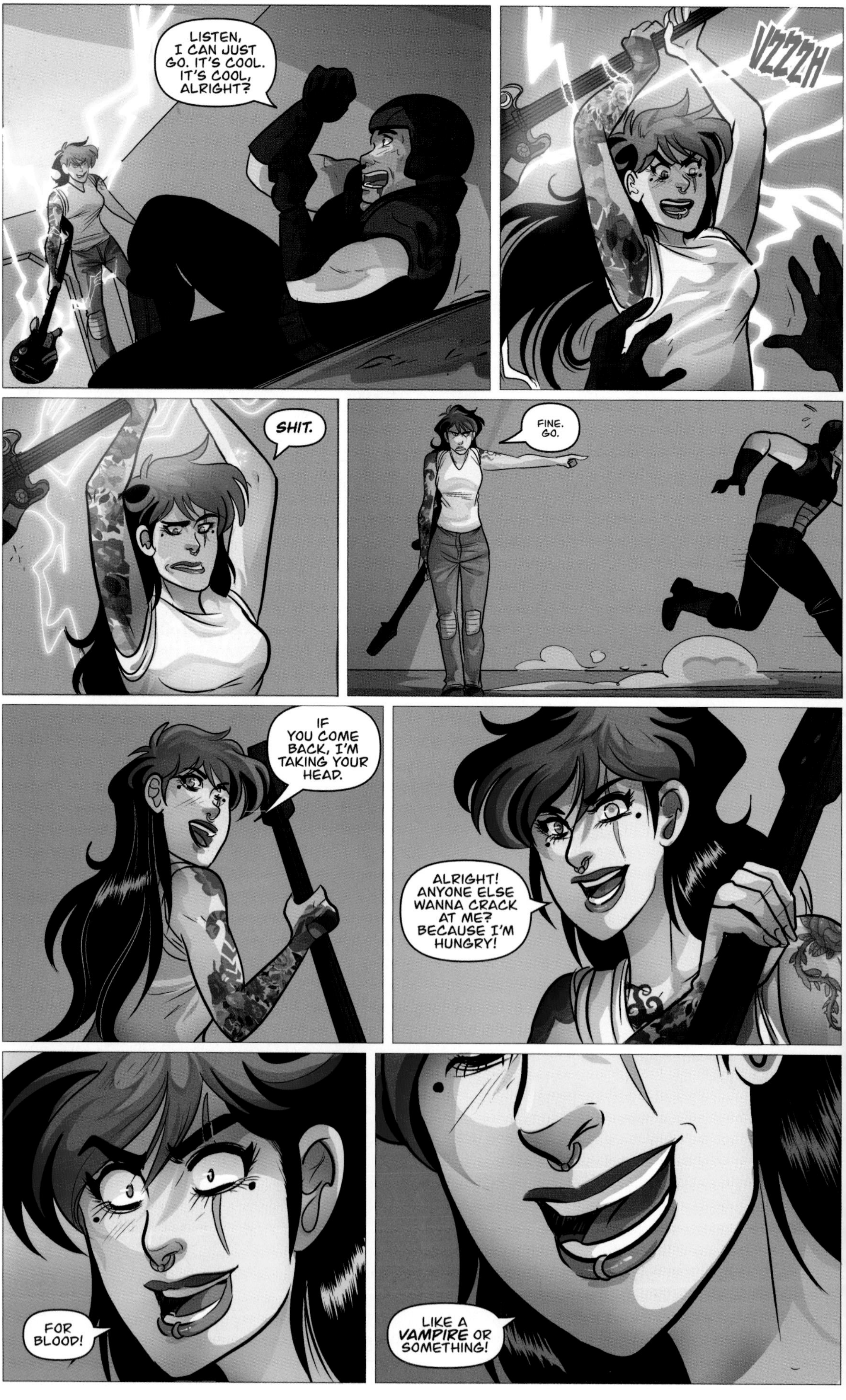
LISTEN, I CAN JUST GO. IT'S COOL. IT'S COOL, ALRIGHT?
VZZZH
SHIT.
FINE. GO.
IF YOU COME BACK, I'M TAKING YOUR HEAD.
ALRIGHT! ANYONE ELSE WANNA CRACK AT ME? BECAUSE I'M HUNGRY!
FOR BLOOD!
LIKE A VAMPIRE OR SOMETHING!

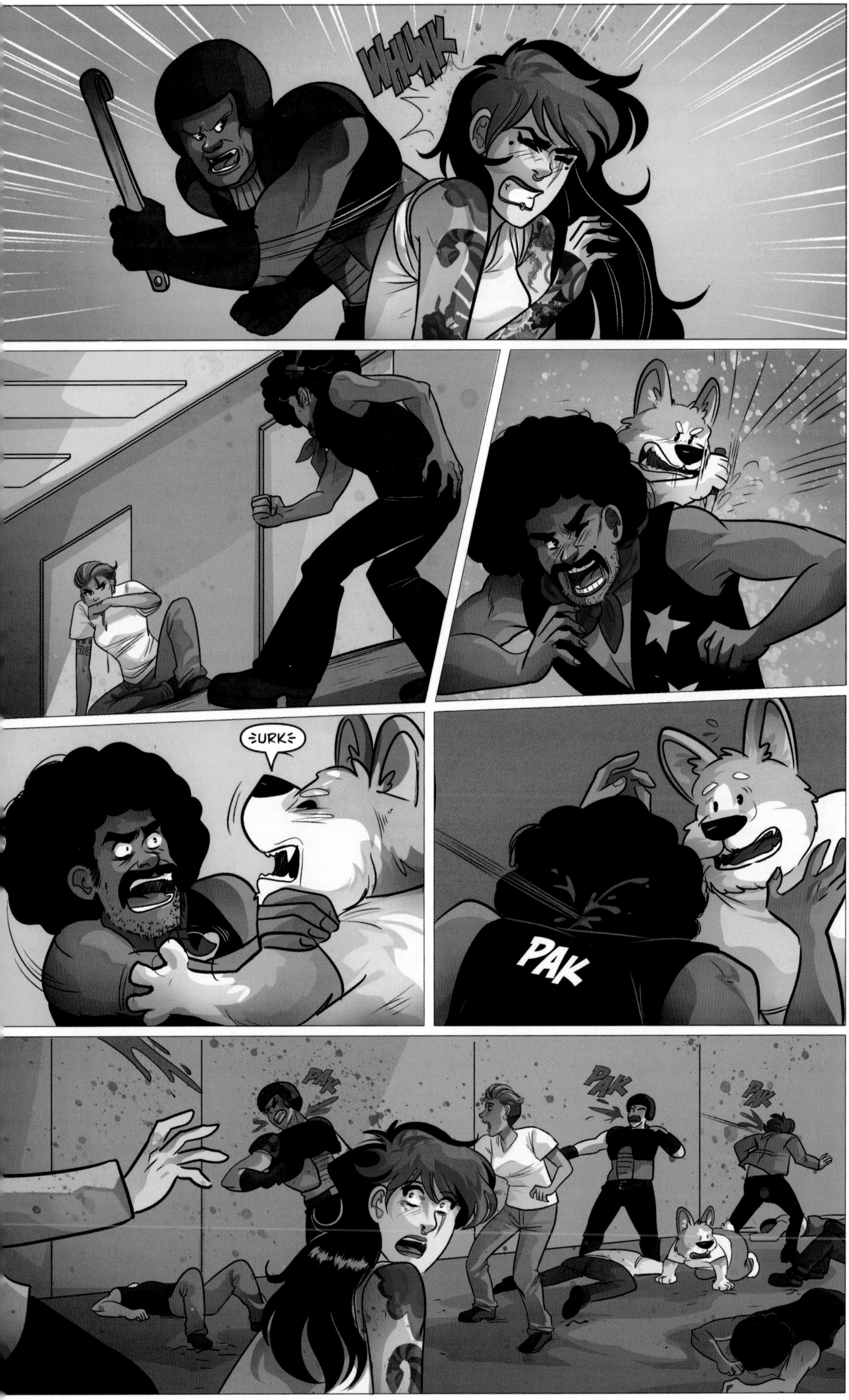
WHUNK
URK
PAK
PAK
PAK
PAK

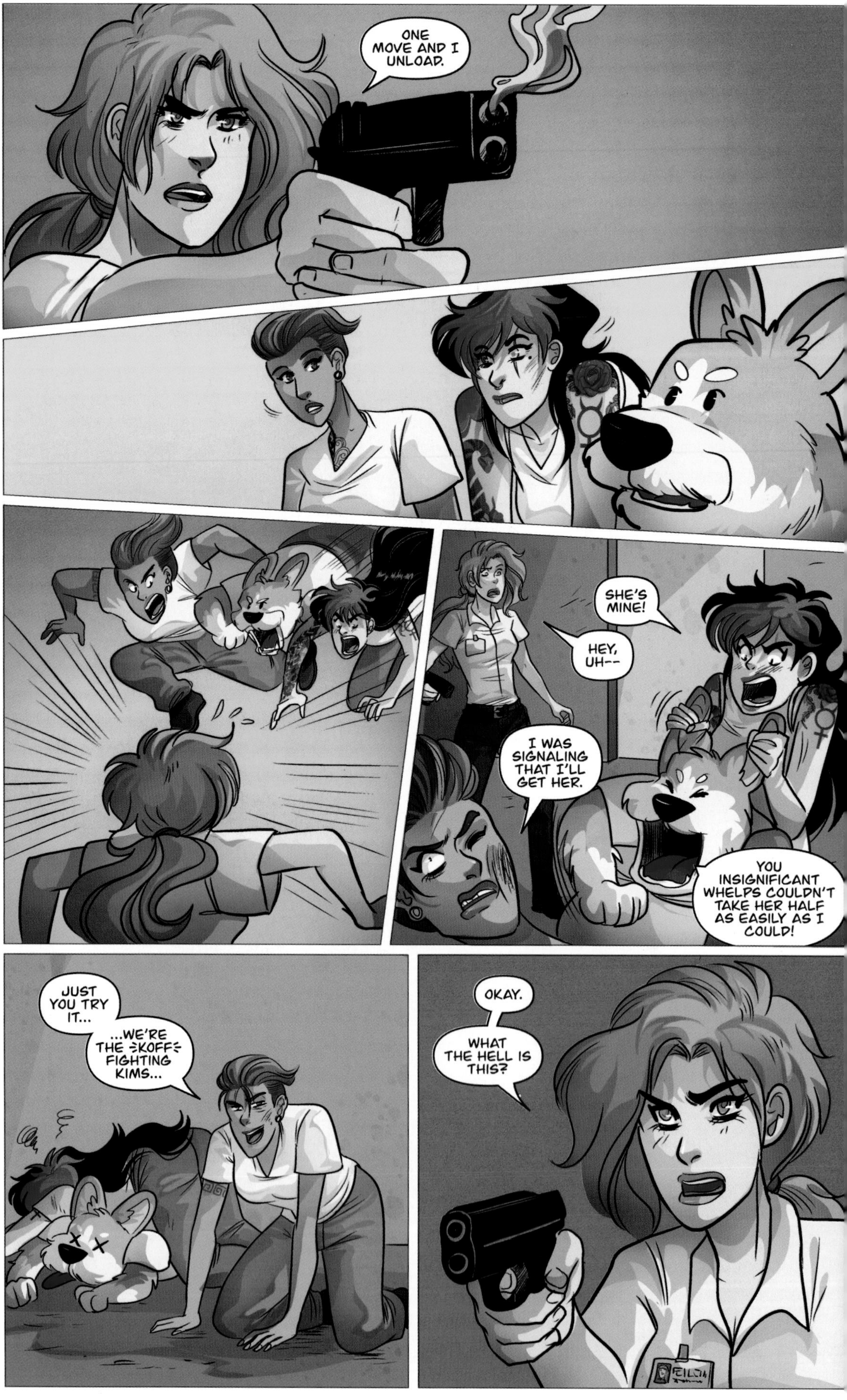
ONE MOVE AND I UNLOAD.
SHE'S MINE!
HEY, UH--
I WAS SIGNALING THAT I'LL GET HER.
YOU INSIGNIFICANT WHELPS COULDN'T TAKE HER HALF AS EASILY AS I COULD!
JUST YOU TRY IT...
...WE'RE THE =KOFF= FIGHTING KIMS...
OKAY.
WHAT THE HELL IS THIS?

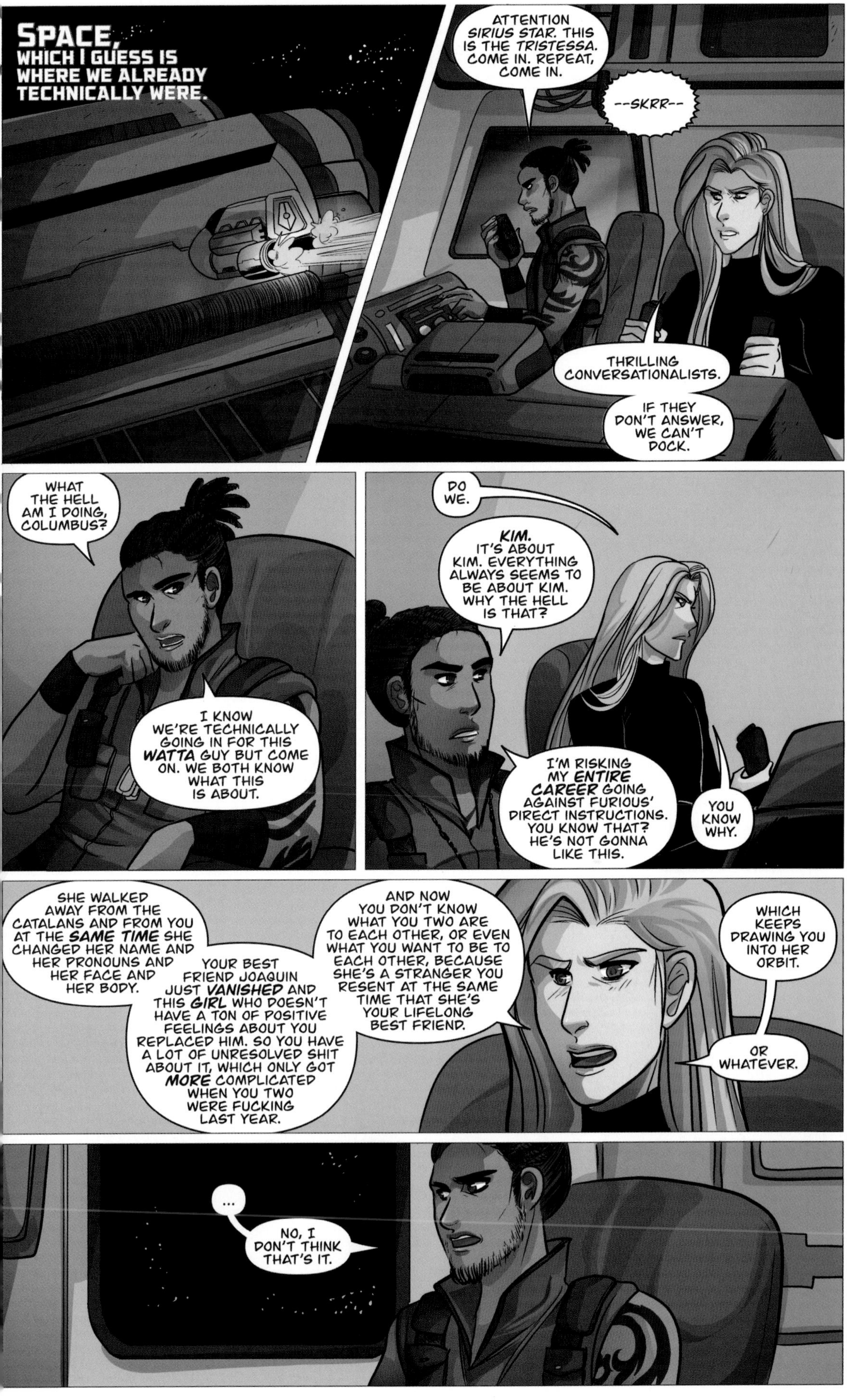
SPACE, WHICH I GUESS IS WHERE WE ALREADY TECHNICALLY WERE.
ATTENTION SIRIUS STAR. THIS IS THE TRISTESSA. COME IN. REPEAT, COME IN.
--SKRR--
THRILLING CONVERSATIONALISTS.
IF THEY DON'T ANSWER, WE CAN'T DOCK.
WHAT THE HELL AM I DOING, COLUMBUS?
I KNOW WE'RE TECHNICALLY GOING IN FOR THIS WATTA GUY BUT COME ON. WE BOTH KNOW WHAT THIS IS ABOUT.
DO WE.
KIM. IT'S ABOUT KIM. EVERYTHING ALWAYS SEEMS TO BE ABOUT KIM. WHY THE HELL IS THAT?
I'M RISKING MY ENTIRE CAREER GOING AGAINST FURIOUS' DIRECT INSTRUCTIONS. YOU KNOW THAT? HE'S NOT GONNA LIKE THIS.
YOU KNOW WHY.
SHE WALKED AWAY FROM THE CATALANS AND FROM YOU AT THE SAME TIME SHE CHANGED HER NAME AND HER PRONOUNS AND HER FACE AND HER BODY.
YOUR BEST FRIEND JOAQUIN JUST VANISHED AND THIS GIRL WHO DOESN'T HAVE A TON OF POSITIVE FEELINGS ABOUT YOU REPLACED HIM. SO YOU HAVE A LOT OF UNRESOLVED SHIT ABOUT IT, WHICH ONLY GOT MORE COMPLICATED WHEN YOU TWO WERE FUCKING LAST YEAR.
AND NOW YOU DON'T KNOW WHAT YOU TWO ARE TO EACH OTHER, OR EVEN WHAT YOU WANT TO BE TO EACH OTHER, BECAUSE SHE'S A STRANGER YOU RESENT AT THE SAME TIME THAT SHE'S YOUR LIFELONG BEST FRIEND.
WHICH KEEPS DRAWING YOU INTO HER ORBIT.
OR WHATEVER.
...
NO, I DON'T THINK THAT'S IT.

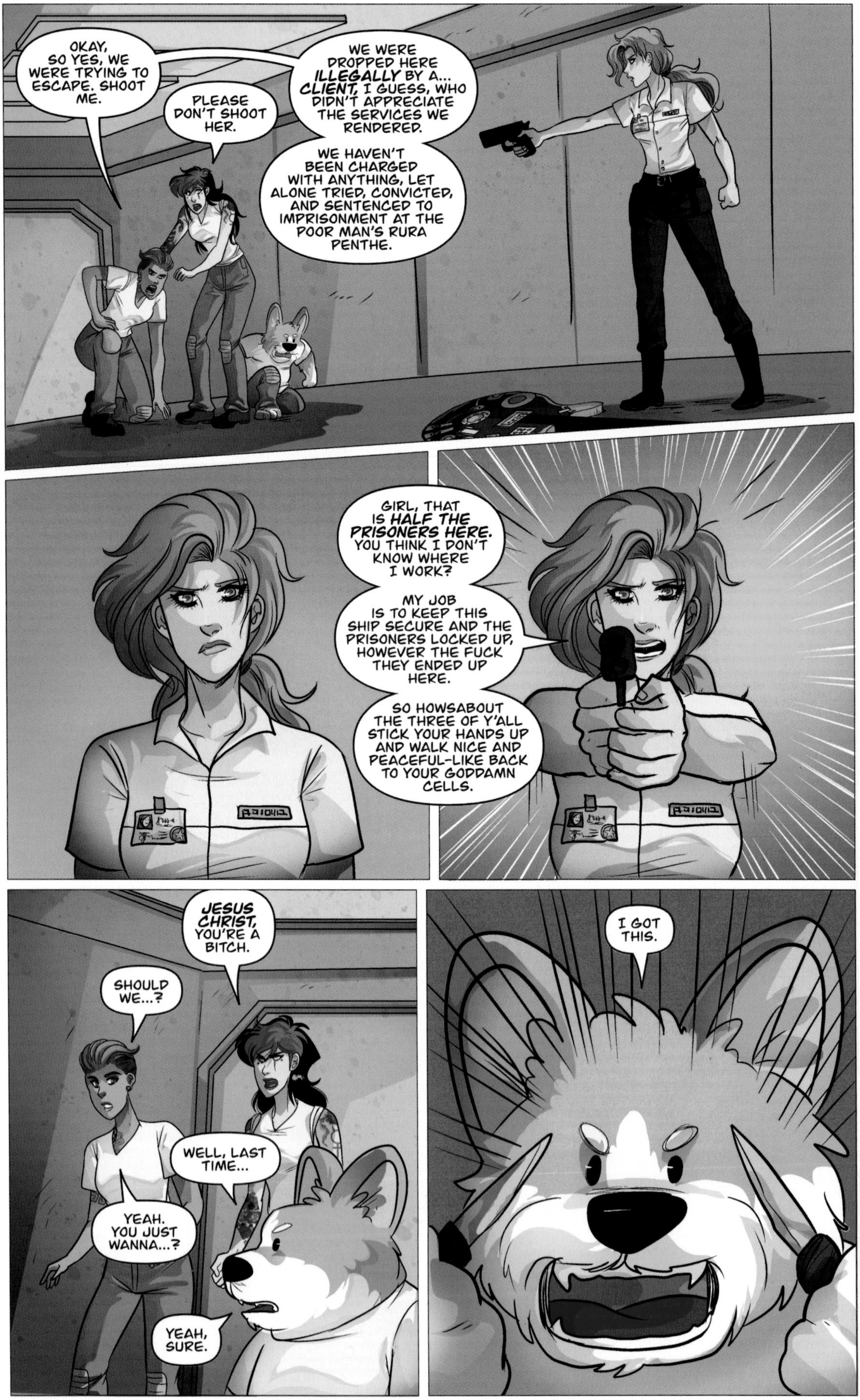
OKAY, SO YES, WE WERE TRYING TO ESCAPE. SHOOT ME.
PLEASE DON'T SHOOT HER.
WE WERE DROPPED HERE ILLEGALLY BY A... CLIENT, I GUESS, WHO DIDN'T APPRECIATE THE SERVICES WE RENDERED.
WE HAVEN'T BEEN CHARGED WITH ANYTHING, LET ALONE TRIED, CONVICTED, AND SENTENCED TO IMPRISONMENT AT THE POOR MAN'S RURA PENTHE.
GIRL, THAT IS HALF THE PRISONERS HERE. YOU THINK I DON'T KNOW WHERE I WORK?
MY JOB IS TO KEEP THIS SHIP SECURE AND THE PRISONERS LOCKED UP, HOWEVER THE FUCK THEY ENDED UP HERE.
SO HOWSABOUT THE THREE OF Y'ALL STICK YOUR HANDS UP AND WALK NICE AND PEACEFUL-LIKE BACK TO YOUR GODDAMN CELLS.
JESUS CHRIST, YOU'RE A BITCH.
SHOULD WE...?
WELL, LAST TIME...
YEAH. YOU JUST WANNA...?
YEAH, SURE.
I GOT THIS.

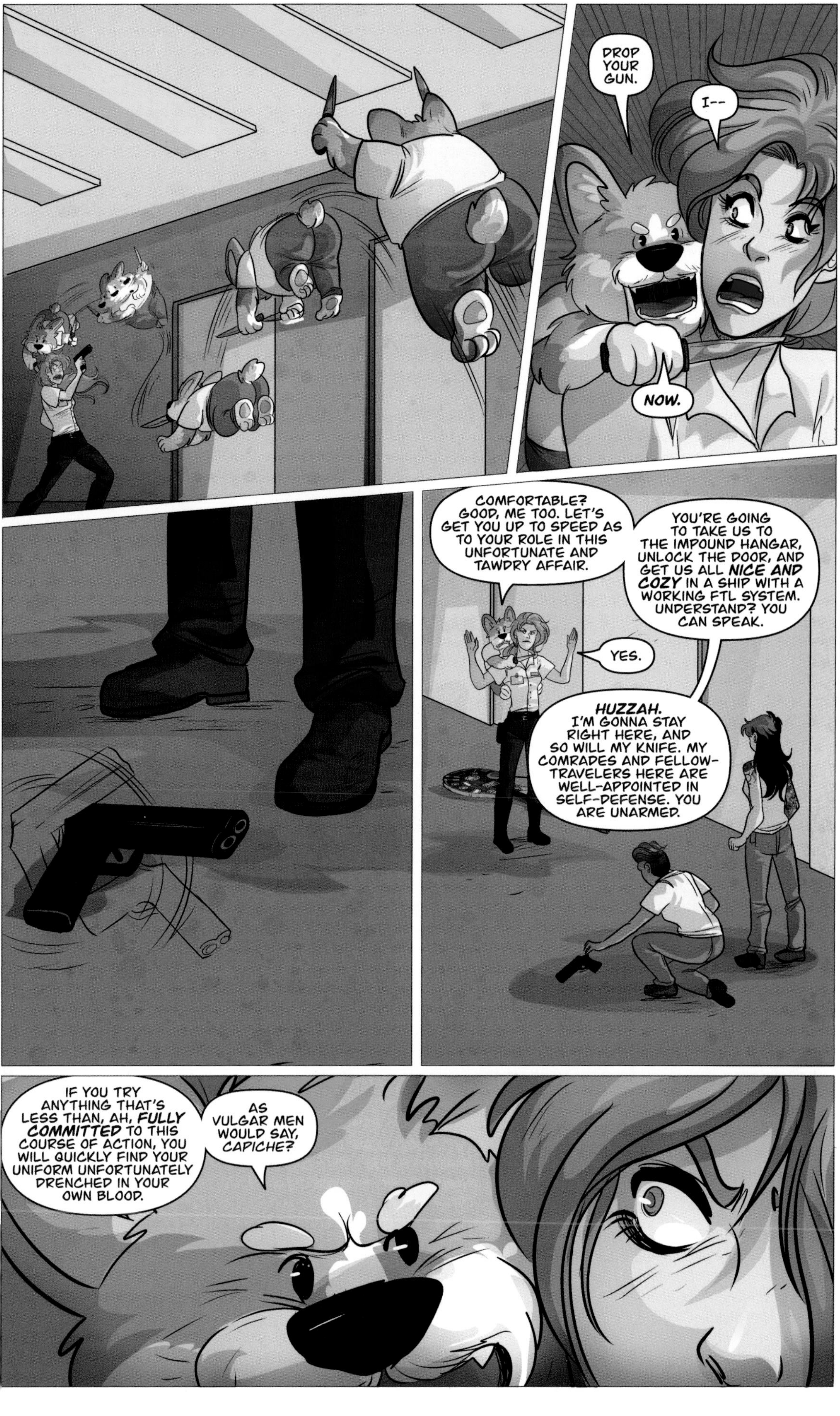
DROP YOUR GUN.
I--
NOW.
COMFORTABLE? GOOD, ME TOO. LET'S GET YOU UP TO SPEED AS TO YOUR ROLE IN THIS UNFORTUNATE AND TAWDRY AFFAIR.
YOU'RE GOING TO TAKE US TO THE IMPOUND HANGAR, UNLOCK THE DOOR, AND GET US ALL NICE AND COZY IN A SHIP WITH A WORKING FTL SYSTEM. UNDERSTAND? YOU CAN SPEAK.
YES.
HUZZAH. I'M GONNA STAY RIGHT HERE, AND SO WILL MY KNIFE. MY COMRADES AND FELLOW-TRAVELERS HERE ARE WELL-APPOINTED IN SELF-DEFENSE. YOU ARE UNARMED.
IF YOU TRY ANYTHING THAT'S LESS THAN, AH, FULLY COMMITTED TO THIS COURSE OF ACTION, YOU WILL QUICKLY FIND YOUR UNIFORM UNFORTUNATELY DRENCHED IN YOUR OWN BLOOD.
AS VULGAR MEN WOULD SAY, CAPICHE?

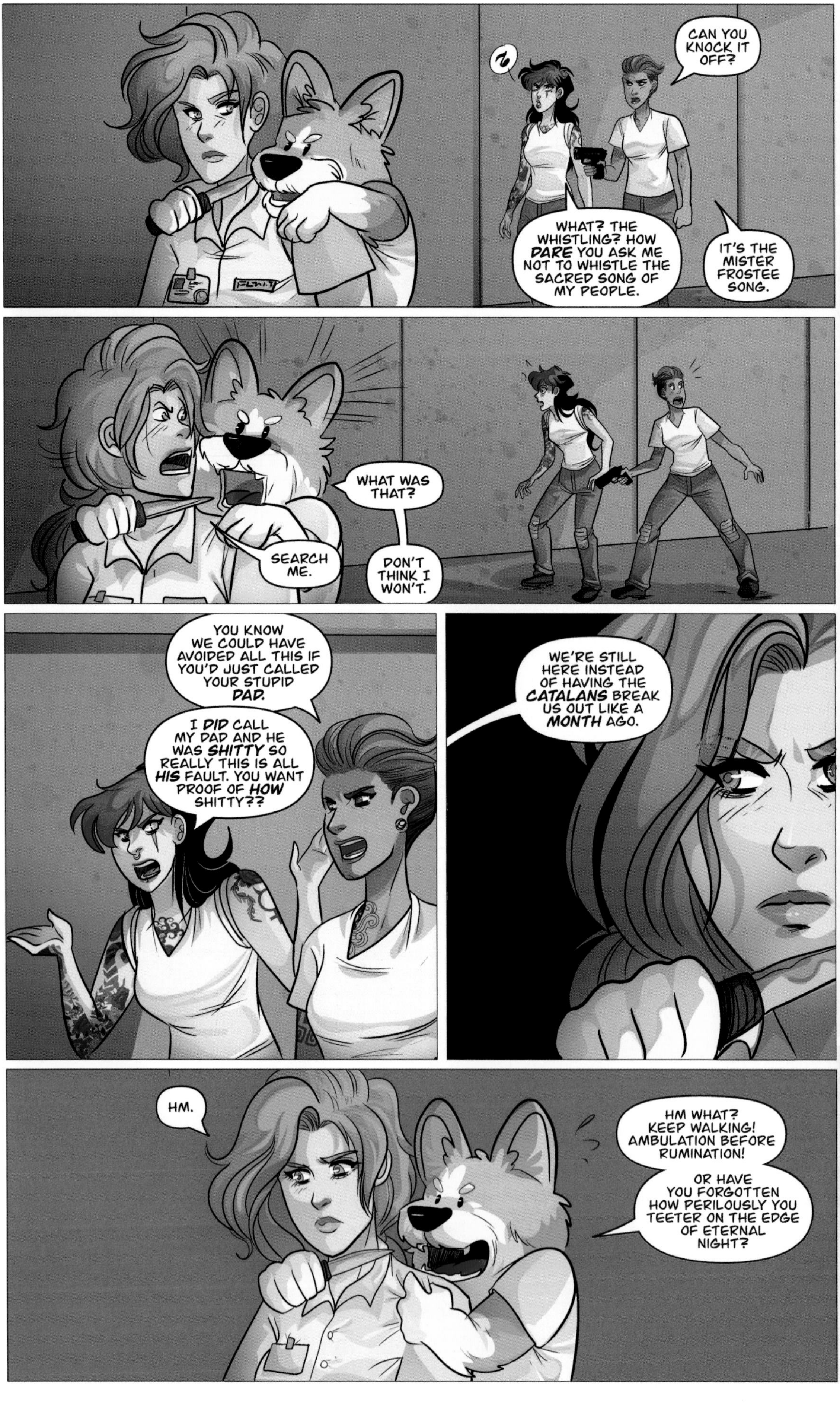
?
CAN YOU KNOCK IT OFF?
WHAT? THE WHISTLING? HOW DARE YOU ASK ME NOT TO WHISTLE THE SACRED SONG OF MY PEOPLE.
IT'S THE MISTER FROSTEE SONG.
WHAT WAS THAT?
SEARCH ME.
DON'T THINK I WON'T.
YOU KNOW WE COULD HAVE AVOIDED ALL THIS IF YOU'D JUST CALLED YOUR STUPID DAD.
I DID CALL MY DAD AND HE WAS SHITTY SO REALLY THIS IS ALL HIS FAULT. YOU WANT PROOF OF HOW SHITTY??
WE'RE STILL HERE INSTEAD OF HAVING THE CATALANS BREAK US OUT LIKE A MONTH AGO.
HM.
HM WHAT? KEEP WALKING! AMBULATION BEFORE RUMINATION!
OR HAVE YOU FORGOTTEN HOW PERILOUSLY YOU TEETER ON THE EDGE OF ETERNAL NIGHT?

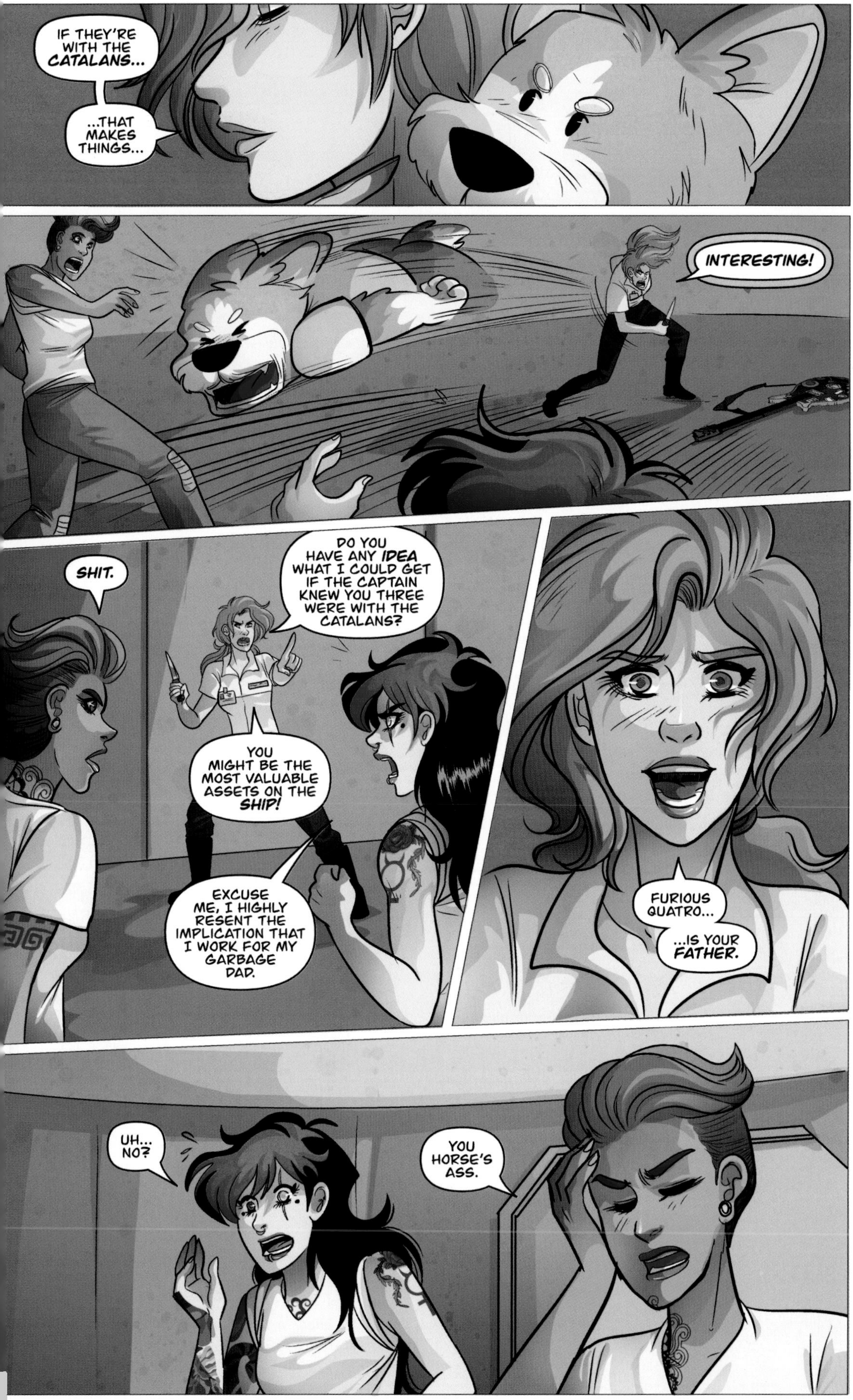
IF THEY'RE WITH THE CATALANS...
...THAT MAKES THINGS...
INTERESTING!
SHIT.
DO YOU HAVE ANY IDEA WHAT I COULD GET IF THE CAPTAIN KNEW YOU THREE WERE WITH THE CATALANS?
YOU MIGHT BE THE MOST VALUABLE ASSETS ON THE SHIP!
EXCUSE ME, I HIGHLY RESENT THE IMPLICATION THAT I WORK FOR MY GARBAGE DAD.
FURIOUS QUATRO...
...IS YOUR FATHER.
UH... NO?
YOU HORSE'S ASS.

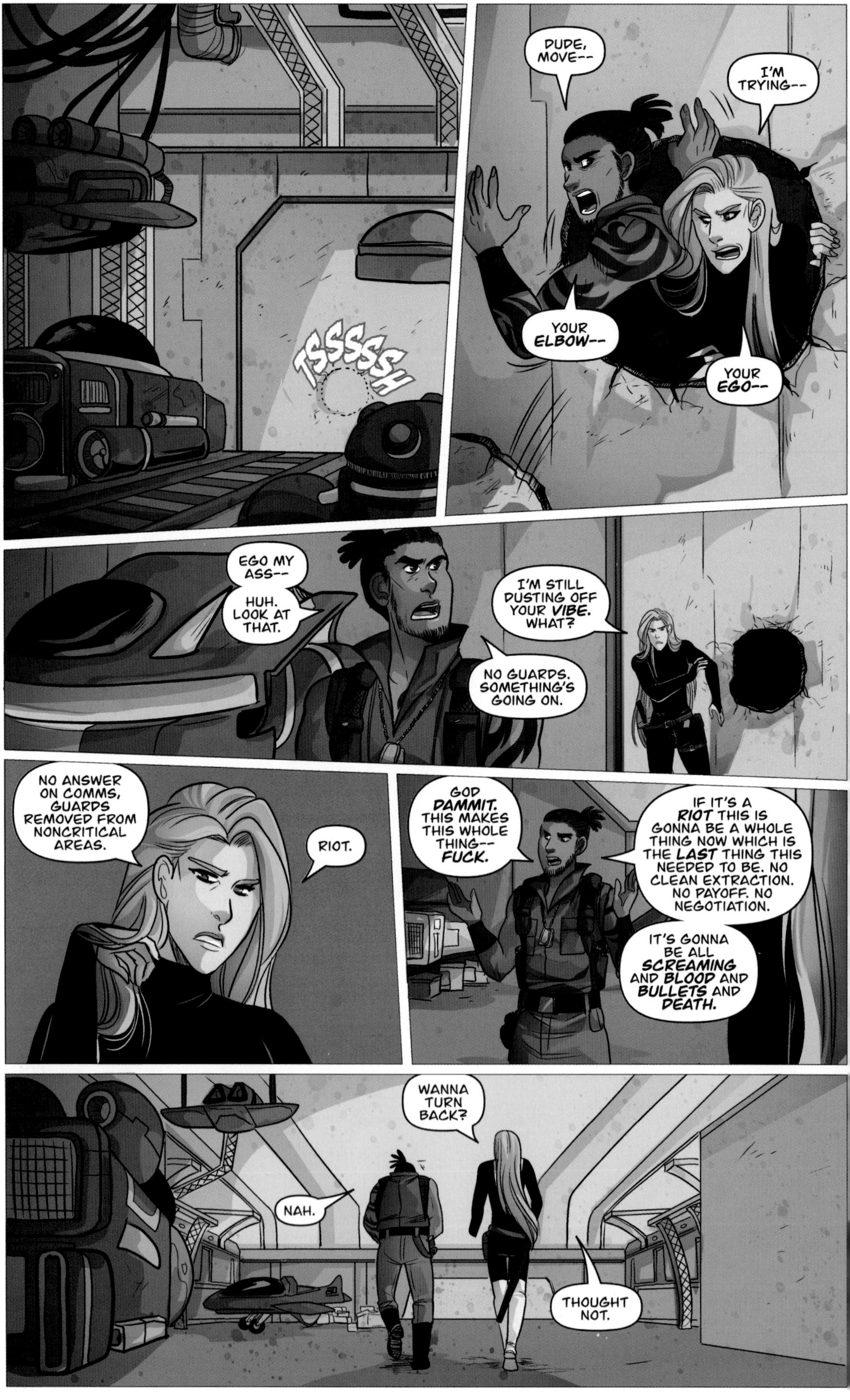
TSSSSSH
DUDE, MOVE--
I'M TRYING--
YOUR ELBOW--
YOUR EGO--
EGO MY ASS--
HUH. LOOK AT THAT.
I'M STILL DUSTING OFF YOUR VIBE. WHAT?
NO GUARDS. SOMETHING'S GOING ON.
NO ANSWER ON COMMS, GUARDS REMOVED FROM NONCRITICAL AREAS.
RIOT.
GOD DAMMIT. THIS MAKES THIS WHOLE THING-- FUCK.
IF IT'S A RIOT THIS IS GONNA BE A WHOLE THING NOW WHICH IS THE LAST THING THIS NEEDED TO BE. NO CLEAN EXTRACTION. NO PAYOFF. NO NEGOTIATION.
IT'S GONNA BE ALL SCREAMING AND BLOOD AND BULLETS AND DEATH.
WANNA TURN BACK?
NAH.
THOUGHT NOT.

WHUP

SMAK

BONK

KRASH

KRONK

FWA

BANG

KRANG

YOU HEAR THAT?

SADLY.

BWONK

THUNK

HUK

WHUMF

AGH!

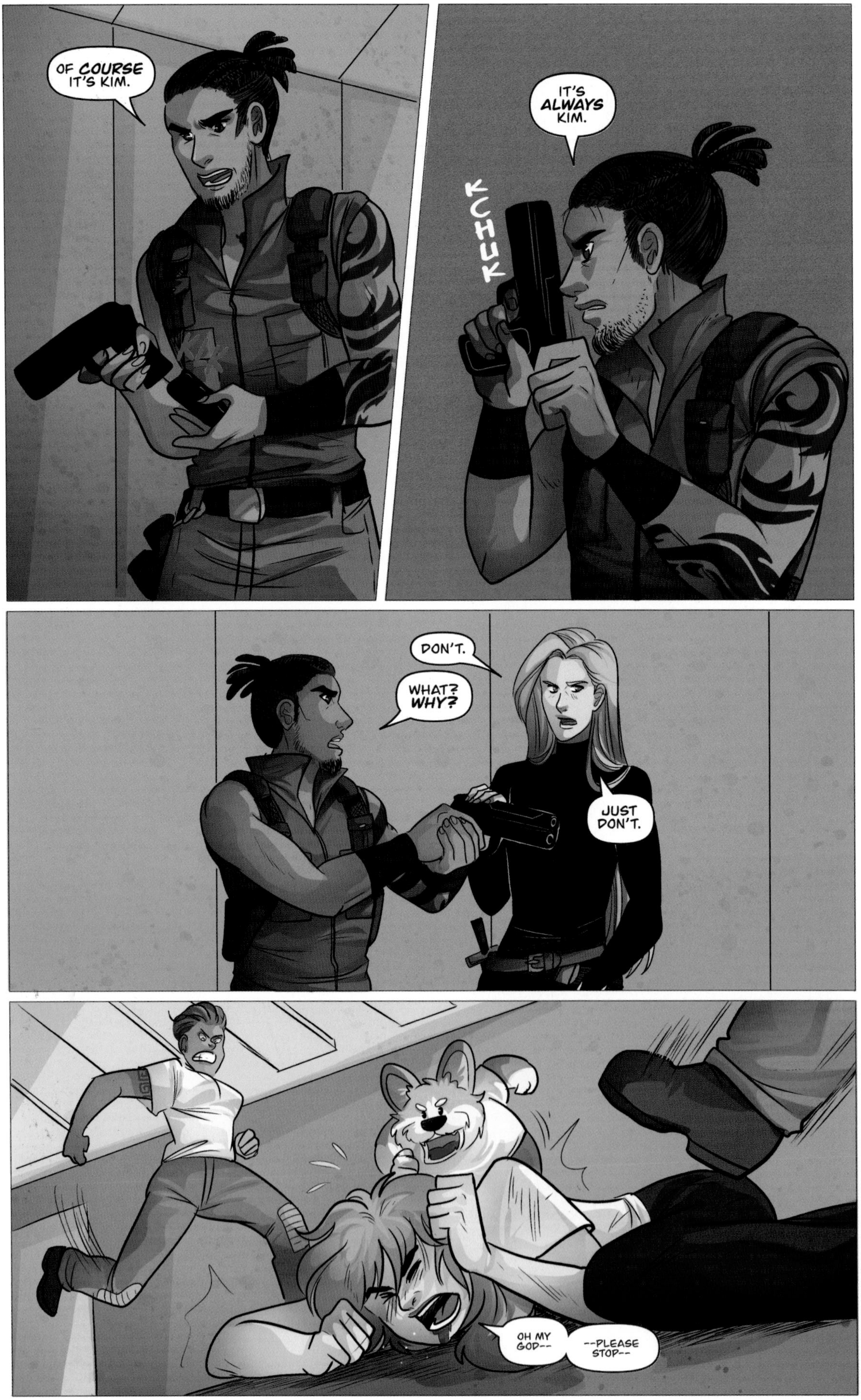
OF COURSE IT'S KIM.
IT'S ALWAYS KIM.
KCHUK
DON'T.
WHAT? WHY?
JUST DON'T.
OH MY GOD--
--PLEASE STOP--

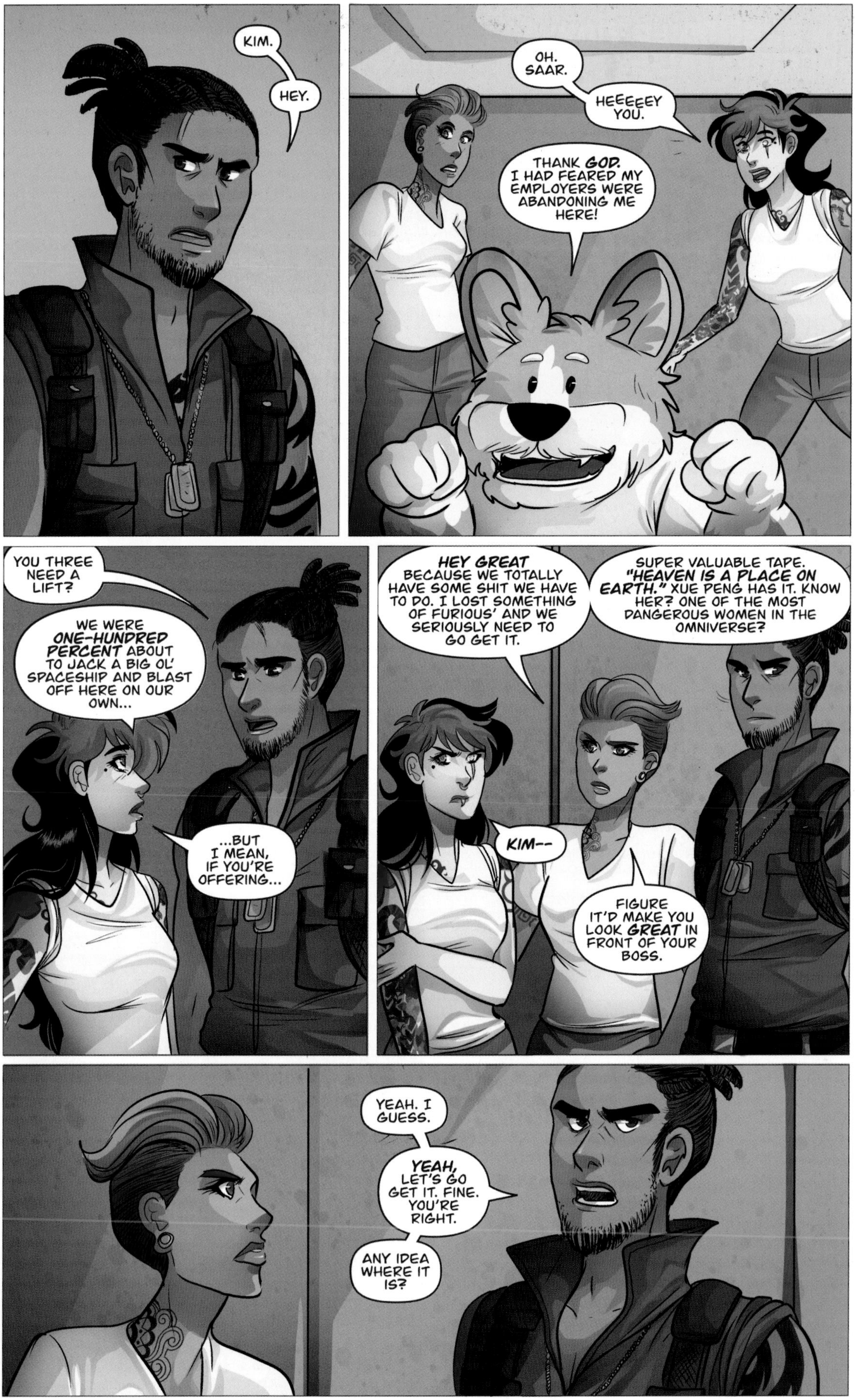
KIM.
HEY.
OH. SAAR.
HEEEEEEY YOU.
THANK GOD. I HAD FEARED MY EMPLOYERS WERE ABANDONING ME HERE!
YOU THREE NEED A LIFT?
WE WERE ONE-HUNDRED PERCENT ABOUT TO JACK A BIG OL' SPACESHIP AND BLAST OFF HERE ON OUR OWN...
...BUT I MEAN, IF YOU'RE OFFERING...
HEY GREAT BECAUSE WE TOTALLY HAVE SOME SHIT WE HAVE TO DO. I LOST SOMETHING OF FURIOUS' AND WE SERIOUSLY NEED TO GO GET IT.
SUPER VALUABLE TAPE. "HEAVEN IS A PLACE ON EARTH." XUE PENG HAS IT. KNOW HER? ONE OF THE MOST DANGEROUS WOMEN IN THE OMNIVERSE?
KIM--
FIGURE IT'D MAKE YOU LOOK GREAT IN FRONT OF YOUR BOSS.
YEAH. I GUESS.
YEAH, LET'S GO GET IT. FINE. YOU'RE RIGHT.
ANY IDEA WHERE IT IS?

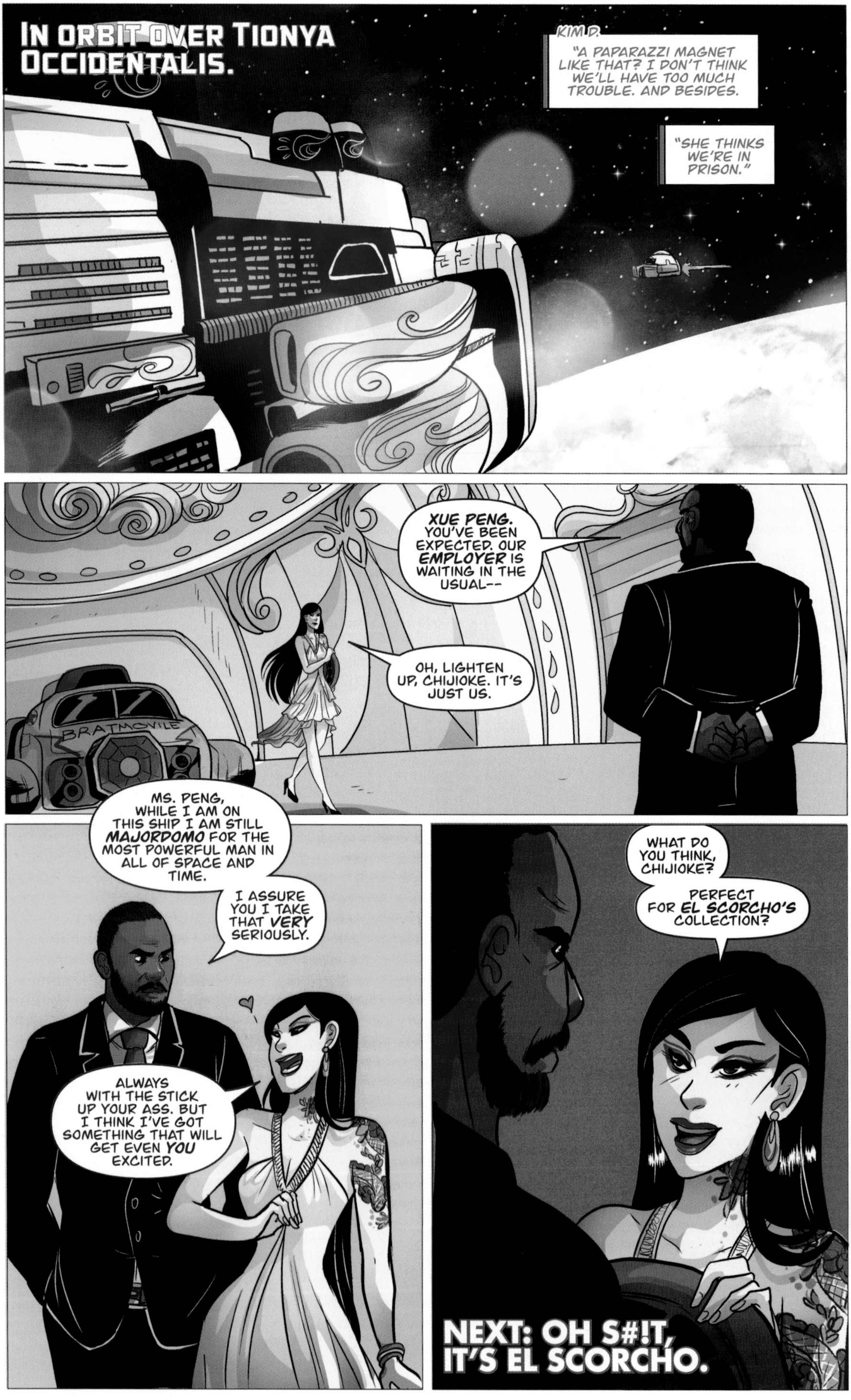
IN ORBIT OVER TIONYA OCCIDENTALIS.
KIM D.
"A PAPARAZZI MAGNET LIKE THAT? I DON'T THINK WE'LL HAVE TOO MUCH TROUBLE. AND BESIDES.
"SHE THINKS WE'RE IN PRISON."
XUE PENG. YOU'VE BEEN EXPECTED. OUR EMPLOYER IS WAITING IN THE USUAL--
OH, LIGHTEN UP, CHIJIOKE. IT'S JUST US.
BRATMOVILE
MS. PENG, WHILE I AM ON THIS SHIP I AM STILL MAJORDOMO FOR THE MOST POWERFUL MAN IN ALL OF SPACE AND TIME.
I ASSURE YOU I TAKE THAT VERY SERIOUSLY.
ALWAYS WITH THE STICK UP YOUR ASS. BUT I THINK I'VE GOT SOMETHING THAT WILL GET EVEN YOU EXCITED.
WHAT DO YOU THINK, CHIJIOKE?
PERFECT FOR EL SCORCHO'S COLLECTION?
NEXT: OH S#!T, IT'S EL SCORCHO.

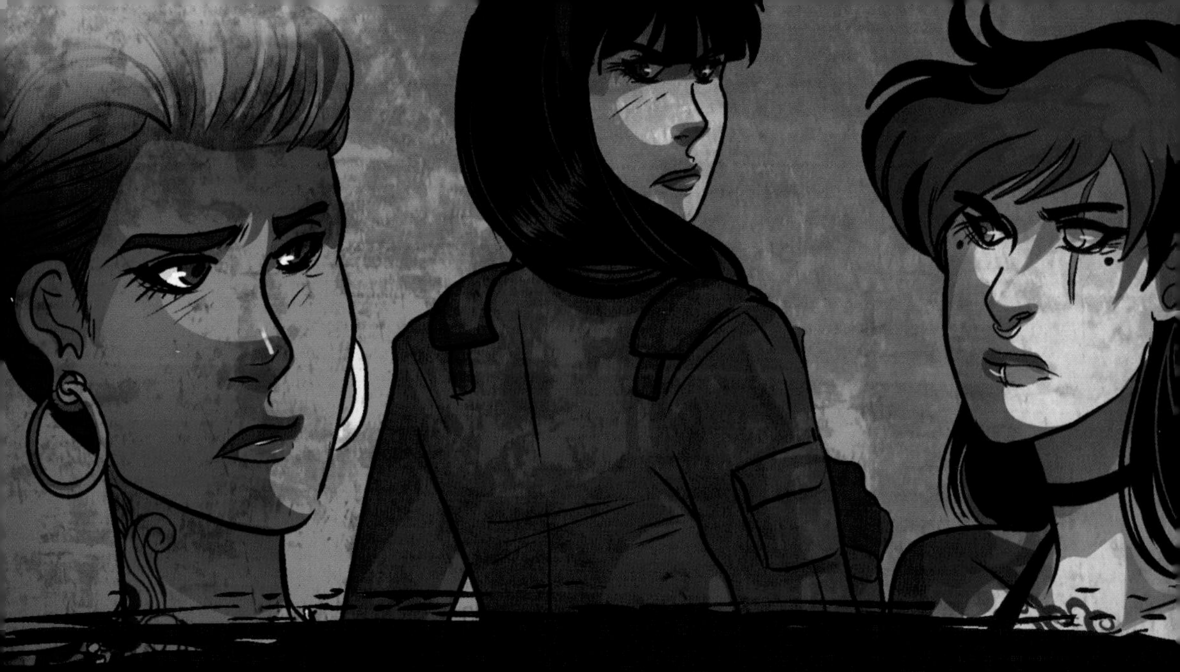

5

"OH SHIT, IT'S EL SCORCHO!"

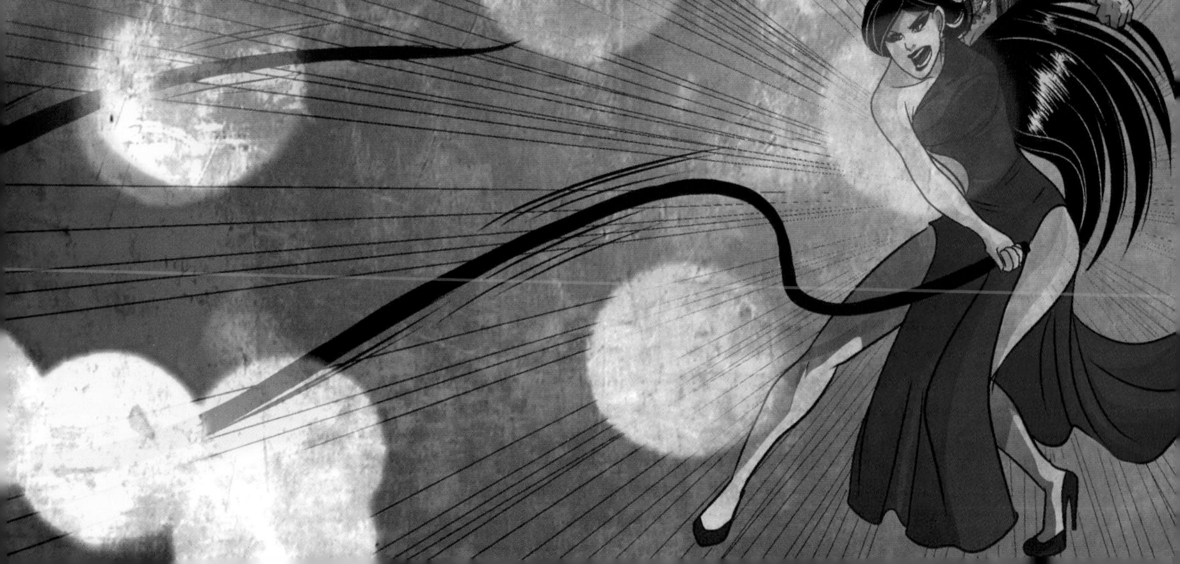

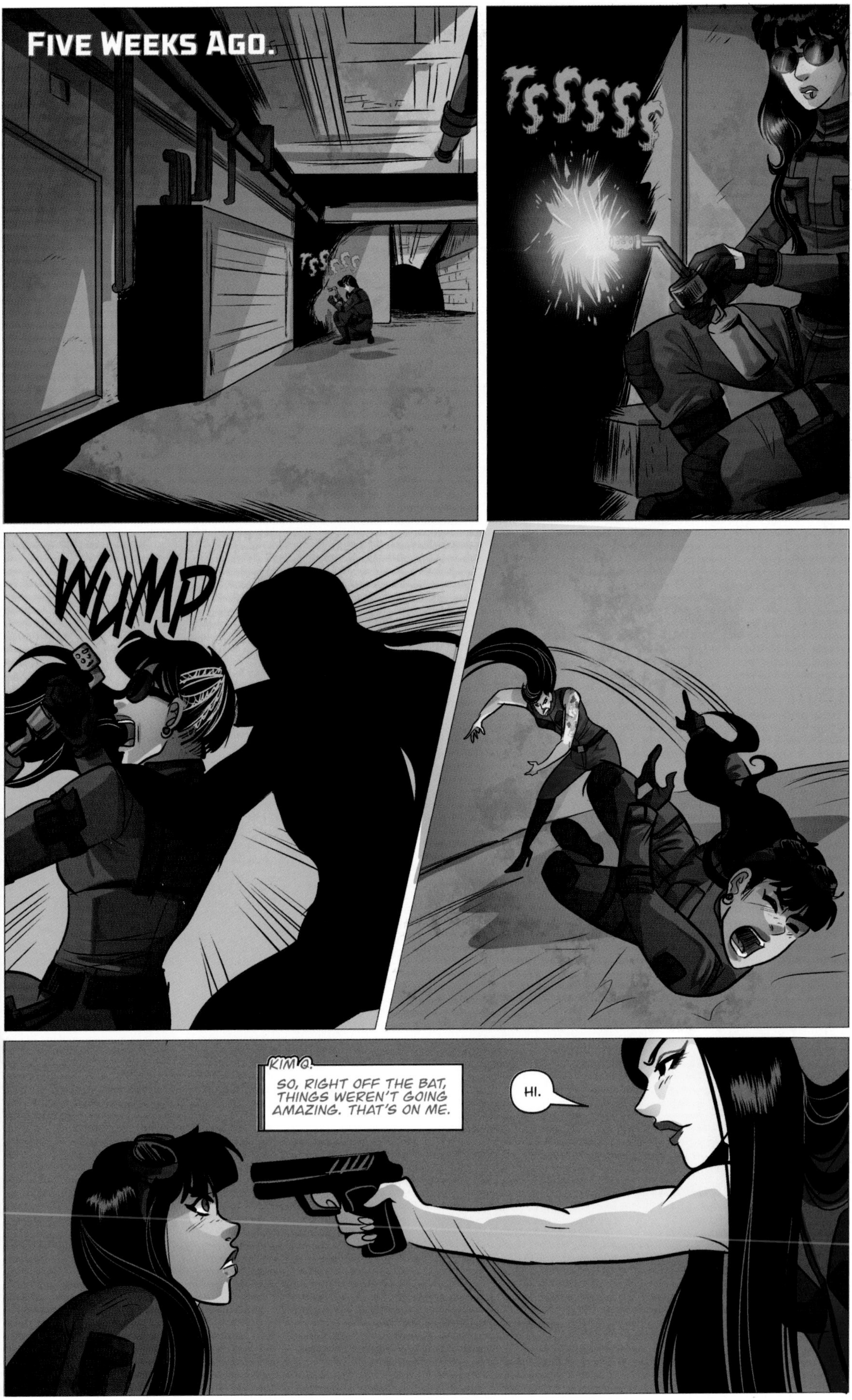

FIVE WEEKS AGO.
TSSSSS
TSSSSS
WUMP
KIM Q.
SO, RIGHT OFF THE BAT, THINGS WEREN'T GOING AMAZING. THAT'S ON ME.
HI.

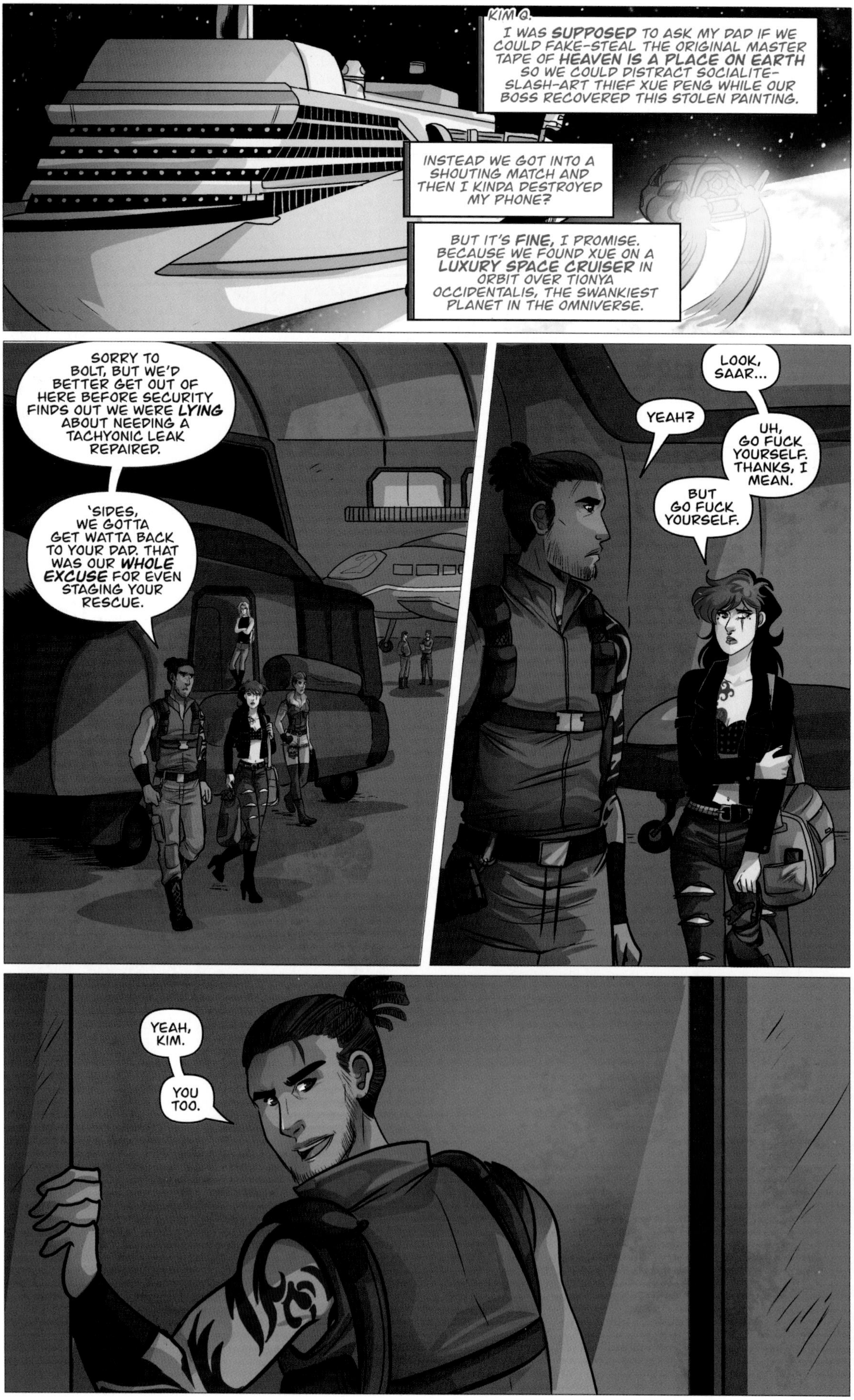
KIM Q.
I WAS SUPPOSED TO ASK MY DAD IF WE COULD FAKE-STEAL THE ORIGINAL MASTER TAPE OF HEAVEN IS A PLACE ON EARTH SO WE COULD DISTRACT SOCIALITE-SLASH-ART THIEF XUE PENG WHILE OUR BOSS RECOVERED THIS STOLEN PAINTING.
INSTEAD WE GOT INTO A SHOUTING MATCH AND THEN I KINDA DESTROYED MY PHONE?
BUT IT'S FINE, I PROMISE. BECAUSE WE FOUND XUE ON A LUXURY SPACE CRUISER IN ORBIT OVER TIONYA OCCIDENTALIS, THE SWANKIEST PLANET IN THE OMNIVERSE.
SORRY TO BOLT, BUT WE'D BETTER GET OUT OF HERE BEFORE SECURITY FINDS OUT WE WERE LYING ABOUT NEEDING A TACHYONIC LEAK REPAIRED.
'SIDES, WE GOTTA GET WATTA BACK TO YOUR DAD. THAT WAS OUR WHOLE EXCUSE FOR EVEN STAGING YOUR RESCUE.
LOOK, SAAR...
YEAH?
UH, GO FUCK YOURSELF. THANKS, I MEAN.
BUT GO FUCK YOURSELF.
YEAH, KIM.
YOU TOO.

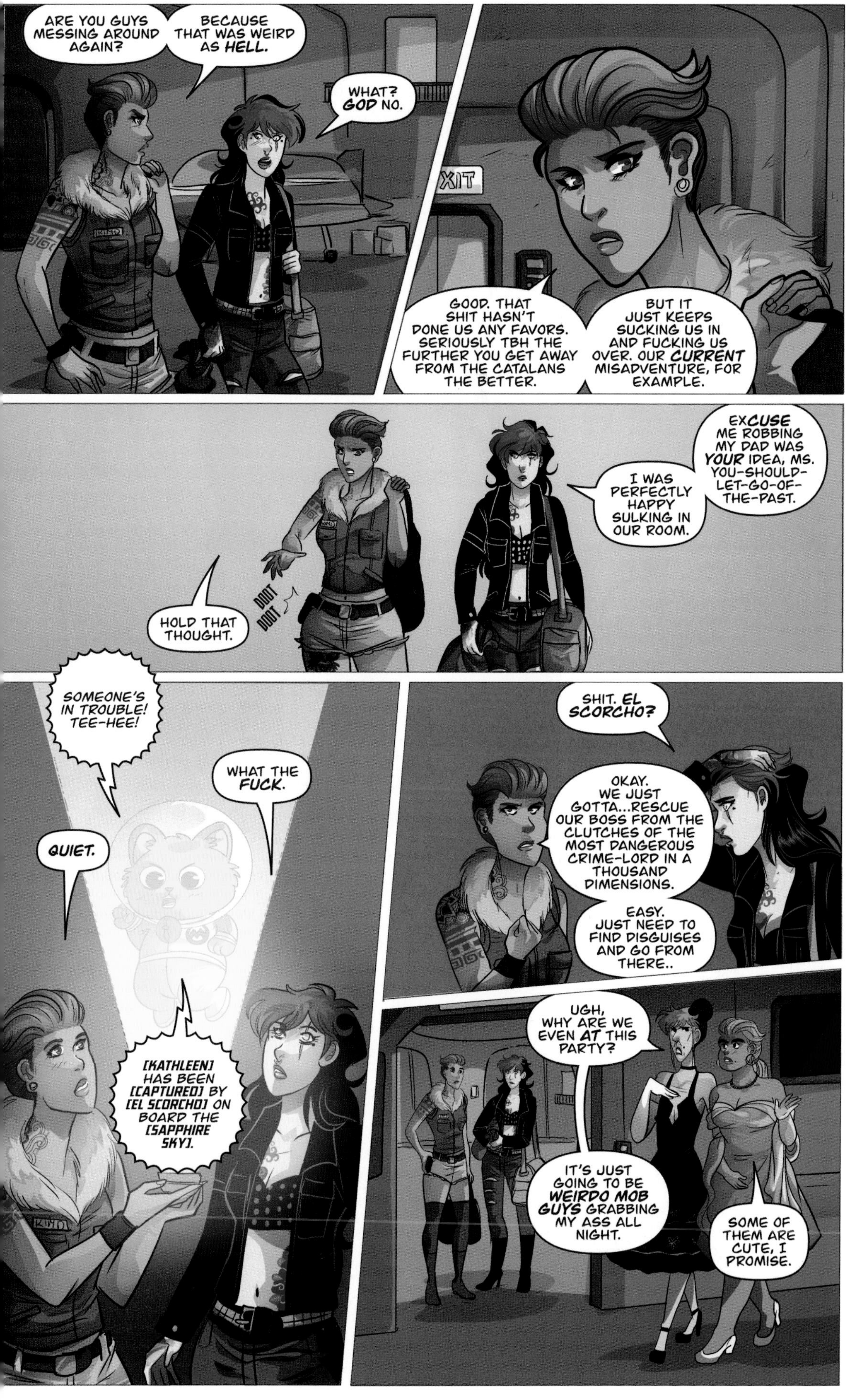
ARE YOU GUYS MESSING AROUND AGAIN?
BECAUSE THAT WAS WEIRD AS **HELL.**
WHAT? **GOD** NO.
EXIT
GOOD. THAT SHIT HASN'T DONE US ANY FAVORS. SERIOUSLY TBH THE FURTHER YOU GET AWAY FROM THE CATALANS THE BETTER.
BUT IT JUST KEEPS SUCKING US IN AND FUCKING US OVER. OUR **CURRENT** MISADVENTURE, FOR EXAMPLE.
EX**CUSE** ME ROBBING MY DAD WAS **YOUR** IDEA, MS. YOU-SHOULD-LET-GO-OF-THE-PAST.
I WAS PERFECTLY HAPPY SULKING IN OUR ROOM.
DOOT DOOT
HOLD THAT THOUGHT.
SOMEONE'S IN TROUBLE! TEE-HEE!
WHAT THE **FUCK.**
QUIET.
[KATHLEEN] HAS BEEN [CAPTURED] BY [EL SCORCHO] ON BOARD THE [SAPPHIRE SKY].
SHIT. **EL SCORCHO?**
OKAY. WE JUST GOTTA...RESCUE OUR BOSS FROM THE CLUTCHES OF THE MOST DANGEROUS CRIME-LORD IN A THOUSAND DIMENSIONS.
EASY. JUST NEED TO FIND DISGUISES AND GO FROM THERE..
UGH, WHY ARE WE EVEN **AT** THIS PARTY?
IT'S JUST GOING TO BE **WEIRDO MOB GUYS** GRABBING MY ASS ALL NIGHT.
SOME OF THEM ARE CUTE, I PROMISE.

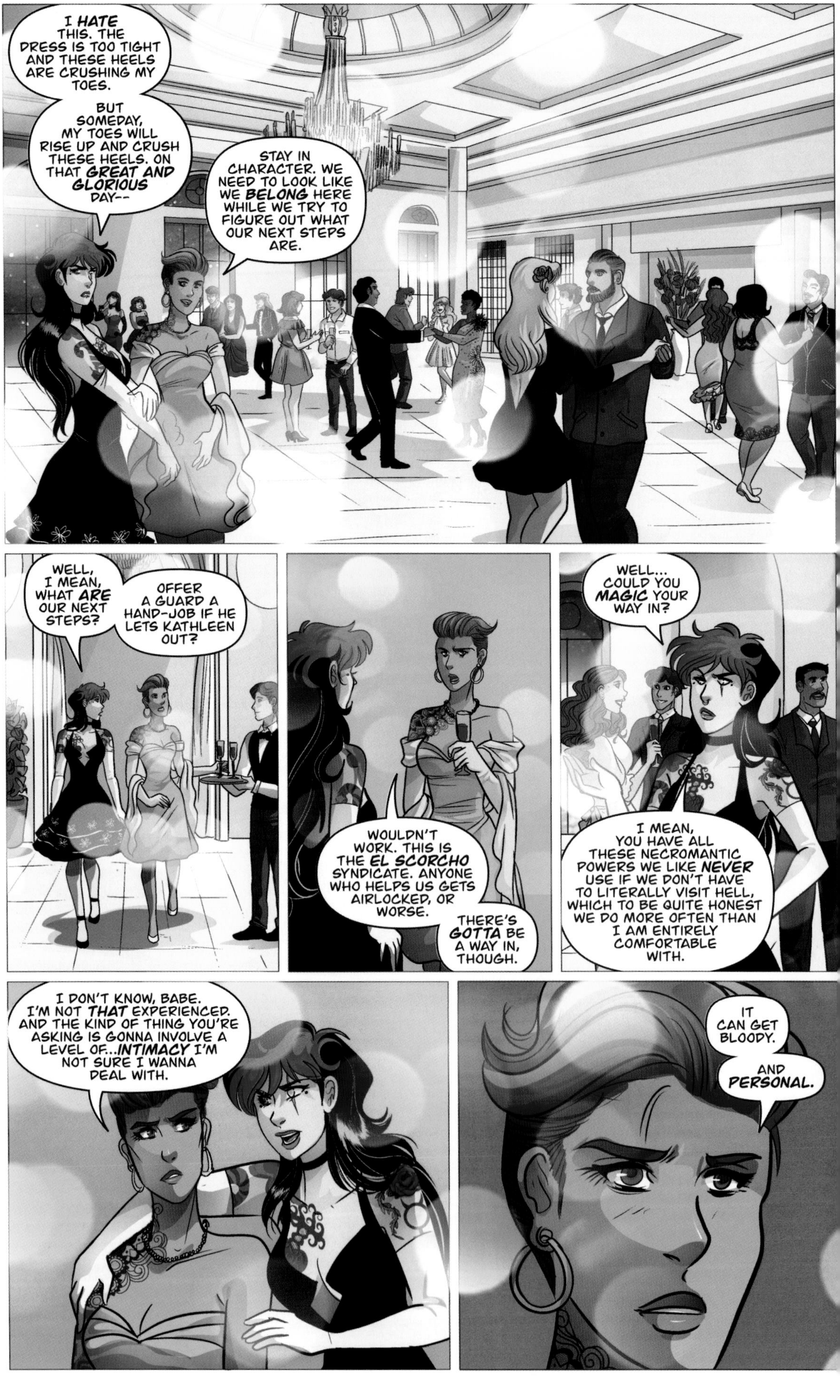
I HATE THIS. THE DRESS IS TOO TIGHT AND THESE HEELS ARE CRUSHING MY TOES.
BUT SOMEDAY, MY TOES WILL RISE UP AND CRUSH THESE HEELS. ON THAT GREAT AND GLORIOUS DAY--
STAY IN CHARACTER. WE NEED TO LOOK LIKE WE BELONG HERE WHILE WE TRY TO FIGURE OUT WHAT OUR NEXT STEPS ARE.
WELL, I MEAN, WHAT ARE OUR NEXT STEPS?
OFFER A GUARD A HAND-JOB IF HE LETS KATHLEEN OUT?
WOULDN'T WORK. THIS IS THE EL SCORCHO SYNDICATE. ANYONE WHO HELPS US GETS AIRLOCKED, OR WORSE.
THERE'S GOTTA BE A WAY IN, THOUGH.
WELL... COULD YOU MAGIC YOUR WAY IN?
I MEAN, YOU HAVE ALL THESE NECROMANTIC POWERS WE LIKE NEVER USE IF WE DON'T HAVE TO LITERALLY VISIT HELL, WHICH TO BE QUITE HONEST WE DO MORE OFTEN THAN I AM ENTIRELY COMFORTABLE WITH.
I DON'T KNOW, BABE. I'M NOT THAT EXPERIENCED. AND THE KIND OF THING YOU'RE ASKING IS GONNA INVOLVE A LEVEL OF...INTIMACY I'M NOT SURE I WANNA DEAL WITH.
IT CAN GET BLOODY.
AND PERSONAL.

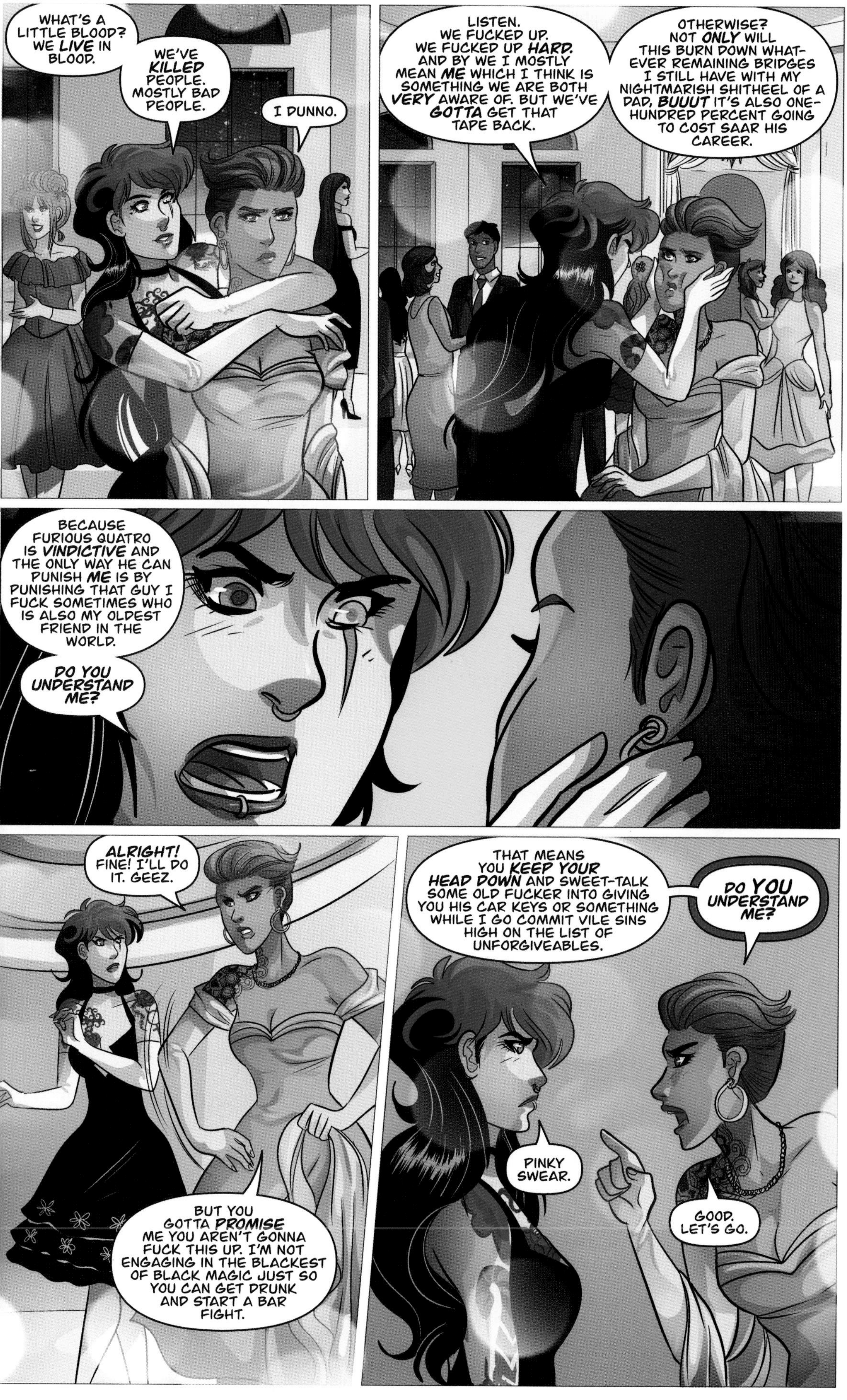
WHAT'S A LITTLE BLOOD? WE LIVE IN BLOOD.
WE'VE KILLED PEOPLE. MOSTLY BAD PEOPLE.
I DUNNO.
LISTEN. WE FUCKED UP. WE FUCKED UP HARD. AND BY WE I MOSTLY MEAN ME WHICH I THINK IS SOMETHING WE ARE BOTH VERY AWARE OF. BUT WE'VE GOTTA GET THAT TAPE BACK.
OTHERWISE? NOT ONLY WILL THIS BURN DOWN WHAT-EVER REMAINING BRIDGES I STILL HAVE WITH MY NIGHTMARISH SHITHEEL OF A DAD, BUUUT IT'S ALSO ONE-HUNDRED PERCENT GOING TO COST SAAR HIS CAREER.
BECAUSE FURIOUS QUATRO IS VINDICTIVE AND THE ONLY WAY HE CAN PUNISH ME IS BY PUNISHING THAT GUY I FUCK SOMETIMES WHO IS ALSO MY OLDEST FRIEND IN THE WORLD.
DO YOU UNDERSTAND ME?
ALRIGHT! FINE! I'LL DO IT. GEEZ.
BUT YOU GOTTA PROMISE ME YOU AREN'T GONNA FUCK THIS UP. I'M NOT ENGAGING IN THE BLACKEST OF BLACK MAGIC JUST SO YOU CAN GET DRUNK AND START A BAR FIGHT.
THAT MEANS YOU KEEP YOUR HEAD DOWN AND SWEET-TALK SOME OLD FUCKER INTO GIVING YOU HIS CAR KEYS OR SOMETHING WHILE I GO COMMIT VILE SINS HIGH ON THE LIST OF UNFORGIVEABLES.
DO YOU UNDERSTAND ME?
PINKY SWEAR.
GOOD. LET'S GO.

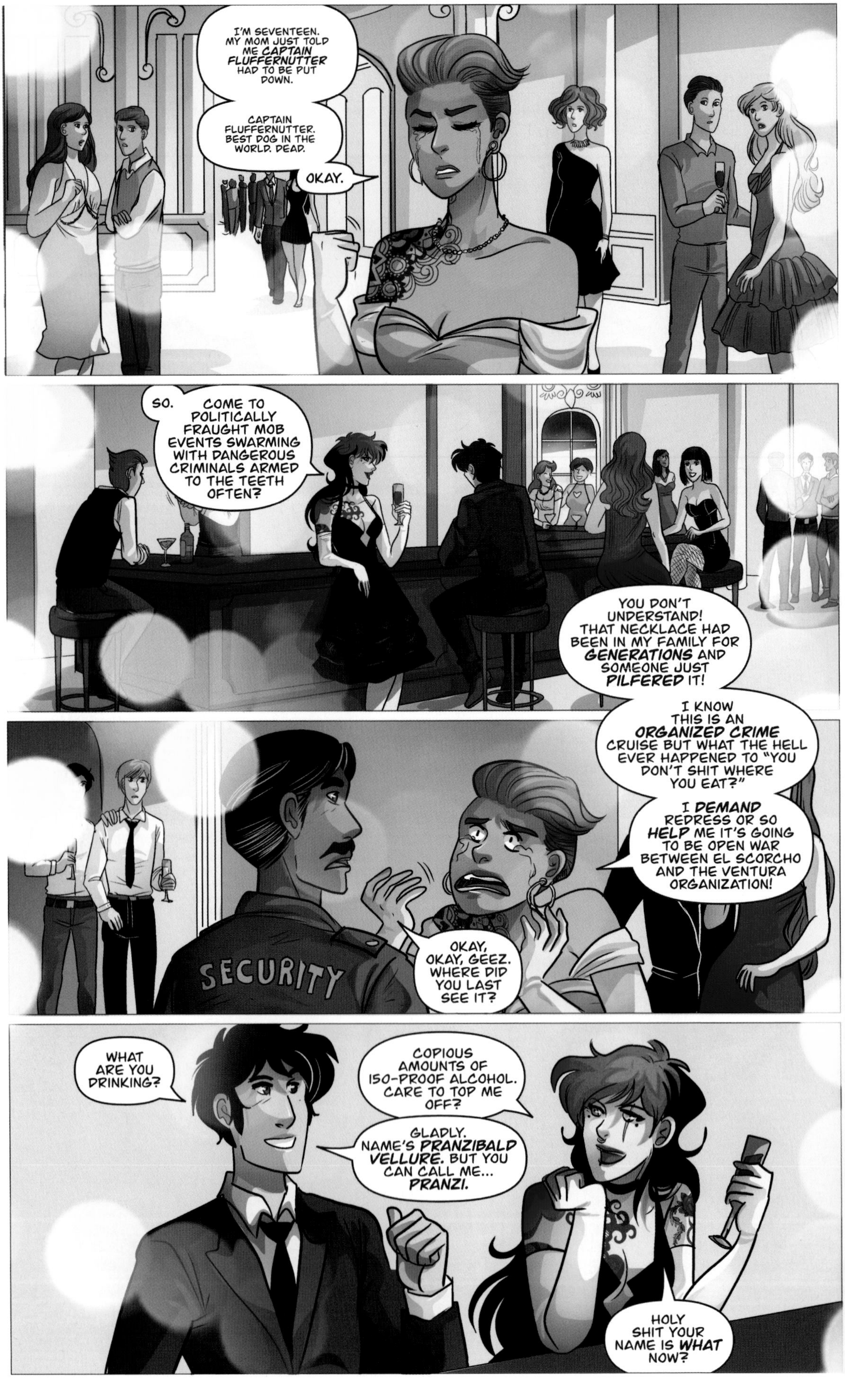
I'M SEVENTEEN. MY MOM JUST TOLD ME CAPTAIN FLUFFERNUTTER HAD TO BE PUT DOWN.
CAPTAIN FLUFFERNUTTER. BEST DOG IN THE WORLD. DEAD.
OKAY.
SO.
COME TO POLITICALLY FRAUGHT MOB EVENTS SWARMING WITH DANGEROUS CRIMINALS ARMED TO THE TEETH OFTEN?
YOU DON'T UNDERSTAND! THAT NECKLACE HAD BEEN IN MY FAMILY FOR GENERATIONS AND SOMEONE JUST PILFERED IT!
I KNOW THIS IS AN ORGANIZED CRIME CRUISE BUT WHAT THE HELL EVER HAPPENED TO "YOU DON'T SHIT WHERE YOU EAT?"
I DEMAND REDRESS OR SO HELP ME IT'S GOING TO BE OPEN WAR BETWEEN EL SCORCHO AND THE VENTURA ORGANIZATION!
SECURITY
OKAY, OKAY, GEEZ. WHERE DID YOU LAST SEE IT?
WHAT ARE YOU DRINKING?
COPIOUS AMOUNTS OF 150-PROOF ALCOHOL. CARE TO TOP ME OFF?
GLADLY. NAME'S PRANZIBALD VELLURE. BUT YOU CAN CALL ME... PRANZI.
HOLY SHIT YOUR NAME IS WHAT NOW?

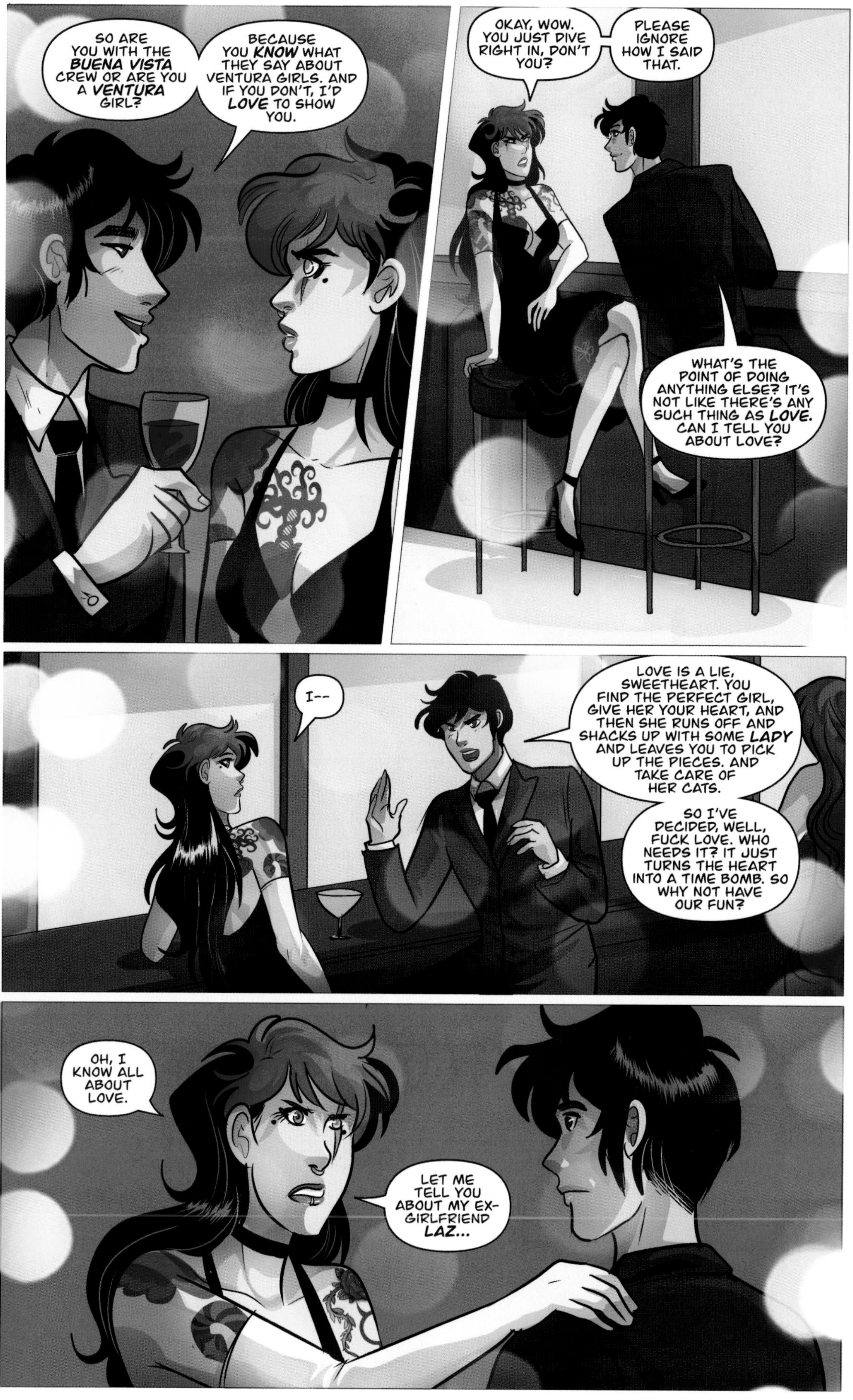
SO ARE YOU WITH THE BUENA VISTA CREW OR ARE YOU A VENTURA GIRL?
BECAUSE YOU KNOW WHAT THEY SAY ABOUT VENTURA GIRLS. AND IF YOU DON'T, I'D LOVE TO SHOW YOU.
OKAY, WOW. YOU JUST DIVE RIGHT IN, DON'T YOU?
PLEASE IGNORE HOW I SAID THAT.
WHAT'S THE POINT OF DOING ANYTHING ELSE? IT'S NOT LIKE THERE'S ANY SUCH THING AS LOVE. CAN I TELL YOU ABOUT LOVE?
I--
LOVE IS A LIE, SWEETHEART. YOU FIND THE PERFECT GIRL, GIVE HER YOUR HEART, AND THEN SHE RUNS OFF AND SHACKS UP WITH SOME LADY AND LEAVES YOU TO PICK UP THE PIECES. AND TAKE CARE OF HER CATS.
SO I'VE DECIDED, WELL, FUCK LOVE. WHO NEEDS IT? IT JUST TURNS THE HEART INTO A TIME BOMB. SO WHY NOT HAVE OUR FUN?
OH, I KNOW ALL ABOUT LOVE.
LET ME TELL YOU ABOUT MY EX-GIRLFRIEND LAZ...

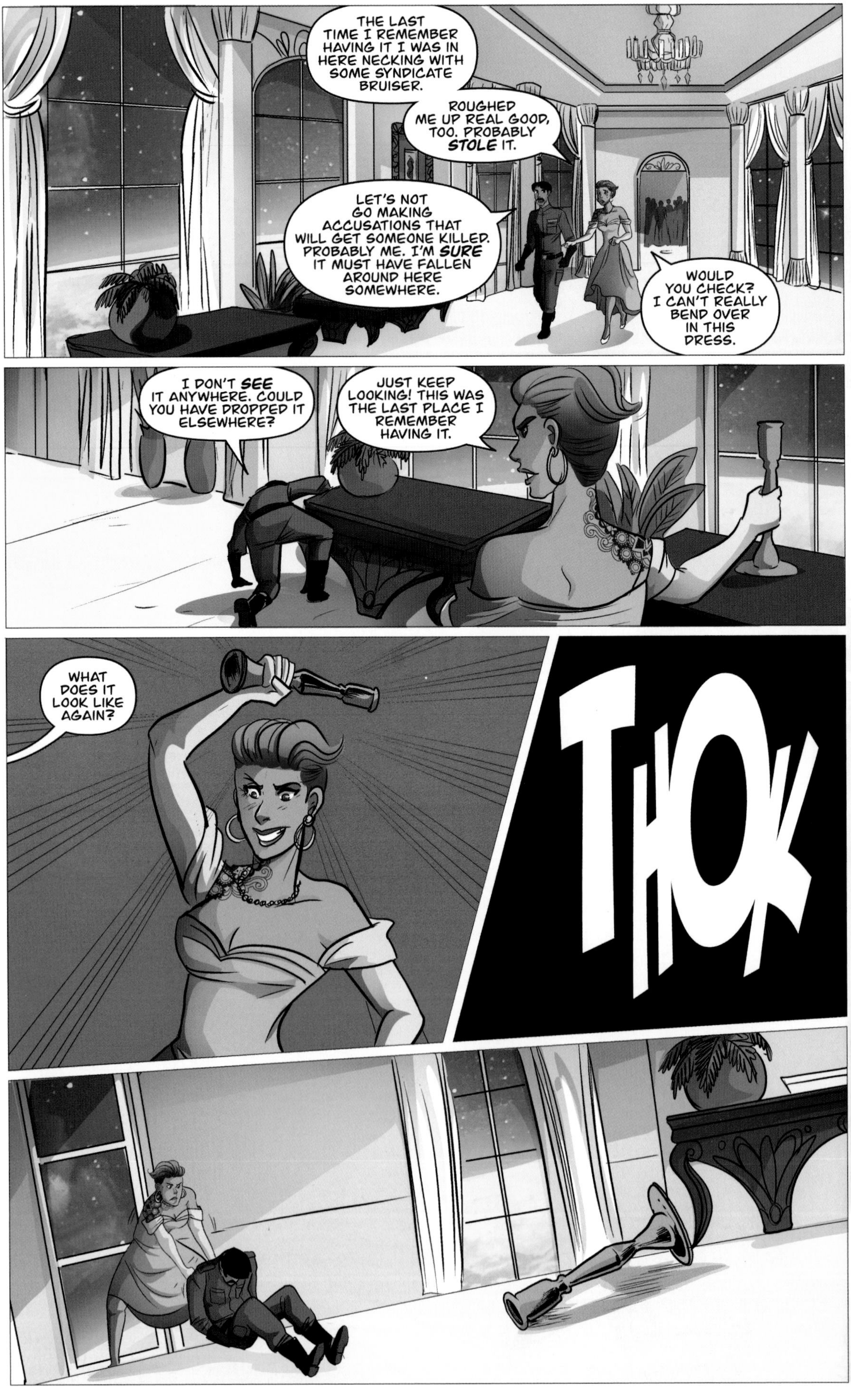
THE LAST TIME I REMEMBER HAVING IT I WAS IN HERE NECKING WITH SOME SYNDICATE BRUISER.
ROUGHED ME UP REAL GOOD, TOO. PROBABLY **STOLE** IT.
LET'S NOT GO MAKING ACCUSATIONS THAT WILL GET SOMEONE KILLED. PROBABLY ME. I'M **SURE** IT MUST HAVE FALLEN AROUND HERE SOMEWHERE.
WOULD YOU CHECK? I CAN'T REALLY BEND OVER IN THIS DRESS.
I DON'T **SEE** IT ANYWHERE. COULD YOU HAVE DROPPED IT ELSEWHERE?
JUST KEEP LOOKING! THIS WAS THE LAST PLACE I REMEMBER HAVING IT.
WHAT DOES IT LOOK LIKE AGAIN?
THOK

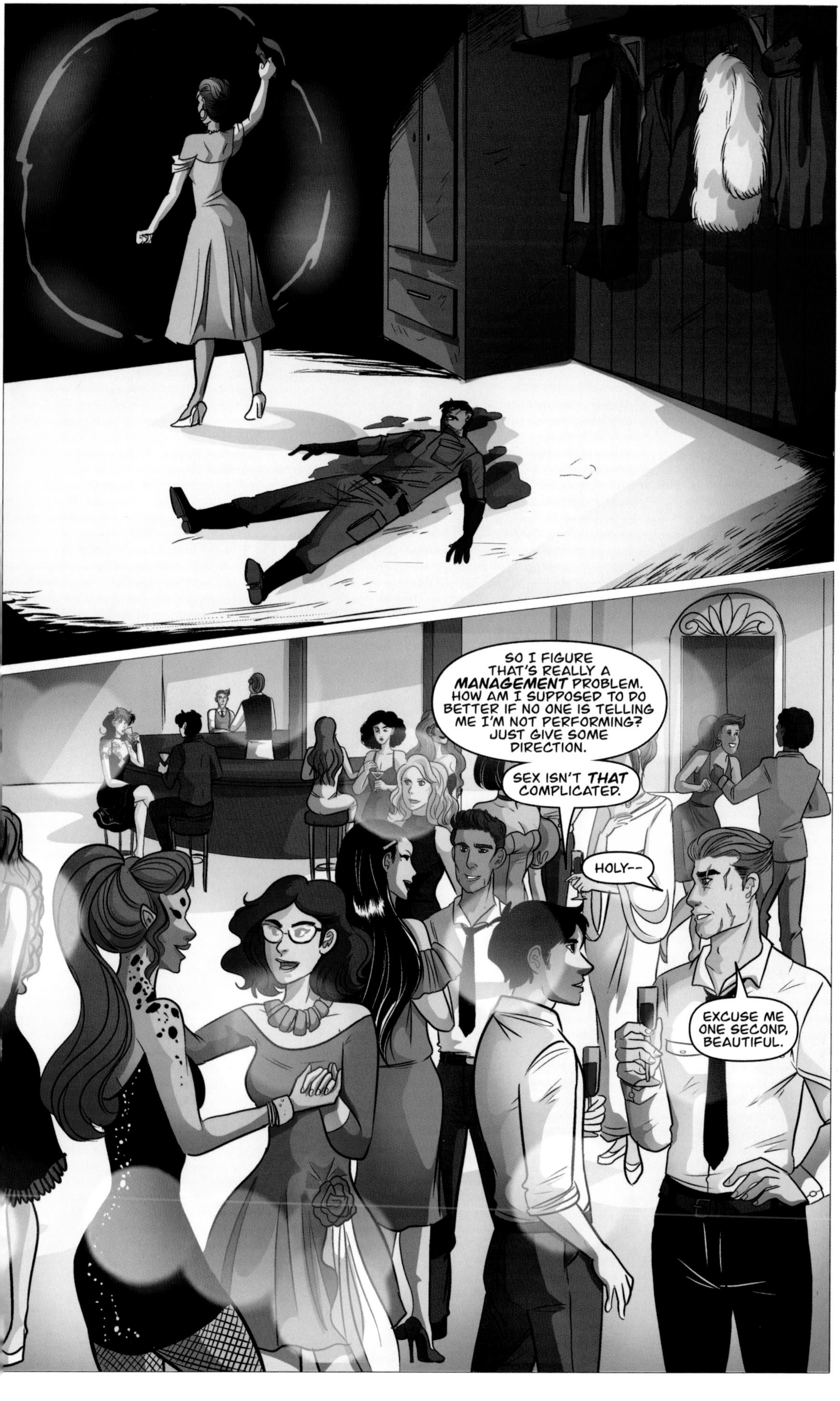
SO I FIGURE THAT'S REALLY A **MANAGEMENT** PROBLEM. HOW AM I SUPPOSED TO DO BETTER IF NO ONE IS TELLING ME I'M NOT PERFORMING? JUST GIVE SOME DIRECTION.
SEX ISN'T ***THAT*** COMPLICATED.
HOLY--
EXCUSE ME ONE SECOND, BEAUTIFUL.

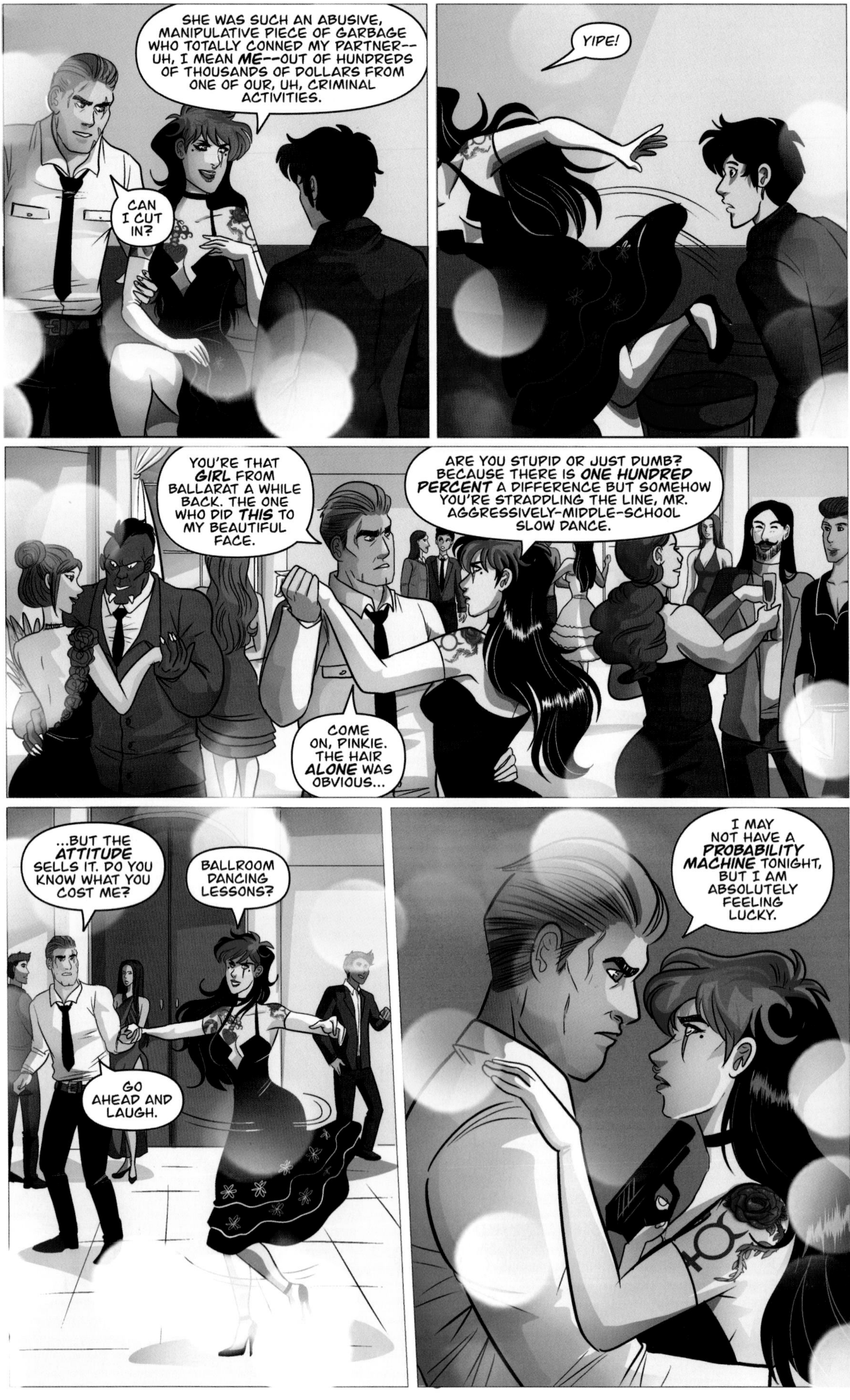
SHE WAS SUCH AN ABUSIVE, MANIPULATIVE PIECE OF GARBAGE WHO TOTALLY CONNED MY PARTNER--UH, I MEAN ME--OUT OF HUNDREDS OF THOUSANDS OF DOLLARS FROM ONE OF OUR, UH, CRIMINAL ACTIVITIES.
CAN I CUT IN?
YIPE!
YOU'RE THAT GIRL FROM BALLARAT A WHILE BACK. THE ONE WHO DID THIS TO MY BEAUTIFUL FACE.
ARE YOU STUPID OR JUST DUMB? BECAUSE THERE IS ONE HUNDRED PERCENT A DIFFERENCE BUT SOMEHOW YOU'RE STRADDLING THE LINE, MR. AGGRESSIVELY-MIDDLE-SCHOOL SLOW DANCE.
COME ON, PINKIE. THE HAIR ALONE WAS OBVIOUS...
...BUT THE ATTITUDE SELLS IT. DO YOU KNOW WHAT YOU COST ME?
BALLROOM DANCING LESSONS?
GO AHEAD AND LAUGH.
I MAY NOT HAVE A PROBABILITY MACHINE TONIGHT, BUT I AM ABSOLUTELY FEELING LUCKY.

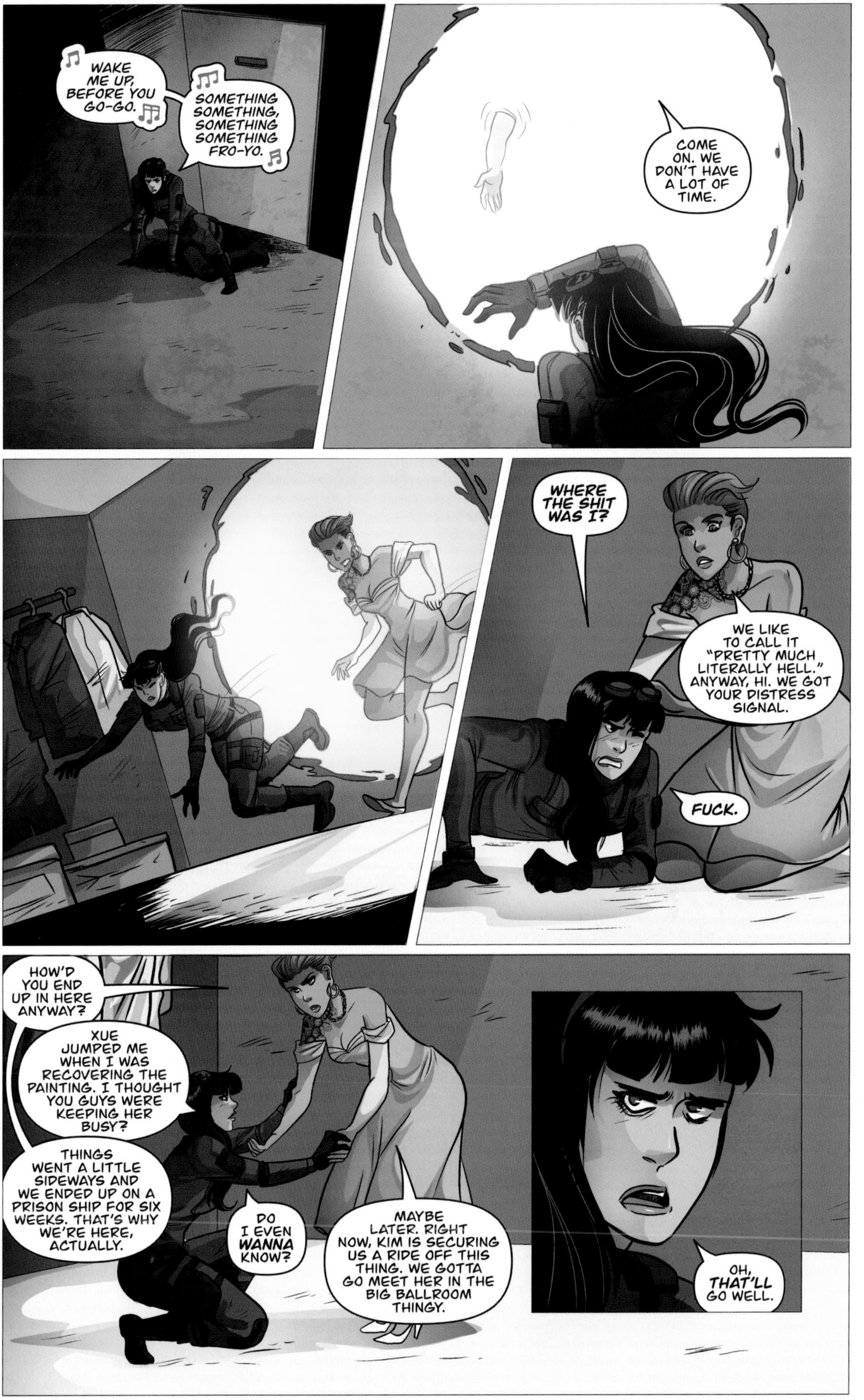
WAKE ME UP, BEFORE YOU GO-GO.
SOMETHING SOMETHING, SOMETHING SOMETHING FRO-YO.
COME ON. WE DON'T HAVE A LOT OF TIME.
WHERE THE SHIT WAS I?
WE LIKE TO CALL IT "PRETTY MUCH LITERALLY HELL." ANYWAY, HI. WE GOT YOUR DISTRESS SIGNAL.
FUCK.
HOW'D YOU END UP IN HERE ANYWAY?
XUE JUMPED ME WHEN I WAS RECOVERING THE PAINTING. I THOUGHT YOU GUYS WERE KEEPING HER BUSY?
THINGS WENT A LITTLE SIDEWAYS AND WE ENDED UP ON A PRISON SHIP FOR SIX WEEKS. THAT'S WHY WE'RE HERE, ACTUALLY.
DO I EVEN WANNA KNOW?
MAYBE LATER. RIGHT NOW, KIM IS SECURING US A RIDE OFF THIS THING. WE GOTTA GO MEET HER IN THE BIG BALLROOM THINGY.
OH, THAT'LL GO WELL.

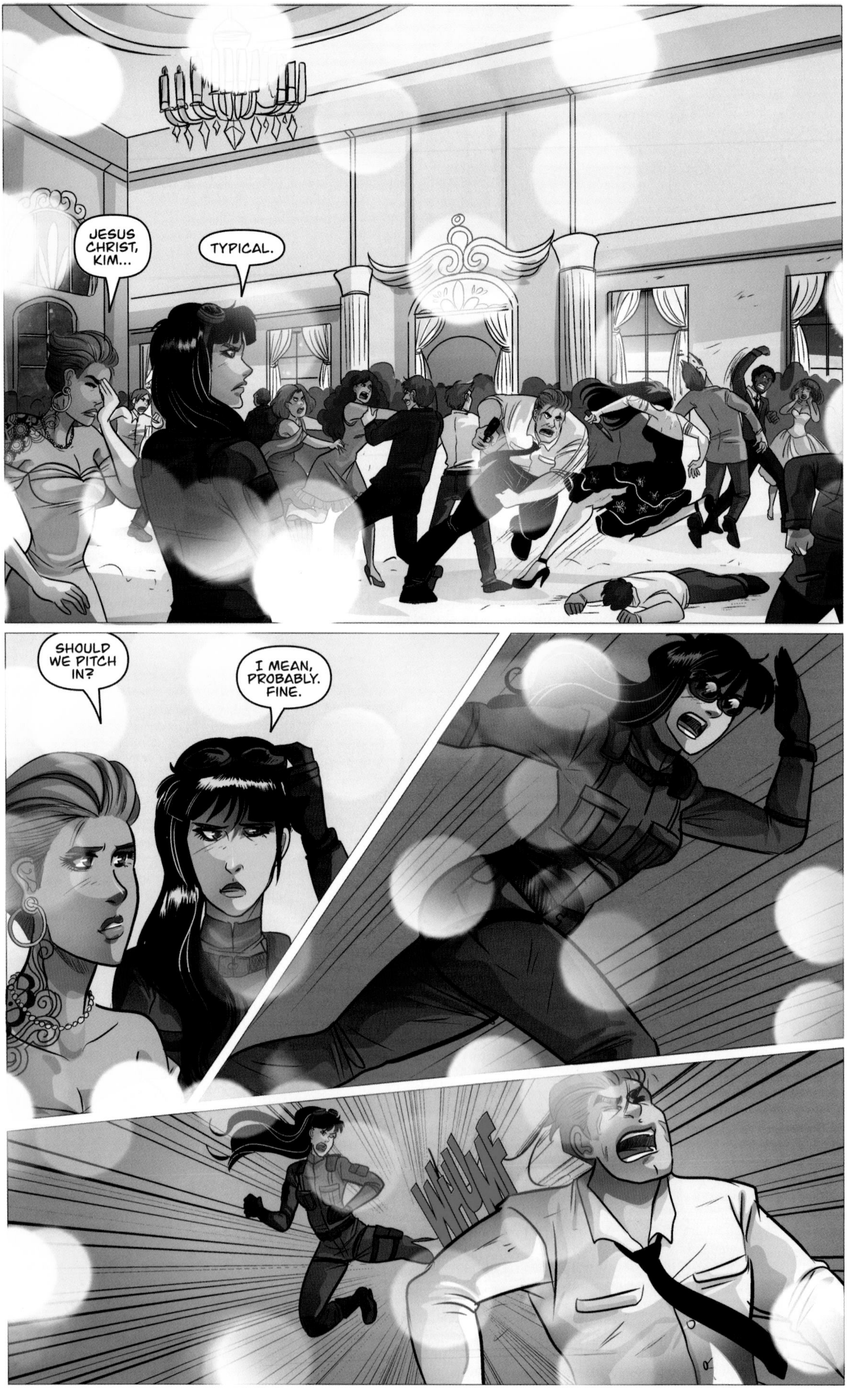
JESUS CHRIST, KIM...
TYPICAL.
SHOULD WE PITCH IN?
I MEAN, PROBABLY. FINE.
WHUMF

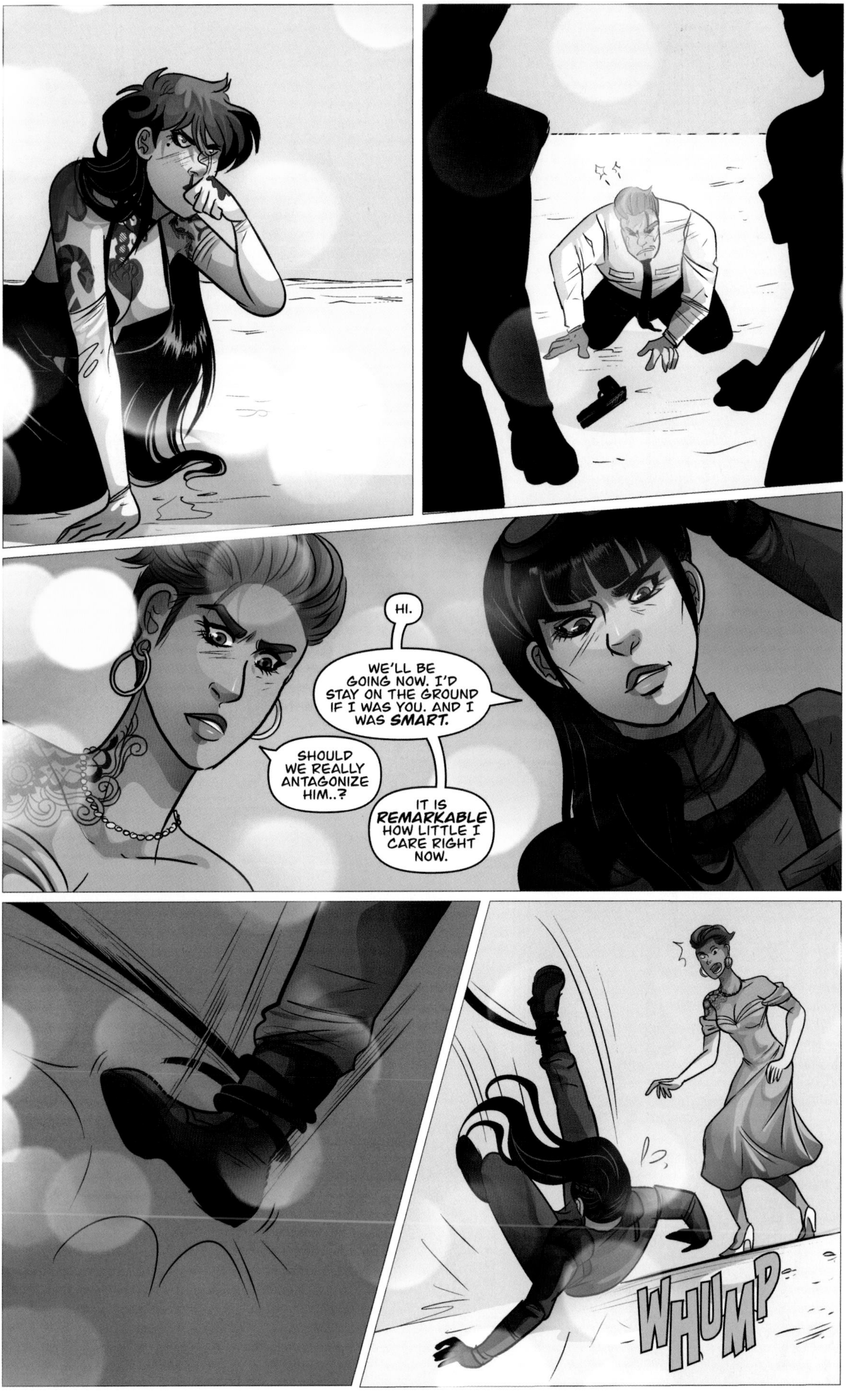
HI.
WE'LL BE GOING NOW. I'D STAY ON THE GROUND IF I WAS YOU. AND I WAS SMART.
SHOULD WE REALLY ANTAGONIZE HIM..?
IT IS REMARKABLE HOW LITTLE I CARE RIGHT NOW.
WHUMP

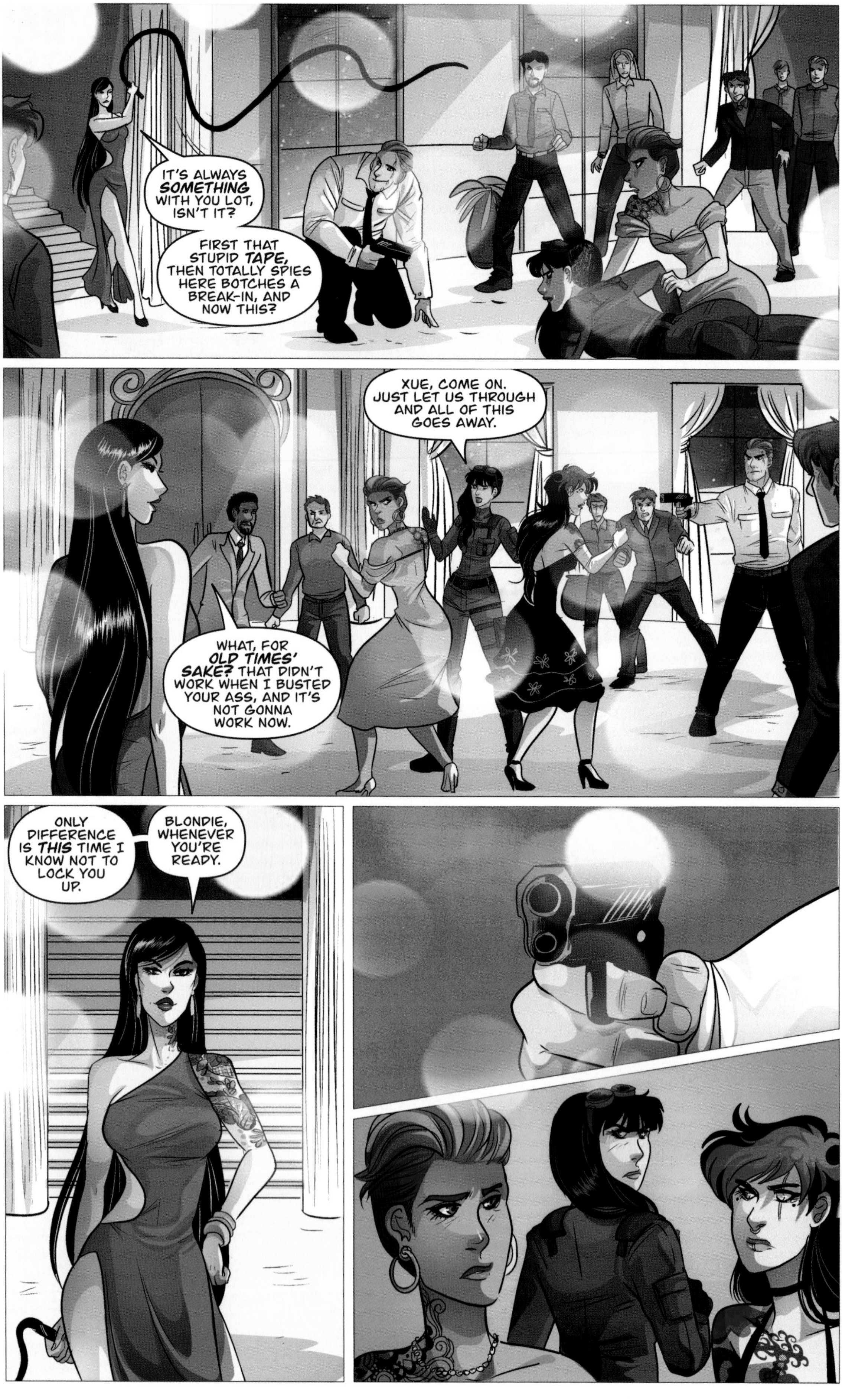

IT'S ALWAYS SOMETHING WITH YOU LOT, ISN'T IT?
FIRST THAT STUPID TAPE, THEN TOTALLY SPIES HERE BOTCHES A BREAK-IN, AND NOW THIS?
XUE, COME ON. JUST LET US THROUGH AND ALL OF THIS GOES AWAY.
WHAT, FOR OLD TIMES' SAKE? THAT DIDN'T WORK WHEN I BUSTED YOUR ASS, AND IT'S NOT GONNA WORK NOW.
ONLY DIFFERENCE IS THIS TIME I KNOW NOT TO LOCK YOU UP.
BLONDIE, WHENEVER YOU'RE READY.

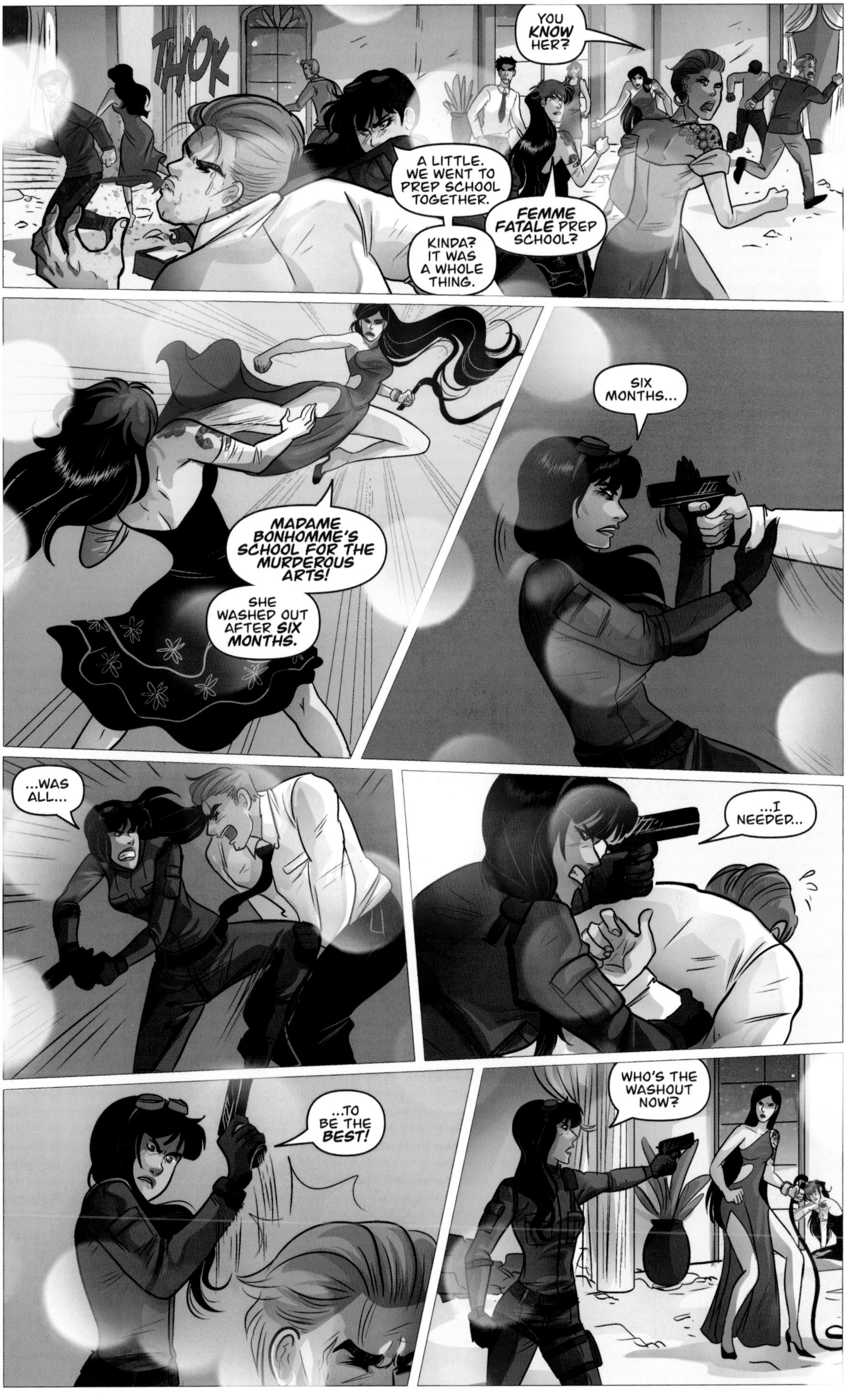
THOK
YOU KNOW HER?
A LITTLE. WE WENT TO PREP SCHOOL TOGETHER.
FEMME FATALE PREP SCHOOL?
KINDA? IT WAS A WHOLE THING.
MADAME BONHOMME'S SCHOOL FOR THE MURDEROUS ARTS!
SHE WASHED OUT AFTER SIX MONTHS.
SIX MONTHS...
...WAS ALL...
...I NEEDED...
...TO BE THE BEST!
WHO'S THE WASHOUT NOW?

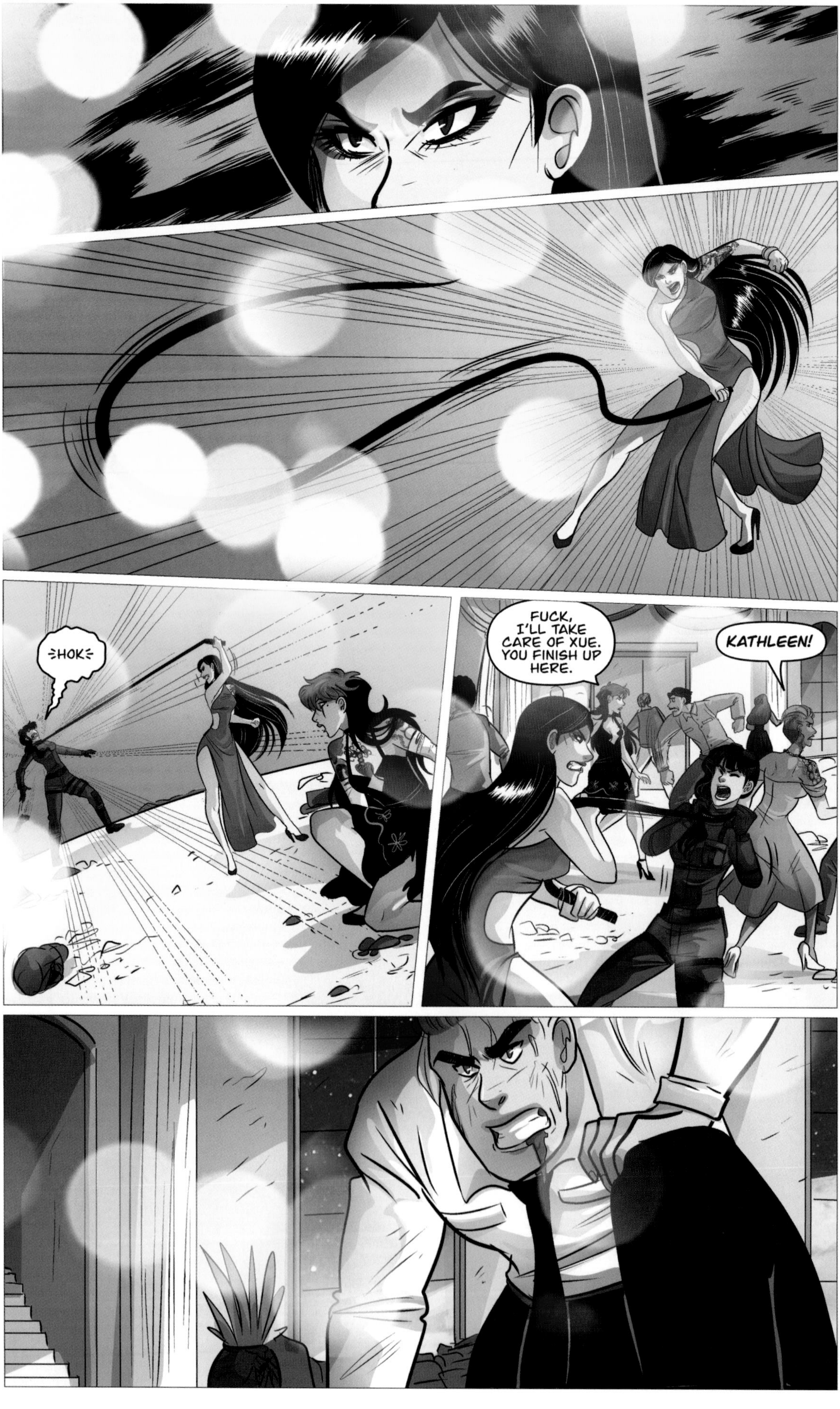
HOK
FUCK, I'LL TAKE CARE OF XUE. YOU FINISH UP HERE.
KATHLEEN!

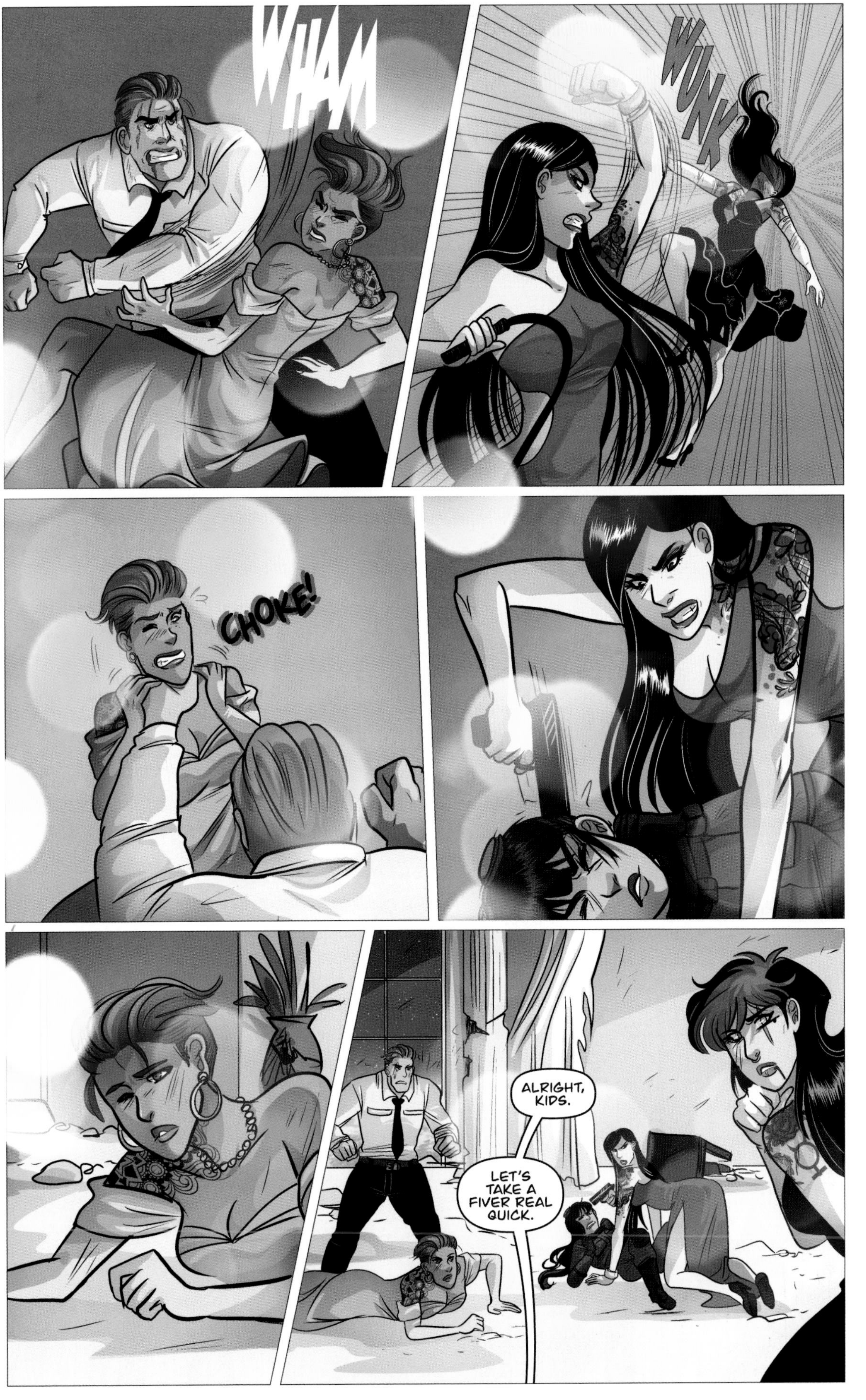
WHAM
WUNK
CHOKE!
ALRIGHT, KIDS.
LET'S TAKE A FIVER REAL QUICK.

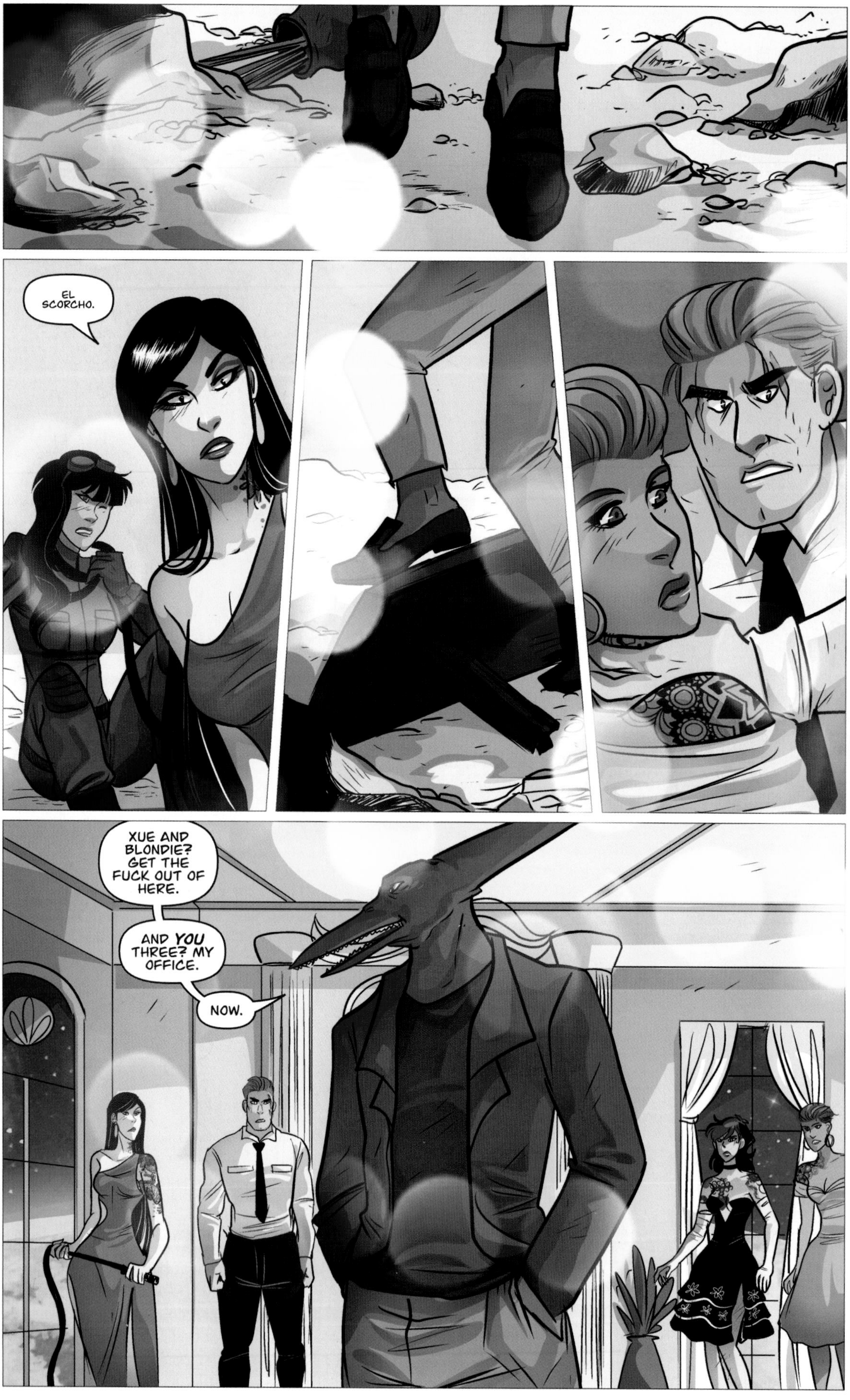
EL SCORCHO.
XUE AND BLONDIE? GET THE FUCK OUT OF HERE.
AND *YOU* THREE? MY OFFICE.
NOW.

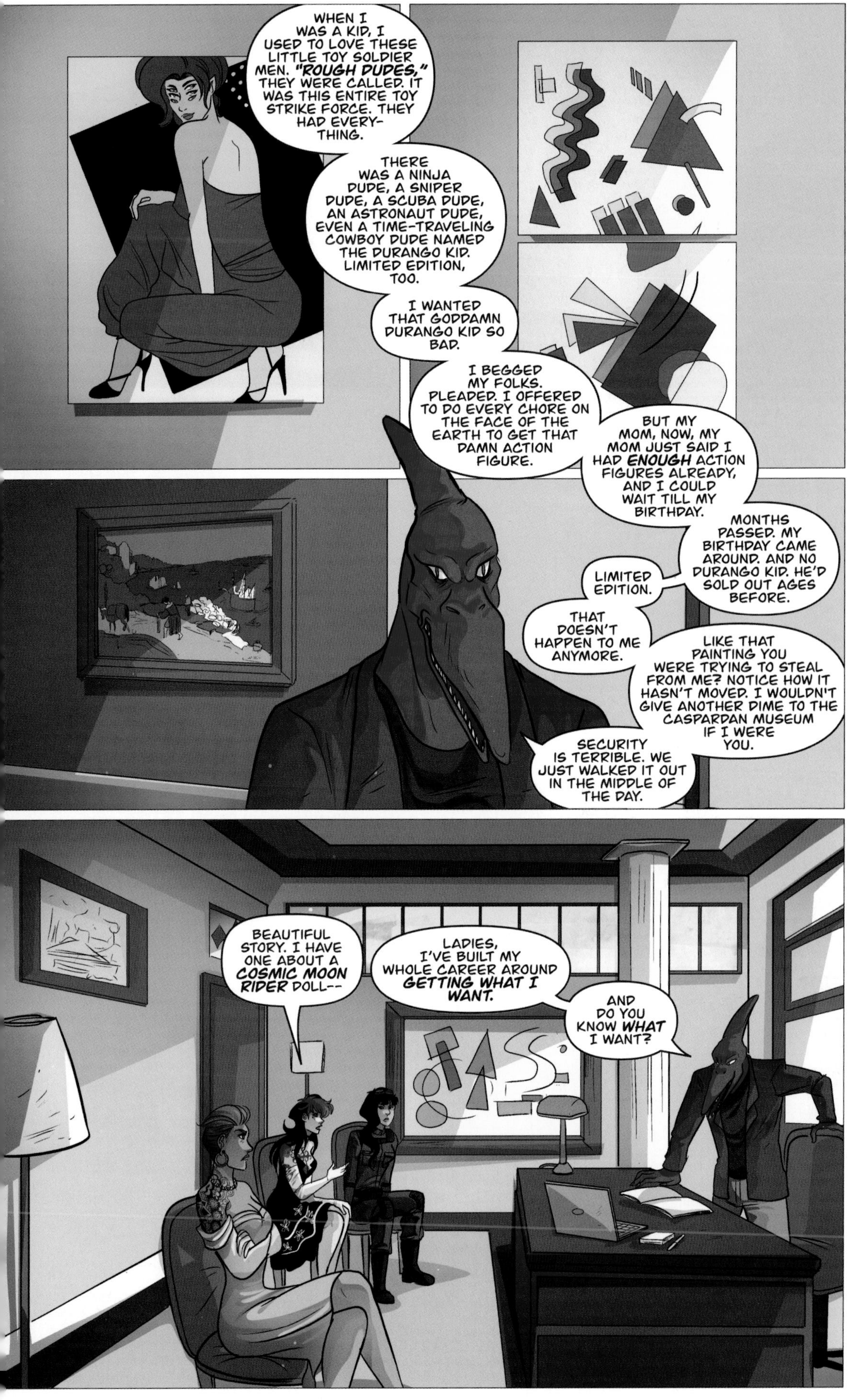
WHEN I WAS A KID, I USED TO LOVE THESE LITTLE TOY SOLDIER MEN. "ROUGH DUDES," THEY WERE CALLED. IT WAS THIS ENTIRE TOY STRIKE FORCE. THEY HAD EVERY-THING.
THERE WAS A NINJA DUDE, A SNIPER DUDE, A SCUBA DUDE, AN ASTRONAUT DUDE, EVEN A TIME-TRAVELING COWBOY DUDE NAMED THE DURANGO KID. LIMITED EDITION, TOO.
I WANTED THAT GODDAMN DURANGO KID SO BAD.
I BEGGED MY FOLKS. PLEADED. I OFFERED TO DO EVERY CHORE ON THE FACE OF THE EARTH TO GET THAT DAMN ACTION FIGURE.
BUT MY MOM, NOW, MY MOM JUST SAID I HAD ENOUGH ACTION FIGURES ALREADY, AND I COULD WAIT TILL MY BIRTHDAY.
MONTHS PASSED. MY BIRTHDAY CAME AROUND. AND NO DURANGO KID. HE'D SOLD OUT AGES BEFORE.
LIMITED EDITION.
THAT DOESN'T HAPPEN TO ME ANYMORE.
LIKE THAT PAINTING YOU WERE TRYING TO STEAL FROM ME? NOTICE HOW IT HASN'T MOVED. I WOULDN'T GIVE ANOTHER DIME TO THE CASPARDAN MUSEUM IF I WERE YOU.
SECURITY IS TERRIBLE. WE JUST WALKED IT OUT IN THE MIDDLE OF THE DAY.
BEAUTIFUL STORY. I HAVE ONE ABOUT A COSMIC MOON RIDER DOLL--
LADIES, I'VE BUILT MY WHOLE CAREER AROUND GETTING WHAT I WANT.
AND DO YOU KNOW WHAT I WANT?

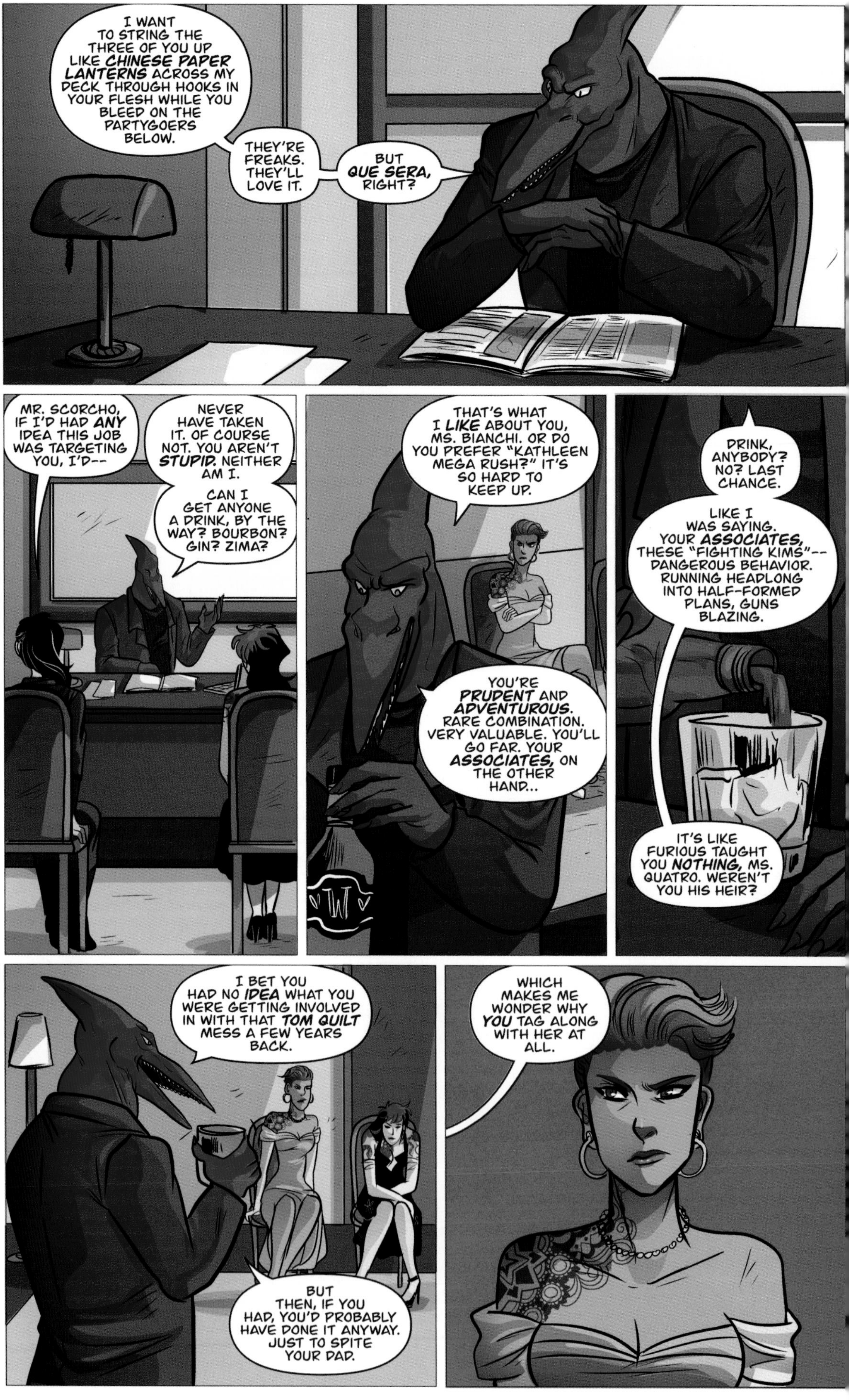
I WANT TO STRING THE THREE OF YOU UP LIKE CHINESE PAPER LANTERNS ACROSS MY DECK THROUGH HOOKS IN YOUR FLESH WHILE YOU BLEED ON THE PARTYGOERS BELOW.
THEY'RE FREAKS. THEY'LL LOVE IT.
BUT QUE SERA, RIGHT?
MR. SCORCHO, IF I'D HAD ANY IDEA THIS JOB WAS TARGETING YOU, I'D--
NEVER HAVE TAKEN IT. OF COURSE NOT. YOU AREN'T STUPID. NEITHER AM I.
CAN I GET ANYONE A DRINK, BY THE WAY? BOURBON? GIN? ZIMA?
THAT'S WHAT I LIKE ABOUT YOU, MS. BIANCHI. OR DO YOU PREFER "KATHLEEN MEGA RUSH?" IT'S SO HARD TO KEEP UP.
YOU'RE PRUDENT AND ADVENTUROUS. RARE COMBINATION. VERY VALUABLE. YOU'LL GO FAR. YOUR ASSOCIATES, ON THE OTHER HAND...
DRINK, ANYBODY? NO? LAST CHANCE.
LIKE I WAS SAYING. YOUR ASSOCIATES, THESE "FIGHTING KIMS"-- DANGEROUS BEHAVIOR. RUNNING HEADLONG INTO HALF-FORMED PLANS, GUNS BLAZING.
IT'S LIKE FURIOUS TAUGHT YOU NOTHING, MS. QUATRO. WEREN'T YOU HIS HEIR?
I BET YOU HAD NO IDEA WHAT YOU WERE GETTING INVOLVED IN WITH THAT TOM QUILT MESS A FEW YEARS BACK.
BUT THEN, IF YOU HAD, YOU'D PROBABLY HAVE DONE IT ANYWAY. JUST TO SPITE YOUR DAD.
WHICH MAKES ME WONDER WHY YOU TAG ALONG WITH HER AT ALL.

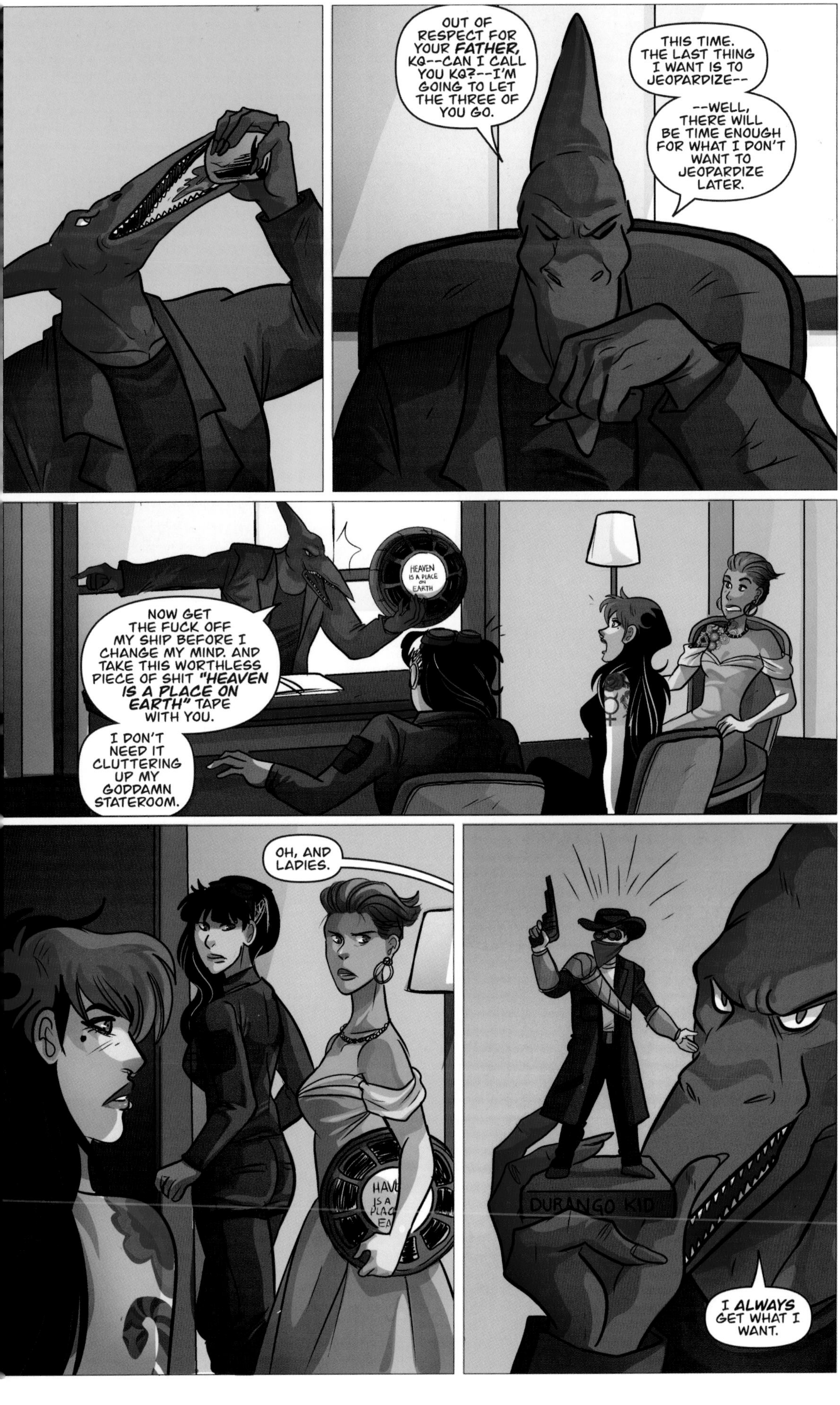
OUT OF RESPECT FOR YOUR FATHER, KQ--CAN I CALL YOU KQ?--I'M GOING TO LET THE THREE OF YOU GO.
THIS TIME. THE LAST THING I WANT IS TO JEOPARDIZE--
--WELL, THERE WILL BE TIME ENOUGH FOR WHAT I DON'T WANT TO JEOPARDIZE LATER.
HEAVEN IS A PLACE ON EARTH
NOW GET THE FUCK OFF MY SHIP BEFORE I CHANGE MY MIND. AND TAKE THIS WORTHLESS PIECE OF SHIT "HEAVEN IS A PLACE ON EARTH" TAPE WITH YOU.
I DON'T NEED IT CLUTTERING UP MY GODDAMN STATEROOM.
OH, AND LADIES.
DURANGO KID
I ALWAYS GET WHAT I WANT.

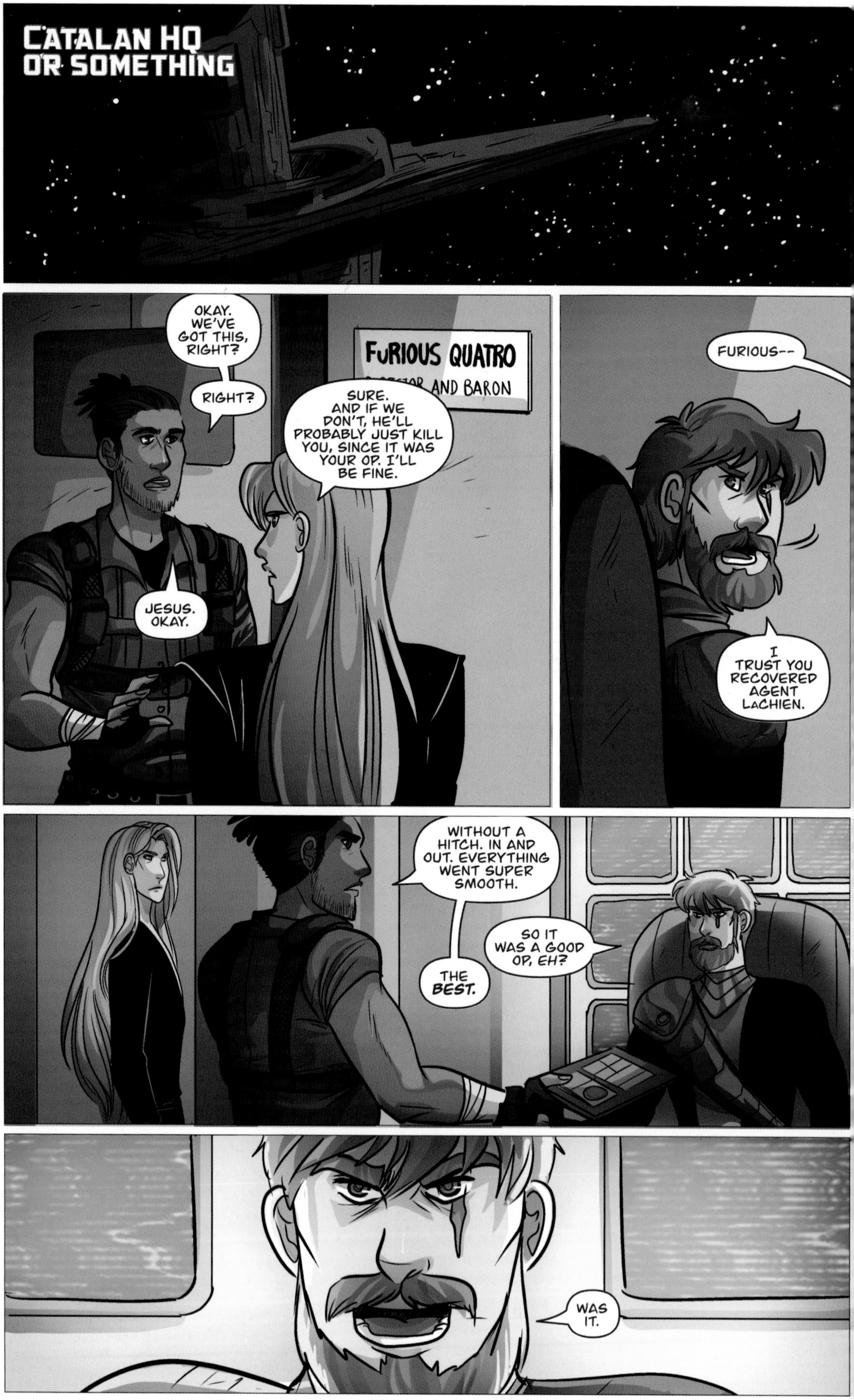
CATALAN HQ OR SOMETHING
OKAY. WE'VE GOT THIS, RIGHT?
RIGHT?
SURE. AND IF WE DON'T, HE'LL PROBABLY JUST KILL YOU, SINCE IT WAS YOUR OP. I'LL BE FINE.
FURIOUS QUATRO
AND BARON
JESUS. OKAY.
FURIOUS--
I TRUST YOU RECOVERED AGENT LACHIEN.
WITHOUT A HITCH. IN AND OUT. EVERYTHING WENT SUPER SMOOTH.
SO IT WAS A GOOD OP, EH?
THE *BEST.*
WAS IT.

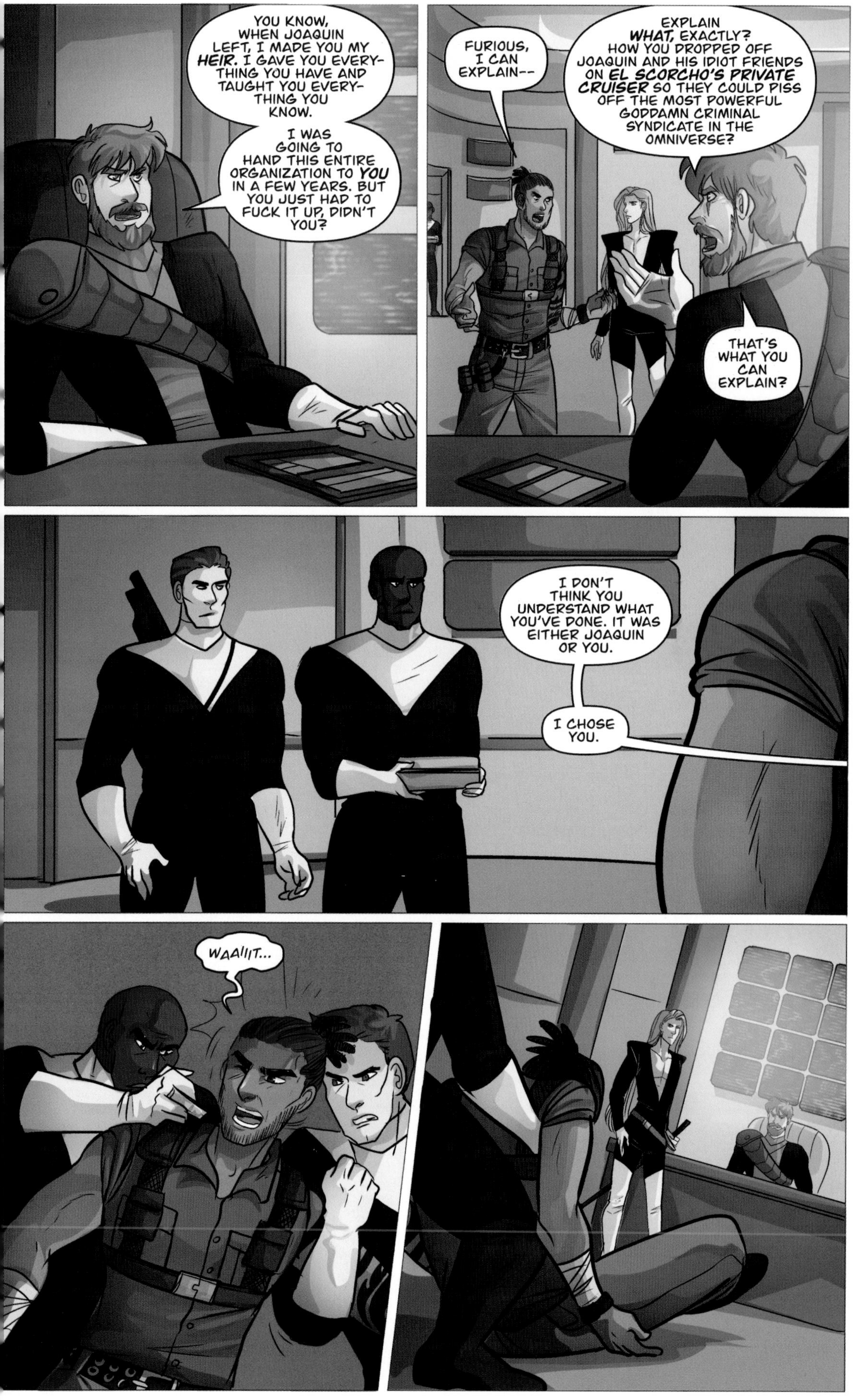
YOU KNOW, WHEN JOAQUIN LEFT, I MADE YOU MY HEIR. I GAVE YOU EVERY-THING YOU HAVE AND TAUGHT YOU EVERY-THING YOU KNOW.
I WAS GOING TO HAND THIS ENTIRE ORGANIZATION TO YOU IN A FEW YEARS. BUT YOU JUST HAD TO FUCK IT UP, DIDN'T YOU?
FURIOUS, I CAN EXPLAIN--
EXPLAIN WHAT, EXACTLY? HOW YOU DROPPED OFF JOAQUIN AND HIS IDIOT FRIENDS ON EL SCORCHO'S PRIVATE CRUISER SO THEY COULD PISS OFF THE MOST POWERFUL GODDAMN CRIMINAL SYNDICATE IN THE OMNIVERSE?
THAT'S WHAT YOU CAN EXPLAIN?
I DON'T THINK YOU UNDERSTAND WHAT YOU'VE DONE. IT WAS EITHER JOAQUIN OR YOU.
I CHOSE YOU.
WAAIIIT...

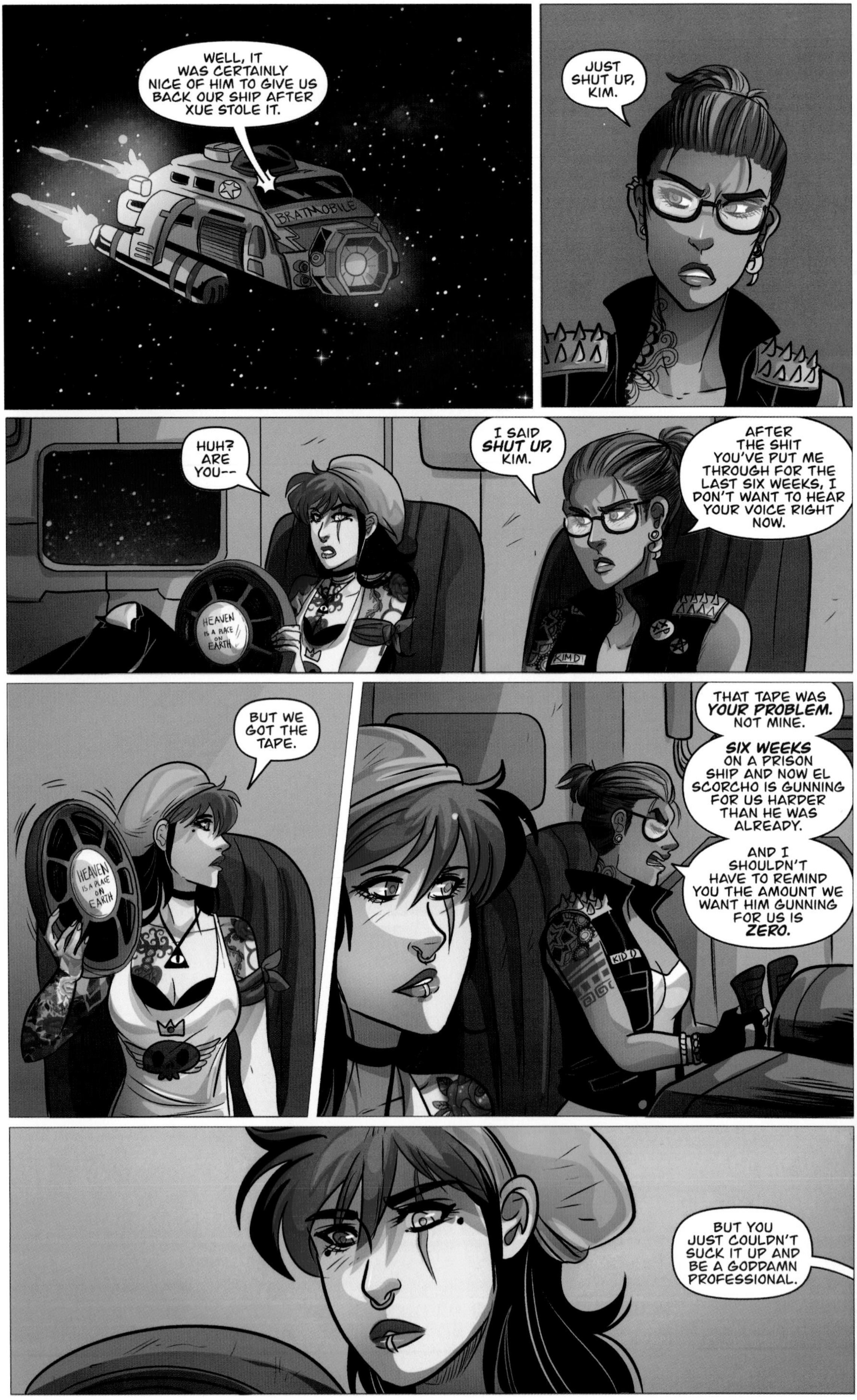

WELL, IT WAS CERTAINLY NICE OF HIM TO GIVE US BACK OUR SHIP AFTER XUE STOLE IT.
BRATMOBILE
JUST SHUT UP, KIM.
HUH? ARE YOU--
I SAID SHUT UP, KIM.
AFTER THE SHIT YOU'VE PUT ME THROUGH FOR THE LAST SIX WEEKS, I DON'T WANT TO HEAR YOUR VOICE RIGHT NOW.
HEAVEN IS A PLACE ON EARTH
KIM D
BUT WE GOT THE TAPE.
HEAVEN IS A PLACE ON EARTH
THAT TAPE WAS YOUR PROBLEM. NOT MINE.
SIX WEEKS ON A PRISON SHIP AND NOW EL SCORCHO IS GUNNING FOR US HARDER THAN HE WAS ALREADY.
AND I SHOULDN'T HAVE TO REMIND YOU THE AMOUNT WE WANT HIM GUNNING FOR US IS ZERO.
KIM D
BUT YOU JUST COULDN'T SUCK IT UP AND BE A GODDAMN PROFESSIONAL.

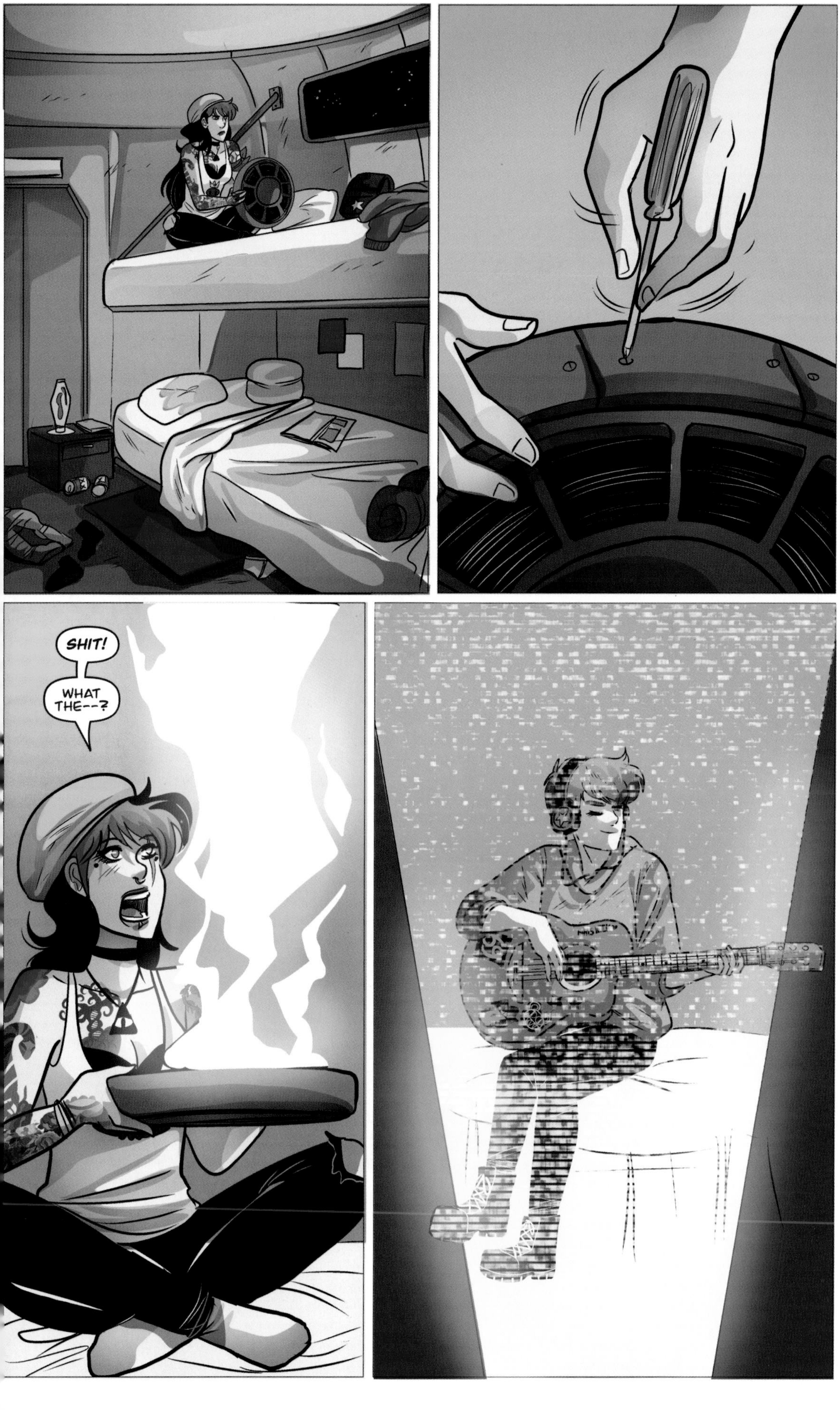
SHIT!
WHAT THE--?

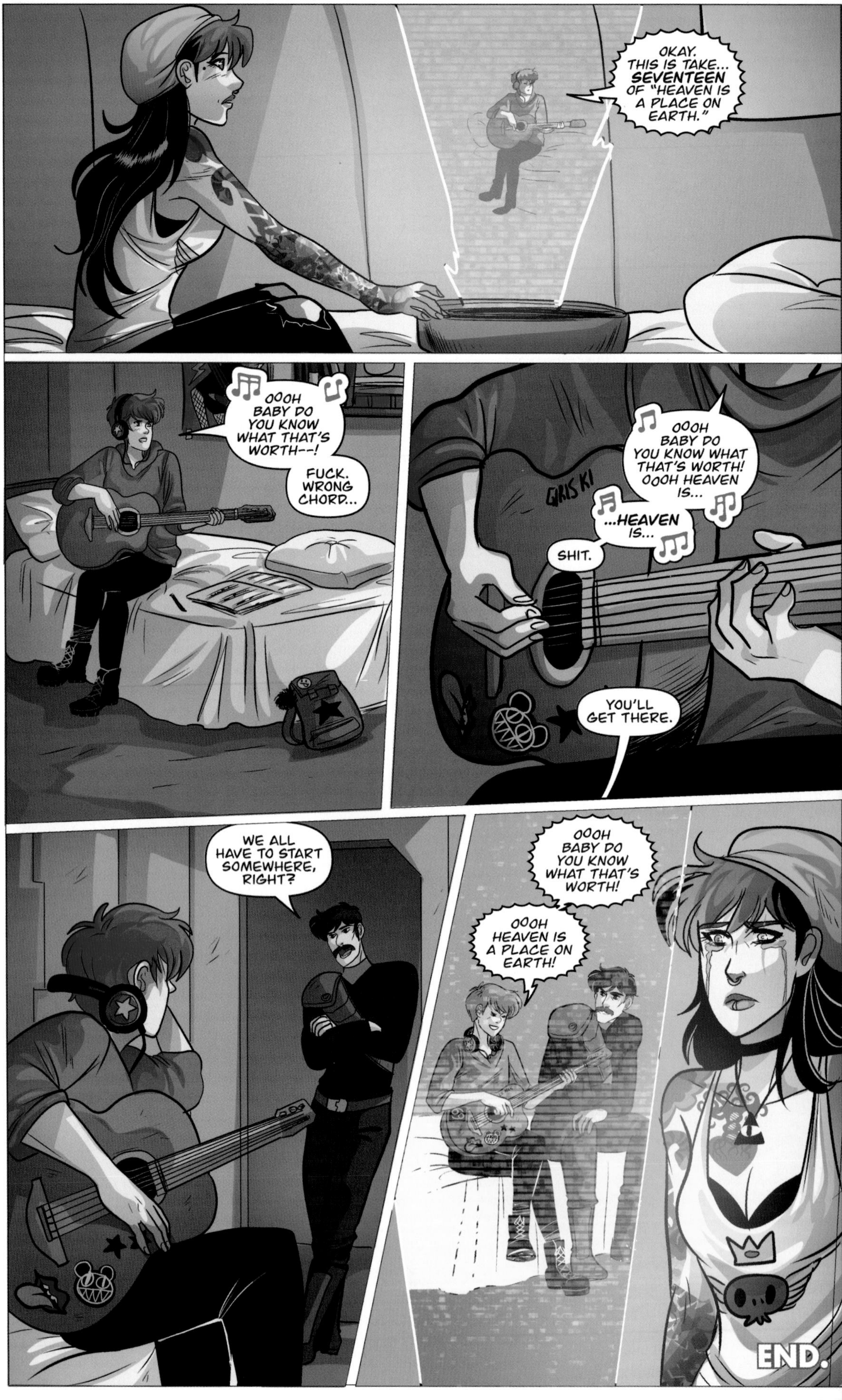
OKAY. THIS IS TAKE... **SEVENTEEN** OF "HEAVEN IS A PLACE ON EARTH."
OOOH BABY DO YOU KNOW WHAT THAT'S WORTH--!
FUCK. WRONG CHORD...
OOOH BABY DO YOU KNOW WHAT THAT'S WORTH! OOOH HEAVEN IS...
...HEAVEN IS...
SHIT.
YOU'LL GET THERE.
WE ALL HAVE TO START SOMEWHERE, RIGHT?
OOOH BABY DO YOU KNOW WHAT THAT'S WORTH!
OOOH HEAVEN IS A PLACE ON EARTH!
END.

Oh S#!T It's KIM & KIM

Cover Gallery

Issue issue #1, convention exclusive
by Michael Avon Oeming

Issue #1 cover
line art by Eva Cabrera
colors by Claudia Aguirre

Issue #2-5 covers
art by Phillip Sevy

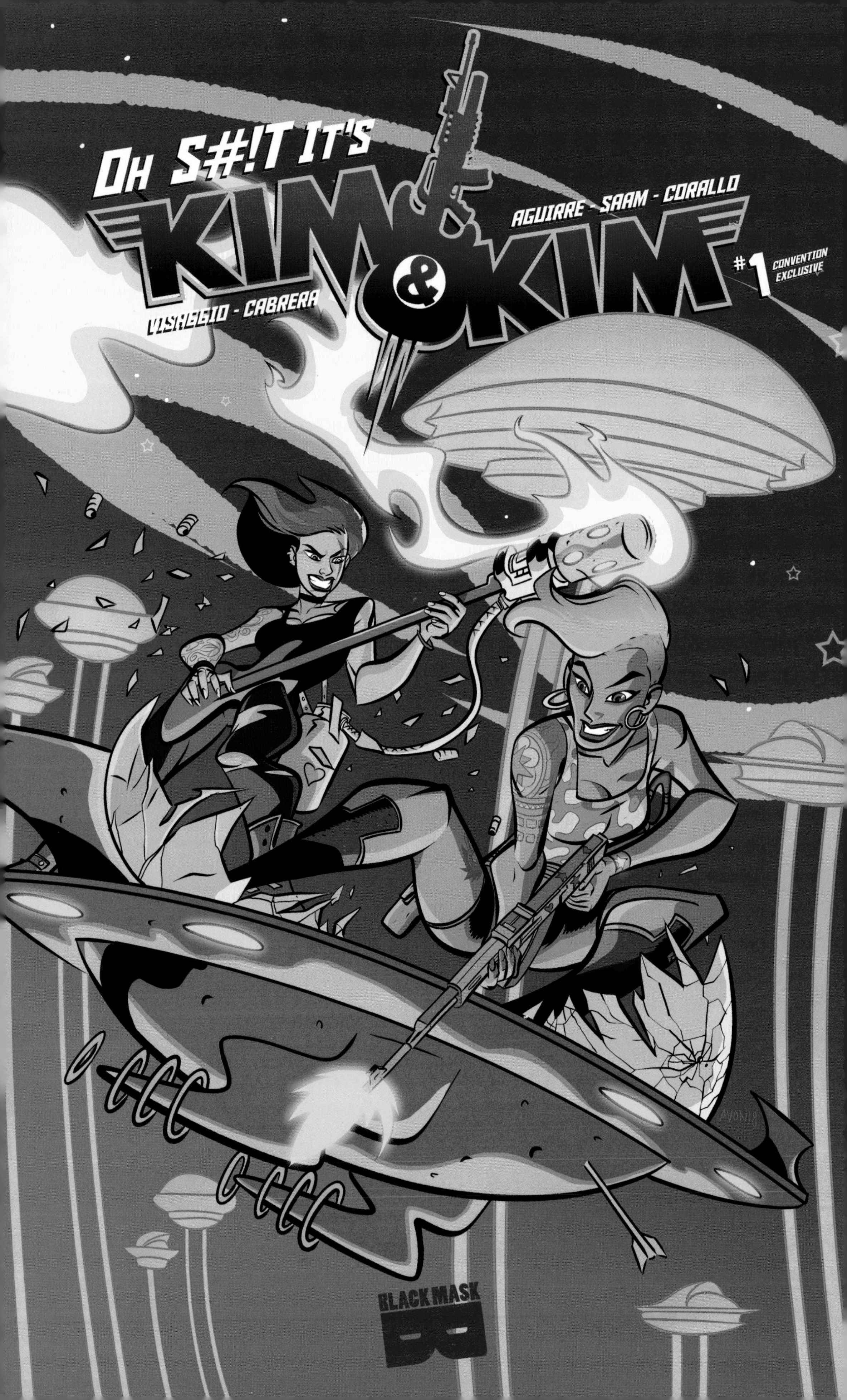
OH S#!T IT'S
KIM & KIM
AGUIRRE - SAAM - CORALLO
VISAGGIO - CABRERA
#1
CONVENTION EXCLUSIVE
BLACK MASK

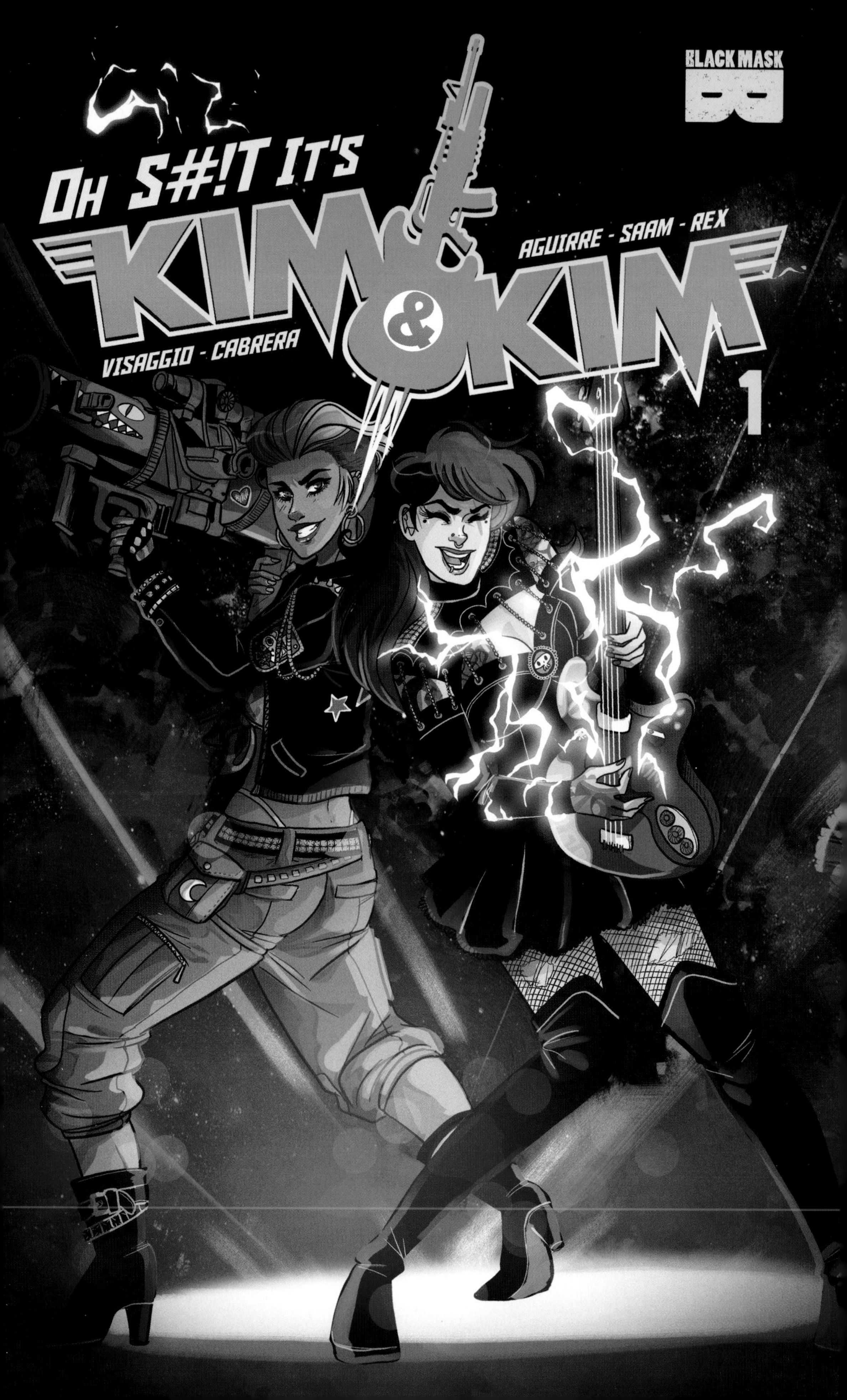
BLACK MASK
OH S#!T IT'S
KIM & KIM
AGUIRRE - SAAM - REX
VISAGGIO - CABRERA
1

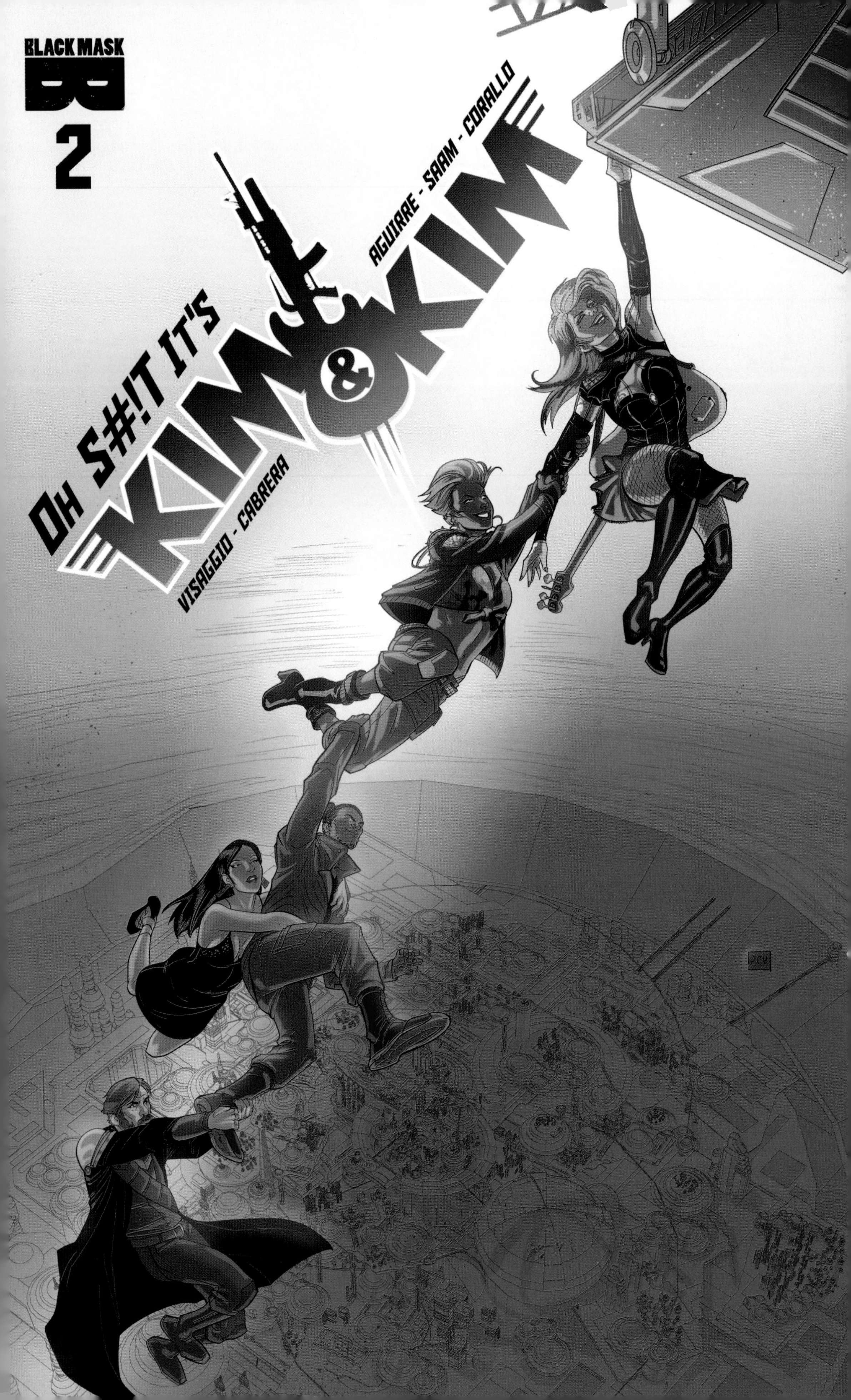
BLACK MASK
2
OH S#!T IT'S
KIM & KIM
AGUIRRE - SAAM - CORALLO
VISAGGIO - CABRERA

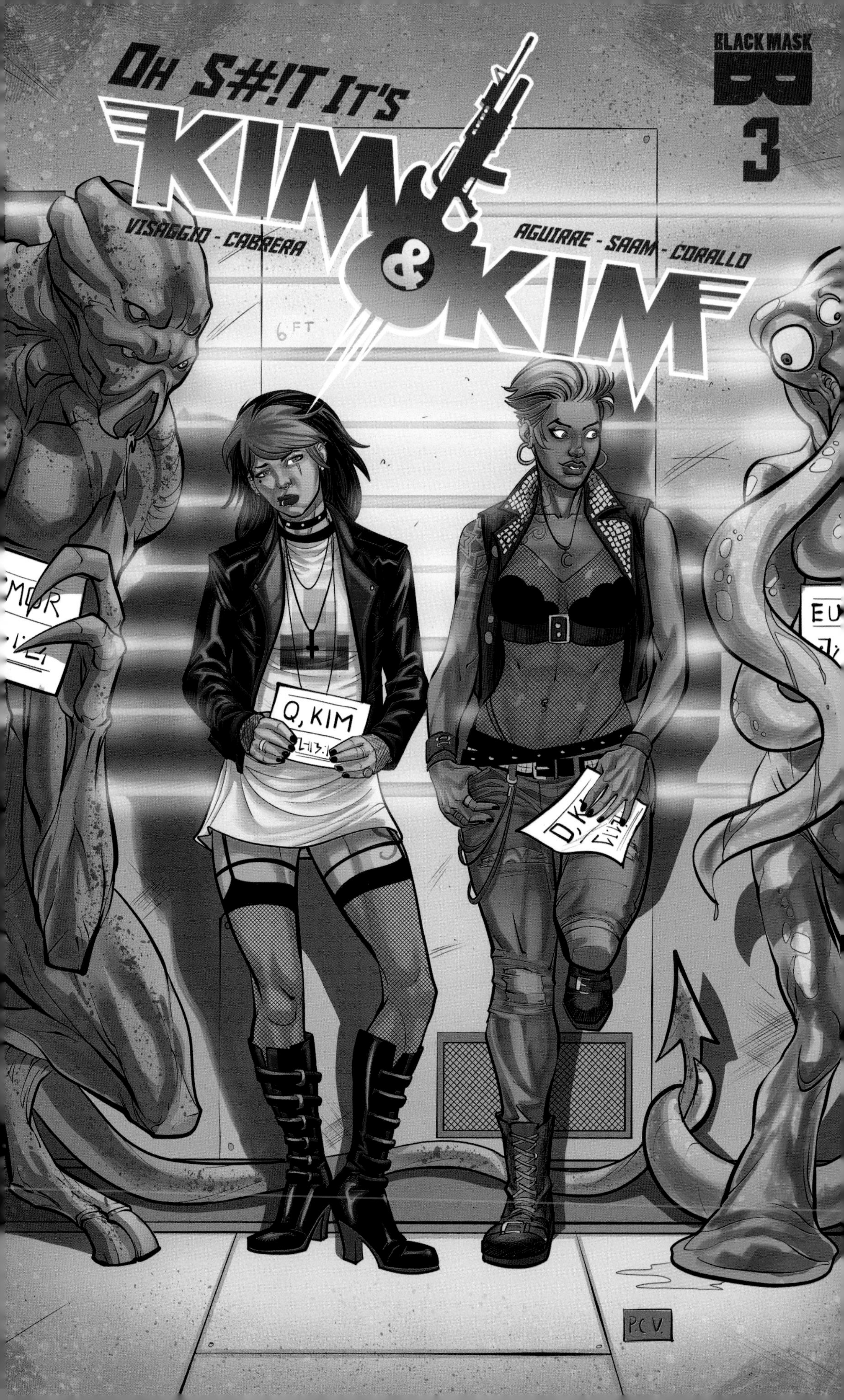
OH S#!T IT'S
KIM & KIM
BLACK MASK
3
VISAGGIO - CABRERA
AGUIRRE - SAAM - CORALLO
6 FT
MOR
Q, KIM
D, K
EU
P.C.V.

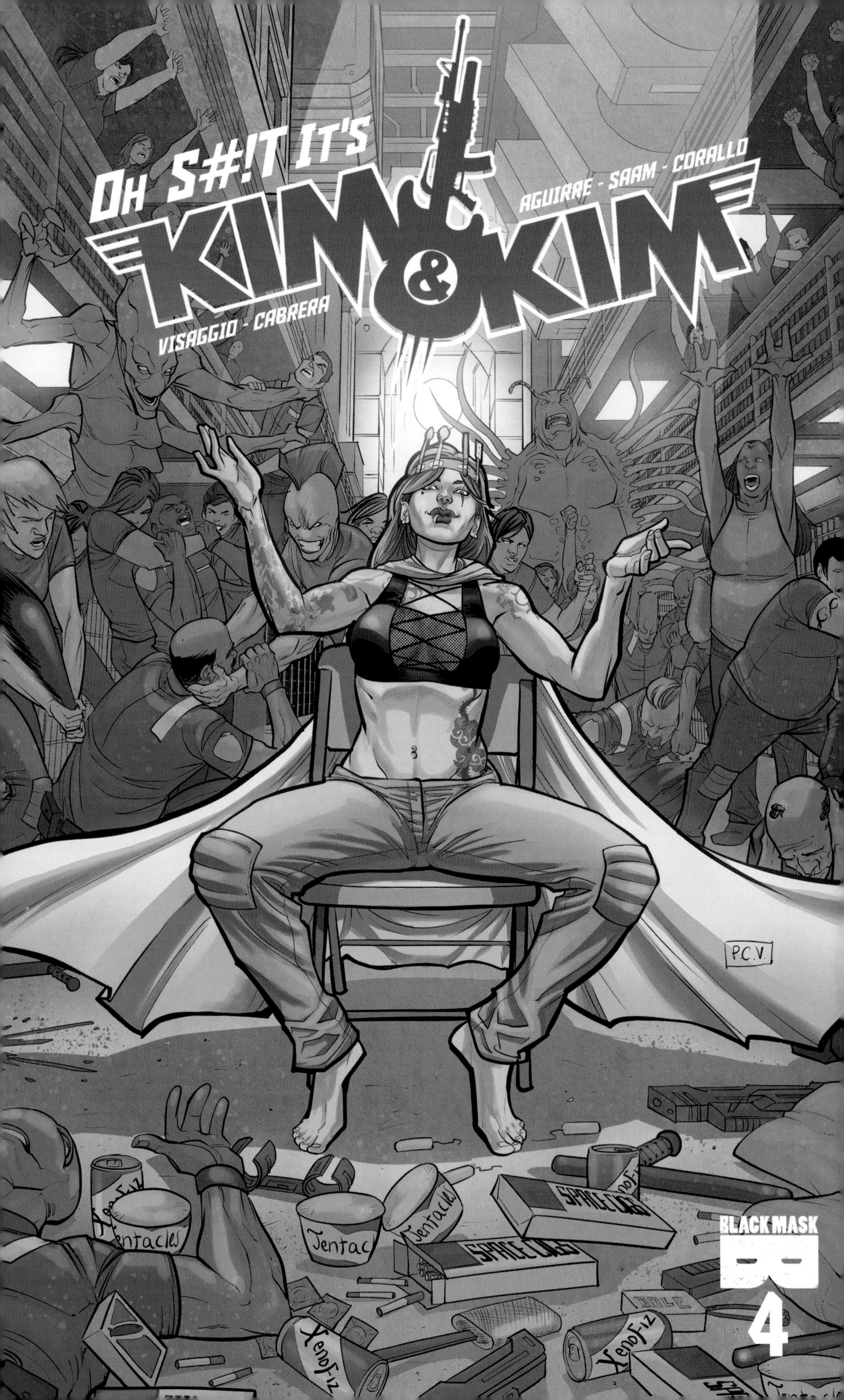
OH S#!T IT'S
KIM & KIM
AGUIRRE - SAAM - CORALLO
VISAGGIO - CABRERA
P.C.V.
BLACK MASK
4

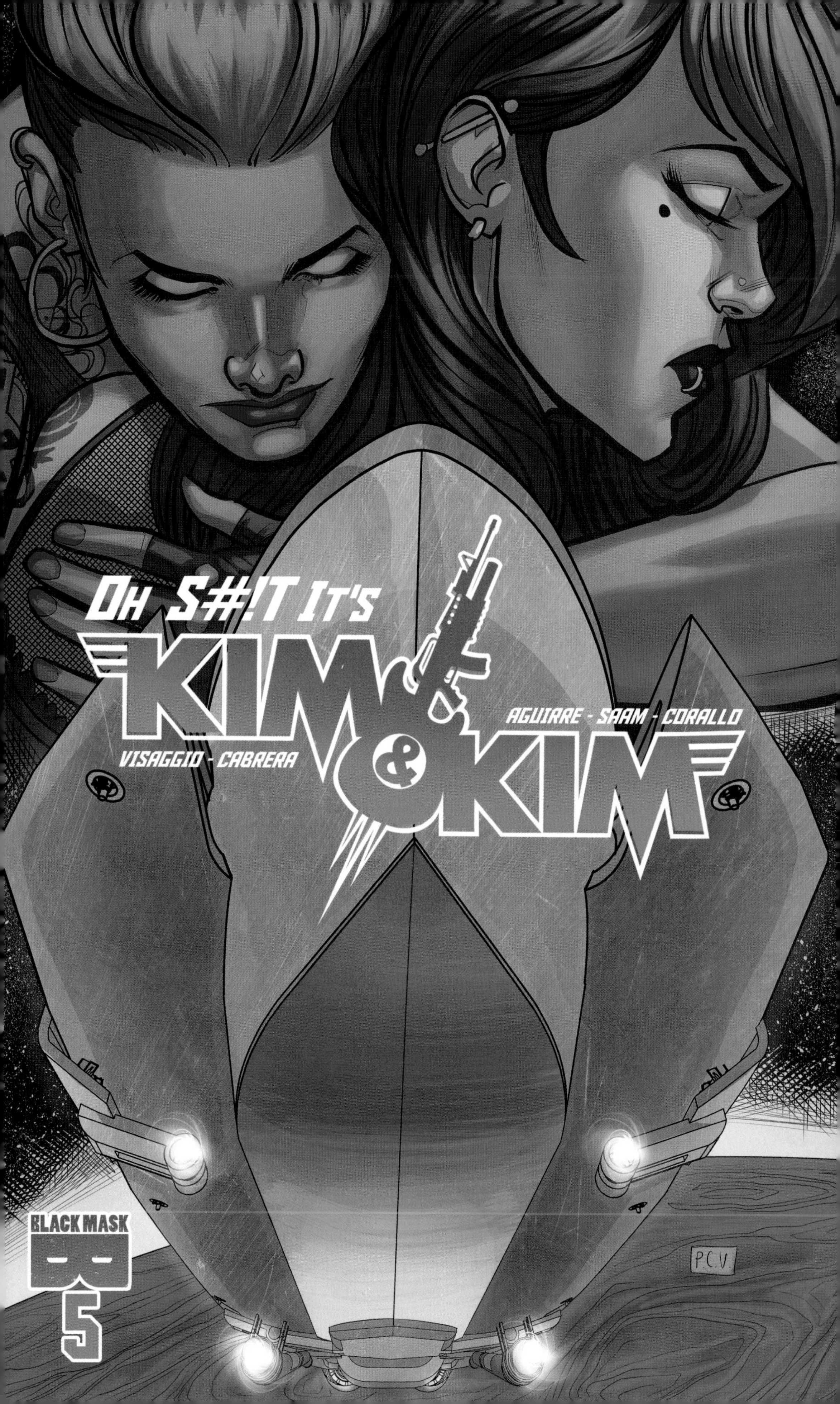

OH S#!T IT'S
KIM & KIM
AGUIRRE - SAAM - CORALLO
VISAGGIO - CABRERA
BLACK MASK
5
P.C.V.